BECOMING SHADOWS AND FURY

"Oh, my Lord.
How much damage can one
woman do?"
S.R. Phillips

THE VALTANA TRILOGY
BOOK TWO

SR PHILLIPS

Paperback ISBN: 978-1-9191671-2-1

E-book ISBN: 978-1-9191671-3-8

Disclaimer

This is a work of fantasy. All names, characters, places, and events spring from the author's imagination and are used in a fictitious manner. Any resemblance to real people, living or dead, or to actual events or locales, is purely coincidental. Though it may draw upon echoes of our own histories, lands, and myths, this tale belongs to another world entirely, where truth bends to story and magic shapes the edges of reality.

For the women who stand tall in the face of doubt,
who follow the quiet wisdom of their heart,
and who choose courage over comfort—may your
strength light the way for others.

Map illustrations by Alexis Veenendaal, PeculiarPDesigns

CHAPTER I
EFA

The storm was coming in fast. All afternoon I'd heard the townsfolk saying that bad weather was coming our way, and now the ominous black clouds that had been hanging over The Azuls all afternoon were hurtling towards Esari. Out in the bay, the tranquil turquoise waters had turned to slate and the waves were starting to build. The soft white cliffs, usually radiant in the sunlight, had turned a cold, ashen gray, no longer the gentle guardians of the shore but watchmen, waiting for the tempest to break with baited breath. Somewhere in the distance, thunder boomed, a low rumbling that seemed to go on and on. It was less like a sound and more like a physical force—a slow, shuddering vibration that threaded through my bones and settled deep in my chest. A sudden gust of wind blew my hair around my face, the loose strands of hair whipping my cheeks, and I blinked, staring up at the man in front of me.

"Prince Trystan," Finn drawled. "A pleasure, as always. Morgan, Bran… it's been a while. Years, even."

We were stood on the cliff path that ran around the

eastern perimeter of the Totease estate, a trail that was little more than a weatherworn scar along the edge of the headland, etched into the chalk by centuries of wind, rain, and the tread of countless feet. Well, *they* were standing. I was still on my knees in the dirt where I had collapsed, the ground rocky and uneven, each sharp edge pressing through the fabric at my knees. Even now, my skin continued to burn like wildfire after Finn's brutal assault, and I still couldn't understand it; how the ungifted, human leader of the Nevedeno could suddenly send excruciating, white-hot pain throughout my body, both inside and out. It felt like he had somehow set me on fire. The oath line on my forearm throbbed intensely, and blood ran freely down over my wrist and hand, staining Eseld's dress.

"You're going to want to back the fuck up, Finn," Emrys said, and I turned to look at him.

I could tell by the way he was standing, his jaw twitching and knuckles white as he gripped his sword, that he was barely containing his rage. But this was a voice I had never heard before, one that promised only violence. It was the voice of the Dark Prince. His gaze flicked towards me and I did a double take, my breath catching. His eyes, usually amber—warm and luminous, like liquid gold I had drunk in with quiet adoration only that morning—were now black. Not the deep brown of shadow, but a void that swallowed the light, leaving nothing behind. They were cold, unknowable, and unyielding. The Dark Prince, indeed.

I could only stare at him, thinking about what a fool I'd been, blinded by the haze of infatuation; deaf to the truths I hadn't wanted to hear. But now... now I saw with unflinching clarity everything that I had missed while I had been caught up in the perfect idea of him. Now I understood the vague answers and lack of specifics, and his reluctance to tell me who they worked for. He could hardly casually drop in that his orders came from his brother, the Fae King who had betrayed my people all those years ago. Or that his cold, unfeeling father had been King Dafydd, the male who had ruled from the Northern Realm's Citadel for three centuries.

Humiliation seared through me as I remembered the way they had all laughed at the stories of the Dark Prince, his betrayal somehow more painful than Finn's physical attack on me. What an idiot they must have thought me, to joke about it so openly in front of me while the whole time Prince Trystan himself sat behind me on the horse with his hand on my leg. Now I understood their knowledge of essence, of oath lines, and why they referred to my gift as the *noswaith* and not 'shadows' like other Valtanans would have. They were Fae, all of them, glamoring themselves to look like men.

I closed my eyes, but the darkness behind them was no refuge. The pain of his deception pressed hot against my chest, sharp and suffocating as my anger coiled tighter, testing my fragile composure. Only hours before, I had given myself to Emrys so completely, telling myself that he had made me feel whole for the first time in my life. But now when I looked at him, I saw only the extent of his duplicity. I saw him for what I knew him to be: a cold-blooded killer, a womanizer, and a liar. In front of me, Finn chuckled, clearly enjoying every moment of my pain.

"Careful, Trystan. I could kill her without even touching her if I so desired it. Before you'd even moved a muscle."

He bent down next to me and gripped my chin hard enough to leave bruises, and I grit my teeth, hearing Emrys make a lethal sounding noise. In my head, the same question was repeating over and over again. How was Finn doing this? And from the curious way Bran was looking at Finn I suspected he was wondering the same thing. It didn't make any sense. Finn was human. He had absolutely no gifts to speak of, and as far as I knew the oath line shouldn't have been able to let him do *this* to me. *Then I guess you know everything, don't you?* His taunting words replayed in my head as dread began to settle in the pit of my stomach. What was he hiding? What had he done?

"Don't worry," Finn shrugged. "I have no intention of harming my property. Not yet at least. Naturally, she will need to be taught a lesson for disobeying her orders and running off like this, but we can do that once we're back home, can't we, Efa?"

I was desperate to sink my knife into his neck, or reach my shadows into his mind, but the thought alone was enough to trigger the oath line's power. The pain intensified on my forearm, enough to make me feel sick, and fresh blood trickled from the line. Hissing through my teeth, I tried to do the impossible and empty my mind of vengeance for the time being, forcing myself to inhale and exhale with deliberate slowness. I focused on the rhythm, on the rise and fall of my chest. Unsurprisingly, calm eluded me.

I glanced up at the three Fae males. Bran and Morgan stood either side of Emrys, swords drawn, and their expressions murderous. Even with his ridiculous moustache Morgan looked absolutely terrifying, and Gods help me, I giggled. Then, before I could stop myself, hysterical laughter broke free from my lips as lightning tore across the sky, a jagged slash of white that momentarily turned night into day. The deafening roar that followed instantly shook the cliffs. The storm was truly upon us now.

"Perhaps you'd like to share what you find so funny, Efa?"

No longer smiling, Finn's tone was lethal. He hated to be laughed at, but that just made me laugh harder, and I gestured weakly at the three Fae males. I had never seen anything more dangerous.

"You," I said. "I might have been blind, Finn, but you're a fool, too, if you don't realize that your days will be in short supply now. Look at them. Do you really think they'll let you live after this?"

Emrys was watching me closely, his body seeming to vibrate with rage. Next to him, Bran shifted slightly, and I wondered if he was readying to move against Finn or preparing to hold Emrys back. Fleetingly, I wondered why Emrys didn't just kill Finn where he stood. He was the Dark Prince. He was supposed to have the same gifts that I had. What was stopping him?

"No one touches her and lives," Morgan muttered darkly.

His hand flexed menacingly around his sword as he stared unblinkingly at the Nevedeno leader. If I hadn't been so impossibly angry I might have thought it was sweet. Finn simply smirked.

"I wouldn't be so sure about that."

Emrys stepped forward, his patience clearly wearing thin, but Finn held up a hand. Without warning, intense pain shot through my body again, and I screamed, the raw sound that tore itself from my chest quivering with agony, fury and helplessness all at once. My body broke out in a sweat as I screwed up my eyes, trying desperately not to give him the satisfaction of seeing me in so much misery despite it being the kind of pain that made me want to beg for death. And then it disappeared as quickly as it came, leaving me breathless and gasping for air. Emrys had stopped in his tracks, staring at Finn with those terrifying, unearthly black eyes. I didn't recognize him at all.

"Anyway, I can see that you all have some things to talk about," Finn said breezily, as if we'd just casually bumped into him in the market. "I'll take my leave, but I'll be seeing you soon, Efa."

He crouched down in front of me again and brushed his lips against my cheek. I turned my face away from him, and as his shirt gaped slightly I noticed a fresh scar on his collarbone. It was an odd shape, almost like a rune.

"I can't wait," he whispered.

He winked at me as he stood and then smirked tauntingly again at Emrys. I was still panting for breath when he boldly turned his back on us and disappeared into the trees.

CHAPTER 2
EFA

I pushed myself unsteadily to my feet, swaying slightly as I waited for the tiny stars in my vision to disappear. Emrys reached out a hand and touched my elbow, but I knocked it away ferociously.

"Don't fucking touch me," I snapped, stepping away from him.

I looked down at my arm and took in all of the blood, surprised at how much there was. It was streaked across my arms and legs in dark, sticky lines, soaking through the thin dress until the fabric clung to my skin. Blood also spattered the ground where I had knelt, the dark droplets dotting the rocky earth like scattered jewels of violence. I wiped as much as I could from my hands onto the skirt, and then reached through the split to find my knife, using it to cut rough strips from the hem since I desperately needed something to stem the bleeding. But every time I tried to wrap the fabric around my arm, I found myself struggling with one hand, the end coming loose every time I went to knot it.

"For fuck's sake," I muttered as it came loose again for the fifth time.

Emrys extended a hand again and I recoiled, shadows bursting from my hand with such force that they actually knocked him back a step. His eyebrows rose in surprise and he dropped his hand.

"You're going to want to *back the fuck up*, Emrys," I snarled, repeating his words back to him and glaring at him. "Or maybe I should be calling you Trystan. You tell me."

His face paled and he looked down at his feet.

"No one calls me that," he said quietly. "Only my brother since my father died."

As if I cared. I tried again to wrap my arm and failed, losing my patience and cursing loudly.

"At least let Bran help you with that," Emrys implored.

I switched my scowl to Bran instead. I was furious with him, too, but since I was clearly getting nowhere and the blood was still flowing freely I reluctantly held out my arm. He held it gently as he worked, keeping his eyes low as he deftly wrapped the fabric and tied the ends. As soon as he was finished I snatched my arm back and marched off in the direction of the house. Lightning flashed again, stabbing through the darkened sky, and the clouds opened in response. Huge, warm, droplets began to fall, a relentless downpour that fell from the sky in thick, heavy sheets, each drop striking like a gentle hammer. Within seconds I was drenched.

"Just brilliant," I said to myself, feeling the wind pick up again, too.

"Efa, please let me explain," I heard Emrys call from behind me, but his plea fell on deaf ears.

"Don't speak!" I raised my voice to make sure it carried over the rain.

I had never felt fury like this before, and for a moment I thought that I might actually shatter Emrys' mind if he said another word. My shadows felt like they were about to explode and I released them in a rush around me, letting them go unchecked as I threw open the gate at the top of the cliff path. Darkness curled around me melodramatically as I stalked across the lawn towards the house. The outer door to Austell's study opened and he and Nev rushed out onto the patio looking visibly alarmed, which wasn't surprising really since I was storming towards the house soaking wet, covered in blood and surrounded in a thick black mist of my own making. I supposed it was one way to introduce them to my gift, and, on reflection, I thought that they handled it rather well.

"Check the perimeter," Emrys ordered from behind me, and this time I really heard it; the voice of someone born to authority. "Finn Yadari was here. Either you have a breach somewhere or one of your soldiers let him in."

Nev frowned, shooting a quick glance at Austell before sprinting off in the direction of the barracks. I wondered whether he knew who Finn Yadari even was.

"Are you hurt?" Austell asked.

His eyes searched my body for injuries but I didn't answer him. I was furious with him, too.

"You knew, didn't you?" I yelled with such force he physically recoiled. "You knew who he was, who he *is*, and you didn't tell me."

Realisation dawned on his face and his mouth set in a grim line. He glanced behind me briefly before meeting my eyes, having the good sense to look contrite.

"Yes, I know, but believe me, Efa, it wasn't my choice to keep it from you. Had it been up to me I would have told you."

I laughed incredulously. Of course it wasn't his choice.

I remembered watching the conversation between him and Emrys on the front steps the night we arrived at Totease. Austell had looked my way and shaken his head, clearly uncomfortable with whatever Emrys was saying. Now I knew he'd been making sure Austell kept his little secret, too. I thought of the way Theo had looked at him back in Cayam. Yes, compulsion was a very useful gift when you had a secret to keep. I looked at Emrys with disgust.

"Keep quiet or you'd make him keep quiet, is that it?" I said to him. "What a pity you were just a few minutes too late just now. A few minutes earlier and you could have shut Finn up, too, and kept your bed warm a little longer."

"I didn't know how—"

"You lied to me," I said sharply, interrupting him. "You *all* fucking lied to me."

I stared at them, rain drops clinging to my eyelashes, each droplet shimmering like tiny glass beads before slipping down onto my cheeks. For a moment, no one spoke, and it was just rain. The constant hiss as it fell in sheets, the sound filling the silence with a steady, almost hypnotic murmur. It slid down the gutters of the house, hit puddles on the patio with crisp, plinking splashes, and ran over leaves with the clean, earthy scent of wet soil and grass. I pushed my wet hair out of my face and scanned their faces. A pained expression was on Bran's face, and Morgan couldn't even meet my eyes.

"Tell me, Trystan, was it not enough to betray my country all those years ago? You had to seduce the lost princess, too?"

"Efa, that was never—"

"At least have the balls to stand there as Fae, all of you. You can give up the pretense now, surely."

"Efa, please..."

"Show me," I demanded coldly, the rain streaming down my face.

I had never seen glamor fading before; the change was so subtle I barely noticed it until they were in their true forms—a shimmer rippling across their skin, softening the familiar lines of their faces. Eyes darkened and lengthened, reflecting an otherworldly light, while fingers stretched just slightly and legs lengthened. Their movement became more fluid and graceful, and even their breathing changed, becoming lighter and echoing with the hum of something ancient and powerful. In the space of a heartbeat, the men I knew were gone, replaced by a presence so utterly mesmerizing and radiant. There was no mistaking them as anything other than Fae.

When I looked at Emrys his eyes were no longer black. Instead, they glowed like golden embers. Anger swelled again and my throat felt tight. I hated him. He had known the depths of my loathing, not just his kind, but for *him*, for the Dark Prince and everything he stood for. Yet he had still pursued me. I hated myself, too, for being so fooled by him, for being so weak and vulnerable, so desperate to feel something—anything—that I had allowed myself to be taken in by him. And I hated the way that he had made me feel again, for making me believe that there was something more, something better out there for me. That there was light at the end of this perpetual, starless night, when all this time I had been nothing but a conquest for him. Emotions threatened to overwhelm me. Not just anger, but humiliation, shame, sadness and grief, too. My hands shook uncontrollably as the tenuous hold I had on my shadows began to wane.

"You need to leave. You need to leave Totease. Now."

"Efa, please. Just let me explain."

Even the way he spoke had changed without the glamor, his Northern Realm accent softer and more melodic than the one I had grown used to.

"Go, Emrys."

"Please don't do this..."

Red pulled at the edges of my vision and as my shadows twitched violently in my blood, I finally gave into my rage. I drew essence into me and then released it, slamming darkness into him. He staggered backwards and I knew I had hurt him, but he said nothing. His eyes never left my face.

"*Go*!" I screamed.

Austell stepped forward quickly, a placatory hand on my arm stopping me from doing untold damage.

"I think it's best that you do as she asks and leave, Emrys. I understand that Cadoc is in the town and I will have word sent to him now. A band of Loyalists are located a few miles north of here. You can join them there. Nev will give you the location."

Shadows still twisted in my hands as Emrys bowed his head sadly, seeming to reluctantly admit defeat. My heart ached suddenly, the anger I had felt replaced by such overwhelming sadness that I struggled to breathe. He nodded slowly.

"As you wish, *elnaya*." He glanced at Austell. "You know where to find us should she need us."

I couldn't look at him anymore. Tears threatened to spill over my cheeks and my legs felt as if they were about to give out at any moment, but I willed myself to stay strong. Lightning flashed again above us as I watched them walk away from me, feeling both extreme relief and utter disappointment. Halfway across the lawn Emrys stopped and glanced back at me. His eyes were pleading and full of hurt.

"It wasn't a lie, Efa. I need you to know that. I meant what I said, all of it. As long as I'm breathing, I'm yours."

I said nothing, avoiding his eyes. Only when he disappeared from view completely did I finally let the tears fall and a sob escape from my lips.

CHAPTER 3
EFA

"Four of my sentry guards were found dead at the southern gate, but there is no sign of Finn Yadari. I can only apologise, Efa. You should have been safe here and you weren't. We have let you down. *I* have let you down."

I took the glass of wine that Austell offered me with trembling hands and drank half of it in one go, ignoring the way his eyebrows rose in slight surprise. Now that the others were gone, I had a suspicion that he had got the good wine out, and I was knocking it back like it was water.

"Nowhere is safe from Finn when he wants something badly enough," I said bitterly.

In fairness, Austell *should* have been apologising. His security had been lapse and his sentry guards inattentive, but I let him off because the truth was very little actually stopped the Nevedeno from getting into places that they shouldn't be, and Finn was one of the best at it. It had only been a matter of time before he found me.

Austell's study was oppressively warm as Eseld knelt

by my feet, patiently cleaning my arm and wrapping a proper linen bandage around the oath line. The bleeding had stopped for the time being, but I didn't hold out much hope for it improving anytime soon. Not while Finn was still alive. Despite the warmth, I was cold to the core, shivering violently. Even my voice trembled when I spoke, my teeth chattering so loudly that Eseld took pity on me and placed a blanket over my legs. My initial blinding rage had subsided since Emrys and the others had departed, but I still hurt, deeply, left with the same insufferable emptiness that I had felt back in the Nijem Forest. Only this time, instead of Emrys being the one person that was able to bring me back from the brink, he was the one who had pushed me into the abyss.

As Eseld finished up, I pulled my feet up underneath me and wrapped myself up in the blanket, finishing my wine. Austell refilled my glass without a word.

"Tell me about this injury on your arm," he said, gesturing at the bandage. "It's not new?"

"No," I sighed. "It's called an oath line. A long time ago, I made a deal to save Noa. You might remember him from when you visited Nissae, but of course he was known as Prince Aeden then."

"A deal with Finn, I presume?"

I nodded, swirling the wine around in my glass absentmindedly. It turned out that Austell knew who Finn Yadari was. Even in Esari the bastard had quite the reputation.

"It bound me to him, and since I decided not to return to him it has been getting progressively worse. But what he did out there on the cliff… the way that he hurt me, made me *burn*… he shouldn't have been able to do that. The oath only stops me from harming him. It doesn't give him those kinds of powers…"

I trailed off, thinking about the rune-shaped scar on his

collarbone. I assumed that was the same as those Morgan had seen on the Order priests I'd killed back in the mountains. In recent years, the Order had figured out how to temporarily take Valtanan gifts, mostly just speed and agility, but sometimes the more interesting ones, too. As long as I'd known Finn, he'd had no unusual abilities whatsoever, and while I had been pretty good at hiding mine, Finn was the boastful type. No, these definitely seemed to be newly acquired, and I'd wager Damen and the Order had something to do with it.

"Theo told us the Nevedeno have created this new lethal Faelock hybrid," I said, thinking out loud. "If he's selling it to Damen and the Order are mixed up in it then it makes sense that he'd want something for himself out of it. I've only ever heard of Gifted fire wielders being able to do this kind of thing. It must be a stolen gift."

Austell took a long sip from his glass and gazed thoughtfully out of the window into the gloom. Rain still hammered against the glass, the thunder still rumbling overhead as the storm continued to lash the coastal town. As Eseld gathered up my wet clothes and left the room, I rubbed at my forehead, feeling a headache coming on. Suddenly I felt incredibly lonely. I missed Arella desperately, and I was becoming increasingly worried about Noa. I was holding on to the hope that if Finn hadn't mentioned him then he was probably safe, but Finn liked to play games, and evidently he was hiding things. I just had to hope it had nothing to do with Noa.

I shut my eyes, but all I could see was Emrys's face and the way he had looked at me when I had told him to leave. His betrayal had hurt me more than I could have possibly imagined given the short period of time that I'd known him. I had trusted him implicitly, and now I felt like my soul had been torn in two and he had taken one half with him when he'd left. I shook my head forlornly, feeling so far away from anyone I loved and trusted. I didn't know what to do next. I'd just exiled myself, and Noa by association, from the Nevedeno and the only home we had, and I knew that Finn would never stop hunting me. Where was I supposed to go? What was I meant to do? Austell sat down in the chair next to me. He seemed to be reading my thoughts.

"I'd very much like you to stay here at Totease," he said sincerely. "For as long as you want, you have a home here. Whatever you need, it's yours."

I smiled at him gratefully, appreciating his kindness even though I wasn't sure that I trusted him completely. I couldn't be sure of his motives, or if he wouldn't just sell me out to the King when it suited him, but right then I had no choice. At least I had somewhere to stay while I considered my next move. I just needed time to think.

"Thank you," I said softly.

I sat back in the chair, listening to the sound of the rain thrumming on the window. Much to my frustration, my mind was still full of Emrys and I picked at my fingers, wondering how they were all faring outside in the storm. They would be getting soaked through. Good.

"How long have you known Emrys?" I asked finally.

Austell finished the rest of his wine and set the glass down on the table next to him before unbuttoning his shirt-sleeves and rolling them up.

"Almost sixteen years. It was my father who introduced us when I was much younger. The Fae have an interest in the Loyalist cause and we share information when we have it. Emrys sometimes stays here when he's in the region and trains with my men. They know him well. Of course, the King remains completely unaware of this arrangement."

I raised an eyebrow at him, and he shrugged.

"I believe the Fae would like to see Damen out of power just as much as we would," he said. "I know the story is that the Fae betrayed Valtana, but I can't help feeling it isn't as simple as we have been led to believe, though Emrys has never been one to give up his secrets easily. One thing I am certain about is that the Fae don't like Damen, and they are *not* his allies."

"Why does everyone call him Emrys and not Trystan?"

"You'd have to ask him about that to be sure, but I believe it's what his mother called him. It was her brother's name. He died very young."

I ran a hand through my still wet hair and pulled the blanket around me tighter, suddenly overcome with exhaustion.

"What is it that they want from the Order temple?"

"Have you ever heard of the Amberstone? No? I must admit I know very little about it, other than that it's very important to the Fae. It's linked to their power. The Order stole it from them, and Emrys has been hunting it ever since."

I thought about Emrys's reluctance to tell me what I was stealing and my anger surged again. His evasiveness made sense now, since telling me what it was would have almost certainly revealed his true identify. But what exactly had his plan been? Had he expected me to just go in blindly without knowing what I was supposed to be looking for? Had he *ever* planned to tell me the truth? I pinched the bridge of my nose as my headache intensified and abruptly decided that I'd had enough for the evening, uncurling my legs and standing. I folded the blanket neatly and placed it on the chair.

"I think I'd like to go to bed now, if you'll excuse me."

"Of course, I'll see you in the morning. If you have need of anything, please just ask."

I finished my wine as I walked to the door and paused to place the glass down on a side table. Just as I was about to go out into the hallway, Austell called out to me.

"Efa, I'm sorry… about all of this. That he wasn't who you thought he was. That he's not the kind of prince our mothers told us stories about. The kind who ends up saving the princess."

I bristled slightly at his words. I didn't doubt that he was sorry, but I also couldn't help but feel he was secretly pleased that I'd told Emrys to leave. I also objected to his insinuation that I was simply a damsel in distress, even if in that moment perhaps I was.

"Is that what you think I need?" I asked, my voice sounding sharper than I intended. "A prince to save me?"

His words had stirred something inside of me. *It is not in your blood to give up or surrender*. I stood up straighter and lifted my chin, letting shadows surround me in the doorway.

"I don't need saving, Austell. I can do that myself."

CHAPTER 4
EFA

I had never known a night to pass more slowly. I tossed and turned for hours in the airless room, desperately trying to quiet my mind, but it was impossible. Every time I closed my eyes, all I could see was Emrys. Eventually, I gave up on sleep altogether and went out onto the covered balcony to sit in the fresh air. I threw a lightweight blanket over my legs and sat listening to the rain until it eventually petered out in the early hours, leaving behind a stifling humidity. Every conversation I'd ever had with Emrys replayed in my head, every vague answer and offhand comment. It had been there in plain sight the whole time. Had I really not seen it? Or had I just been so desperate to be seen myself that I'd chosen not to? Tears fell silently from my eyes and I wiped them away crossly, irritated with myself for getting so upset.

Eventually exhaustion must have won out because I fell asleep, waking just as the sun was appearing on the horizon like a burst of orange on the sapphire sky. My headache from the night before hadn't improved. My head was heavy and I felt like I could hardly breathe, suddenly feeling the overwhelming need to get out of the house and away from Totease. I washed my face and dressed simply in a pair of loose, beige linen pants and a sleeveless white blouse, before closing my door softly behind me. Austell had increased his security after the breach, and I nodded to the two guards on duty at the back door before crossing the lawn and heading towards the cliff path down to the town.

Some of the weight I'd been feeling lifted from my shoulders as soon as I left the house and I breathed in the fresh, salty air that blew in off the bay. It was going to be a hot day. The sun was already beating down and drying the ground beneath my feet, and I kept to the shade as I walked through the deserted streets and down to the beach. The glittering clear blue water lapped gently against the shore now, but driftwood and debris littered the sand, the only sign that there had been a storm the night before. I slipped off my shoes and went down to walk in the waves, enjoying the feeling of the warm water around my bare feet as I looked out at the fishing boats on the horizon, lost in my own thoughts for a while. In the aftermath of everything, I realized that I wasn't even really angry anymore. I was sad. Sad, disappointed, and disillusioned.

When I reached the end of the beach I turned and began waking back towards the town, looking up at the larger ships docked in the harbor. If I squinted, I could just about make out the names of each of the sterns. My heart stuttered. At first I thought I must have been mistaken, because there was no reason for the ship to be there. But there was no mistake; I would have known the *Panacea* anywhere, which meant only one thing. Torr was here.

With an excited yelp I scurried up the beach, barely pausing to brush the sand off my feet and put my shoes back on before I hurried along the jetty. By the time I clambered up the *Panacea's* gangway I was short of breath and sweating, startling the loan sailor standing watch on the deck. Shock registered on his face before he recognized me.

"Efa! What are you doing here?"

"Is he here, Harri?" I asked, panting hard. "Is Torr here?"

"Torr? Yes, he's–"

"Efa?"

Torr's voice boomed across the deck and I turned towards it with a cry, the tears starting to fall before I'd even thrown myself into his arms. He wrapped his arms around me without thinking.

"Hush, Efa, whatever it is we can solve it."

After a moment I lifted my head from his chest and wiped my eyes with the back of my hands. I'd left damp marks on his linen shirt. I shook my head, about to protest and say that I couldn't see how any of this would be resolved when Torr's cabin door creaked open and I glimpsed a head of auburn hair. I shrieked, pushing Torr aside unceremoniously.

"Arella! What are you doing here?"

I wrapped my arms around her and held on to her tightly. I couldn't believe that she was there. Torr never came to Esari, not even on his way to the Azulian capital of Soless. How was it possible that they were here right when I needed them?

"You're going to laugh at me or say I'm crazy, but I had one of those feelings again. I felt like I needed to be here, and I couldn't shake it." She rolled her eyes. "I had to promise Torr all manner of things to persuade him."

"Gods, Rell. I promise you I'm not laughing. I've never been more grateful for your 'feelings'. You have no idea how relieved I am that you're here."

"Maybe it was fate, huh?" she said lightly, ushering me into the cabin.

Inside it was a mess, the bed unmade and clothes strewn everywhere. They had clearly just risen, and Arella bustled about the room tidying things away. I sat down heavily into the only chair while Torr squeezed himself through the door and perched on the edge of his desk.

"Have you seen or heard from Noa?" I asked anxiously.

I already knew the answer. If either of them had seen him, he would have told them that I would be heading to Esari and neither of them would have been surprised to see me here.

"Not for weeks," Arella said. "Why? What's happened?"

I dropped my head in my hands and squeezed my eyes shut, a bad feeling growing in the pit of my stomach.

"I left him at Cryf's Gap days ago, and he was supposed to head back to the camp. If things didn't go well he was supposed to get to you or on one of Torr's ships. And it has gone wrong. Terribly fucking wrong. I've left the Nevedeno, and the oath line is a mess and Finn—"

"Hold on, hold on."

Arella gently interrupted my babbling and came to sit in front of me on the floor, taking my hands in hers. My knee was bouncing violently and I was hyperventilating slightly, the relative composure I'd been holding on to disappearing now I was safe onboard the *Panacea*. Arella muttered something to Torr about rum and he pulled a bottle from off the shelf, hunting around for a glass.

"We need to go back a few steps because you're not making any sense. You've left the Nevedeno?"

I nodded miserably. Hearing it out loud only made me realize how fucked I was. No one left the Nevedeno. Not alive, anyway. Torr handed us both a glass of rum and I took a sip, grimacing as the hard liquor went down.

"Alright, well let's come back to that. Start from the beginning. Why did you leave Noa in Cryf's Gap, and how have you ended up in Esari?"

I told them both about finding Edvarr dead and the subsequent journey through the Nijem, the events of Cryf's Gap felt like a lifetime ago. The wound in my side prickled as I recounted the Nothori attack and Bran saving my life, and when I told them about my true identity being revealed Torr's face visibly paled. He seemed speechless for probably the first time in his life.

"That's quite the revelation there, Efa. You're telling me I had royalty on my ships all those years?"

"I'm afraid so," I said, smiling weakly.

"Gods." He ran a hair through his hair. "So, what's happened with Finn then? What's got you in such a panic?"

I took a deep breath and continued, recounting what happened with Finn on the cliff. Arella's brow furrowed when I told her about the way he had hurt me, but when I got to the part where he made his own revelation about Emrys, she nearly spat out her rum.

"Stop it. You're fucking kidding me. He's the Dark Prince? Surely Finn is lying."

I shook my head, wishing that were the case.

"Right… that's a lot to take in. Well, first things first, we left Serenfell a week ago, so it's likely that we would have missed Noa if he'd made it there looking for us. *If* he got into trouble, he's probably on a ship somewhere absolutely fine. He's a smart boy, Efa. He knows how to take care of himself."

She finished her drink and poured us both another. The first one had gone straight to my head, as I'd eaten nothing since my lobster roll the day before at the festival, but I took another sip regardless. It was helping to calm the tremor in my hands. Torr came and placed his hands on my shoulders.

"I have to go and get this damned crew up and about, but believe me when I say you are not alone in this. You are like a daughter to me, princess or not. The same goes for Noa. He's family. We'll put the word out. If he's on one of my ships, we'll know about it soon enough."

He glanced back before stepping out onto the deck.

"One other thing. I think we'll need to revisit our payment terms since it looks like my next shipment is going to be delayed."

A broad smile spread across his face and I laughed wearily. I hoped he knew that his shipment was likely cancelled completely. Could I even call myself a smuggler anymore? Arella carried her glass over to the bed and lay down on it.

"Gods, what a total mess," she sighed as I went to lie next to her. "Noa will be alright, E. Don't forget he's Gifted, and he's pretty good with those knives of his."

I closed my eyes and sent up a prayer to the Gods. I had never considered myself particularly devout. It didn't go with the job. But these days I seemed to be hoping fervently that there was something up there on my side.

"The most shocking part about all of this is that, after all these years, it's Prince Trystan that you've ended up falling in love with."

"What?" I spluttered, sitting up straight. "I'm not in love with him."

Arella turned to look at me, her face only inches away from mine. She raised one eyebrow and smiled impishly.

"Aren't you?"

I scoffed indignantly, opening and closing my mouth but not finding any words.

"No... I don't... absolutely not. He wasn't... no, Arella. Just, no."

"Oh well, my mistake then," she said easily, but the grin didn't leave her face.

I scowled at her as I lay back down, closing my eyes again. I wasn't in love with him. My shadows fluttered gently and I clamped down on them. It was a ridiculous idea.

"It was just a flirtation, really," I said. "After the temple, we'd have gone our separate ways and never seen each other again."

I rarely lied to Arella. I never needed to, but that really was an outright lie. Because ever since Cayam I had been beginning to wonder what would happen if we didn't go our separate ways after I'd been into the temple. What if there *had* been a future for us? A fresh wave of hurt and betrayal washed over me. Obviously Emrys hadn't been thinking the same thing. I opened my eyes and looked at her, changing the subject.

"You're getting these 'feelings' an awful lot lately. Are you sure you're not a Seer?"

She laughed lightly.

"No, there are no Witnessings here. No visions of any kind. It's just instincts, I suppose. Although did I ever tell you that my great-aunt was a Seer? Maybe there's something in my blood."

"Huh. I'll keep an eye out for your eyes changing color, shall I?"

We lay in silence for a few minutes, lost in our own thoughts. Then Arella sat up and crossed her legs.

"So, what is so special about this Amberstone?"

"Honestly, who knows? None of them told me a single

thing about it. I only know what it's even called because of Austell, and he doesn't know why the Fae want it back so badly either."

"Aren't you curious about it?"

I tilted my head to look at her. She was using the tone she used when she was planning something.

"A little, why?"

"No reason…"

"Out with it, Arella."

"I was just thinking that you've never been one to go back on a deal, apart from the one with Finn, for obvious reasons. And you said Emrys gave you money, so he's already paid you in part. I just thought you might like to know what all the fuss is about."

"You think we should sneak into the Order temple anyway and steal whatever this stone is?"

I stared at her with disbelief, but she only smiled wickedly back at me.

"I thought you prided yourself on your professional reputation?"

I snorted and shook my head. She had me on that.

"We'd be risking our lives for something that's probably not even in there."

"Who cares?" She grinned at me. "It'll be fun. We haven't done something like this together for years. Not since we stole those rubies back down in Tithra. Besides, I hate the Order. If all we do is kill a few of them, then I'd say that's a success."

I ran a hand over my face and reached over to where I'd left my drink, sitting up slightly and draining the glass.

"Alright. Let's do it. I suppose you better come back to Totease with me and meet Austell. And then someone is going to need to tell us where this stupid temple is."

CHAPTER 5
EFA

"I'm not foolish enough to tell you not to do this. The two of you seem born to burn just a little out of control. But please, for the love of the Gods, try not to take too many unnecessary risks."

Torr had come back in while Arella was packing her bag, and the look that he had given us when we told him what we planned was a long-suffering one. It was the look of a man who had been putting up with our behavior for too long and knew when arguing with us was futile.

"We won't," I promised. "It'll be easy, just like old times when we used to raid your warehouse in Astraea."

"Yeah, I caught you though, remember? That's when all my troubles began."

"Oh, that was years ago," Arella said, throwing various items of clothing into her bag. "We're seasoned professionals now. And I happen to think that Noa, Efa and I were three of the best things to have happened to you and your business."

Torr's expression softened and he smiled fondly at her,

wrapping an arm around her affectionately and kissing her on the top of her head.

"You're absolutely right," he said to her with a chuckle. "I apologise unreservedly for any offence given. As you know, I have business in Portreth, so we'll leave on the evening tide and return in three days. Please, please try to keep yourselves alive until then."

I gave him a small smile, making no such promises, and stepped out of the cabin to give them some space, looking out over the busy harbor. Esari had come to life while I had been on the ship, and the town was busy as we walked back towards the cliff path. I pointed out some of the things Eseld had shown me the day before, finding it hard to believe that yesterday I had been so happy and carefree. So much had changed in less than a day.

To one side of the main square a group of children were gathered around a street performer, squealing and laughing at whatever he was saying, and we paused to watch. I recognized the folktale he was telling. It was a popular story about a prince who had been turned into a crow by an evil enchantress. The performer certainly had a way with words, building the suspense and drawing the crowd in with dramatic whispers. Even I was hanging on to his every word as he reached the climax of the tale, when suddenly there was a loud crack and black smoke exploded from his hands. I jumped along with the rest of the crowd, and then began to laugh, smiling at the delighted looks on the faces of the children.

"Gods," Arella said. "For a minute there I thought he had your… you know. I wonder how he does that."

I laughed, setting off again up towards the cliff path.

"This lobster festival is so adorable! It's so quaint. I love it here."

"I know, me too," I agreed as we pushed through the

crowds. "I was thinking just this morning that if things were different I could have been happy living here. Imagine if we'd ended up in Esari and not in Astraea all those years ago, how different things could have been. Maybe in another life, hey?"

I was imagining just what our lives would have looked like by the time we reached the top of the cliff and Totease came into view. We were both breathless, but Arella still managed to let out a low whistle, her eyes growing wide as she took in the impressive manor house and the glorious gardens surrounding it. It was the same two sentry guards at the entrance to the gardens and I smiled at them, rolling my eyes at the way Arella played up to their shameless glances. She flirted almost as much as Noa did.

"No wonder you could see yourself living here," she muttered as we entered the house. "This place is incredible."

"I'm sure Austell will be delighted to hear you say that," I said, smiling at her over my shoulder.

We found him in his study as usual, leaning over his desk looking intently at maps of Esari. He glanced up at Arella as we entered, curiosity flickering in his eyes. I couldn't help but look for any hint of interest in her as he came round to take her hand. Everyone liked Arella, what wasn't to like? But if he did find her attractive he gave no sign of it. He was as courteous and chivalrous as he was with everyone.

"Austell, this is my friend, Arella."

"Arella Raenord," she said politely as she offered him her hand.

I glanced at her, surprised. Unlike Noa and I, Arella had never changed her first name after we escaped Nissae. It was common enough across Melrith that she didn't need to, but she had always used a different family name since

Raenord would certainly identify her to anyone who knew my mother's court. Clearly she had decided to take a leaf out of my book and embrace her true identity.

"Any relation to General Raenord?" Austell asked.

"His daughter," she replied, meeting his eyes and no doubt watching for his reaction.

General Raenord had been one of my mother's most trusted advisors, the leader of Valtana's army, and like an uncle to me. Like my parents, he had given his life for his people that night. Austell smiled sadly.

"I had the pleasure of meeting him on several occasions when I was younger. He was a good man. Please do sit down and make yourself comfortable. I will call for some tea."

I smirked at the mention of tea. That was unquestionably a much more sensible drink for that time in the morning, and I hoped it would help to sober me up a little after the rum. I took a seat next to Arella and observed Austell where he sat in his usual seat behind his desk for any hint of surprise on his part. If he was wondering why my closest friend was suddenly in Esari, he kept it well hidden. His father had clearly prepared him for a life at court, because his expression was one of politeness and amiability as he asked her about her role in Torr's business and the languages she spoke, sharing his own interest in studying different dialects. I sat in silence for the most part, gazing out of the study window, but when their conversation came to a natural lull, I decided just to come out and say what I was thinking.

"Arella and I are planning to visit the Temple of Truth and Wisdom. I had an agreement with Emrys. If the Amberstone is there, we'll retrieve it and bring it back. We'd appreciate some assistance from your men, if you would be so kind as to accommodate that."

A muscle twitched near his mouth and his eyes widened just a fraction. He was intrigued, and maybe a little impressed. He spread his hands in front of him on the desk.

"Of course, I'm very happy to oblige. What assistance do you need?"

A servant had just come in with the tea, and I leaned forward to take a biscuit from the plate that she'd put on the small table just next to me.

"We need men that know the temple well, information about how many priestesses reside there, and ideally their habits and routines."

"Certainly. Nev will escort you there. He has a group of soldiers who regularly monitor the temple and they will be able to share all they know. Is there anything else?"

"Well, obviously it would be good to know what the Amberstone actually is, but I'm not sure that's going to be possible. We've no idea what it looks like, how big it is... we'll have to go in blind on that front."

It was far from perfect, but short of inviting Emrys or one of the others back to tell us about it, which I wasn't inclined to do, there wasn't another option. Knowledge of the Amberstone seemed to be rare, so I decided to view it as simply adding an extra layer of excitement to our mission.

"You better send word to Emrys, too, in case they were planning on going in themselves."

"That's probably wise. When do you plan to go?"

I glanced at Arella who pulled a face and shrugged her shoulders. She was easy, it seemed, and I figured there was no time like the present.

"We'll go in tomorrow night."

CHAPTER 6
EFA

The Temple of Truth and Wisdom lay some twenty miles south of Totease, perched on the cliffs overlooking the ocean. Until about fifteen years ago, it had been an old castle belonging to the Mirle family but, much to the old Lord Mirle's displeasure, it had been requisitioned by the Order with permission from the King, and turned into one of the six temples across Melrith. It was an impressive fortress, with an abundance of turrets and crenellations. Ivy grew up the walls and cobalt flags fluttered from the battlements in the gentle breeze coming in off the sea.

We left Esari in the early afternoon, accompanied by Nev and two of his men, and set up camp in an abandoned farm building up on the hillside watching the evening activity as priestesses in their blue cloaks lit the sconces around the perimeter. Since arriving, we had paid attention to the comings and goings through the main gates, keeping note of where sentries were stationed and how frequently they changed. It was a beautiful night, the air warm and full of the smell of lavender. Already the stars were beginning to appear, and a thin, sliver of moon hung in the cloudless sky.

"You'll have about an hour once the evening prayers have started. Hopefully that's enough time to do what you need to do," Ross said.

He was a young man, with a slightly nervous disposition, but according to Nev he made an excellent spy. He passed Arella another blade and she strapped it to her thigh, flicking her braid over her shoulder and smiling sweetly at him. His cheeks flushed slightly under her gaze and I stifled a laugh. According to Nev, Ross and Peta knew the temple better than anyone, and they even had a girl inside who was able to periodically get messages out to them.

"Evening prayers take place in the main atrium," Ross continued. "It's the one time that almost all of the priestesses are in the same place at the same time. The High Priestess doesn't join them in the evenings, so she will be alone in her room."

Peta squinted, pointing towards the left hand side of the temple He was considerably older than Ross and I wondered if his eyesight was starting fail.

"Her rooms are at the top of that turret there," he said. "She's given herself the best views, naturally. You can expect two guards outside her room, and two at the bottom of the staircase."

"What's your plan?" Nev asked.

"Get in. Get out," Arella said simply.

I snorted. The truth was, we weren't assassins, nor had we ever had any formal training unless I counted Morgan's two brutal sessions in the forest. We were smugglers by trade, our methods learned through years spent on the streets. We were experts at blending in and sleights of hand, as well as the occasional interrogation, and when we fought it was quick and dirty with knives and garrotes. Ideally, we wanted to avoid drawing attention to ourselves and too much hand-to-hand combat as much as possible.

"Right" I agreed. "Stay out of sight and keep out of trouble until we find her."

We knew nothing about the Amberstone; nothing about what it looked like or where we might find it. Nor did we have time to search the whole place. So we were going to cut to the chase and find someone who would have the answers we needed: the High Priestess. According to our inside girl, the High Priestess was a cold, calculating woman who was unlikely to give up the information we wanted easily, so it looked like my shadows would be coming out to play soon enough. They flared in my finger-tips at the thought.

"We'll be down by the western gate waiting for you," Nev said. "If we see any signs of trouble, we'll come in. Otherwise, the two of you are on your own in there."

I nodded once, glancing at Arella and finding her grinning. She was looking forward to this, and about two hours after sunset, we made our final preparations and readied ourselves to leave, checking and rechecking our weapons. Before we left the oasthouse Nev placed on his hand on my arm.

"Remember," he said. "It's best if no one knows that anyone is looking for the Amberstone."

I caught his eye and held it for a moment, knowing full well what he was suggesting. The High Priestess wouldn't be seeing dawn.

"Understood. Let's go."

We separated; the three men headed for a small copse of woods where they would stay until we had made it inside the temple. After that they would make their way down to the western gate. Arella and I jogged down through the pasture until we reached the thick perimeter wall that ran around the compound. We melted into the shadows against the wall, listening to see if we had been spotted. When we heard nothing out of the ordinary we crept along to the southern gate.

The temple was inhabited by Order priestesses, most of whom were academics rather than soldiers. The sentry guards were almost exclusively male priests. It was short-sighted, in my opinion. I'd often found that women made the most astute and vicious guards, and were less likely to get distracted. The two men on duty at the gate who leaned casually against the wall confirmed my opinion. They were discussing their latest visit to the local whorehouse and speaking fondly about a girl called Lyra. Clearly they weren't sticking to the vow of celibacy they took on joining the Order.

I wrapped us both in shadows and Arella and I darted out in front of the gate, taking one guard each. Generally speaking, as smugglers we tended to incapacitate rather than kill when doing something like this, but these men had willingly joined Damen's Order, so I didn't feel particularly guilty about their deaths as we quickly slit their throats. I caught mine as he collapsed, his weight catching me slightly off guard as he fell awkwardly. I dropped him clumsily, hastily dragging him into an alcove. With a quick glance at one another, we ran silently across the sloping lawn and up to the temple, flattening ourselves against the stones that were still warm from the day's heat.

Honeysuckle clambered up the side of the walls in places and the scent of it filled the air as we disturbed it. We were exposed here, illuminated by the flickering sconces, but I was keen to preserve my gift for as long as possible. I strained my ears, waiting to hear anything that might indicate we had been seen. Still nothing. We waited for a moment and then began to edge towards the stone archway that served as the main entrance to the temple, but sudden footsteps had me throwing myself back out of sight. Arella was close behind me, her breathing shallow.

The heavy oak doors opened, and two priestesses emerged from the temple, dressed in the flowing blue robes of the Order. Large hoods hid their faces and they talked quietly to each other. I felt a brief moment of nervousness. Either we were too early and the gong hadn't sounded yet to call everyone to prayer, or our intelligence was wrong. I held my blade tightly, waiting to see which way they went. When they turned towards us, my breath quickened and we darted out into their path. A moment later, our soft leather boots were silent on the flagstones and the loose Order robes fluttered around our ankles as we entered the temple.

"You know, I've always thought this color blue rather suited me," Arella whispered.

I rolled my eyes but didn't look at her, more interested in the inside of the temple. I wasn't one to spook easily, but even I had to admit that there was something unnerving about the place. It was a maze of narrow corridors filled floor to ceiling with shelves of ancient looking books and the pungent smell of incense in the air. I wrinkled my nose., the aroma sweet, sour, heady and jarring, all at the same time. Despite the warm evening, it was drafty within the old fortress, a cold, damp breeze coming from somewhere. And sound travelled strangely. More than once I thought I heard footsteps or voices right behind me, but when I turned there was no one there.

"I don't like it in here," Arella murmured, clearly feeling the same way.

I made a small sound of agreement. I'm sure he'd have argued that it was the principle, but I couldn't honestly say that Austell had lost much by relinquishing this particular asset to the Order. Somewhere deep within the temple a gong sounded and we stepped quickly into a convenient recess. I shrouded us in darkness once again, breathing a sigh of relief that our intelligence was correct. We were just a few minutes early. Right on cue we heard footsteps echoing in the hall, and a dozen priestesses drifted by like wraiths. The sight of them sent a shiver down my spine.

"It's like old times, isn't it," Arella joked quietly. "Reminds me of the time we snuck into the Emir's house in Amanca."

"That was a lot less creepy," I replied. "This place is like a labyrinth. How the fuck do we find the High Priest-ess's rooms?"

She peered out of the recess, her hand emerging from the robes to gesture out into the corridor.

"There are stairs over there," she said. "I can't hear anything. I think we're safe to go"

Cautiously we crossed the corridor and climbed the staircase as far as it went, pausing halfway so I could hang my head out of a window to try and locate the turret Peta had pointed out.

"This way," I said, more confidently than I felt.

Up ahead I heard a cough and the sound of someone moving about, so we slowed our pace, creeping towards the end of the corridor. I pulled my shadows around us as we peeked around the corner.

"Two guards," I mouthed to Arella

We walked quietly towards a sweeping staircase that led up to the rooms at the top of the turret. Underneath the shadows, we were almost invisible to the two men, but I saw one lift his head. He must have heard us approaching, but it didn't matter. We were upon them both a second later, neither of them making a sound as they fell. This time I was prepared for the weight, catching him deftly and lowering him to the ground soundlessly.

With nowhere to hide the bodies, we had to leave them and hope no one discovered them while we were upstairs. I glanced at Arella, keeping the shadows in place as we tentatively went up the staircase, both on alert for the two guards supposedly upstairs, but we needn't have worried. They were both half asleep and dispatched as quickly as the two downstairs.

"Ready?" I asked Arella, taking a deep breath.

"Ready."

I was expecting a simple room, devoid of any character since the Order were devout, simple folk, or so they would have us believe. As it was, I was rather taken aback by what we found when we entered the High Priestess' room. Rich, brightly colored tapestries adorned the walls, multiple decorative candles burned around the room, and the bed looked almost as luxurious as my own back at Totease. The High Priestess knelt on the floor with her back to us, her knees cushioned by a magnificent bearskin rug that must have come from Nothore or somewhere up on the Ice Flats. I dropped the shadows and she turned to us. Our cloaks gave her no immediate cause for concern, but she looked irritated at the intrusion.

"What is the meaning of this? Why are you not at prayer?"

She was a striking looking woman, with silvery white hair and piercing blue eyes the same color as the robes she wore. They weren't much different from the ones worn by the women we'd seen downstairs, but rather than rough cotton, hers were made of a beautiful, turquoise silk. Her gaze narrowed as she looked between us, suspicion growing.

"You must be new to the Order. I don't believe I recognize you, sisters."

I laughed softly.

"No, you wouldn't. I can't say I've ever been one for religion. Especially one that has made it its mission to murder the innocent."

The High Priestess began to rise but Arella held out a hand.

"Please, High Priestess, stay where you are. We only have a few questions for you."

Too late I saw the throwing star hidden in her sleeve. I was across the room in an instant, my blade at her throat, but the star had been dangerously close to slicing Arella's face. I wasn't usually so quick to get annoyed, but it had been a trying couple of days, and I was out of patience. Shadows filled the room in response to my rising irritation and I took a firm grasp on the old woman's mind, taking satisfaction in the hissing sound she made. Arella rubbed her ear, her fingers coming away red from where the throwing star had just nicked her.

"Valtanan filth," the High Priestess spat out.

I tightened my grip on her, and a trickle of blood ran down her neck as my knife started to cut into her skin.

"Oh, that's unkind," Arella said with a pout. "We came to play nicely, but now I think I've changed my mind."

"You are playing a dangerous game, girls," the High Priestess said, raising her chin defiantly. "I don't know what you want, but you won't get it."

I dragged the woman backwards and forced her down into the chair, holding the blade at her throat as Arella tied her wrists to the chair. When she was secured I stepped back and sat on the edge of the bed watching her.

"The Amberstone. Tell me about it."

There was a flicker of something in her eyes. Surprise,

maybe? Intrigue? Concern? I couldn't read her. She said nothing.

"What does Damen want with it?"

Nothing. Her eyes looked passively into mine.

"Is it here?"

Without warning the woman shrieked and I looked down to find Arella's knife embedded in the woman's thigh. The High Priestess drew in a shuddering breath as she composed herself. I gave Arella a questioning look.

"Sorry," she said pleasantly. "My hand slipped."

I crouched down in front of the woman and smiled coldly.

"Listen. We're busy people, you and I. Prayers to say, wine to drink, and all that. So why don't you start telling me what I want to know so that we can get this all over with nice and quickly?"

"What could you possibly want with the Amberstone?" she sneered.

"Maybe I want to return it to its rightful owners."

She cackled, throwing her head back and laughing as if I'd said something hilarious. Arella sighed impatiently.

"After the way the Northern Realm betrayed your people? You know… that might have been the best thing the Fae have ever done."

I backhanded the priestess. Hard. The sound reverberated around the room, but she only laughed again and I studied her closely. I believed her when she said I'd get nothing out of her, not by asking nicely, anyway. I stood up and wandered around the room, balancing the tip of my blade on a fingertip. It was a trick that Noa had taught me years ago.

"I'm running out of patience, *sister*."

Arella trailed her blade over the woman's cheeks. The

High Priestess smirked at me. There was blood in her teeth.

"You took a little trip recently, didn't you? To Rostorrmel. Why?"

Silence. I breathed out a laugh and paced back and forth in front of her.

"You know, I hear that they have a wonderful way of getting information out of people in the dungeons at Rostorrmel."

"You can threaten me all you want, but it will make no difference. Do your worst," she snarled.

It was my turn to laugh now.

"Oh, don't worry, I will."

I tightened the grip I had around her mind, filling the darkness with threat and malice and squeezing until her eyes went wide with fear. I stopped short of shattering her, taking inspiration from Emrys's interrogation of Theo. I might not have been able to compel her to speak like he could, but I could definitely influence her, and that combined with what I was doing inside her head would likely have the desired effect. In the end, I was right. She spilled her secrets, and I devastated her mind at exactly the same moment that Arella slit her throat.

CHAPTER 7
EFA

"We were right," I called across the garden to Austell to where he sat eating his breakfast on the patio. "It wasn't at the temple. It never was."

It was a bright, pleasant morning. The slight haze that hung over the ocean was already beginning to burn off, and, though the air had lost some of its overbearing humidity over the last couple of days, it was still sticky and close despite the early hour. I pulled out the chair opposite him and sat down, leaning forward to rest my elbows on my knees.

"The High Priestess believes that it is, and has always been, somewhere near Rostorrmel."

"I see," Austell said, regarding me with amusement whilst he dabbed at his mouth with a napkin.

"Whatever she was in Rostorrmel doing, it was linked to the Amberstone. She wouldn't… well, she *couldn't* tell us anymore about what she was doing there. We found an oath line on her arm. My guess is she's sworn an oath of silence to prevent her from speaking about what happened there in case she fell into the wrong hands."

I heard a door open and close, and then Nev appeared from around the side of the house and walked towards us.

"Whatever they're doing in Rostorrmel, they're keeping it a closely guarded secret even within the Order. Right at the end she mumbled something incomprehensible about blood magic and 'the door'. I don't know what that meant. Anyway, that was all we could get out her, but my guess is it's something to do with the newly improved Faelock and Valtanan gifts. "

He nodded thoughtfully, pouring himself a cup of tea.

"Would I be right in assuming you were *very* persuasive in getting even that information from her?"

"You would be."

"And does she live to tell the tale of your conversation?"

My eyes flicked up to Nev. He was fighting back a smile.

"She does not."

"I see."

"Anyway, you may send word to Prince Trystan," I said, his real name sounding strange on my lips. "Let him know the unfortunate news. If you could also please remind him that I have fulfilled our original agreement and await the rest of my payment."

Austell smiled as he sipped from the delicate teacup. It was patterned with roses.

"Of course. Nev, perhaps you could arrange for a message to be sent?"

"Certainly. I have also had my men spread rumors that the attack was orchestrated by the Loyalists."

"Good," Austell said, nodding his head. "Yes, that seems sensible."

"Is there anything else that I can do for either of you now?"

I shook my head.

"No, but please thank Peta and Ross again for their assistance last night."

He bowed his head briefly before leaving us, and Austell gestured at the plates of food that were laid in front us.

"Please help yourself. I imagine that you are hungry after last night's escapades."

I'd had no appetite since the night of the storm, but I helped myself to a single pancake and some fruit, pushing the berries around on my plate as he spoke.

"So, it all went well last night?"

"Yes. It all went relatively smoothly, I'm pleased to say."

We had departed from the temple quickly, seeing no one as we slipped back out into the gardens and sprinted down to the west gate to meet with the men. As we reached the farm building, discarding the stolen cloaks and mounting our horses, we heard the deep sound of the gong and women shouting. They'd discovered her body. I sipped from my glass of apple juice, barely registering the sweet nectar-like taste.

"There is something that I need," I began, pausing to think about how to phrase what I was about to ask. "You are aware that I have a particular gift, but I am struggling to harness it to it's fullest. Cadoc said that I need to build up my stamina and to practice, but I really don't know where to start."

Austell placed his cutlery together neatly and poured himself a fresh cup of tea before answering.

"I see," he said for the third time. "And you are

wondering whether I might know of someone who can help you discover how to unlock your full potential."

"Yes. I realize that this is Melrith, and the chances of you knowing such a person may be slim, but still…" I tailed off, biting my lip.

"Of course, as a loyal subject of King Damen, if I *were* to know of such a person I would have had to report them to the Order." He gave me a knowing smile, leaning back in his chair and rubbing his jaw thoughtfully. "Leave it with me, Efa. I will make some enquiries."

"Thank you."

"There is something else."

He leaned forward again and picked up an envelope from the table. Opening it, he pulled out a thick piece parchment embossed with what looked like flecks of real gold. I scowled when I recognized Damen's crest.

"What is that?" I asked, eyeing the card suspiciously.

"Damen has requested that I and the other Lords join him in Rostorrmel."

"Oh. For any particular reason?"

Austell handed me the parchment, and I stared down at it.

"He hasn't given one, although it has been some time since we last gathered so I have been expecting this for a few months. Apparently there is to be a ball."

I scanned the invitation, feeling a stir from my shadows. Austell placed his cup down and cocked his head. I lifted my eyes to meet his.

"What does that look you're giving me mean?" I asked uncertainly.

"I think that you should attend with me."

I stared at him, certain that he would be able to hear my heart pounding. I might have vowed to myself that Damen would die at my own hands, but I don't think I'd actually thought that I'd potentially be in the same room as him in Rostorrmel in a matter of weeks.

"Oh."

"Obviously, I am not suggesting that you just walk into the palace and kill him. There is clearly much at play in Rostorrmel that we don't understand. We need him alive for the time being, but it would be useful to gain what information we can."

I took a deep breath in and let it out slowly as I thought things through.

"Just to be clear, we're talking about the man who almost killed the Seer upstairs in one of your bedrooms to learn of my existence, and then instructed the Order to capture me and take me back to Rostorrmel *alive*. We're contemplating me *willingly* walking into the palace, which is likely crawling with Order priests, for a *ball*?"

Austell inclined his head.

"Yes, I appreciate that there is some risk to what I am proposing, but it feels to me that there is a chain of events in motion here and we may be well served to go with it."

I sighed. He had a point. I thought about what Cadoc had said a couple of days before, that sometimes things happen before we are ready for them to happen. Maybe it was best to face this head on and figure it out as we went.

"Alright. I'll come," I said firmly before I could change my mind. "But won't I need an excuse to be there?"

Austell opened his mouth and then closed it, seemingly wanting to say something else. I raised my eyebrows and looked at him, silently prompting him to speak.

"If you are to join me, I think it would be best if you did so as my fiancée. It would be most unusual for a Lord to bring a female companion if there was not some... arrangement in place."

I blinked once, then twice. I was taken aback by his suggestion, but also slightly tickled by his choice of words.

"Arrangement?"

"A wife or betrothed. Lord Canver and Lord Tanrith sometimes bring their mistresses, but I'm not sure that would suit either of us."

I laughed at his awkwardness, suddenly finding the conversation rather funny. No, Austell wasn't really the type to show up somewhere with a mistress in tow.

"Yes... I can see that might cause a bit of a stir. But what if I'm recognized or it becomes known that I'm Nevedeno? What if Finn chooses to confide in his new business partner?" I held up my arm, my sleeve falling down to reveal my tattoo. "Plus *this* kind of gives it away."

He waved his hand dismissively; smiling at me as his eyes shamelessly roamed my body.

"It's cold up there, so you'll want long sleeves. But if it comes out, you will beg for forgiveness and claim you were entrapped, which you were, and I'll declare my love for you and beg the King for his mercy and generosity. I'll tell him the truth. That I am completely and utterly enthralled by you."

I laughed, feeling my cheeks heat as I avoided his eyes. Suddenly I was the one feeling awkward. He leaned back in his chair and shrugged nonchalantly, the move belying his upbringing as the son of a wealthy lord.

"I'm known as a rather headstrong, impulsive man when it comes to matters of the heart, and not someone who concerns myself too greatly with what others think. This won't be seen as particularly out of character. Besides, we could likely put on a fairly convincing act, don't you think?"

I breathed a laugh. What had given him that impression? Of course, he was a handsome man, and he was growing on me the more I got to know him. And I was flattered, fully aware that he was attracted to me, but his words caused my chest to constrict and my heart to ache. I pushed the feeling away with a deep breath. What I'd had with Emrys hadn't been real. I had to forget all of that. Would it really be so bad pretending to be in love with Austell for a few days?

"I suppose so," I said, forcing a smile on my face. "But if we're to make this believable, Lord Mirle, we're going to need a very large diamond."

CHAPTER 8

EFA

"You know what they say," Arella called from my bathtub. "The best way to get over a man is to get under another one."

I almost choked on my water, spluttering slightly as I lay on the bed gazing out of the window.

"I'm not sure that's quite what I had in mind."

"Why not? He's very attractive, in a traditional sort of way. Classically handsome, I'd say. And he's obviously got a thing for you. You can tell by the way he looks at you. Like you're a rare vintage wine he can't wait to taste."

"Honestly, Rell," I said, laughing as I walked over to the bathroom and leaned against the doorframe. "I don't know where you get these ideas from. Torr isn't keeping you busy enough."

She smiled at me as she lathered soap into her hair.

"Look, I know what you're going to say: that he's a bit too pristine. You've always liked them a bit rougher round the edges. To be honest, that's probably why you put up with Finn for so long since he's as beautiful as he is crazy.

But you know, I think our Lord Esari might have a bit of an edge to him."

"An 'edge'?" I asked, raising an eyebrow.

"Yeah, you know the type. You *think* he's going to be gentle and unadventurous, but then the next thing you know he's telling you to turn around and put your hands on the headboard."

My laugh echoed around the marble-floored room.

"I'm not convinced. He strikes me as the sort of man who would fold his clothes neatly before he fucks you."

Arella screeched hysterically, her sudden movement causing water to slosh over the side.

"I'm serious though, Efa," she said, dipping her head back into the water. "I think he's a good guy. I know Emrys felt like… I don't know, like he was the missing piece. Dark and mysterious and setting your shadows off… but don't write off Austell just yet. Give him a chance. Maybe you could have that other life that you were dreaming of. Who knows, being Lady Esari might suit you."

I picked up a towel and walked over, dropping it on the floor and using my foot to move it around so it soaked up the water on the floor. I perched on the edge of the bathtub and rubbed at my face.

"Don't joke. I'm not sure that with my history being Lady Esari is actually an option. Anyway, I guess I just feel a bit nervous and awkward about this pretend engagement. It's all happening a bit soon after… you know. I just feel delicate."

Arella's face turned serious, her hand reaching out to touch mine.

"I'm only teasing you, E. You don't need to fall in love with him, or sleep with him, unless you want to see which of our theories is correct," she said with a wink. "You just need to see this as a job. It's no different from anything else we've ever done. Your primary objective is to get into the palace, work out what the fuck is going on, and figure out how we take the bastard down."

"Easy when you say it like that, huh?"

"You can do this. *We* can do this."

I nodded, looking down at my hands.

"Torr is back tomorrow. What will you do?"

"It's up to you. He has business in The Azuls that will take a few weeks. I'm supposed to go with him to translate, but if you really need me here then of course I can stay."

"No, I'll be alright if you need to go. I'm sure I can fill my time readily enough. There'll be plenty of training with Nev, and then I need to figure out how to build my 'stamina' so I don't lose my shadows quite so quickly. And of course there will be the dress fittings for all of the new clothes that I'll need now that I'm Lord Esari's fiancée, and don't forget Austell's lessons in Melrithian politics…"

"Stop it, you're making me jealous."

I grinned at her, standing up and going back into the bedroom to flop down on the bed again. I tried to put a brave face on her leaving, but I was tearful the next morning when I hugged her and Torr goodbye down in the harbor, already feeling the loneliness settling back over me before she had even left.

"Are you sure you don't want me to stay?" she asked, her forehead creased in concern.

"No, it's fine. You go. I'll be seeing you in a few weeks. Just make sure you're in Rostorrmel like we agreed. I'm not sure I can do this without you."

I trusted that I was as safe as I could be at Totease, so we had agreed that Arella would sail with Torr to The Azuls to complete their business. Austell and I would leave for the capital in three weeks, and I would meet Arella there, the *Panacea* sailing directly north from the Azulian capital of Soless to Rostorrmel. Once there, she would join me as my lady's companion since Austell and I would be unmarried and it would be improper to be without one.

"We'll be there, Efa," Torr said. "We'll see you in Rostorrmel in a month. You have my word."

I nodded as he kissed me on the cheek and squeezed my shoulder reassuringly.

"Remember to eat, Efa," Arella murmured to me as we embraced each other for the final time. "Keep your strength up, and *remember who you are*."

I desperately tried to hold back tears again as I walked back through the town and traipsed despondently back up the cliff path. A month felt like a lifetime in my current state and I had a feeling that the days would drag until I was with Arella again. Fortunately, Eseld had arranged for the local dressmaker to attend that afternoon and I had plenty to distract me.

The dressmaker, Sowena, was clearly Gifted. I could tell from the way that she interacted with the different fabrics she had brought with her that she had a talent. The colors seemed to intensify as she ran her hands over the silk, her face lighting up as she pulled out different fabrics, pairing patterns and shades together that just seemed to work. I had never been one for fashion so I deferred to her and Eseld, sitting silently for most of the afternoon as they discussed what I would need for the trip. Sowena wafted around, moving and turning me as she decided what would complement my figure and coloring, and by the sound of it, there was no limit on what Austell was willing to pay.

I dined with him and Eseld again that night, asking questions about his vineyards and the estate in general as I pushed my food around my plate. I tried to be interested in the responses, but the truth was my mind kept wandering.

"Of course, the Muscat wine has a sweet and fruity flavour..."

Where was he now?

"But when the grapes are crossed, or mixed with other varieties..."

Had any of it been real?

"Sometimes we perfume it with honeysuckle or pear from the orchards..."

Was he thinking about me, too?

A few times I caught Eseld looking at me sympathetically, and I had smiled at her like nothing was wrong. But as I stood on my balcony that night with the warm, salty air blowing gently off the sea, everything felt wrong, as if the stars had somehow dropped out of the sky. And I couldn't help but wonder what hurt more; missing Emrys the way that I did, or pretending to everyone that I didn't.

CHAPTER 9
EFA

I fell into a routine over the next few days, breakfasting with Eseld and Austell in the dining room or on the patio and then walking over to the barracks to train with Nev. He was a kinder teacher than Morgan had been, with what seemed like infinite patience. He took the time to explain things to me, correcting my grip or my stance and slowing down the drills so that I could pick them up, but the sessions were no less grueling. I had also taken to eating lunch at the big table in the kitchen as Molly, the cook, and her two young kitchen maids scuttled around, gossiping while they prepared the evening meal. At a loss as to what to do with myself, I sometimes stayed there for the afternoon while they taught me how to make bread or pastry, and one afternoon I asked the gardeners if I could help them with harvesting the day's vegetables. The busier I was, the less time I had to think.

After a few days, Austell asked me to join him in his study one evening and I followed him in, taking a seat in what had become my usual chair. He was wearing a light blue linen shirt that was the same color as his eyes, and I thought how nice he looked in it.

"You've been quiet lately," he said gently. "How are you?"

"Fine, thank you."

"You look tired. Are you sleeping?"

I pushed my hair back behind my ears, avoiding his eyes as I pressed my nail into the pad of my thumb. The skin felt raw and sensitive.

"I sleep well enough."

That was a lie. Sleep had eluded me recently, and I suspected he knew that. He said nothing though, rubbing at his neck as he looked at me with concern.

"I'm fine, Austell, really. You don't need to worry about me."

"I do worry," he sighed, but he seemed to think better of pushing me on it. "Anyway, I have some news. A woman called Negan will be arriving tomorrow afternoon. I believe she will be able to help you with your additional training."

"Oh!" I said, my spirits lifting a little. "Well, that's good news. I'm surprised that you managed to find someone so quickly."

"I hope she will be able to build your confidence and answer any questions that you may have." He moved to stand behind his desk, opening a drawer and pulling out a small box. "I also have something else that I think may cheer you up."

He walked back around to me and leaned casually against his desk, opening the box and holding it out to me. My eyes widened and I let out a small gasp.

"Is that big enough for you?"

Inside the box was one of the most exquisite diamond rings I had ever laid eyes on, an oval diamond on a platinum band. I lifted it out and held it up to the light.

"What is that, four… four and half carats?"

"Almost five," Austell said. "It was my mother's engagement ring."

My head snapped up to look at him.

"You're letting me wear your mother's ring?"

"It is no more than you deserve, Efa. Besides, my mother's engagement ring is rather well known. It is a family heirloom, and I would never propose without it. Our engagement has to be believable, does it not?"

He carefully took the ring from me and slipped it on to my finger, leaving me speechless. Everything felt rather surreal right then.

"Of course, there's always the chance that you'll end up keeping it should you fall in love with me by the end of our trip."

He grinned playfully at me and I found myself blushing awkwardly. I seemed to be doing that a lot these days.

"Tomorrow I shall announce our engagement," he went on. "I'll also be notifying the King that I intend for you to accompany me to Rostorrmel. In the meantime we should begin making plans for our wedding; we should visit the shrine and the seamstresses, select flowers and cakes… that sort of thing. It needs to be public, too. Should any spies be watching, it's important that they see a couple very much looking forward to their marriage."

"You're not worried about Finn?" I asked, thinking about what Theo had said that night in the dungeons.

"That he will try and kill me? Should I be worried?"

I lifted a shoulder, standing up and going to stand at the window. I looked down at the ring on my finger, marveling at the way it sparkled in the light.

"Finn is a jealous man. He has killed men who were acquainted with me in the past."

"Care to elaborate?" he asked as he joined me at the window.

"A few years ago I met a merchant in Astraea. I liked him a lot. He was unassuming, gentle, and he didn't know what I did, either. I went to his house one day to meet him, only to find him murdered in his bed. Finn never said a word, and I never asked, but I knew.

"Over the next couple of years I had two other lovers. This time I was much more discrete, thinking I could keep it hidden. But they both ended up the same way. When I returned back to camp after finding Rollo dead in his warehouse, Finn asked me what it was like to have innocent blood on my hands."

I turned to face Austell, my fingers fiddling nervously with the ring. I liked the Esari Lord, and right now he was all I had. I didn't want anything to happen to him, and I wasn't sure I could handle the guilt of knowing that, if anything did, it was because of me.

"It is my risk to take, Efa, and I am willing to take it. Finn will not intimidate me. He may have got through my security once, but we will not make that mistake again."

He shifted where he stood, and I became aware of how close he was to me.

"You deserved better," he said softly. "Better than being lied to or controlled."

I knew he wasn't just talking about Finn and I glanced up at him from under my lashes, his blue eyes gazing at me intently. My stomach fluttered unexpectedly as his hand lightly brushed against mine and I licked my lips hesitantly, noticing the way his eyes dropped to my mouth. I was becoming increasingly aware of the mounting tension between us, and I stepped away from him breathlessly, the moment passing. Austell cleared his throat and I took a deep breath, suddenly weary and desperate to be alone.

"Efa—"

"Good night, Austell," I said quickly, cutting him off. "Thank you for all that you are doing for me. I really am so grateful. I'll see you in the morning?"

"Of course," he smiled. "Sleep well."

CHAPTER 10
EFA

Nev's wooden training sword slammed into my shoulder and I cried out, stepping back to dodge his next swing and realizing too late that he had placed his foot behind my own. I fell hard onto the ground, cursing loudly as I dropped my head back into the dust. The fall had winded me slightly and I lay there panting hard until Nev offered me his hand. I used it to stand clumsily and dusted myself off.

"You know, when we started this I remember thinking that I preferred training with you over Morgan, but now I'm wondering if you were just going easy on me. You're as vicious as he is!"

Nev grinned at me, motioning with his sword for me to get back in position so that we could begin the drill over again. He slowed his pace, giving me a chance to keep up this time.

"I wasn't soft on you exactly," he said, pulling a move that had me twisting awkwardly to block him. "But I was trying to ease you in and figure out what you were already capable of doing so I could train you appropriately. I'm not sure Morgan knows what that means. He's an exceptional fighter, that kid, but it's all or nothing with him when he's got a sword in his hand. I don't know where he gets his energy from."

I laughed, or tried to since I was still struggling to catch my breath after almost an hour of training. Nev referring to Morgan as a 'kid' had me realizing that I had absolutely no idea how old any of them were. When I thought they were all Valtanan I'd assumed that Bran and Emrys were only slightly older than me, and Morgan about Noa's age, but if they were Fae… well, who knew?

"How old is Morgan?" I asked.

"He's actually about my age, forty or so, but young enough that the Fae would still consider him a juvenile. I'm not sure about Emrys and Bran, but I know Cad is at least 250 years old. That guy has seen a fair amount in his lifetime."

My mouth dropped open in shock and I lost concentration, yelping as his sword caught me and made the still healing wound on my side smart.

"He's 250 years old? Are you kidding me? Ouch!"

This time his sword caught my other shoulder. I was growing tired and suddenly my irritation got the better of me as I pulled essence to me, using it to dart behind him. My sword was against his throat before he had a chance to react.

"That's cheating, Efa," he said, suddenly stern. "We've talked about this. You won't be able to do that if you've been touched with Faelock. You need to rely on your own physical abilities, *without* your gifts."

"I know, I know…" I moaned, using my forearm to wipe the sweat from my brow.

"Let's finish up for the day," he said, softening. "It's getting too hot."

We walked over to the edge of the training ring to find some shade and he threw me a water skin. I found Nev to be easy company, liking his no-nonsense approach, and that what you saw was what you got with him. I hated having to second-guess people, and I never had to do that with him. He had been reserved at first, bowing and still referring to me as 'my lady', but after a few days of training that formality had dropped away. His accent changed, too, the softer, rhotic brogue of the region coming out as he relaxed around me. When I'd asked him about it he told me that he was born and raised in Esari, and that his father had been the old Lord Mirle's Captain of the Guard. That was how he and Austell had become friends, training together as boys.

"Can I ask you about Austell and Emrys?" I asked, thinking about the incongruous relationships between the two men. "Am I imagining it or is there some kind of animosity there? I can't figure it out. It's like they respect each other, but they don't really like each other."

He laughed, taking a seat on the low wall next to us.

"Yeah, you'd think they'd be over it by now, but ten years on and they're still mad about it."

"Mad about what?"

"A girl, naturally. It's always over a girl, isn't it?" He gave me a sideways look and grinned. "Seems like history is repeating itself."

"Just tell the story, Nev," I said sharply, suppressing a smile.

"Austell was courting the daughter of one of Esari's wealthiest landowners. She was a pretty girl, all doe-eyed and shy smiles, and he was quite taken with her. I was surprised at the time; he usually preferred someone a little more… spirited."

There was that grin again.

"Anyway, around that time, Emrys was in the region on some training exercise, and he met the girl when the old Lord Mirle threw his regular summer ball."

"I think I see where this might be going," I said, rolling my eyes.

It was hardly surprising. All of the rumors painted Prince Trystan as a prolific womanizer. This sounded like just another story that was about to confirm that.

"Indeed. They were discovered in the gardens later that evening. When Austell learned of their dalliance there was a bit of a brawl, and then the girl's father subsequently demanded that *Emrys* marry her, but he refused, saying that nothing had happened. Austell could hardly marry her after the scandal got out, and so she was quickly married off to a wealthy merchant in Tithra."

He chuckled to himself, but I didn't find it funny. It was reminding me of what a fool I had been, simpering over Emrys like all the other poor, naïve girls before me. Nev's story was also making me wonder whether Austell's interest was all just to get a rise out of Emrys, rather than because he was genuinely attracted to me. And, of course, it was possible that there was another reason that Austell might be pursuing me. He was clearly an ambitious man. Was he quietly hoping that one day I would sit on the throne, and that he might sit beside me?

I wasn't really sure what to think, but I decided that right then it didn't matter. I trusted that he wasn't trying to sell me out to the Order, and that was enough for the time being. If he flirted with me, so what? I was done feeling sad about Emrys, and I belonged to no one.

Nev left me at kitchen door and Molly greeted me warmly as I traipsed in and sat down heavily at her table. I let myself be fussed over as she placed a bowl of chicken soup and a plate of fresh bread in front of me while Mea, one of the young maids, chattered away about how the baker's apprentice down in the town had glanced at her this morning on her walk up. I smiled at her innocence, noticing Molly placing another bowl of soup on a tray.

"Who's that for?" I asked.

"It's for Iona, the poor love. Mea, will you please take this upstairs for me before you start on those potatoes?"

"I can take it," I said quickly, rising from my chair.

"Gods, no, child. Lord Mirle would *not* be pleased if he found out I had you carrying trays around like a serving girl!"

I stepped around her to pick up the tray.

"I insist. I'll take it up now. I'd like to see Iona, anyway."

I left her flapping about and strolled along the corridors and up the main staircase. By chance, I happened to come face to face with Austell at the top of the stairs and, as Molly predicted, he eyed the tray in my hands with a frown. I laughed. It was typical that I had run into him then when I hadn't seen him all morning.

"You know I employ people to do this?"

"Before you tell her off, I gave her no choice," I said as I swept past him and walked quickly along the hallway to Iona's room. "I can be very persuasive, remember?"

When I reached her room, I knocked softly and opened the door awkwardly with my elbow.

"Hello," I said as I entered, feeling heartened to see Iona sitting up in bed reading a book.

I helped her to arrange her pillows more comfortably and placed the tray down on her lap, taking a seat in the chair next to her bed. There were fresh roses in the vase by the window and I wondered if Austell or Eseld had picked them for her.

"How are you, Iona?" I asked.

Her bruises had almost disappeared now and the bandages had been removed from her hands. It would take some time for her fingernails to grow back, if they ever did, but they didn't look anywhere near as sore as they had when Bran had seen them for the first time. He really had done a remarkable job healing her before he left.

"Tired, mostly," she said, her voice sounding much stronger than it had done previously. "But in a lot less pain, thanks to that wondrous boy."

"Yes, he's very good, isn't he?" I agreed, finding myself reluctantly missing Bran's reassuring presence.

"More importantly, how are *you*, child?"

I laughed faintly, gazing out of the window. How was I? A mess. My head and my heart were warring constantly, and I hadn't felt like myself for days. I said as much to her.

"One minute I feel resolute and absolutely clear in my mind about what I must do. The next, I'm lost, confused, and I doubt myself completely. I've never felt like this. I've always been so decisive, so sure in myself. I feel like I don't even recognize myself anymore."

Iona put her spoon down and reached forward to take my hand. She looked at me kindly.

"It's funny, I remember your mother saying something very similar to me when she was a young girl about to take the throne."

I looked at her in surprise, my eyebrows knitting together.

"You knew my mother?"

"Oh yes, rather well, in fact. I Witnessed for her several times. When she was barely more than a girl she was suddenly faced with the prospect of becoming one of Valtana's youngest ever queens when her mother, your grandmother, became unexpectedly ill. She doubted herself, too."

"What did you say to her?" I said, my voice almost a whisper.

"I told her what I had seen. That she would become one of the greatest queens that Valtana had ever seen, and that she would find true love and happiness in the *daenadas*."

"The *daenadas*?" I repeated.

"It's the Fae term for what we demi-fae call Gods Fated."

I looked at her, confused. The term was scattered through folk tales and legends, but I'd never thought it was actually a real thing.

"I thought that was just something made up."

"Oh no, child. It's a real as you or I. To be Gods Fated is a rare and powerful bond. It is said that when the Gods forged the very fabric of reality, they left threads within it that tied certain souls together—not by chance, not by love alone, but by *purpose*. Two people who are Gods Fated are more than soul mates; they are echoes of each other across lifetimes, reforged over and over to fulfill their divine purpose."

I frowned, always skeptical of stories about the Gods who seemed to be long absent from this world.

"The union isn't always romantic, although that is certainly the most common. Sometimes they are adversaries, sometimes allies, sometimes both. But their connection is undeniable. When they meet, the world stirs. Mountains rumble their names. The stars blink with memory."

I breathed a laugh, staring out across the ocean as I considered her words.

"Why are some Gods Fated and not others?" I asked.

"No one knows exactly. Some say it's because they hold within them the spark of a forgotten God, split in two.

Others believe it is because they have been chosen to restore balance. The one thing that all seem to agree on is that their connection shapes the fate of realms."

Her words hung in the rose-scented air. A butterfly fluttered past the window and I watched it absentmindedly, a small crease between my brows.

"And you're telling me that my parents were Gods Fated?"

"Yes. You didn't know?"

"No. They never told me... was it common knowledge?"

"I doubt it. Your parents were very private people. But I think that they had always known that something drew them together." She paused, watching the butterfly, too. "The *daenadas* changes everything. When people speak of it, they speak of finally finding themselves, of feeling whole, complete. It makes both people stronger when they are with each other. Certainly for your mother it made her gift so much more pronounced. I remember her saying that it was as if she had found the other half of herself in your father, that she found peace in his presence, and that nothing felt right when he wasn't there."

My shadows hummed and tears pricked at my eyes, a question trying to form in the back of my mind. I forced it away.

"Did... did Damen know?"

A pained expression passed across her face at the mention of the king and she nodded sadly.

"I believe he did, and I think that only fueled his jealousy and resentment. When he found out, he realized that she would never be his, and he couldn't bear it."

I bowed my head, pressing my thumbnail into the pad of my finger.

"Last time, you told me to trust the darkness. You

meant Trystan, didn't you? The Dark Prince. He is the darkness."

She inclined her head.

"Yes, I believe so. That is what I have seen."

"How could I possibly trust him after all that he has done?" I stood up and began pacing around the room. "I don't believe it. I *cannot* believe that he is my fate. Not after all he has done… all that he is."

Iona watched me steadily with a kind, patient expression on her face.

"We only speak the prophecies as we see them, child. They are but predictions, glimpses into the future that may or may not come true. Fate is a funny thing, and we Seers see only a few moments of what is yet to come. You will know yourself how quickly things alter, how easy it is to set off a chain of events. Sometimes, Aeva, all it takes is one word, one look, one touch… and absolutely everything can change."

CHAPTER II
EFA

I was sat in the rose garden brooding and staring out at the glittering waters when I heard the sound of voices, and I looked up to see Austell walking towards me with someone I hadn't seen before. She was a small and slight olive-skinned woman, with wiry, grey curls piled up on top of her head wrapped in a brightly colored scarf. As she got closer I had the strangest sensation, as if she was looking right through me. As if she knew all of my secrets just by looking at me.

"Efa, allow me to introduce Negan Aeland. Luckily for us, she has agreed to work with you."

The woman bowed respectfully and I inclined my head in response, wondering what Austell had told her so far about me.

"Thank you for coming," I said politely. "I hope you haven't had to travel far."

"My home is on the south coast, but I am used to travelling." She paused and smiled, her almost colorless eyes meeting my own confidently. "I must confess, when I received Lord Mirle's request for help I was most curious. So, here I am."

"Well, I am extremely grateful for any help you can offer me."

Austell stepped towards me and touched me gently on the shoulder.

"I have business to attend to on the estate, but I shall leave you both to get acquainted and see you later this evening."

I nodded and watched him walk away as Negan walked to stand at the very edge of the garden, her eyes squinting against the sun. I felt a little unsure of myself as I went to join her, not knowing what to say.

"I'm not sure I would ever tire of this view," she said.

"Yes, it's quite breathtaking."

"Shall we sit?" Negan asked, gesturing to one of the wooden benches a little way off. "Perhaps you can tell me why you believe that you need my help."

I was silent as we strolled to the bench and took a seat. I looked down at my lap and tried to frame my thoughts.

"I have an unusual gift. It is what some have called the *noswaith*."

Negan's eyes widened slightly with interest but she said nothing. I cleared my throat before continuing.

"Not long ago I had to fight for my life, and for others that I… that I cared about. I know that I'm powerful, seemingly more than ever for some reason, but I can't sustain it. The essence just runs out too quickly. My nose bleeds and I get unbearable headaches. Cadoc… someone told me that the essence doesn't just run out, and that if I practiced more and learned how to properly use my gift that it wouldn't happen. But I don't know where to start."

She had laughed softly at the mention of Cadoc's name, her smile lighting up her wizened face.

"I assume that you are referring to Cadoc Angove, and yes, he should know."

I sat up a little straighter, staring at her in shock.

"Cadoc Angove? Do you… do you mean General Angove? King Dafydd's General?"

She nodded at me, and I made a small sound. I'd never thought to ask any of their family names, although I doubted they would have been honest even if I had. But Cadoc Angove was almost as legendary as the Dark Prince himself. He was a phenomenal soldier and one of the previous king's best strategists.

"The very same. You know that he was renowned for teaching Faelings how to harness their full powers? He was doing that long before he became General. And he's right. Your gift is like any other skill. It can be honed and sharpened by use and practice."

I stood up and paced back and forth, feeling suddenly restless.

"You have kept your gift hidden for many years," she continued. "And with good reason, too, since I imagine if you had not, you would have been discovered long before now. But you must get used to using it. You must learn to draw on the essence all the time. It should become as natural as breathing."

I glanced at her, wondering what she meant and how I was supposed to do that. She smiled kindly at me, probably seeing the confusion on my face.

"I suspect that what you are doing now is pulling essence to you and letting it go in a sudden, wild burst, but the better way is to steadily release the essence. You must control it, instead of *it* controlling *you*. Does that make sense?"

"I think so. It has always felt as though my shadows

had a mind of their own, a slightly wayward mind of their own…"

"They may always be like that. I suspect in some part that's down to your own character." She paused and smiled at me. "But to Cadoc's point, the more you use it, the more you will be able to govern it. Tomorrow we can start to train you, but until then, I want you to focus only on drawing and releasing essence as much and as steadily as you can, and on being consciously aware of how you are doing it."

"I'll try, but won't it be obvious?"

"Oh yes. We'll need to ask Lord Mirle to warn his staff that they may see and feel some disturbances around the estate."

I laughed, stopping my pacing and sitting down next to her again.

"Can I ask… how do you know all this? What is your gift?"

She turned those colorless eyes on me and tilted her head as if she was listening to something.

"You carry a great deal of heartache and anxiety, Aeva Penrose."

I stilled, my breath catching before I could stop it. A prickle ran up the back of my neck, spreading across my scalp, and the hairs on my arms lifted.

"You worry about your cousin and you don't know who to trust. And you are angry, too. *So* very angry. At the one who has hurt and betrayed you. At the one who has attempted to own you. And at the one who persecutes your people. But mostly with yourself. You question whether you are enough, and whether you can truly be your parent's heir."

I could hear my pulse thudding in my ears, and for a moment I could only stare.

"You're an Empath," I whispered. "You're in my mind."

Gods. Where had Austell found *her*? She nodded sagely, turning her gaze onto the ocean.

"I am. And I was once one of your mother's spies. It is an honour to serve her daughter."

I took a deep breath, swallowing hard. Like Iona, she had known my mother.

"You know, it's funny. You look like both of them and neither of them at the same time."

I smiled sadly, blinking away the tears that had formed in my eyes, my emotions closer to the surface than usual after the events of the last few days. I held the woman's gaze, wondering if I could let my guard down with her. If my mother had trusted her, then perhaps I could, too. I released my breath in a rush, deciding to take a risk.

"I *am* angry, and hurt. I don't know what to do with all of this rage."

My leg was bouncing up and down and Negan placed a wrinkled hand on it.

"I knew you as a child, Efa, the willful, spirited, and determined force that you were even then. And I knew your parents well. I recall a time that someone, Damen, if I recall correctly, said that you were too wild, too reckless. I'll always remember what your father said. He said that you were exactly who you were supposed to be."

My lip trembled at her words and tears threatened to fall again. I tried to picture my father's face. Not a day went by when I didn't miss him. When I didn't miss them both.

"He wanted you to be bold and brave, and to live a life without shame or regret, Efa, even though they often go hand in hand with the responsibility of wearing a crown."

She leaned in to me, her voice low and urgent.

"You must *let go* of your anger, Efa, for it does not serve you. It drags you down and stops you from moving forward. Instead, embrace the woman that you are *in spite* of all that you have lost, *because* of what you have lost, and how you have been wronged. Do not concern yourself with revenge, but seek only to do what is *right*, for you and for your people. Let that be what drives you, and let everything else go."

CHAPTER 12
EFA

I slept through that night for the first time since I had sent Emrys away, although odd dreams still troubled me. I woke feeling tired and heavy, exhausted from practicing drawing essence throughout the previous afternoon and evening, letting shadows slip from my fingers and curl about my hands at the dinner table. To his credit, Austell said very little about it, but I could see Eseld's eyes flicking to them every few minutes, clearly perturbed by their presence. After a while, I let the shadows drift, sending them up to the ceiling where they hung like thick, shimmering clouds that caught the candlelight in strange, delicate ways, and her expression turned to one of delight.

I carried on practicing the next morning, letting them explore as I took my time getting ready for the day. I bathed and dressed in a loose lemon yellow dress instead of my usual training attire and went downstairs to find Austell and Eseld already in the dining room eating

"I assume that you aren't meeting Nev this morning?" Austell asked, nodding his head at my dress.

I shook my head, reaching across the table for a slice of toast.

"Not today. I sent him a note this morning. I feel tired and decided it would be more beneficial to rest. I might take a walk or go into town before I meet with Negan again later this afternoon."

"Sowena will be coming after lunch with your gowns," Eseld said. "If it suits you, she can do your final fittings."

"It suits me very well. Thank you for arranging it, Eseld."

I smiled at her and she blushed shyly, looking down at her breakfast. She was a sweet girl, good natured and kind at heart. She had lost her father around the same age that I had lost my own parents, and sometimes I saw a lot of myself in her, except she didn't seem to have the mischievous, wild streak that had got me in plenty of trouble over the years. Austell placed his cutlery together and picked up his cup of tea.

"I'll be heading out to the vineyards soon," he said. "Perhaps you would like to accompany me, as you have a free morning?"

"I'd like that," I said, pleased by the genuine delight on his face.

Not long after, we stood in front of the house as the stable hands brought our horses round. I had taken great enjoyment in the way Austell hesitated when he realized that I wasn't going to get changed, and that I intended to ride not just in a dress, but astride the horse, too. Since the skirt had long slits on each side, I simply swung my leg over the white mare and settled comfortably into the saddle, ignoring the fact that a good deal of my thighs were now brazenly on display and reaching down to take the wide brimmed hat that Nev passed up to me.

The young boy holding my horses' reins didn't seem to

know where to look, and I laughed as Nev cuffed him gently round the head. The boy wasn't the only one distracted though, it seemed. I noticed Austell's eyes lingering on my legs when he thought I wasn't looking. Almost certainly what I was doing wasn't proper, but fuck it. I had never been one to care too much what people thought of me.

"Are you ready, my love?" I asked Austell sweetly, and I heard Nev stifle a laugh behind me.

It took about twenty-minutes to ride from the house to the vineyards and I stayed close to Austell, listening carefully as he talked about the estate and pointed things out on our way. When we arrived, I waited for him to dismount and help me, leaning into him as he held me by the waist and lifted me down. I breathed in the scent of his cologne, citrus with a hint of vanilla, and gazed up at him adoringly as I put on a show for the farm hands that waited for us. He broke contact first, a little reluctantly, I thought.

Austell's estate manager was an Azulian man by the name of Lassa who had been working for the Mirle family for many years. He was tall with glowing caramel skin that was darkened from the time spent outdoors, and he had the muscular, lean build of someone who was physically active for a good part of the day. We left Nev with the horses, his face turned up to the sun, and I followed Lassa and Austell as they strolled up and down the rows of vines, assessing the plants and discussing the upcoming harvest. It was a beautiful morning. The sun was warm on my skin and the smell of lavender drifted towards me on the breeze from the nearby fields. I was enjoying being out of the house.

"How do you know when they are ready to harvest?" I asked Austell, pulling off a grape and popping it into my mouth.

"It's all about berry fullness. You see, a ripe grape is plump, juicy, and pulls easily from the cluster. When they are under ripe, they are smaller and harder, obviously, and an overripe grape will start to shrivel. So, we must monitor them closely to pick them at the right time. These should be ready to harvest within the next few days."

"I see, and how can you tell if the wine will be good?"

"Ah, well there are many influences on whether it will be a good or bad vintage, often climatic. But we have had a good year weather-wise, so hopefully we will see it reflected in the taste."

I continued asking questions, finding Austell to be patient and attentive to me. He seemed pleased that I was interested, and I realized that I was seeing him at his most relaxed, surrounded by nature and watching things grow. When Lassa wandered off to check the vines further down, Austell began pointing out the different grape varieties and encouraging me to try them all. He looked almost boyish as he talked to me about each one, and his enthusiasm was infectious. I found myself looking at him in a different light.

"This is what you love, isn't it?" I said suddenly, sweeping my hand in the direction of the vines.

He stood up from where he was crouched down checking the soil, surveying his land like a proud parent.

"Yes, it is, really. I suppose I find peace in nature. There is a balance to her. We must take the rain with the sunshine, the floods with the drought. She is beautiful and chaotic, and unapologetically so. Rather like you, I suppose," he finished with a smile.

I tapped him lightly on the arm, blushing at his smooth attempt at flirtation.

"It's true, though. There is always beauty in nature,

even in its destruction. No matter what, she always finds the balance again. I admire her predictability and honesty."

"'Nature never deceives'," I murmured, quoting the Mirle family motto that I had seen written in various places throughout the house. Austell laughed softly.

"Quite so. I find I know where I stand with nature much more than I do people."

"I can imagine that being Lord Esari must sometimes get in the way of doing all of this."

"To tell you the truth, I never expected to inherit my father's title, nor did I particularly want it. It was always supposed to be my brother, Aric; even though he made it obvious *he* never wanted it either. There are times when I loathe the politics; all the scheming and plotting that goes on, kneeling before a king that I neither like nor respect. I would much rather be here, making wine."

He crouched down to inspect the vine closest to us, passing me a grape to try.

"I stay away from the capital as much as I can, preferring to focus my energy on the region, finding solace in my vineyards and gardens. But I have found that sometimes I can also do a lot of good, too."

He stood up and led the way back up the gentle slope towards Nev and the horses. The temperature was beginning to rise, and I adjusted my hat, pulling down the brim to keep the sun out of my eyes. A light breeze caught the skirts of my dress and sent it fluttering behind me.

"In what way?"

"Esari is and always has been a patient and tolerant region. Her people are kind and gentle, content with a simple life and a strong community. When Damen attacked Nissae, there was no question that we would be a safe place for any Valtanans who needed it. Thousands live in the region, including Gifted, all unbeknownst to Damen and the Order. I even have many in my own staff. They train my horses and manage my land and household, living peacefully amongst the rest of the townsfolk, just like they do across most of Melrith, some hidden and some less so."

"And you lead the Loyalists," I prompted, thinking about the rebels making waves across Melrith.

Emrys had told me that the Loyalists were a real mix of individuals. Some were Valtanans, both Gifted and ungifted. Others were Melrithians, humans who were still loyal to Novos, and unhappy with Damen's cruel and vicious reign.

"Indeed. I still dream of a better Melrith, Efa. For it to be peaceful again, like it was under your parent's rule."

"You are an idealist," I said.

He tilted his head as he considered.

"Perhaps, but I am also a pragmatist. The Loyalists are about restoring the balance, much like nature does. Damen took what was not his and calls for violence and division. He revels in pain, torment and fear. The Loyalists... well, we can only do so much, especially when there has been no natural heir to challenge Damen. I have had to accept my limitations and do what I can to protect Esari, and influence the other Lords as much as I can. But you... you could be the catalyst that brings about real change."

"You think I should challenge Damen for the throne?"

"Why not? It is your birthright."

We had reached the horses now and Austell helped to lift me back up into the saddle. His hand grazed the bare skin of my thigh through the split in the skirt and he caught my eye. I held his gaze, noticing that he didn't immediately move his hand away. My shadows twitched slightly, longing for someone else's touch, but I ignored them, letting Austell's hand remain where it was.

"I am a smuggler, Austell. I'm hardly a model queen.

I'm not meek, or virtuous. I have a tendency to say what I think, to be too direct, and you'd have good cause to question my morals."

"Your people don't need a queen who sits quietly on her throne looking pretty while others make the decisions. They need someone who puts their needs first. Anyway, I've often found that the best leaders are the reluctant ones."

"Like you?" I asked with a smile, and he chuckled.

I glanced away to look at the vines, my brow creasing as I thought about what he said.

"Don't make a decision now," he counseled, moving away and mounting his own horse as Nev joined us. "Let's just get through Damen's ball first and then see where we are."

"All right," I nodded, thinking that I could at least do that.

"Come, I need to check on some other things before we go back. We can ride the long way back to the house and I'll show you the rest of the estate."

Austell nudged his horse into a trot, and I put all thoughts of challenging the throne to the back of my mind and focused on living in the moment. For the time being I was free, fresh air in my lungs and the sun on my skin. On a whim, I held onto my hat and spurred my horse into a canter as I followed Austell across the field. After all, if I wanted to be believable as Lady Esari, I supposed it was high time I got to know my estate.

CHAPTER 13
EFA

"Enough!" I gasped as Nev's sword knocked my own out of my hand for the fourth time in five minutes. I bent over with my hands on my knees trying to catch my breath as the sun beat down relentlessly from the cloudless sun above.

"You're distracted today," Nev observed unnecessarily, stooping down to pick up my sword. "I can see it on your face. Your grip is weak, and your guard is down. This lack of focus will get you killed. Leave your emotions behind, Efa. You need to find a sense of calm when you're fighting."

I pulled a face, irritated with myself and far too hot. Negan had worked me hard the day before, training me in one of the old granaries on the estate. She had made me push my gift harder than I ever had before, asking me to reach deeper into the essence as she taught me how to gather and expend it steadily. I'd gone too far though, feeling the familiar throb in my temple by the time we finished. To make matters worse, I hadn't slept well either, waking every hour in a state of panic and with a feeling of dread in the pit of my stomach. I still hadn't shaken it by the time I met Austell's captain earlier this morning, and I felt off balance and out of sorts.

"You're not trying to kill me," I grumbled. "Obviously, if someone actually *is*, I'll be paying better attention."

Nev raised an eyebrow but chose not to respond, which was probably just as well. I didn't trust myself not to snap at him, and he wouldn't have deserved it. Instead, he left me to ruminate as we walked back to the house and I took a few deep breaths, releasing some of my pent up emotion in the form of vapor-like shadows that trailed behind me on the path. As the house came into view one of the serving lads came running out from the house. His eyes flicked briefly behind me, but he paid the shadows no heed. Austell had done as Negan suggested and warned his staff, and they had seemingly taken it in their stride. Most were now starting to get used to the house shaking or rumbling randomly, or walking into a black fog as they rounded a corner or entered a room.

"Captain, Lieutenant Androw has returned from Baern. He is with Lord Mirle in his study."

Nev clapped the boy on the shoulder and thanked him, frowning slightly as the boy ran ahead of us back to the house.

"What is it?"

"Nothing, really. I just wasn't expecting Androw back for a few weeks. There must be news."

We found the two men mid-conversation when we entered the study, Austell pouring them both a glass of brandy. I judged the Lieutenant was only a few years older than me, but his light brown hair was already beginning to grey. His freckled face had caught the sun in places, leaving his nose and forehead slightly burnt, and he wore no uniform and was dressed much the same as Lassa had been, as if he had just come in from working on the estate. Nev stepped forward to embrace him before taking a seat in one of the chairs. I nodded at the soldier briefly and then wandered over to the window, feeling too restless to sit.

"What news?" Nev asked.

Androw's eyes flicked to me.

"Speak freely, Lieutenant," Austell instructed, sitting down in his usual chair.

"Four days ago, Damen ordered the release of eight Valtanans and for the Order to escort them back to their towns, three to Polruen and five to Baern, with orders to publicly execute them. I am led to believe that the method of execution was to be determined by the local Lord, although the king favors death by fire."

I clenched my fists. They would have been held in Rostorrmel's dungeons for months, years even. Now, they were being returned to their homes to be murdered in front of their families. It was a cruel, deliberate act.

"Lord Baern chose the pyre, and I'm pleased to report that we interrupted the executions, much to his displeasure." Androw smirked at this last part. "The townsfolk revolted in response to the executions. The castle came under siege for a day or two, and parts of the city were on fire for a time. Some sense of order has been restored now but only because a large number of Nothori soldiers arrived and quickly contained the riots. They have spread across the region."

"Nothori? What are Nothori soldiers doing in Melrith?" Deep frown lines were etched into Austell's forehead, his unease as obvious as mine must have been.

The Nothori had never been welcomed by any of Fjellskille's territories. Hailing from the cold, mountainous country of Nothore northwest of the Northern Realm, across the Rhannu Strait, they were a barbaric and savage race that treated their females little better than their slaves.

"They appear to have an arrangement with King Damen, but our sources indicate that Lord Tanrith was unaware that they would be arriving in the city."

"It wouldn't surprise me if Finn was involved in that arrangement," I wondered aloud as I paced back and forth. "They've been creeping along the border, stealing women and girls for months as slaves, and now they're working with the Order and providing military support? That's not a coincidence."

That had Finn written all over it.

"I'd be inclined to agree," Nev said. "What about Polruen?"

He leaned forward, drumming his fingers on the arm of his chair. Androw shook his head sadly.

"Lord Denfor chose death by the sword. It seems he was taking no chances. He deployed his entire guard and at the first sign of attack the Order priests removed their heads rather than risk them being rescued. There was nothing we could do. We understand that further convoys are on route to Baern, Cayam and Portreth."

I closed my eyes, my shadows desperate to be unleashed. I breathed deeply, trying to channel my rage as Negan had taught me, but it threatened to overwhelm me. Shadows erupted from my hands and the floor trembled beneath us making the whole house shake violently. I glanced to at the three men now finding them all looking at me.

"I apologise," I said tersely, but I said it without conviction.

Suddenly the room felt airless and I opened the door that led out onto the patio and stepped out to cool off, resuming my pacing on the lawn.

"I've never seen him fight like this, Nev." Androw's voice floated out of the open door. "It's extraordinary and terrifying at the same time. He doesn't sleep and I barely see him eat. He's on a rampage, cutting down Nothori and Order priests like he's caught up in a permanent bloodlust."

"Well, the Prince certainly has a reputation for violence and bloodshed," Austell replied indifferently. "I can't say I'm surprised."

Emrys. A shiver ran down my spine when I realized who they were talking about.

"Has word got out yet that it's Trystan fighting with the Loyalists?"

"No, my Lord. He is taking care to keep his identity concealed as usual, and they all keep themselves glamored as men."

"Good. At least he's not lost all sense then."

"I've seen Prince Trystan fight alongside the Loyalists a lot over the last few years, my Lord, and he's never been anything but calm and controlled. But this time he's taking risks, taking on ten Nothori all at once. It's like he doesn't care if he lives or dies."

It was like a punch to the gut hearing that. I hadn't wanted to admit it to myself but I had struggled to get him off my mind all day, and now to hear that he was risking his life… I sank down to the ground and pressed my palms into my eyes.

"Fuck," I muttered to myself.

I had to break out of this. Emrys's movements shouldn't bother me in the slightest. I hated him, and what he had done to me, so why was I such a mess? Why did the idea of him getting hurt concern me so much? Gods, I felt like was going slowly insane, and now the small voice in the back of my mind that I had been doing my best to ignore was asking whether he was missing me as much as I missed him. Whether my absence was driving him mad, too.

“Efa?” I heard Austell’s tentative voice behind me and I snapped my eyes open, blinking against the sun. I answered without turning my head.

“I’m fine, Aus. I just need a minute.”

I heard the floor inside creak as he moved away from the door and I dropped my head again, staring down at my trembling hands. It was no good; I needed to work out some of this restless energy and get a grip on myself. I stood up abruptly and marched off across the grass. It was time to find Negan again.

CHAPTER 14
EMRYS

Adrenaline still surged through my veins and my heart raced as I crouched in the shade of a beech tree and tried to catch my breath. In front of me, bodies were strewn across the road, some with tattooed faces, others wearing cobalt cloaks. They'd all met the same end. They'd all deserved to die.

We had intercepted the convoy on its journey south, a unit of Nothori accompanying the Order priests as they transported Valtanan prisoners. I pushed my hair out of my face with a bloodstained hand and watched the Loyalists breaking open the wagon door. Morgan lifted one of the prisoners down, a boy who looked no more than twelve with a bruised and bloodied face. Something about his expression reminded me of Evyn at that age, and I felt the same sudden, crushing guilt that always floored me whenever I thought of my brother. Bran strolled over and sat down beside me on the grass, spearing his sword into the earth.

"How many was it this time? Fifteen? Sixteen Nothori?"

I shrugged. I wasn't keeping count anymore. All I cared about was killing as many of the bastards as I could.

"I see the conversation we had the other day has made no difference. You're still taking too many risks, even for you. Be careful that the bloodlust doesn't blind you, Emrys."

I ignored him, and stared at the activity going on over by the wagon. I knew that I was being rash and reckless, but the truth was I didn't care. Not since she'd told me to leave.

"You haven't lost her, brother," he said, reading my mind like usual. "She's just hurt… there's a difference."

I said nothing, but I heard the regret in his voice and I looked down at my hands. Of all people, Bran would know what it meant to lose someone, but though I had left Efa alive and well in Esari, it felt like I had lost her forever.

"One day you have to stop punishing yourself, Em." When I remained silent he gave a long-suffering sigh. "All right. Let me look at that cut on your arm then."

I held my closest arm out to him and watched him inspect the deep gash that ran down the outside of my forearm. I couldn't even remember getting it. A moment later I felt the familiar prickling across my skin as he began to knit the wound together. Boots crunched on the ground and I glanced up to see Cadoc walking towards us, a stony expression on his lined face.

"I've had a message. We're being called home, Emrys," he said. "Your brother's orders are for us to return to the Northern Realm as soon as possible."

"No," I said, with a small shake of my head.

"Emrys, they're our orders."

"I said no." There was a bite to my voice this time, my patience already wearing thin. "We're not going back."

Cadoc sighed, rubbing the back of his neck uneasily as he looked to Bran for support, but he only shrugged.

"I'm inclined to agree with Emrys on this occasion," Bran said. "We have our strongest intelligence yet that the Amberstone is in Rostorrmel."

"He won't like it—"

"I don't fucking care what he likes, Cad," I snarled. "We're not leaving. We're going to find the Amberstone, and we're going to do what we should have done twenty years ago."

I pulled my arm out of Bran's grip and stood up abruptly, sliding my sword back into its scabbard. *As long as I'm still breathing…*

"We're going to stay and fight for *her*."

CHAPTER 15
EFA

"Tell me what's bothering you," Negan said, raising her voice over the noise of me relentlessly slamming shadows into the granary wall.

It was a welcome addition to my repertoire, not least because it was helping me release some of the pent up frustration that had been building all day. For years I had believed that, aside from shattering the occasional mind, the most I could do with my gift was hide myself. But when I had described the way my shadows had unexpectedly manifested in the forest against the Nothori, and then when I'd used them against Emrys, Negan had shown me how to use them as a weapon. Unsurprisingly, I had taken to it quickly, so she'd also had to show me how to limit the damage only to what I wanted to break or hurt whilst leaving everything else, or more importantly *everyone* else, unscathed. But as she watched me hurl another hay bale across the barn, I had a feeling she might have been regretting some of her decisions.

"You're channeling your anger, and that's good. That's

productive. But I can see that you're still holding it in. Talk to me, Efa."

"You already know what's bothering me since you can read my mind," I snapped, the ground shifting slightly beneath me as I cast out more darkness.

"Sensing it isn't the same as you acknowledging it and moving on."

I paused my assault on the walls to glare at her.

"What do you want me to say?"

"I want you to *tell* me why you're so angry."

"Why do you fucking think?" I exclaimed, throwing my hands up in the air in exasperation. "My people are *dying*, Negan."

"Yes. What else? That's not the only thing on your mind, is it?"

Her voice was firm as she continued to press me, refusing to rise to me even when I was being deliberately rude and disrespectful to her. What did the woman want from me? She was in my head, reading my thoughts. She knew why I was so angry, and that pissed me off even more. What difference did it make me saying them out loud?

"You can get annoyed with me, too, if you like, but it won't help. Your trouble is that you're trying to hold on and let go at the same time. Until you acknowledge what is causing this rage, you cannot deal with it. So tell me, what's bothering you?"

She wandered over to one of the bales I'd tossed about earlier and hopped up onto it, smoothing her long navy skirt down over her legs. I shut my eyes and released all of the essence I was holding in one go; screaming as I did so and feeling the earth shudder violently beneath us. The barn roof creaked and groaned above us and I thought for a moment that I had gone too far and that it was about to come crashing down on us, but by some miracle it held, and I muttered a brief prayer of thanks to the Gods. Negan hadn't even flinched.

"My people are dying," I repeated. "A tyrant who sits on my father's throne while I live here in luxury is murdering them. I'm strolling through vineyards and going to fucking lobster festivals, while he publicly executes innocents as if their lives mean *nothing*. And Gods, I miss Noa! I have known where he was every single day since I was eight years old, and it is *killing* me that I don't know that he's safe."

I paced across the dusty floor and ran my hand through my loose hair, darkness following me with every step. I sighed heavily, my anger starting to give way to despair as I wiped away a single tear that had the nerve to fall.

"And I have never felt about anyone the way I feel about Emrys, Negan. But it was all a lie, wasn't it? He wasn't who I thought he was. In fact, he turned out to be the worst possible person that he could have been. And the cruelest thing about it is that when he left he seemed to take part of me with him. My shadows search for him constantly and I haven't felt like myself in days. It's driving me out of my mind."

I stopped where I was and turned to look at her, finding those watchful eyes of hers staring at me. The words tumbled out now as I went from one thought to another,

"The Loyalists are doing what they can, but the reality is Austell can't truly lead them, not without considerable risk or openly coming out against Damen. In truth, I think they are rather a law unto themselves right now with Austell simply financing them. They need something stronger to unite behind, to give them real purpose. And Damen cannot remain on the throne; it simply can't be allowed to happen. Not for my own vengeance, but for the good of my people, for the good of Valtana *and* Melrith."

"But what will *you* do about that, Aeva Penrose?"

I took a great shuddering breath, blinking away the rest of the tears that threatened to fall.

"You keep telling yourself that you aren't enough and that you can't possibly take the throne. But I look at you and all I see is someone who cares deeply about her people, and quite frankly, that's what they need right now. So, tell me: what will you do about it?"

I raised my head, meeting her eyes as I let the shadows disappear. I knew what I had to do, and it terrified me. Back in Nissae, I had stood before my mother's image and vowed to unleash the full force of my shadows upon him, but since then I had procrastinated and made excuses because I didn't trust in myself to be able to do that, and because I thought I was on my own. But now I had allies, and a resistance fighting in my name. Austell was right, we needed a catalyst to bring about change.

"Tell me who you are," Negan demanded, reading my thoughts.

I dropped my gaze and stared down at the floor.

"Stand up tall, Aeva. Look me in the eye and tell me who you are."

I lifted my head, clenching my fist as I made the decision I had been putting off for weeks.

"I am Aeva Penrose, the heir returned and the rightful queen of Melrith and Valtana."

"Yes, you are," she said, nodding her head slowly. "Don't ever forget that. What will you do?"

I breathed deeply.

"I will fight for my people. For what is mine."

The time for change was now, and if I was to be the catalyst, then so be it.

CHAPTER 16
EFA

The patio door stood wide open, but it made no difference to the stifling heat inside Austell's study. It was a still, sultry night and there had been no hint of a breeze the entire day. Outside, the sky had grown dark and the cicadas buzzed noisily out in the garden as Austell poured the wine. This time he had selected a Tithran rosé—a soft, sweet vintage that had hints of strawberry and elderflower.

The week had passed in a blur of training. Despite making the decision to fight for my birthright I still had to keep myself busy in order to keep the intrusive thoughts telling me I wasn't enough at bay. When I wasn't with Nev or Negan, the rest of my days had been filled with dress fittings and fictional wedding planning. Earlier that day, Austell and I had gone to the shrine where we would supposedly share our vows with each other, and visited the bakeries in town to discuss wedding cakes. News had spread fast of our engagement and there was plenty of excitement and speculation from the local townsfolk, all keen to catch a glimpse of the woman who had seemingly swept their Lord Esari off of his feet.

I had joined him in his study after dinner that evening to discuss the latest news making its way down from Baern. The Order continued in their efforts to hold public executions, but so far the Loyalists had managed to prevent them all from taking place. And although I reminded myself that I no longer cared, I found myself waiting for news of Emrys and the others, but whether there wasn't any, or Austell was simply choosing not to tell me after the last time, nothing more was said about the Dark Prince. The last I'd heard of him had been a few days after Androw had returned. A large bag of coins had been left in my room. The rest of my payment for entering the temple.

Austell finished pouring and handed me my wine, condensation immediately settling on the outside of the glass. He took a seat in the chair next to me instead of sitting behind his desk and I smiled, offering him one of the biscuits that I had helped Molly to make earlier in the day.

"Tell me about the other Lords," I said, tucking my feet up underneath me and adjusting my loose cotton skirt around my legs as I made myself more comfortable.

"How much do you know?"

I tilted my head and pulled a face. I knew who governed each region and the lords by their reputations, but otherwise I had never paid much attention to Rostor-rmel's politics unless I needed to. I was usually more concerned with the local gangs and crooks that operated beneath the surface. Austell put his glass down on the table next to us and stood up, rifling through the papers on his desk until he found the parchment he was looking for. When he sat back down, he placed it on the arm of his chair so we could both see it and I saw that it was a list of Melrith's wealthiest families and landowners, illustrated with their family crests.

"All right, well, let's start with one of the worst ones," he said, pointing to the crest in the bottom corner.

In Melrith, it was custom for most of the wealthiest families to be represented by an animal. This one was a wild boar, black on a scarlet background.

"Zennor Tanrith, our delightful Lord Baern. He's a cruel man, with a fetish for violence and a fondness for watching others suffer."

"He's the one who chose death by fire?"

"Indeed. And likely he will have done so because he knows it's Damen's preference. He plays the political game, that one."

"He sounds wonderful," I said acerbically. "Does he have a wife?"

"No," Austell said, swallowing a mouthful of wine. "And I'd say that's a blessing because he wouldn't make a very good husband. He has multiple women living in his household, some scarcely more than girls. I believe that when he heard about Damen's harem he decided he fancied one for himself."

I shook my head in disgust and mentally added Zennor Tanrith to the list of men I was going to take pleasure in killing.

"He is one of the two new Lords. His predecessor was a good man, a friend of my father's and very loyal to your parents. Ciaran stood with them at Nissae with his three sons. None of them survived the night."

Austell moved his finger to the shield next to Tanrith's.

"Perran Denfor, the Lord Polruen. Just as brutal, and just as vicious. Perran was one of the Lords who turned on your father, but I doubt that was much of a surprise to Novos. I don't think they ever saw eye to eye."

I eyed the Denfor crest, an umber fox on forest green. It was Lord Denfor that allowed underground gangs to rule his region, the most notable an organisation that called themselves the Fraternity who dealt in Silvermist and a particularly lethal hallucinogenic drug called Amanita. The Fraternity was one of the reasons that Torr hated doing business in Polruen, and I'd had a few brushes with them myself. None of them had gone particularly well.

"You might not know this, but you and Denfor are actually related. A third cousin removed, if I remember correctly."

"Wonderful. I might keep that one quiet."

"His wife is a woman called Anneth. She's half Tithran, and I've never really been able to get the measure of her. She says very little and prefers to stay away from Rostorrmel, but if I were a betting man I'd say she's every bit as ruthless as her husband. And, of course, the other thing to mention here is that Damen keeps his military ships down in Polruen."

"That makes sense," I said, nodding thoughtfully. "The harbor is bigger there."

I placed my finger on the crest in the top right hand corner, the magenta eagle of the Canver family.

"This guy is a prick, too," I muttered. "He's the one that won't marry his mistress because of her low birth."

"That's the one. Sandow Canver. He's the other new Lord, although the previous Lord Cayam wasn't much better. He also turned on your father, but he died fighting that night. No great loss. Anyway, you've been through Cayam recently. You will have seen the state of the city."

I nodded. I had been shocked at the amount of whore-houses and Silvermist dens that had cropped up in the city;

the streets filthy and buildings run down. It had been a vibrant, effervescent city when my father had ruled it, and now it had been left to go to ruin.

"He is a pompous, conceited man who is content to let his region go to waste, using Cayam's taxes to fund his lavish lifestyle instead. Caja, his mistress, is a beautiful but vacuous girl and for years he has treated her like his wife, affording her the same privileges and luxuries, but he refuses to marry her because she is the daughter of a cobbler."

"How can she stand to stay with a man like that?"

Austell laughed dryly, swatting away a mosquito that kept buzzing around his head.

"Who knows? She obviously feels it is better than whatever life she left behind."

I uncurled myself and took my glass to go and stand by the window, thinking that the trip to Rostorrmel was sounding worse and worse by the second.

"Now, although half of the Lords are despicable bastards, the other three are not so bad." He placed a hand on his chest and smiled playfully. "Obviously, that includes yours truly—a man of impeccable fashion and style, and a man of the people, beloved by all in his region."

I laughed, unable to disagree with him. He really did dress beautifully, and he was very popular with the Esari people. I glanced at him over my shoulder and smiled. I'd often thought that some people became more attractive as you get to know them. Austell was one of those people, and he'd been handsome to start with. I'd thought him stiff and overly formal at first, but I'd got him wrong. He valued decency and respectability, and he had a strong moral compass and sense of justice. But once you got to know him, much like with Nev the formality fell away. He was even-tempered, with a calm and steady approach. He had a wry, subtle sense of humour, and was a good conversationalist, always genuinely interested in other people's experiences and what they thought about things. My eyes lingered on his face for a fraction too long; long enough for his gaze to became heated. I blushed and looked away again.

"So, we come on to our final pair," he said, smiling and continuing on.

His finger tapped the crests for the Rael and Portreth Lords.

"Montavis and Hollis, who interestingly, are first cousins. They look alike, too. They were once your father's men, but just because they weren't executed after Nissae doesn't necessarily mean they were traitors."

Austell joined me at the window, standing a little closer than he needed to.

"Those two are tight, and they will also be aligned in their approach. They have sworn their allegiance to the king, just like I have, but I believe it is with the best interests of Melrith in mind. They are fair, reasonable men, and like me they counsel Damen to choose peace and tolerance."

"It seems to fall on deaf ears," I muttered, and Austell gave a small laugh. "When do we leave for the capital?"

"In five days. I wish we didn't have to stop in Baern, but Zennor is insistent and to do otherwise would seem discourteous. We'll spend the night at Fort Celnaer in the middle of the city, and travel in convoy from there to Rostorrmel."

"Who else will be there?"

"Canver, probably. Montavis has been overseas so it's likely he will arrive into Rostorrmel by ship. Denfor won't take the Baern road. He'll head north up via Portreth and the coastal road."

Austell moved away to pour himself another glass of wine and I sighed, looking out over the garden.

"We must be very careful, Efa," Austell said from behind me. "I fear that we are about to enter a vipers nest."

I finished my own glass and stretched my neck out, tilting my head from side to side.

"I've been dealing with vipers my whole life, Austell. The trick is simply to become one, too."

CHAPTER 17
EFA

"Focus. This is important." Negan's voice chided me from across the barn. "I can still hear your thoughts as if you're screaming them."

"I'm doing my best, but this isn't a skill that one just hones overnight," I huffed, taking a deep breath and trying again.

I worried at my fingers. Over the last few days, Negan had begun teaching me how to shield my mind from people like her, Empaths who could rifle through my thoughts and discover things that I would prefer to keep hidden. Whilst her gift was extremely rare, almost as rare as my own, it would be just my luck that Damen had one working for him, or had found one and stolen their gift.

"Tell me again why we didn't start this training two weeks ago?"

"You know why. Your mastery of essence was too weak and immature. To build strong walls around your mind it takes considerable skill and energy if you are to keep them up at all times. This is why we have been practicing the way you use essence, and you must continue practicing once I leave tomorrow. Your shield must become second nature to you, like breathing."

"I wish you were coming with us," I said gloomily as I ran my hand across the rough straw of the bale I was perched on.

I had grown close to the Valtanan woman, enjoying our lessons despite how draining they were. I liked the way she challenged me, scolding and reprimanding me like my mother would have, whilst pushing me to achieve what she knew I could. She would have been a useful person to have with us in the capital, but I knew the risk was too great and she had already given so much by coming to Esari to train me. Tomorrow morning, Austell's men would escort her back to the village where she lived with her family, and the next day we would leave for Baern.

"It would certainly be an interesting trip," she dryly. "But I think I'd prefer to live to see another day."

"I don't blame you."

I rubbed at my eyes, feeling tired after concentrating so hard on building my mental shield over and over again.

"There have been more executions," I said with a sigh. "Have you heard?"

She nodded sadly.

"Why is he doing this, Negan? What drives someone to be so cruel?"

"Do you really not know? It's love, Efa. It's always about love. And when it isn't about love, it is about the absence of love. Damen loved your mother more than anything else until it became an obsession. When she didn't love him… worse, when she fell in love with Novos, his closest friend *and* his king, he became twisted and jealous.

"And so love turned to betrayal, and he turned on his friend and the woman he loved, because if he couldn't have her, no one could. Everything is about Aemylia, Efa. All of this… it is all about your mother. He is destroying everything that meant something to her. Everything that was important to her, and everything that reminds him of her."

Yours is a tale of love and betrayal, the prophecy had said. Perhaps the story wasn't just mine. Perhaps it all started with my mother.

"Because he hates her?" I asked.

"No. Because he loves her *still*. And because it *hurts* him so very, very badly."

~

"Do you know what I keep thinking about?" I said to Negan as we strolled back to the house a few hours later.

Negan had made the most of her last day, keeping me in the granary for hours while I constructed the defensive walls over and over again. Blood trickled from my nose by the time we had finished but the usual headache hadn't come. I figured that was progress. She looked at me questioningly.

"The Amberstone. It's niggling away at me. What do you know about it?"

"Very little, in truth, just rumors and gossip. It has something to do with Fae powers, but what exactly I couldn't say. It is a relic, of great significance and importance to the Northern Realm."

"I thought our gifts were linked to theirs?"

"Perhaps once, long ago, but not so much anymore. The link has been diluted through the generations, and now our gifts are just an echo of something much greater. Why do you ask, anyway?"

"Emrys was looking for it. Has been looking for it for some time, apparently."

She looked thoughtful, her brow creasing, as if she was just putting two and two together.

"You would have been too young to notice, but older Valtanans, those with gifts, we noticed it. Around the time when Nissae fell, there was a change in our abilities. It was subtle, hard to put your finger on exactly, but it felt as if our gifts had weakened slightly and never recovered. If the Amberstone went missing around that time I suppose it might have explained the change to our gift."

I watched her, trying to make sense of everything. Her eyes flicked up to meet mine.

"You though… you are the exception, it seems. You have grown exceptionally powerful."

"Surely that's just because you have been teaching me how to use my shadows?"

"No," she said adamantly. "You grow stronger every day. I have taught people before. They refine their gift, polish it, almost. But you… no, what is happening to you is very different. You have become quite formidable."

I bit my lip, my eyes boring into hers.

"Why?" I asked quietly.

"I have only ever known gifts to change like this when someone has either met their Gods Fated, like your mother did, or when they have spent considerable time in the Nijem."

My shadows twitched and I swallowed.

"Well, I have been in the Nijem recently," I said, thinking about the forest's recent possession of me.

Her eyes danced and a smile appeared on her lips.

"Why are you smiling?" I asked, but she only smiled more.

"No reason, child. Yes, you have been in the forest. Perhaps she saw something in you."

I was surprisingly emotional when I embraced her and said my goodbyes the next morning, and as I watched her and her escorts trot down the winding path away from the house I couldn't help but feel sad. In a rare moment of forwardness Austell put his arm around me, pulling me in close against him, and I leaned my head against his collarbone, taking comfort in his presence. It was peaceful at the front of the house; the only sounds that of the starlings in the trees and the incessant buzzing of the bees on the lavender bushes behind us. I thought again how happy I could have been here had things been different. In the last few weeks Totease had been a haven for me when I had needed it the most.

"It's beautiful here, isn't it? I'll miss it when we leave."

There was a moment of silence before he spoke, his voice hesitant.

"You know that you can always come back here, Efa. This could be your home, here with me. If you wanted it."

I pulled back my head to be able to look up at him. I had doubted his intentions towards me at first, but now, as I looked into those intense, blue eyes, I saw genuine affection. I smiled shyly, dropping my eyes and leaning into him again as he held me closer and kissed me softly on the top of my head. My shadows rose, fluttering beneath the surface, full of lust and longing.

Searching for someone far away.

CHAPTER 18
EFA

We left Totease under an overcast sky, a full company of Esari guards escorting the carriage that Austell and I rode in. At first it was something of a novelty, as I hadn't ridden in one since I was a child, but I very quickly grew nauseous as it bumped and shook on the uneven road. I closed my eyes and tried to sleep, but after a few hours I could take no more and I demanded that we stop so that I could ride one of the spare horses instead.

I had dressed in pants rather than a dress, so at least I was able to retain some decency on this occasion and not expose my legs to everybody, but as I settled into the saddle and adjusted my hat, Austell raised an eyebrow at me. I knew what he was thinking. If I were to be spotted riding astride a horse instead of travelling in the carriage, as the future Lady Esari should, there would be plenty of talk, and, according to him, a lord should always arrive in style for a state visit. But he said nothing, and I thought I saw the ghost of a smile on his lips as he returned to the book he was reading. As far as I was concerned, people could talk as much as they wanted to. I was a smuggler more than a princess or a lady, and unapologetically so. Besides, there were considerably worse things in my past that people could be talking about, and I thought Austell secretly rather liked my rebelliousness.

The journey was incredibly, infuriatingly slow and I felt like we'd never arrive in Baern, but I took the opportunity to practice my mental shields and joined in with the conversation between Nev and his men which kept me relatively entertained. I found my self unexpectedly eager to reach Rostorrmel, despite the butterflies that quivered in my stomach, in part because I was keen to get it over with, to know what I was dealing with and to look Damen in the eye finally, after all this time. More importantly though, I was desperate to see Arella and Torr again and find out what news they had of Noa. I was hoping that Torr would be able to tell me he was somewhere safe within his fleet.

Had we been travelling without the carriage, we might have made it to Baern in three days, two if we were lucky and pushed the horses. Instead, it took us five, and as we headed further north, it was clear that autumn had given way to winter while I had been in Esari. The trees were bare now, and there was a bleak greyness to the landscape, a chill lingering in the air. On the final day we set off slowly, since clearly no one was in any rush to spend any more time than absolutely necessary in Baern.

I had insisted on riding every day, but as we neared the region's main city I reluctantly climbed back into the carriage with Austell, grudgingly accepting that it would be poor form to arrive on horseback. It was just as well because not twenty minutes later a group of riders came galloping down the road towards us wearing Tanrith's colors. As the convoy came to a halt, Nev signaled to two of his men and they rode forward to meet them. After a brief discussion, he returned the carriage and put his head through the open window.

"Lord Tanrith has requested that we head to Pendruffle, his country house in the north of the region. It appears there is still a great deal of unrest in the city and he believes we will be more comfortable away from the noise and crowds."

"I'll bet," Austell said sarcastically.

"I imagine that he's also not pleased at the Nothori soldiers camping only a few miles from here," Nev added.

"Indeed," Austell agreed. "Very well, as long as they are happy to escort us. I'm not sure I could find Pendruffle again even with a map."

"Should we be concerned?" I asked as the carriage started to move again.

"I shouldn't think so, he'll simply be embarrassed that he has lost control of his city." He picked up his book again, finding where he had last left off. "I hope you packed some warmer things as it's going to get a lot colder. We're heading into the foothills of the mountains, and the shadow of the Nijem Forest. It's a good thing you don't scare too easily. There's something particularly off about the trees that border his country estate. I can't say I like being that close to them, myself."

I smiled to myself as I gazed out of the window at the barren fields, the crops long since harvested here. My shadows had begun to buzz with excitement at the mention of the forest. Oh no, I didn't scare easily. In fact, I felt like I was going home.

We followed Lord Tanrith's men north until the city appeared in the distance, the Ferras Mountains looming behind it. Plumes of smoke still snaked lazily into the air after the riots, and the smell of ash drifted in through the window we had left open. When we were still a few miles out we veered off to the left as if we were heading to Tywell's Pass, but then turned off again into a narrow, unmarked road toward the forest. It was the kind of road that you could have easily missed, the hedges on either side dense and overgrown. Twigs scraped along the side of the carriage and the guards were forced to travel single file until it widened out about half a mile later and Pendruffle finally came into view.

It was a daunting scene. The timber-framed hunting lodge sat nestled on the very edge of the forest, partially obscured by the heavy mist that crept down from the mountains and out of the trees. Despite it being early evening, the sun had already disappeared behind the snow-capped peaks in the west plunging the lodge in the gloom, but no sconces had been lit to give it a warm, welcoming atmosphere. Instead, it looked bleak and uninviting.

"Gods, how bad was Baern if he thought we'd be more comfortable *here*?"

Austell smirked at me from across the carriage.

"Yes, it's certainly atmospheric."

Laughter burst from my lips. It really was. My immediate thought was how different it was to Totease. Where the Esari house was light and open, basking in sunshine and surrounded by fields and flowers, Pendruffle was melancholy and dreary. As the carriage pulled up outside the front of the house and a footman opened the door, the cold, earthy smell of the Nijem wafted in on the breeze, and my shadows pulsed in recognition. Austell hopped out of the carriage and offered me his hand to help me out, as any loving fiancé would do. I stepped out as gracefully as I could and straightened my skirts, the cool breeze blowing them around my legs and making the bare branches nearby clack as they rubbed against each other. I braced myself to meet my host.

Lord Baern stood in the doorway, clasping his hands behind his back, and I couldn't help but think that he looked every inch the villain. He was a tall, imposing man, dressed in dark pants and a soft, cream jumper. His black hair was thinning at the temples, and he had an impressive handlebar moustache that Morgan would have been envious off. I judged him to be somewhere in his sixties, deciding that he had probably been handsome in his younger years, although by the sounds of it he didn't struggle to attract women these days.

"Good to see you again, Zennor," Austell said easily.

He smiled broadly as he clasped the older man's hand in greeting, and then reached back for my own, bringing me forward to stand beside him with a look of such adoration that I had to remind myself it was just an act.

"Please allow me to introduce my fiancée, Efa."

I fixed a smile on my face and dropped into a small curtsy. At least I could still do that; my mother had made me practice over and over as a girl until it was perfect, and it was the kind of thing you didn't forget. Tanrith's eyes shamelessly raked across my body and I felt Austell stiffen slightly. I merely raised an eyebrow at his boldness.

Eventually Tanrith took my hand and lifted it to his lips as he bowed in return. I suppressed the shudder that threatened to raise the hairs on the back of my neck as his lips touched my skin, but when he glanced up at me from under his heavy eyebrows, the smile he gave me sent a shiver down my spine. The cruel slant to his mouth belied his true nature, and there was something taunting in his eyes, as if he knew something I didn't, or he was having some joke at my expense. Yes, this was the man who would choose a slow, painful death for the Gifted.

"I am delighted to make your acquaintance, Efa," he said, his voice rich and deep. "I must confess that I have been most eager to meet you after the news of Austell's rather sudden engagement. One can only assume that you have bedazzled him."

As he rose, his eyes caught on the ring on my other hand.

"Goodness, and wearing Lady Tiva's ring, if I am not mistaken?"

"Of course," Austell replied. "Although I fear that the diamond pales in comparison to the wearer herself."

"Oh, quite so..."

I smiled demurely, glancing at Austell affectionately and ignoring the predatory look on Tanrith's face. So far I hadn't had to say a single word, and I got the feeling that was exactly how he liked his women. Silent.

"Well, let's not stand out in this dreadful weather. Come in, come in," he drawled as he strode into the house. "You must be tired and in need of a rest prior to dinner."

"After you," Austell murmured, placing a hand on the small of my back.

I took a breath and followed Tanrith down the dark corridor, trying to keep my face neutral but probably failing as I took in the décor. The inside was no better than the outside, in my opinion; I had never seen so much taxidermy in one place. No fewer than sixteen stags and five wild boars lined the walls, and at the end of the corridor a glass cabinet displayed a selection of birds in various poses.

"Do you like my collection?" Tanrith asked, noticing me looking. "This was originally my great-grandfather's hunting lodge. We are a family of excellent marksmen."

"I can see that," I said politely. "I always thought it was considered bad luck to hunt for sport in the Nijem."

Noa and I had hunted in the forest many times, just like the rest of the Nevedeno, and just like Morgan and Bran when we were in there a few weeks ago. But there was a difference between hunting to survive, and hunting for amusement, especially in the ancient forest. I was surprised that she tolerated it. It turned out that she didn't.

"Oh indeed, hunting in that Gods forsaken place is not for the weak and feeble minded. I have known good men who did not return after a hunt. The local folk claim that they still roam the forest even now looking for the way out. Fortunately, I am neither weak nor feeble minded."

He had already turned around to carry on walking as he said this, and I was grateful, since he didn't see me rolling my eyes. Austell caught it though, and I saw him mouth the word 'careful' to me. We reached the end of the corridor and stopped in front of a large staircase where a stern faced woman in an apron stood waiting to show us to our rooms. I nodded at her amiably, receiving only a hard stare in return.

"We expect Sandy to be arriving within the hour, so please take your time, freshen up and change, and we'll meet back downstairs for dinner. You'll hear the bell when it's time. I'm afraid that two of our bedrooms are undergoing extensive repairs after the recent storms, and as Pendruffle is so much smaller than Fort Celnaer, I regret that we are not able to provide you with separate rooms."

I lifted my chin and stared at him in amusement. Now that *was* disrespectful. It was most inappropriate for any host, let alone one as significant as a Lord, to suggest that his unmarried guests would share a room, but one look at his face and I knew that it was deliberate. Whether he was attempting to get a measure on me, or antagonise Austell, I wasn't sure, but I'd wager those other bedrooms were absolutely fine. Next to me, Austell had gone still, no doubt deciding how to respond to the insult.

"Zennor, that is completely unsuitable…" he began.

A flush was spreading up from underneath his collar, and I knew that he was deeply affronted and likely concerned about how I would feel. Sharing a bed wasn't part of the deal we had. I placed a placatory hand on his arm.

"Sweetheart, it's no matter," I purred softly, looking at him meaningfully from under my lashes. "After all, it is not as if we are *unfamiliar* with each other..."

I had to stop myself from laughing at the look on Austell's face. I wasn't sure who was more surprised at my words, him or Tanrith, but Tanrith certainly recovered quicker, laughing heartily and gazing at me with open lust. *Good*, I thought. That was exactly what I wanted. I had seen enough men like him over the years to know that he was a cunning man who missed very little with those beady little eyes. He would see me as a conquest, despite me being engaged to Austell. *Especially* because I was engaged to Austell. But as long as he saw me as simply something to be desired and used by men, like the other women and girls hidden somewhere in his household, then he wouldn't be seeing me as a threat. Tanrith's eyes dropped to my chest and his tongue flicked out to lick his lips.

"She certainly is a spirited one, Austell! Yes, I think I shall like her very much."

Austell smiled tightly, and I took his hand as we followed the maid and made our way silently up the stairs, our footsteps silent on the richly carpeted steps. When I glanced back down I found that Tanrith hadn't moved. His eyes glinted in the lamplight and he watched me intently, like a predator eyeing up his next meal.

~

CHAPTER 18

"It's fucking unbelievable!"

Austell raged around me as I began to unpack the clothes I intended to wear that evening. His voice was a harsh whisper, since he didn't want to be overheard, but I had never seen him so angry. This had certainly upset him. Clearly impropriety was a particular trigger point for him.

"The arrogance… the disrespect! He may have no morals himself, but to subject my fiancée to such… such insult and contempt!"

"Calm yourself, Austell," I said lightly, keeping my voice low, too. "It's of no consequence. He's trying to bait us. He wants us to feel compromised and humiliated, and we aren't. Like I said, I'm no girl; I don't need my modesty protecting. And besides, if I had my own room I'd only spend the whole night lying awake waiting to hear him sneaking in after the way he was watching me downstairs."

I lifted my evening dress out of the trunk and carefully took it out of the paper it was wrapped in. Austell composed himself slightly, striding over to the window where he stood with his hands on his hips, his mouth set in a thin line. I could see why he was upset, but I figured that it was all just part of the game we were playing. I really couldn't care less about what people thought of me sleeping in the same room as my 'fiancé' before we were married, but I did care about sleeping in the same bed as Austell, because it complicated things. I had to admit that I was attracted to him. He was easy and uncomplicated, treated me like an equal, and he had only ever been transparent with me. It would have been simple to let myself fall in love with him. I sighed, hanging my dress up on the front of the wardrobe and brushing out some of the creases.

"Still," Austell muttered. "It's the principle, isn't it? And it's not what we agreed would happen."

He turned to me and I could see the warring emotions in his face. Yes, he was irate, but I think he was also a little excited about the prospect of us being forced together in this way. He had wanted this since I'd arrived in Esari, but he wasn't sure about how I felt. I finished tying a sheath around my forearm and slipped a blade into it, pulling on my fur coat to hide it.

"It wasn't, but I'm certain we can make it work for one night." I gave him a reassuring smile. "You freshen up first. I need to stretch my legs after that journey."

"Take care not go to too close to the forest, Efa. It will be dark soon."

I wasn't sure whether he was worried about the spirits or the Nothori that potentially lurked in there, but neither concerned me these days. My gift was stronger than ever, and I could handle myself well after my training with Nev. Besides, I trusted the Nijem to take care of me. I crossed the room and kissed him lightly on the cheek as his hand came to rest lightly on my waist.

"You don't need to worry," I said.

I left it at that because I didn't want to lie to him. But that was exactly where I was going.

CHAPTER 19
EFA

I opened the door slowly and poked my head out to check the coast was clear before I walked quickly and quietly down the hallway, keen to avoid running into Tanrith if I could help it. I was heading towards a spiral staircase that I'd noticed earlier on our way up. When I'd casually enquired about where it went, the maid had told me that it led downstairs and to a door out to the gardens and 'those dreadful woods', and sure enough that was exactly where I found myself a few moments later.

Tanrith's sentry guards were worse than the pair at the temple gates back in Esari, standing around casually and paying no attention to their surroundings. If they had been, they would have heard me approaching, but wrapped in my shadows I slipped right past them into the fog and strolled into the waiting trees. My shadows rejoiced as I stepped over her threshold, and there was no trace of the oppressive weight that I had felt when I had last left her a few weeks before. In fact, it was quite the opposite. I felt a rush of energy and life as I filled my lungs with fresh, invigorating air.

Welcome back, elnaya.

My head whipped around, half expecting to see someone standing right behind me. It had sounded as if someone had whispered the words right next to my ear. There was no one there, of course. I hadn't expected there to be.

The fog was heavier in the forest than it had been back at the house, creeping down from the mountains and drifting lethargically through the pines. In half an hour it would be completely dark but I continued on regardless, enjoying the chance to stretch my legs after a day stuck in the carriage. My shadows begged to be allowed out to play but I denied them the opportunity, conscious that I might have been followed from the house even if I couldn't see or hear anything. Instead, I focused on clearing my mind and preparing for the night ahead.

I had never been very successful at quieting my mind, though. Over the years, Arella had tried to teach me various mindfulness techniques, but they'd never worked. So it was that as I walked aimlessly through the Nijem my mind wandered, thinking back over everything that had happened since I'd left Cryf's Gap. If someone had told me the night I'd first met Emrys in Astraea that I'd be on my way to a ball at Rostorrmel Palace, I'd have laughed at them. Yet here I was. A sudden breeze swept through the trees and blew my hair around my face, and I smiled wryly to myself. I barely recognized the woman who had left that small mountain village. Something fundamental had changed in me during those weeks with Emrys in the forest. I knew it in my bones. I sighed deeply at the thought of him, his memory haunting me still.

Trust the darkness, Efa.

This time I laughed out loud when I heard her voice

echoing around me. There was that prophecy again, and I still refused to believe it.

"He's not my fate," I declared defiantly into the stillness.

I didn't trust him. I never would. It was impossible after what he had done.

But you did, once, said a small voice in my head.

"He's not my fate," I said again, quieter this time.

The forest stayed silent.

CHAPTER 20
EFA

I shook my head at the two sentries on my way back in, oblivious to my return to the house. I debated sending Tanrith a message and slitting their throats right then and there to prove a point that his security was so lapse, but I liked to avoid making things unnecessarily complicated for myself, so I let them be.

My boots were quiet on the stairs as I slipped back upstairs, but as I reached the top and started walking to my room, I heard a door open behind me. A man growled playfully and there was a round of high pitched giggling and squealing. I glanced back over my shoulder to see two girls tumbling out of one of the bedrooms, half-dressed and pink cheeked. When they saw me they froze, and then burst into hysterical laughter before running down the hallway in the opposite direction.

Tanrith appeared in the doorway wearing nothing but a loosely buttoned shirt that, thankfully, covered all of the important parts. I'd seen a fair few cocks in my time, not always willingly, but I wasn't in a rush to see his anytime soon if I could help it. He watched the girls go for a moment, and then turned to look at me. He had known I was there, and from his grin I knew that he wanted to be caught. It was all part of the thrill for him; some kind of deliberate power play achieved by shocking people or making them uncomfortable. I gave him a charming, untroubled smile before continuing back to my room. If he thought he could shock me, he was wrong. I'd seen plenty of things over the years, and was hardly scandalized by the sight of a man without any pants on.

I knocked softly before entering the room I shared with Austell, finding him sitting in a chair by the window with his book. He had bathed while I had been gone, and the frown lines that had marked his forehead were gone. His eyes gave me a once over as I entered, the tension in his shoulders visibly leaving when he saw that I was in the same condition I had been in when I left.

"Everything all right?" he asked.

I nodded as I slipped off my boots by the door, not wanting to talk about where I had been or what I'd been thinking about.

"The servants are just bringing up fresh water now for you. I assumed you'd want a bath. Lord Canver and Caja are here. I heard the carriage arrive just now. We still have about an hour until dinner, apparently."

I groaned inwardly. I wasn't looking forward to the evening ahead and the prospect of sitting in the same room as Tanrith or Canver for hours on end. I threw myself into the chair next to Austell. On the table in between the chairs there were two glasses of wine and I picked up the one closest to me.

"I took the liberty of pouring you a glass. Apparently the grapes come from the Baern region."

I gave him a sideways look. Baern wasn't known for it's wine. It had neither the soil nor the weather, a fact that was confirmed with the first sip I took of the dark red. I pulled a face.

"Yes, I thought the same," Austell said with a smirk.

I rested my head back as I surveyed the room but I kept the glass, hopeful that it would become more drinkable the more I had since I couldn't bear to go into dinner stone cold sober. It was a comfortable enough room, I supposed. The maid had called it the 'blue room', and it was fairly obvious why. The walls were painted a dark navy, and the rest of the furniture and fabrics were varying shades of blue to match, including the heavy drapes around the four-poster bed, which made the room feel a little oppressive. All of the furniture was oak, and on the wall opposite the bed there was a painting of a large wild boar. I took another sip of wine, grimacing as I swallowed it.

When the hot water arrived, I took my time bathing. I sank deep in the water, examining the oath line. It hadn't improved in the slightest since the night Finn had shown up in Esari, but at least it wasn't getting any worse. The hathersage root that Bran had given me helped to dull the constant pain, but I rationed it frugally, knowing that I was unlikely to get more anytime soon. I switched my attention to the new scar just above my hip from where Theo had tried to kill me. It was about two inches long; with tiny marks either side where Bran had stitched it up. Compared to the oath line it was looking remarkably good, the injury rarely giving me pain now. The scar was still red, but it had healed unbelievably fast.

When the water had gone cold I climbed out of the bath, tied my robe around me, and went back out. Austell was still sitting by the window but he had changed for dinner, looking rather striking in a white shirt and perfectly tailored, dark green woolen jacket and pants. My eyes lingered on him, and his eyes danced as he turned to look at me. I blushed, feeling like I'd been caught out admiring him.

"You look very handsome," I said, walking over to the mirror to brush out my hair and start pinning it up.

"Thank you," he replied, looking pleasantly surprised. "I thought I would dress to match you."

He pointed to the dress I had hung up earlier, one of the new ones that Sowena had delivered before I left. It was a beautiful floor length gown in emerald green, with a plunging neckline and a thousand shimmering sequins and beads sewn onto the bodice. Like most of my gowns, it had been deliberately made with long sleeves that hid both my Nevedeno tattoo and the oath line.

"How thoughtful of you. We shall cause quite a stir," I teased.

I finished fixing my hair and face, and glanced at the dress, looking pointedly at Austell as the dinner bell chimed distantly.

"Turn around," I demanded, and he did so dutifully with a laugh. "And no looking!"

"I wouldn't dare!" he said, laughing harder as he faced the wall.

I shimmied into the dress and adjusted it over my hips and shoulders. I had lost weight since the original fitting, a combination of all the extra training with Nev and my loss of appetite, and though Sowena had taken it in it was still a little loose around my waist and hips. Despite that it was still one of the most beautiful things I'd even worn, and a far cry from what I usually wore as a smuggler.

"You can look now," I murmured, turning round to face him.

Austell turned around and crossed the space between us, his eyes roaming up and down my body as he took me in.

"You look absolutely beautiful, Efa," he whispered softly, his heated gaze making me blush. "Which, quite frankly is a concern, since Zennor actually might try to get into our room tonight."

I grinned, checking myself once more in the mirror and adjusting a stray lock of hair. Austell strolled over to the bedroom door and placed his hand on the doorknob.

"Shall we get this over with then?" he asked with a wink, and I took a final deep breath.

"Lead on, Lord Esari, and may the Gods help us."

CHAPTER 21
EFA

The wooden floor creaked loudly beneath my feet as I stepped into the dining room causing heads to immediately turn. It was a small, intimate room, decorated in much the same way as the rest of the house. Heavy velvet curtains hung at the two floor-to-ceiling windows, and oil paintings depicting various hunting scenes adorned the walls. Across the room, a fire was crackling in the hearth, giving the room a stifling, airless feel.

We were the last to arrive, entering the room just as Tanrith was handing the man next to him a glass of brandy. *This* was Lord Canver, then. He was a squat, bloated man whose fine clothes clung uncomfortably to the large swell of his gut, the blue silk of his shirt straining at every button. His brown hair was slicked back with so much pomade it glistened under the lamplight, and his face was a deep shade of puce. Beads of sweat collected at his temples, and a damp, crumpled handkerchief hung from his fingers. There was something about him that made my skin crawl and my body want to recoil away from him. He was repulsive; a man who had fed himself on other people's hunger, who had taken more than his share and never lost a night's sleep over it.

In contrast, the slender young woman next to him was nothing short of perfection. She stood at his side like an ornament made to be admired. Her skin was flawless; the warm bronze of sun-kissed silk, unmarked by hardship, and long, glossy brunette hair tumbled in immaculate curls down her back to a narrow waist. A delicate face framed incredible brown eyes, deep and liquid, holding a gaze that could both invite and dismiss with the smallest flicker. Diamonds dripped from her ears and draped her neck, trailing down between her full breasts and disappearing beneath the rich purple gown that clung and flowed in all the right places.

She was, quite simply, the most beautiful woman I had ever seen. I could absolutely see why Canver desired her. What man wouldn't? How she could possibly bear to be with him, well… that I couldn't understand. But as I got closer I noticed that there was something wrong. Her movements were slow, almost jerky, as though her body and mind were no longer in step. Her pupils were wide, and there was a faint, vacant glaze in her expression that made her seem far away, as if she were listening to something no one else could hear. My heart sank and I sighed inwardly as I glanced at her arms to confirm what I already knew. They were silver in the low light.

Silvermist. That was how she endured him, dulling whatever torment she was living in to something she could survive. But surely a woman like her had options? Surely there were other potential suitors who could have offered her a good life without reducing her to this?

I sighed again, fixing the smile on my face as Austell made the introductions, and then I listened quietly to the three men make small talk for a time. They discussed the weather and the season's hunting before we took our seats and the servants began bringing in the first course. Tanrith kept the wine flowing but I drank very little despite it being better than the stuff in our room, preferring to keep my wits about me. I noticed that Austell was doing the same, but beside me Caja was drinking glass after glass.

"So, Austell, tell me. How is it that you came to meet this mesmerizing young woman?"

Tanrith's eyes watched me over the top of his wine glass. Austell reached under the table to take my hand, bringing it up to his mouth to kiss my knuckles.

"It feels like fate, if I'm honest," he said, glancing my way and giving me a dazzling smile.

Do you believe in fate? My heart stuttered.

"She happened to be in Esari for the annual lobster festival where I was presenting some awards. I confess that I was absolutely enchanted with her from the moment I set eyes on her."

"Oh, Austell," I said, feigning modesty.

We were playing the part well, but Austell's words sounded far too sincere. A blush crept over my cheeks.

"How delightful," Tanrith purred, and I heard that mocking edge to his voice again. "Do you travel to Esari often, Efa?"

We were taking a risk with our story, and we both knew it. We were counting on my face not being recognized since the individuals I usually fraternized with didn't tend to run in these circles. We were also hoping that it wasn't common knowledge that I had been travelling with Emrys prior to arriving at Totease severely injured, but I knew from the Nevedeno's extensive network that there were spies everywhere. I checked and re-checked the mental shields I'd had up since we arrived.

"My brother deals in antiquities and fine wines," I said pleasantly. "Occasionally some decorative weapons. Our ship had docked in Esari for a few days, and he continued on to The Azuls after I decided to stay."

The part about the antiquities wasn't a lie. Noa and I regularly smuggled stolen and black-market items for the Nevedeno, and although I might have found antiques terribly dull, I could talk quite confidently about them if I needed to for some time.

"You have not had any unrest down in Esari then, if your festival has been uninterrupted?" Canver directed his question to Austell and I relaxed slightly, relieved that the attention had been drawn away from me.

"None at all," Austell replied. "Only a small disturbance at the nearby temple. And long may it stay like that. I hear things have not been so peaceful in your cities though?"

"No, indeed not," Tanrith said. "But there's nothing like a good public execution to get the blood pumping and the people talking, is there?"

He smiled wickedly at me and I made a small sound as if I was amused by his statement, but my hand tightened around my fork.

"What do you say, Sandy?"

Canver rolled his eyes.

"I just find it all such an *inconvenience*," he said dismissively, as if the executions were nothing but a minor annoyance getting in the way of his useless existence.

"I understand that most of the executions in Baern have been interrupted?" Austell said.

"Yes… by these fucking Loyalists," Tanrith bit out, the careful mask he wore slipping ever so slightly. "They skulk through our towns like rats, fighting for what? A dead king and queen and their long forgotten offspring?

They have no cause, and they are certainly no threat. They are an irritant, nothing more than a vexation. But they will soon be eradicated like the Gifted scum they seek to protect."

"Are you any closer to rooting out the Loyalist cells in Baern?" Austell had leaned forward with his elbows on the table. "We have been following up on our own intelligence in Esari but they are an elusive bunch, disappearing into the wind as soon as we get close."

"They elude us, too. They seem to be everywhere and nowhere."

My shadows simmered with rage but I kept my face neutral, almost bored even, as I sat there silently. I played idly with my cutlery, noticing that Caja's hand was trembling violently as she held the stem of her wine glass. Her face had gone deathly pale and I recognized the telltale signs of Silvermist withdrawal. When I discreetly asked if she was feeling well, she excused herself from the table, swaying as she stood and left the room. When she returned a few minutes later she had a better color in her cheeks and the tremor had disappeared, but when she looked at me she seemed even more vacant and unfocused than before. Wherever she had disappeared to, she had topped herself up.

"What of the Nothori?" Canver was asking. "I hear they are camped just outside of Baern."

"Yes," Tanrith said, rolling his eyes. "Far be it from me to question the plans of our great king, but I neither like nor trust those tattooed savages. I'm sure I'm not the only one who would have appreciated a little consultation before they arrogantly sauntered into my city and started giving orders to my men."

So there was some discord within the ranks, I thought to myself. That was interesting. I sipped my wine slowly as the conversation turned to other less contentious matters, and after dinner we moved into a small sitting room where Canver had become so inebriated that he stumbled awkwardly over the rug and almost pulled Caja down on to the floor with him. He recovered slowly, finding it difficult to get up, and it took three servants to help the large man. He fell into one of the chairs, and as Caja sat down next to him I thought I caught a quick glance of disdain from his mistress. Despite the fact that Canver had clearly had enough, Tanrith continued to ply him with alcohol, seemingly finding Canver's worsening condition amusing.

"So, darling Efa, you are an antiques dealer," Tanrith said, his eyes sparkling. "I am in the market for some antiquities myself. Perhaps you could be so kind as to make some suggestions?"

"A fine idea!" Austell said, taking my hand.

I inclined my head and smiled sweetly, taking a sip from my cup of mint tea.

"It would be a pleasure, my Lord. What sort of items are you interested in?"

"Oh, Zennor has a taste for the macabre," Canver slurred, his hooded eyes barely managing to stay open now. "He likes to collect items from Nissae, things scavenged from the ruins. The more intimate and morbid the better."

Tanrith laughed heartily and raised his glass as if to say *what am I like*? I saw then that I'd been wrong about Tanrith. He *could* surprise me. I had underestimated the depths of his sadistic tendencies, and for the first time I wondered if I'd finally met someone who was more disturbed than Finn.

"It's true, I am a devious soul, am I not? The king was, of course, intent on razing the city to the ground, but there were some just *wonderful* finds in the days afterwards. In fact…"

He rose from his chair and strolled over to the bureau in the corner of the room, opening a drawer and taking out a small black box. I watched him idly as he brought it back over to the table and handed it to me, his fingers deliberately brushing mine as he did so. My shadows pulsed in warning as I took it gingerly, slowly lifting the lid. Inside was a gold necklace with a small oval pendant on the end of the long chain. The pendant had been carefully engraved with daxholla flowers, a rare species of plant that grew only in and around Nissae. I remembered my mother having vases of them in her room.

"It's lovely," I managed to say, my mouth dry. "But I dread to ask where it was found."

"Oh, Gods, you must be thinking that we took it from some poor dead Valtanan's neck. No, no… not this item, at least. This was simply found in the ruins of one of the houses in the city. It had somehow escaped the flames."

I swallowed down my nausea and forced a smile on my face, feeling Austell's eyes on me.

"Well, what a find!" I said brightly, snapping the lid of the box shut and holding it out to Tanrith, but he shook his head.

"Please, I insist that you keep it. Consider it an engagement gift."

"You are far too kind, Lord Tanrith."

"What were you saying when we last met, Zennor… about your collection being almost complete?"

Canver was slumped into his seat, his hand draped across Caja's leg. Tanrith sat down opposite me and used his fingers to smooth his moustache.

"Ah, yes. Perhaps something you or your brother could help me with, Efa. I have been searching for a Valtanan blade. I seem to remember Novos used to carry one around, in fact. Now, *that* would be the real find."

A slow, delighted smile stretched across my face and my shadows twitched. I squeezed my legs together, feeling the Valtanan blade where it was strapped to my thigh. Oh yes, I could definitely help him with that. In fact, I'd take great delight in helping my father's blade find its way straight into Tanrith's cold, black heart.

CHAPTER 22
EFA

I stared at myself blankly in the mirror as I dropped the final hairpin down onto the dressing table and let my hair fall loose around my shoulders, the ends curling slightly after being tied up all evening. Behind me, Austell stood shirtless at the window holding a glass of brandy and looking out into the darkness, a frown pulling at his handsome features. I'd found him like that when I'd come out of the bathroom, my breath catching slightly as I took in his lean, muscular torso and the deep tan lines around his neck and forearms. Given that he was so proper, I was surprised to see him half dressed, and I couldn't help the way my eyes kept glancing at his reflection in the mirror. When he turned to me suddenly I dropped them quickly, a blush creeping over my cheeks at being caught out.

"Tonight was intense," Austell said wearily. "How are you feeling?"

I walked over to the bed and climbed beneath the covers, sighing as my head touched the pillow.

"Like every day I find someone new to add to list of people I'm going to kill," I replied quietly.

Intense was an understatement. Between Canver getting so drunk that it took four servants to carry him up to his room, Caja saying barely three words the entire evening, and Tanrith just being a sick fucking bastard, it had been a thoroughly uncomfortable and trying evening. But in spite of it all, I actually felt relatively calm. The night's conversation had only served to confirm that I had made the right decision in embarking on this journey. Things needed to change.

"You handled yourself magnificently tonight," Austell said, disappearing into the bathroom and appearing a moment later in a pair of light cotton pants for sleeping in.

"I can't imagine how difficult it must have been for you, but you charmed them. Zennor is quite taken with you. You'll need to be on your guard with him, though. He's arrogant enough to believe that he could have you if he wanted you, and there is no question that he wants you. He can barely take his eyes off of you."

"How delightful," I muttered.

Austell moved about blowing out the candles that were scattered about the room, bringing the last one over to the bed with him. Setting it down on the bedside table, he pulled back the covers on his side and got in, lying down with his head propped up on his hand.

"Then Tanrith is a fool," I said. "Doesn't he know that I am a taken woman? I am to become Lady Esari, after all."

I fluttered my eyelashes dramatically and held up my left hand so that the diamond glittered in the candlelight.

"Oh, but how I wish that were true."

His words were meant as a joke, but he couldn't hide

the longing in his voice and I faltered slightly, awkwardly changing the subject to something safer.

"Caja was completely out of it on Silvermist tonight. I wonder what she was like before Canver, before the drugs. Does she take it willingly, or is that how Canver keeps her so pliant?"

"Both, I imagine. Sandy is well known for liking his women meek and submissive. He seems lazy and apathetic, but underneath that he is an unsympathetic, cold man who knows what he wants and expects to get it. When he's not completely inebriated, I've known him to be violent towards his mistresses if they dared challenge him or step out of line, although I've never heard of him hurting Caja. But he does have rather unusual tastes in the bedroom, or so I am led to believe. He might be monogamous, his one redeeming feature, but it's certainly not an easy job being his mistress. I wouldn't be surprised if she takes Silvermist just to be able to get through the day."

I blew out a breath and gazed up at the ceiling.

"She must be so miserable, though. Was there not a handsome farmer somewhere in the region who would have married her? Gods, it might have been a simpler life without all the diamonds, but surely she would have been *happier*…"

I trailed off, getting lost in my own thoughts, and then I suddenly realized he hadn't replied. Turning my head I found him looking at me intently.

"What is it?" I whispered.

"I was just thinking how beautiful you are." He hesitated, licking his lips before he continued. "You must be aware of how I feel about you, Efa. Sometimes I think that you feel the same, but then you pull away again and I can't read you. Your life will never be simple, I know that, but I like to think that I could make *you* happy, if you were to let me, and there is nothing I wouldn't do for you."

I bit my lip as I scrabbled around for the right words. My head warred with my heart again, my mind whispering that I was safe with Austell. He was a good man, kind and steady, but my heart... my heart was bruised, stubbornly clinging to something it could never have. Something that set my blood aflame and made my shadows stir restlessly around me. Somehow I needed to convince it to let go...

"You're right," I said softly. "There isn't a day that goes by when I don't wish that my life was simpler; that I had no enemies and no responsibilities. But that life wasn't for me. I don't doubt that you could make me happy, Austell. All I ask is that you are patient with me."

I leaned across the bed and kissed him on the cheek, pressing my lips against him for a moment longer than I intended. My hand rested on his chest and I felt his heart racing as he leaned towards me, as though he wanted to take me in his arms. I pulled back despite the blood pounding in my own veins.

"Of course," he whispered. "Take all the time you need."

His disappointment was written clearly on his face, but he returned my smile nonetheless, reaching up to stroke my cheek. A moment later, he rolled over and blew out the remaining candle and the room plunged into darkness. I breathed a small sigh, letting my shadows venture out, the shimmering darkness testing the boundaries as it filled up the room. All the while they searched for someone far away.

Enough. I said to them sharply, rolling on to my back and squeezing my eyes shut. *He's not your fate, so stop looking for him. It's time to find a new destiny.*

CHAPTER 23
EFA

I sat up in a blind panic. The sound of screaming and crying filled my ears and flames surrounded me. Arms grasped my shoulders and I thrashed around, clawing and hitting as I desperately tried to escape, vaguely aware of someone repeating my name. The sound was muffled and distant.

"Efa!"

Austell's voice pulled me from my nightmare and I stopped fighting, hands falling limply into my lap as my eyes tried to adjust to the dark room. He still held me, but his grip was looser now, now that I had grasped that I wasn't in Nissae and stopped fighting. I leaned forward and collapsed into him with a sob, his arms coming around to hold me tightly. His heart was beating almost as fast as mine. I must have scared him half to death.

"Fuck," I groaned into his chest.

I stayed like that in his arms for a few minutes until my breathing returned to normal and then pulled away from him, reaching for the glass of water next to the bed. It was just starting to get light outside, the room filling with a drab, grey light. I took a long drink and then lay back down again, pulling the covers up to my chin against the chill in the room.

"Sorry I woke you," I murmured. "I bet you didn't think sharing a bed with me would be so exciting."

He laughed quietly, raking a hand through his hair before lying down next to me.

"What did you dream about?"

"The same thing as always. Nissae."

It had been the same dream that had plagued me for the last twenty years. Flames licked at my bare feet and Noa's cough tore through the air, ragged and desperate as the smoke curled around us. As we were carried toward the forest, the sky burned orange, but this time we never reached the trees. This time the flames engulfed us as we ran.

"How did you escape that night?"

"I don't remember much about it, to be honest, but Noa says he remembers two soldiers finding us in the house and carrying us into the forest. We were briefly in Danae, and then somehow we ended up in Astraea. It's all a bit of a blur to me."

"Is that when you started using your new names? In Astraea?"

I nodded slowly, my thoughts drifting back to the day we began using them. At the time, the syllables had felt foreign on our tongues, clumsy and ill fitting, like clothing borrowed from a stranger. Each introduction had carried a flicker of hesitation, a pause where our true selves still lurked beneath the surface. In those first few weeks, the names had seemed like masks, but over time, they had begun to settle, shaping themselves until they fit, until the old ones felt distant, like echoes from another life.

"How did you choose them?"

"I went for something simple. Efa is just the common version of Aeva, which made it easier to remember and respond to. But Noa was more adventurous." I smiled thinking about his excitement when he realized he could choose anything. "Do you remember the tales of the Noa the Phantom?"

Austell snorted quietly.

"You mean the legendary assassin? Yes, my mother used to tell us the stories when we were boys."

"Noa used to idolize him. In all the games we played, he was always Noa the Phantom. It's one of the reasons that he's so good at knife throwing these days. I knew he'd choose that name before I even suggested we change them. Becoming a criminal really suited him, to be honest. He'd been practicing to be one his whole life."

I glanced at Austell, finding him gazing up at the ceiling with a smile on his face.

"My brother and I used to pretend to be the famous bandits, Five Fingered Pell and Three Toed Tom. "

"Which one were you?" I laughed.

"Pell, every time," he grinned. "Aric was always better at feigning a limp."

It was hard to picture Austell as a child, carefree and wild, pretending to be a notorious outlaw. But in a way, maybe he wasn't that much different from Noa. My cousin had become a smuggler, and Austell had ended up leading the Loyalists. For all his propriety, maybe Austell secretly enjoyed working in the shadows.

"Would you go back to being called Aeva? When all of this is over?"

"I'm not sure," I said. "I've been Efa now for a lot longer than I was ever Aeva. I think it would feel strange. I'm not sure I could start calling Noa 'Aeden' again, either."

We fell into silence for a while as I thought about him. Gods, I missed him.

"Do you think you'll be able to get back to sleep?" Austell asked eventually. "It's still early."

I shrugged, knowing that I should at least try, but almost an hour later I was still lying awake while Austell slept peacefully next to me, so I dressed quietly and left our room.

Once again, I heard the sound of a door opening and closing as I reached the stairs. This time I remained out of sight as I heard footsteps leading away from me down the hallway, but curiosity got the better of me. I peeked round the corner, raising an eyebrow at what I saw, because instead of it being one of the girls from the night before leaving Tanrith's room again, it was Caja, half-naked and drifting along in a dream-like state before she disappeared into her own room.

I frowned, shaking my head and going quickly down the stairs and out into the forest, taking a deep breath and filling my lungs. I couldn't shake the feeling of dread that had accompanied my nightmare, and I felt helpless and anxious whenever I thought about Noa. I walked quietly through the forest with only the birds for company, wondering what my parents would make of me if they could see me now. No doubt I was a far cry from the heir they'd expected me to be. Instead, I was something else entirely. I had crossed so many lines, done so many wrongs, my hands stained with choices that could never be undone. Would they be horrified by what I had become? Sighing heavily, I pushed the hair back from my face and rubbed at my eyes.

A rustling from behind startled me and I turned sharply, my knife already in my hand, but there was no one there, only a white stag standing only a few meters away from me. It seemed unsurprised to see me, and we stared at each other for a long moment, the look in its eyes almost daring me. Then, it looked away and walked calmly back into the trees. My shadows trembled, and for a moment I pictured myself back in Cayam, lying contentedly in bed next to Emrys.

Apparently, the appearance of the stag always heralds some profound change for those in the story.

I could still hear his voice; still feel his fingers as they caressed my stomach, and the feel of his lips on mine. I closed my eyes. The forest was teasing me. Tormenting me. When I opened my eyes again I could see the stag a little way off where it had paused to glance back at me. I laughed softly. I got the message. Time to stop doubting myself and be who I was meant to be.

CHAPTER 24
EFA

We were on the road to Rostorrmel shortly after breakfast. Above us, the sky was grey, but the day held promise, the sun desperately trying to break through the thick cloud cover. Tanrith was his usual jovial self, all provocative comments, sidelong looks and sly smiles. I couldn't say the same for Lord Canver, though. Neither he nor Caja had joined us downstairs for breakfast, and when they did appear at the front entrance ready to get into their carriage, he looked pale. I was willing to bet he had one terrible hangover and it was going to be a long, arduous journey, made only somewhat bearable by the fact that most of the inns along the way weren't big enough to accommodate us all. Of course, I feigned my most sincere disappointment when Tanrith told me that we would therefore have to stay in different places for the first two nights, but I clapped delightedly once I was alone with Austell.

The road ran directly alongside the forest, the huge pines dwarfed by the mountains behind them. As usual, fog rolled down off the slopes and gave the woods an eerie, unnatural feeling that had the guards slightly on edge, but I found her constant presence reassuring. I suffered through the first day in the carriage, conscious of looking the part in front of the rest of our party even though the nausea overwhelmed me. I had even tried to get into a book that Austell had given me, but I found myself reading the same part over and over again, too apprehensive to concentrate. By the time we stopped to change the horses around midday I'd had enough.

"Fuck it," I muttered, opening the door and breathing in the fresh, cool air. "I'm riding again."

"They'll talk..." Austell said lightly without looking up.

"Let them talk. What's the point in being a lord's wife if you can't do what you want to do every now and then?"

I jumped down from the carriage and began tying up my hair so that it didn't fly about in the wind, silently thanking myself for putting on pants instead of a dress that morning.

"Spoken like a true lady," Austell laughed, putting his book down and climbing down from the carriage behind me. "Although don't forget, you're not a lord's wife *yet*."

He winked, signaling for one of our guards to come over.

"My fiancée would like to ride for a time, and I think I'll join her."

I raised an eyebrow at him, pleasantly surprised.

"I thought a Lord should always travel in style?"

"Well, I suppose on horseback *is* a style, isn't it? Besides, what's the point in being a lord if I can't do what I want sometimes?" he smiled at me teasingly, and I grinned back. "It seems you are having a bad influence on me, Efa."

"That's what you get for spending too much time with

a smuggler," I quipped quietly as he helped me up on to the horse.

My spirits immediately lifted once I was out of the carriage. My anxiety eased and I felt strengthened by the Nijem and the murmuring voices I could hear coming from within. Occasionally I could make out the words *elnaya* and *fate*, but otherwise I couldn't make much sense of them. Around me the men were skittish. Though I was sure they couldn't hear the voices that I could, they were picking up on something—a presence or energy, perhaps. They whispered about the *Raeth* and death spirits as they glanced nervously over their shoulder, twitching at the slightest movement between the trees. In the end Nev had to snap at them to get a grip and focus on what they were there to do, but even after his barked command I could still see them glancing nervously at the forest.

We met a few travellers on the way, mostly a mix of farmers and merchants. In the late afternoon we passed a group of men sitting up on the grass bank beside the road. From their garb I assumed they were farmhands so I paid them no mind, giving them only a cursory look and smile. I wouldn't have given them another thought had my shadows not murmured faintly, and I glanced up just in time to catch one of the men, a big man with dark, unruly hair and a full beard, make eye contact with Nev who was riding beside me. At first, I thought it was nothing more than that, but then I noticed him discreetly tapping two fingers against his forehead. My eyes flicked to the captain and I saw him nod in response before exchanging a look with Austell.

When I saw the same man again that evening from my room at the inn, it confirmed what I'd thought: Loyalists. He was speaking casually to Nev outside the stables, no sign of it being anything clandestine, just two strangers discussing horses. But when Nev joined Austell and I for dinner a short time later, his face was grim.

"What news from Jory?" Austell asked.

I already knew what Nev was going to say. There was an atmosphere in the town. The townsfolk were nervous and their conversations in the tavern were easy to overhear. There were more executions planned.

"The Order have decided not to hold executions in the main towns anymore on account of there being too much rioting. Instead, they're going to the villages where they have more control. They'll be more regular and more spread out."

"It's tactical," Austell said, rubbing his jaw thoughtfully. "They know we can't be everywhere at once."

"There's a village about five miles from here called Noak. It's a farming village mainly; about a hundred people live there. A few years ago the Order took two brothers captive, and tonight they are being returned. The executions are being held at dawn. Jory was aware of at least three other executions planned for different villages."

I flexed my fingers, desperate to release my shadows as I felt my anger rising. Damen was making a point. He wasn't threatened by the Loyalist attacks. The Order would just adapt its strategy and make it more difficult for them to intervene. He was making it known that no one could defy the king's will. Austell reached across to hold my hand as Nev left us to go and speak to his men.

"I know that you know this, Efa, but we need to be extremely careful in Rostorrmel. I don't believe that there is anything linking me to the Loyalists, but I can't be certain. We could be walking into a trap."

He stroked my knuckles with his thumb and smiled adoringly at me, as if he were simply exchanging sweet nothings with his fiancée.

"We must give him no reason to doubt us, or believe that we are anything other than two people very much in love. He will want people that flatter him and support his agenda. He won't take kindly to being challenged."

"I understand."

His eyes lingered on my face.

"I will do everything in my power to keep you safe."

I rose from the table and kissed him on the cheek, smiling to myself. He had never seen me train with Nev, and he certainly didn't know what I had been learning and practicing in the old granary with Negan. I didn't think Austell had any idea exactly how dangerous I was these days.

"Likewise," I said with a wink. "I'm going to get some air."

I found Nev back in the stables, entering the stall as he was offering an apple to his horse. I leaned against the back wall and crossed my arms, watching them silently until he glanced up at me and raised an eyebrow.

"I assume that Jory will be on his way to Noak tonight," I said quietly.

"Yes..."

I left it hanging for a moment, and he cocked his head, studying me. We both knew what I was going to say next.

"I'd like to go, too."

He laughed soundlessly, running his hand through his hair.

"Have you mentioned this to Austell?"

"No, and I don't intend to."

He stepped away from his horse and leaned against the wall opposite me. He mirrored my position, crossing his arms and fixing me with a look.

"They fight in my name, Nev," I whispered vehemently. "It's only right that I stand beside them at long last."

Something like pride flashed in his eyes and he nodded his head.

"I don't disagree with you, and I know what it will mean to those that fight for our cause. But I report to Austell. He should know what you're planning."

"He would counsel me not to go."

"Probably," Nev agreed.

I knew that I should tell Austell. It was the right thing to do. But whilst Emrys would have picked up his sword and said 'let's go', Austell would tell me not to put myself at risk. He would tell me that there was a bigger game being played, and that I needed to make sure I arrived in Rostorrmel to play my part without getting captured by the Order before I even got there. And he was probably right, but that didn't change my mind. Nev and I stared at each other for a long moment until eventually I broke the eye contact, laughing faintly.

"Come on, don't make me give you new orders, Captain. We both know that I outrank Lord Esari."

He snorted, his eyes dancing in a way that told me he had foreseen exactly how this conversation was going to go from the beginning. He'd known I was going to ask him to take me, and he'd known I was going to pull rank on Austell if I needed to. He sighed, smiling at me resignedly.

"Why did I know you were going to get me in trouble the first time I laid eyes on you? Very well. We leave three hours before dawn. I'm sure I don't need to tell you how to dress for a raid, but I'd advise you to bring as many knives as you can."

This time it was my turn to laugh. I pushed away from the wall and began walking out of the stall.

"Try and stop me," I called.

CHAPTER 25
EFA

It was a dark night. The sliver of moon above us barely lit the track, and we rode as fast as we dared, not wanting to injure the horses should they trip on a rock or tree root. About half a mile out from the small village, a light flickered ahead where a young lad of was holding a torch. He said nothing as we approached, simply nodding at Nev before turning and walking down the long gravel path towards an old, run-down looking farmhouse.

From the road, the farmhouse looked like it had been forgotten decades ago. The roof sagged in places, moss clung to the damp stones, and the shutters hung crooked. But the torch picked out details that told another story: the mud near the door was well trodden; boots cutting clear paths through the weeds. The latch on the gate was newer than the fence around it, gleaming faintly with fresh oil. The smell wasn't just of old hay and damp wood, either. It carried the sharper tang of horses not long stabled, leather recently waxed, and smoke from a fire somewhere inside. A cart leaned against the wall, its wheels scrubbed clean of mud, and the water bucket near the trough was brimming full, too fresh to have been forgotten. It might have seemed ruined at first glance, but the longer I looked, the more obvious it became. This place wasn't abandoned at all. It was alive, watchful and ready.

The boy rapped on the weathered door in a quick, deliberate pattern. For a moment, nothing stirred, the silence pressing heavier than the night. Then the latch scraped and the door opened just enough for a woman's face to appear, framed by the dim glow of lamplight. Her eyes were sharp and wary, measuring us in an instant. She hesitated, hand still on the doorframe, her body poised to slam it shut if she didn't like what she saw. But when her gaze landed on the boy and Nev standing just behind him, recognition softened the hard line of her mouth, and her wariness melted into a small, relieved smile. She pulled the door back wider, beckoning the two of us in with a brisk nod, though her eyes lingered on me for a second too long.

"They're in the kitchen," she said, lifting her chin toward the heart of the house, and I followed Nev toward the sound of voices.

Inside, the house was worn but surprisingly cosy and well kept, nothing like the weary exterior suggested. The faint smell of baking clung to the air, mingling with wood smoke. A woven rug, its edges frayed, lay across the floorboards, and the walls were lined with shelves stacked with neatly jarred preserves, bundles of dried herbs, and a scattering of hand carved trinkets. The floor creaked beneath my feet as I walked, my chest tightening a little as I went. The kitchen fell silent the instant I stepped through the doorway. All eyes turned to me, some narrowing; some blank with careful restraint. The air seemed to thicken suddenly, becoming heavy with mistrust.

"Evening all," Nev said smoothly.

There were six of them, all dressed simply and gathered close around the long scarred table, and I could feel their mistrust as keenly as the warmth from the fire. They watched me in silence, eyes sharp and assessing. One woman's jaw was tight, as if she were holding back words. Another man leaned back in his chair but didn't take his hand from the mug in front of him, knuckles white around the handle. There was no welcome here. I was an intruder in their refuge, and they were waiting to see if I was threat or ally.

The man I had seen at the inn stood, the scrape of his chair loud in the quiet, and stepped forward to clasp Nev in a rough embrace, thumping his back with the easy familiarity of long trust. The smile on his face seemed to soften the room, just, and as they moved apart, Nev turned to me, his hand lingering on the man's shoulder.

"Efa, this is Jory Marrak. He leads this group, and is one of the most senior members of the Loyalists."

Jory nodded amicably, as though we were old acquaintances and not strangers meeting for the first time. The warmth in his eyes stood in stark contrast to the wary stares around us, and it struck me that he might have known something that the others didn't. That or he trusted Austell and Nev's judgment more than the others. As he lowered himself back into his chair, Nev lifted his hand to the woman sitting furthest away. She had long, curling brown hair that fell in wild waves and striking blue eyes that seemed to miss nothing.

"This is Nessa, and that's Treave and Rumo."

Though they had different coloring—Treave was blonde and pale and Rumo tanned and dark haired—the two men sitting either side of Nessa were clearly related. Brothers, was my guess, and likely only a few years apart. The last man at the table had hair so dark it looked black, and eyes like coal glared up at me from under a heavy brow.

"Don't mind Caydan, there," Nev said with a small smile in the man's direction. "He always looks angry."

The woman at the front door had followed us in and now stood over by the sink, leaning casually against the worktop. She was somewhere in her thirties, her fair hair falling loosely around a face sharpened by dark, unyielding eyes.

"I'm Merryn," she said, still watching me like a hawk.

I studied her for a moment. Her body was lean and athletic, but it was the steel in her gaze and the rebellious tilt of her chin that marked her. There was a sharpness about her, a hardness that spoke of defiance and of someone who would follow only when it suited her, There was something cold and challenging in the way she looked at me, a distance to her that made her difficult to warm to. Perhaps she would be one to watch.

"Where are we with our plans for tomorrow?" Nev asked, and I turned my head to look at him.

Jory hesitated and all of the eyes in the room fell on me again.

"You can speak freely in front of her. Are we ready?"

"As ready as we can be. The Order is only a few miles out, and we have eyes on them. From what we can tell, the boys are in a bad way but alive."

"Good. We'll be joining you, so we better go over the exact plans."

Jory paused again, and I could sense the animosity in the room as his eyes lingered on me. I understood their reluctance, their mistrust. It wasn't unfamiliar to me. Caution had been my own shield for as long as I could remember. I had been much the same as a smuggler, always wary, always weighing friend against foe. All my life, in fact, suspicion had been the instinct that kept me alive.

"Forgive me, Captain, but I think we're all wondering the same thing. What is Lord Mirle's fiancée doing here?"

Nev turned to me with a knowing smile, gesturing for me to answer for myself. I stepped forward slowly, steadying my breath as one by one I met their eyes in turn. My voice was calm when it came, though my pulse drummed in my ears. This was no place for doubt or weakness.

"I get it. As far as you're concerned, I appeared out of nowhere a few weeks ago and was swept off my feet by a charismatic young lord." I smiled to myself, raising an eyebrow. "Or maybe I enchanted him, who can say?"

Nev snorted softly.

"And now I stand here with your lives in my hands. You don't know me. You don't know what I want. So let me show you."

Without warning, I slammed my hands down onto the table. Shadows erupted from my fingertips, extinguishing the candles and plunging the room into an icy darkness. The floor beneath us shook violently and made the glasses on the table clink. Around the room there were audible gasps, more than one panicked curse, and the sound of a chair being pushed back so fast that it had fallen over. To my right someone muttered a brief prayer to the Gods and I smiled. Essence was surging through my blood, making my shadows dance elatedly, and for a moment I was nothing but pure, unfettered power.

I let my shadows reach out to kiss each of the Loyalist's faces, easing into their minds to caress their consciousness. There was silence in the room, not a single one of them daring to move. But I breathed easily, delighting in the darkness, and for the first time since I had lain in Emrys's arms, I felt like I was exactly where I was meant to be. Feeling like I was exactly *who* I needed to be. I let my shadows fall, just enough to be able to see the faces around me. I almost laughed at the assortment of expressions around the room, but when I glanced at Jory he was grinning.

"My name is Aeva Penrose," I said, my voice sounding clear and loud. "I am the daughter of Aemylia Ashae and Novos Penrose. For too long, Damen Treforno has ruled with violence and brutality, murdering the innocent and taking from them what is rightfully ours. He thinks that fighting back is futile, that you are fragile and easily destroyed. He believes that every flicker of hope can be stamped out beneath his heel. He means to crush the Loyalists, to make you think there is no better future.

"But we are still here. Like you, I have bled. I have lost. I have clawed my way back from the dark more times than I can count, and I'm still standing. Not because I want a throne. Not because I want your fear. But because I refuse to let men like him rule what should be ours. You want a reason to trust me? Then trust this: I'm not here to break you. I'm here to break *him*. To tear down everything he has built, stone by stone, until not a trace of his cruelty remains.

"A few days ago, Lord Baern called the Loyalists rats —skulking through the villages, troublesome, an inconvenience. But they have forgotten the trail of damage that even a single rat can leave in its wake. They should fear the damage, the ruin, the *rage* we carry. He has forgotten what happens when the cornered fight back. But while he believes that, while he underestimates us, we can become something *more*—something he cannot fight, cannot crush, cannot stop."

Nessa had been watching me with interest and now leaned back in her chair, a smile on her lips.

"What exactly are you proposing we do, then?"

The *noswaith* poured from my hands and stole menacingly around the room, making the very air seem to tremble. I closed my eyes, picturing the white stag from the night before and remembering the challenge in its eyes. I wasn't hiding in the darkness anymore. I was shadows and fury. I *was* the darkness.

I opened my eyes, and smiled.

CHAPTER 26
EFA

"I count twenty four Nothori," Jory whispered as he crawled back over to us.

We lay stretched out on the flat roof of the bakery, the tiles cool and damp with night dew. Noak was a small village, and its main street was barely more than a cluster of buildings centered around an old tavern, it's sign creaking as it moved in the faint breeze. At the far end, there was a shrine dedicated to Temos, one of the agricultural Gods. Like the rest of the village, it was simple in its design. A wooden carving of the God, weathered by years of being touched by devout hands, stood outside, surrounded by various offerings—mostly herbs and dried flowers. It was a humble place, well kept and practical, much like the people who lived there. It was also where the Order had decided to erect the scaffold, and I watched on with disdain as three Nothori soldiers stacked kindling around two makeshift stakes.

"Twenty four Nothori and six Order priests," Nev said. "Seems like overkill for a village execution. Reckon they're expecting trouble?"

"If they are, they'll get it," Jory said, his lips curving up in a smile.

I scanned the street, trying to make out the rest of our group. It still wasn't particularly light out but the sun was starting to rise, sending streaks of red across the sky. Shepherd's warning. I didn't need Owen to remind me of that omen. From our vantage point I could see Caydan and Merryn on top of the tavern roof, their quivers full of arrows. The others were well hidden, but I knew they were close by, crouched behind the hedgerows until it was time. Like the three of us, they were all dressed all in black, their faces smeared with charcoal.

After almost an hour, I heard the sound of a wagon approaching, the wheels grinding on the stony road, and one by one, villagers started to emerge from the small cottages, their faces solemn and drawn. According to Jory, the two brothers had been barely more than children when they had been taken by the Order, dragged kicking and screaming from their aunt and uncle's farm. Now they were young men, scarred and weakened after years of harsh imprisonment. I calmly watched the scene in front of me unfold. More and more villagers appeared, some of them crying and upset, some of them, the men especially, visibly angry. The boys and their family had been well liked before they were taken, and the village had been angry, but no one did anything then, and no one did anything now. None of them wanted to fight thirty trained soldiers, especially ones as terrifying and intimidating as the Nothori. It would be suicide.

The Order priests stepped forward in front of the gathered crowd, their hands resting on their swords ready to draw should there be any trouble. Their eyes darted around, waiting, watching. The tallest of the four came forward, the symbol on his tunic breast denoting his seniority.

"By decree of the Crown, these traitors stand condemned. They have turned against their rightful sovereign, conspiring with rebels and betraying the peace of the realm. For such sins, there can be no mercy. Let all who watch remember: rebellion against the Crown is rebellion against the Gods themselves."

"The Gods themselves, hey?" Jory muttered with a dry chuckle. "I must have missed the day the Gods started handing out blessings for murdering the innocent."

A faint smile tugged at my lips as I shook my head. The words were laughable, a mockery of truth. My fingernails cut into my palm as I clenched my fist, watching the Order priest nod at the two Nothori soldiers guarding the wagon. They unlocked the door and reached in, dragging out the brothers.

I hissed under my breath when I saw them. Their faces were a mess of blood and bruises, some old and some new, their clothes were ragged and filthy, and they were thin, their muscle wasted away. The smaller of the two lost his footing as he was pulled from the wagon and he fell awkwardly down into the ground. The Nothori closest to him backhanded him, shouting at him to stand and then dragging up by the thin fabric of his shirt when he didn't move fast enough. There was silence from the crowd as they stumbled towards the scaffold, resigned to their fate as the Nothori shoved them up the steps. I could see the fear in their eyes even from where I was, their faces deathly pale.

"Ready yourselves," Nev muttered as the Nothori secured them to the stakes.

It was clear to anyone watching how much pleasure the Nothori were taking in the situation. They leered at the two brothers, leaning forward to whisper no doubt crude taunts in their ears, and as they left the scaffold the tall Order priest took the lit torch being offered to him. He at least had the decency to look sombre. As he took a single step towards the scaffold there was movement next to me as Jory raised two fingers to his temple. Then, an arrow struck the priest through the chest and the torch dropped to the ground. There was a moment when it felt like no one breathed, only for a second or two, but it felt like a lifetime. And then I released my shadows.

~

My boots were quiet on the damp ground as I walked towards the scaffolding, blade in hand. Bodies littered the market street, some bearing knife wounds, others the victims of Merryn and Caydan's arrows. Some had club wounds to the head. That was the work of the villagers. About a third had no visible injuries, but blood leaked from their ears and noses. That was my doing.

I had pushed myself this time, not content with shattering only one mind at a time and delighting when I found I was able to destroy several at once. My temples throbbed and I brought my hand up to wipe the blood from my nose, a smile on my face. Rumo, Treave and Nessa had climbed up onto the platform and were releasing the two brothers. The younger one had lost consciousness at some point, his head lolling forward, but the other was grinning. Behind me, Jory, Caydan and Merryn were walking amongst the bodies and checking that they were in fact dead, and Nev walked beside me as we strolled over to the single Order priest that we had intentionally left alive.

He was young, probably a year or two younger than Noa, with reddish gold hair and freckled skin. Blood was splattered across his face and he was visibly trembling. In fairness to him, if I had been surrounded by Nothori and I'd watched them stop dead in their tracks, screaming and clawing at their heads as some unknown enemy tore apart their minds piece by piece, I might have been a little unsettled, too.

I stopped a meter or two away from him, and sent out dark shadows to wrap around his ankles like ropes, dragging him towards me as the villagers gasped. He shrieked, and I noticed a wet patch forming around his crotch. A man and woman rushed forward from the crowd to embrace the brothers as they were being helped down from the scaffold, but I paid the aunt and uncle little attention. All around me, the villagers were looking at me with shock, curiosity, and even abject horror. Good. I wanted to cause a scene.

I focused on the boy at my feet, crouching down and gently stroking my blade down his cheek, the Valtanan steel no doubt cold on his skin. I smiled at him like I would a child and he shuddered; terrified tears rolling down his face as his eyes kept glancing up to the dark smoke billowing above me.

"What is your name?"

"Clem."

I nodded thoughtfully.

"Do you know why you're still alive, Clem?"

He shook his head, and I casually ran the blade down his neck and chest.

"You are alive for the sole reason that we would like you to deliver a message."

"Wh-what message?" he stuttered.

"You will go back to your temple and you will tell your superiors that you have a message for the king. You will tell Damen that this is just the beginning. He can send a thousand Nothori and it will make no difference. We will kill them all." I paused to smile, thinking of Tanrith. "Tell him that we are like rats; multiplying and spreading across his kingdom, hidden in the darkness. Impossible to eradicate."

I pressed the tip of my knife down into his thigh, hearing his slight intake of breath as it pierced the fabric and broke skin, blood staining his pants.

"You will tell him that Aeva Penrose is coming for him. Tell him that I will take back what is rightfully mine, and that he should be afraid. Because I am about to bring nothing but shadows and fury down upon him."

CHAPTER 27
EFA

"You'll ride in the carriage with me this morning," Austell instructed as he strode past me and out to the front of the inn, his tone brokering no argument

My mouth dropped open and I stared at his back as he walked away from me, unimpressed by his tone. Clearly he was annoyed. He'd had a face like thunder, and I noticed the collar of his jacket was slightly upturned, as if he had been in a rush to get ready. It was an unusual oversight for Lord Mirle who rarely had even a hair out of place. I followed him outside with a mix of irritation and amusement, taking in the line of his shoulders and clenched fists. Nev was waiting next to the carriage, and he opened the door as Austell approached. Austell pointed a finger at his captain but didn't even glance his way. Oh, he *was* mad.

"You too, Captain."

I raised my eyebrows as I met Nev's eye, shaking my head as he silently mouthed 'here we go'. Despite the fact I hadn't slept all night, I had been planning on riding that day, choosing to ignore Tanrith's remarks about what he called my 'scandalous disregard for propriety' and that the fresh air and stiff breeze gave me a 'wild, untamed look' similar to that of a forest nymph. After the way Austell had just spoken to me I seriously considered ignoring his demand and just getting on my horse anyway, but I decided to oblige him on this occasion. I had, after all, done something of a disappearing act on him during the night and I wasn't surprised he was pissed off.

I climbed in with something of an attitude, sitting on the bench opposite him and fixing him with a fairly direct look. I felt the carriage sway a little as Nev followed me in, and we sat in silence for the first couple of minutes while I looked at Austell expectantly. It took me a moment to realize that he was waiting to be far enough from the inn so that we wouldn't be overheard, but as soon as we were out of range he exploded.

"Are you crazy, the pair of you? You went without a word in the middle of the fucking night and went to an Order execution, left a man alive, and then *revealed* yourself to him? To give him a *message*? What were you thinking, the pair of you? You—"

I raised my hand abruptly, giving him a hard stare as I interrupted him.

"First of all, who the fuck do you think you're talking to, Austell? You better rein yourself in right now if you think I'm going to stand for being spoken to like this. I'm not Eseld and I'm not one of your servants. Perhaps you have forgotten exactly who I am?"

His words incensed me. I wasn't one to regularly pull rank, but I refused to be spoken to like I was a disobedient child. He flushed, a deep red staining his cheeks and spreading up from under his collar. Austell was a courtier through and through. He knew that he had spoken out of turn, but he was still livid with me.

"Secondly, though I recognize that you have every right to be concerned and worried about me, I don't owe you an explanation. I neither belong to you nor report to you. It is my prerogative to come and go as I please, and I am entitled to keep things to myself, just as I'm sure you do."

I saw him take a breath and look away from me for a second, and I knew I'd hit the mark with that one. Austell was usually very open with me, but there were definitely things that he withheld, either because he thought he was protecting me, or because it suited him for me not to know. News of the Dark Prince, for example.

"Thirdly, though you may lead this rebellion, for which I am incredibly grateful, those men and women fight in *my* name. For *my* legacy. And it is *my* identity that I chose to reveal last night. And that is also *my* prerogative."

I took a breath and tucked my hair behind both ears, softening slightly.

"Perhaps I should have told you my intentions. I assumed that you would say no, that you would think it a bad idea, and to tell the truth, I neither wanted to have to ask permission to go or feel like I was defying you when you told me not to. Can you honestly say that you wouldn't have?"

Austell sighed deeply and ran his hand over his face as he gazed out of the window. I took that as a no.

"You could have been killed, Efa. Everything we are doing… this whole elaborate ruse… it's all to give us the best possible chance of understanding what we're up against here. If something had happened to you, or if you'd been captured…"

"There was very little chance of that," Nev murmured. Austell shot him a murderous look.

"Don't even get me started on *you*. Your actions amount to outright insubordination."

"Aren't his orders to protect me?" I asked.

"To protect you, yes. Not take you to fight."

He leaned back in his seat, a weary look on his face, and for the first time I felt guilty. He had been worried about me. That was all. Perhaps I had done him a disservice by not bringing him in on my plans.

"I'm sorry, Austell. I should have told you, you're right."

"I think the least I deserve is to know where you are in case something had happened."

I nodded, reaching forward to place my hand on his knee.

"You're right," I said again, "and you will going forward, even if we don't always agree on my approach or actions."

"Fine, then let's leave it at that. I understand everything went well, anyway."

Nev scoffed.

"More than well. It couldn't have gone any better."

Just then, one of the guards tapped on the window.

"My Lord, we're about to join the rest of the convoy."

"Wonderful," I said, slapping my hands on my thighs. "I think I'll get out and ride. Give Lord Tanrith something to really get excited about."

Nev chuckled but Austell held up a finger.

"Hold on, before you do that, what about the risk? Novos and Aemylia's heir just shows up five miles from where I'm staying with my new, previously unknown fiancée?"

"We've thought of that," I said, opening the carriage

door and glancing back at him mischievously. "Now we just have to hope what we planned works."

And lucky for us it did, because the next morning we received reports of Melrith's heir being seen ten miles south of Noak. Miles away from us.

CHAPTER 28
EFA

"Quite the exciting turn of events, I would say!" Tanrith said, the usual mocking smile stretching across his face as he played with his moustache. "Novos's heir has appeared out of nowhere to spread terror through our villages."

He had just finished reading aloud the letter his guard had handed him as he sat down for breakfast, a report on yet another execution that had taken place the night before in a village called Fletching. Once again, Aeva Penrose had been there, surrounded in shadows as they massacred the Order priests and Nothori. Once again, a single priest had been spared so that he could deliver a message to the king.

Of course, I hadn't been there. I had been tucked up in my bed listening to the rain hammering against my window. It was Merryn who was out killing Nothori and using my name. She was a similar height, build and coloring, and, dressed in black with our faces covered in coal, she easily passed for me. All we needed to complete the deception was something that could pass as my shadows, and it was the memory of the street performer back in Esari that had given me the idea.

As luck would have it, Treave and Rumo had grown up in a travelling troupe and knew exactly how the trick was done. Something to do with finely ground sawdust, damp leaves, and a common weed found throughout Melrith that when ignited caused the smoke to turn black. Sure, it wouldn't hold up under much scrutiny, especially if you knew what you were looking for, but in the middle of the chaos and confusion of a skirmish I'd have said it was pretty convincing, and these village folk were simple creatures. I was willing to bet that very few, if any, had ever seen the *noswaith* in real life, so it was enough to get the gossip spreading and to make everyone think that the heir was moving across Melrith and not right into the heart of Damen's stronghold.

"Spreading terror through the villages, or through the capital?" Austell asked calmly as he buttered a slice of toast.

Canver grunted, speaking with his mouth full as usual.

"Indeed. It's rather concerning how readily these common peasants are reacting to these insurgents, don't you think? They seem so very enamoured with the idea of her."

I stared at the Lord Cayam, trying to conceal my revulsion as I took in the grease on his chin and the food that had already somehow slopped down the front of his shirt. Disappointingly, the inn that we had arrived at the night before was large enough to accommodate the entire party, and though the night before I had been able to beg tiredness and take supper in my room, there was no option other than to eat breakfast with them this morning. Tanrith aggressively speared a sausage and brought it up to his lips.

"I'd like to know where this girl has been hiding all these years? I always thought the child had died alongside her hopeless parents in the flames that night. No doubt she has been hidden in some whore house in Danae or Tithra."

I sipped my tea demurely. It was true; I had frequented a number of brothels over the years, but it wasn't for the reason Tanrith was alluding to. I wondered what he'd think if he knew I was more accustomed to removing cocks rather than sucking them. He'd probably find it oddly arousing, from what I'd seen so far.

"I never liked the Valtanan way of passing the crown down through the female line," he continued. "I myself have always thought that women should either be wives or whores. Don't you agree, Sandy?"

Across the table, Caja's cheeks flushed slightly at the inference but she kept her eyes cast down. If she wasn't a wife… I remembered her sneaking out of Tanrith's room the other night. Did Canver know about their arrangement?

"What about you, Austell? I expect you like your women placid and amiable, as easy to prune and maintain as your roses?"

Austell laughed almost despairingly as he took another slice of toast.

"I'm afraid I don't, Zennor. And you're quite mistaken. Roses are certainly not simple. They take considerable time and attention to get the best from them. But no, I have always very much enjoyed the company of women, outside of the bedroom just as much as inside. I find them to be intelligent, good company, and quite capable." He glanced at me and smiled, his eyes lingering on my face. "In fact, in my own fiancée I must say that I have rather found my equal."

I blushed unexpectedly at his words and Tanrith guffawed loudly, his eyes glimmering.

"Your *equal*? Oh my, Austell. She certainly has bewitched you, hasn't she? No… nature didn't intend for women to be our equals. They are here to please men, to be useful, and to make life agreeable and sweet for us. They *belong* to us. They don't rule us."

I calmly topped up my cup with more fresh mint tea. I always found it astounding when men talked like this, especially with women present. Their arrogance really knew no bounds. Tanrith and Finn would probably be fast friends.

"And if by some outlandish turn of events the princess somehow ended up on the throne," Austell mused, "would you change your mind and kneel before her, Tanrith? Would you pledge your allegiance to your queen?"

Canver's small, piggy eyes flicked back and forth between the two Lords. Tanrith smirked, dabbing at his mouth with a napkin. He waggled a finger back and forth as if to rebuke Austell.

"That, my Lord Esari, is surely treasonous. But since you have asked… no, I would not. She is not my queen. I would die before I bent my knee to Aeva Penrose."

I smiled sweetly, nodding in agreement as I spread a thick layer of jam on my toast and bit into it with a satisfying crunch, finding my appetite for the first time in days. I could certainly make that happen. Little did he know that I had every intention of taking the throne, and every intention of killing him in the process.

CHAPTER 29
EFA

The usual heavy mist rolled down off of the mountains and spilled through the Nijem Forest as we left the inn and rejoined the road. The Baern Road was rough and uneven, little more than packed earth and stone, but it was wide and well worn from years of use. Farmer's carts, marching soldiers, and countless hooves had beaten it into a track that stretched from Rael in the west all the way to Rostorrmel on the eastern peninsula. A heavy, foreboding feeling had started to weigh on me as I stared at it stretching into the distance. It was hard to believe that the next night I would be sleeping in Rostorrmel Palace again for the first time since my father had ruled from its throne room.

Despite the dismal weather, I chose to ride, preferring the fresh air and Nev's easy conversation to the confined space within the carriage and Austell's quiet apprehension. The weather was turning colder now, and the rain that had been falling for the last hour had now turned to sleet. I bundled myself up in my fur coat, pulling it tight around me in an effort to keep out the mist that swirled around in the biting wind. For just a moment, I remembered the strength of Emrys's arms around me, the way he would tug his cloak around us both as he rode behind me down from Cryf's Gap. Pain speared through my heart, and I shook my head, irritated with myself.

"Have you been to Rostorrmel recently?" Nev asked from beside me.

I turned my head to look at him. He was halfway through eating an apple he'd pulled from somewhere.

"Not since I was a child," I said. "And not because I was afraid to, or sad, or anything like that. I was never particularly attached to the city. I always thought of Nissae as my home. Rostorrmel was just where all the politics happened. For whatever reason, Nevedeno business just didn't bring me this way. Has it changed much over the years?"

"Not really. Some of the towns around Baern, Cayam and Polruen haven't fared so well, but Rostorrmel has carried on much the same as it always did, apart from a much greater Order presence."

"It will be strange being in the palace again. I imagine *that* will be different."

Nev shrugged, finishing the apple in two bites and tossing the core into the forest.

"Yes and no. The portraits of your parents and your father's family were removed immediately, as you'd expect. But I'm led to believe that it remains otherwise much the same." He paused to smile at me. "You might even find your old room still intact."

I laughed quietly.

"That *would* be surreal. I almost hope I don't."

"I imagine it wasn't the best place for a child to grow up," Nev said.

"Not really. But the hidden passageways were exciting to explore."

"The passageways?"

I imagined myself as a child, holding my breath and trembling with excitement as I peered through a crack in the Great Throne Room wall to watch my father's meetings.

"Almost every room had one—hidden passages behind the walls, with spy holes. Noa and I found them by accident once. I thought my father didn't know about them, until one day he asked me what I'd overheard in the throne room. He'd known I was behind the wall the whole time."

"Where did they lead to?"

"Everywhere. They went all over the palace and down to the coves and the forest. The trouble was remembering them all. I found myself down in the dungeons once, but I could never find my way down to them again."

"You sound like an adventurous child," he laughed. "Austell said something about you being spirited when he met you in Nissae. 'A force to be reckoned with', I think was the phrase he used."

"Not everyone thought it was a good thing. I seem to recall Damen being rather critical of my spiritedness."

"How so?"

"I'd ended up in a fight with one of the other children after they'd picked on Noa. I'd used my shadows to stop them from hurting him, and somehow broken their nose. I remember standing in the throne room after, still covered in their blood. Damen said that I was disobedient and uncontrollable, and that my father needed to take me in hand. That he gave me too much freedom."

"What did your father say?"

"That I was exactly who I was supposed to be. That he was raising a daughter, a queen, who wasn't afraid to look any enemy in the eye, and who would bring down nothing but shadows and fury on anyone who tried to harm her people."

"That's what you said back in Noak," Nev said quietly. "Shadows and fury. They were your father's words?"

I nodded, biting my lip as I fiddled with the horse's reins. From the forest I began to hear those whispering voices again, and my shadows rose in response. *I hear you*, I said to them. *We're finally doing what we're supposed to be doing*. I swallowed hard and changed the subject.

"You'll still accompany me into Rostorrmel tonight?"

"Of course. Just as we planned."

I nodded, pushing my hair out of my eyes and staring off into the darkness of the trees. The rest of the journey passed uneventfully until we stopped at the final inn, and I counted down the minutes until I could retire to bed. Only I didn't go to sleep. Instead, Nev and I waited until the early hours and then rode the final ten miles into Rostorrmel to retrieve Arella, ready to return quietly to the inn and do the journey by carriage all over again the next morning.

The harbor was still unexpectedly busy when we reached it, despite the late hour. It was high tide, and ships were coming in and out. Cargo was being loaded and unloaded, and men were stumbling out from the nearby taverns and back on board their ships after weeks at sea. Nev asked a reasonably sober looking man where we could find the *Panacea*, and we set off in the direction he'd pointed, finding Arella waiting on the deck, her pretty face illuminated by a nearby lamp. She embraced me tightly when I reached the top of the gangplank.

"Gods, Efa. You look like you haven't eaten *or* slept since I left you in Esari. What did I tell you?"

"Have you found him, Rell?" I asked, ignoring her question and skipping right to the point.

She pulled back from me and I could tell from her face that she didn't have good news.

"No, Efa. None of the ships we came in contact with in Soless had any news. But it doesn't mean that he isn't safe. Torr has over a hundred ships in his fleet, you know that."

I did, but I also knew that word got around quick in Torr's fleet. I would have expected to hear something out of the gossip in Soless's busy harbor. My heart sank and I could feel my anxiety rising as we all sat in Torr's cabin. The small room felt even smaller than usual with the addition of Nev in there too.

"I'm sure Arella has told you that we've had no word on Noa," Torr said gravely. He was perched on the edge of his desk, his head nearly skimming the low ceiling beams. "My ship, the *Zephyr,* was in Soless and I spoke with Jato. He had come straight from Serenfell and there was no sign of him there."

My hand trembled as I bit at the skin around my thumbnail, wincing as I pulled the skin too far and drew blood. Nev reached over to take my hand from my mouth and I clutched both hands together instead in my lap, my knee bouncing. Torr passed me a glass of rum, the amber liquid sloshing against the sides. It burned as it touched my tongue, searing its way down my throat, but instead of steadying me, it only seemed to sharpen the edge of my nerves, setting my pulse racing faster. Arella's face was pale, her eyes large in the lamplight as she looked between us all.

"So, what do we do next?"

I shrugged, downing the rest of the drink and wincing. I'd never liked rum.

"The only thing we can do. Bide our time, hope for the best, and pray to the fucking Gods."

CHAPTER 30
EFA

I shifted uncomfortably in my seat. I was in a bad mood, a scowl etched on my face since I had woken up that morning after a short, restless sleep. All I could think about was Noa. If he wasn't on one of Torr's ships, where was he? Did Finn have him? Was he dead? Was he injured and hurt somewhere? Worrying about him was driving me to distraction, and to make matters worse the rolling of the carriage was making me feel nauseous, and the fabric of my dress was itching my neck. All in all, I was pretty terrible company.

"How many ships?" Austell asked, leaning forward on his knees.

"At least ten, apparently," Arella said, "sitting about three miles off the coast of Rostorrmel out of sight of the harbor."

This was the other news Torr had imparted the night before. One of his ships, the *Halcyon*, had arrived in from the north to Rostorrmel's harbor the day before, running straight into a fleet of Nothori warships. They had tried to intimidate the *Halcyon*, even going as far as to fire a couple of warning shots at her across the water before she had put enough distance between them. I huffed out a breath, staring out of the window as the rain thrashed against the glass. I caught a glimpse of Nev riding just behind us, his face grim under the wide hood of his cloak. Maybe I was better off in the carriage on this occasion.

"That's a lot of Nothori," Austell said, raising his voice so I it carried above the sound of the rain on the roof. "And Torr thinks that each ship carries, what… 200 men?"

"At least," she said. "Two thousand Nothori soldiers sitting out in the Eastern Sea, a long way from home. What are they doing out there? And why isn't Damen doing anything about it?"

"Because he invited them," I said darkly. "This isn't just about executions or slave trafficking. This is about something much bigger. We just don't know what yet."

Austell blew out a breath and ran a hand through his hair.

"Could he really be planning a war?"

"Against who? The *Fae*?" Arella asked, frowning. "If that's true, then they definitely aren't allied anymore."

Austell leaned back in the chair and rested his head against the seat.

"I don't think they ever were allied," he said. "I think we got it all wrong, all those years ago."

"But then why would the Fae let everyone think that they betrayed us?" I screwed up my face, trying to add everything up.

"Efa, you've just spent weeks with a group of Fae males," Arella said, sending me a withering look. "You must know what they're like by now. They're a stoic, patient race that will go to great lengths to keep their own business to themselves. They have plenty of secrets up there in the snow and ice. Maybe they want us to think that to hide something else."

I scowled, feeling a headache coming on. The rain continued to pour and forked lightning split the sky in the distance. I shut my eyes, trying to block everything out, but all I could think about was those few days of contentment I had known in the forest with Emrys and the others. All I could see was the way he smiled at me as he looked at me across the campfire, and the way he had held me after the Nothori attack in Cayam. When he thought that he had lost me. My heart hurt.

"We're approaching Rostorrmel now," Austell said a few minutes later.

With a sigh I cracked my eyes open and looked out of the window. Up ahead in the distance, the city sprawled out in front of us, the endless, rough grey waters of the Eastern Sea behind it. And there, perched perilously on the peninsula's ragged cliffs in the shadows of the easternmost snow-capped peaks of the Ferras Mountains, stood Rostorrmel Palace.

Rostorrmel, meaning 'violent storm' in the old language, was a relatively new city compared to some of the others across the human territory of Melrith. About six hundred years earlier, one of my ancestors had decided that they preferred the strategic location; its position on the cliffs gave it unrivalled views, and it could defend itself well against any threats coming in from the sea. Though it was nowhere near as cold as the Northern Realm, the city was rarely warm, even in the summer. The harsh prevailing wind that came in off the water kept temperatures low and blustered through the meandering streets, and the city was regularly battered by ferocious storms, hence its name.

The city itself wasn't particularly special, either. It

lacked the picturesque charm of Esari and the vibrant nightlife that still clung on determinedly in Cayam. There were beaches and coves aplenty, but none of the spectacular coastline that made Rael so beautiful. And since it was so much larger than many of the other cities and towns, it didn't have the same sense of community, the folk less friendly and preferring to keep themselves to themselves.

But what it did have was a palace so impressive that it rivaled some of the castles and fortresses in both this continent and others. At least, those were Eseld's words before we'd left Totease. Like the rest of the city, the palace itself was built from grey stone and had blue slate roofs. I'd never thought it was particularly remarkable in appearance but it was certainly imposing, built over multiple levels directly into the cliffs. The notorious dungeons ran underneath, deep within the naturally occurring caves in the cliff. They were damp and terribly cold, with only the faint echoing sound of the sea and the moaning of the other inhabitants for company.

On the rare days that the sun was out, Rostorrmel was pleasant enough, but more often than not it was a dreary and uninviting place. I could only ever recall my demi-fae mother, born and raised in Valtana's much more temperate climate, wearing a thick fur stole when she was in the palace. She used to complain about the near constant rain and that she could never get warm, and that the only good thing about the palace was its proximity to the forest where she used to walk daily. The great expanse of it came right up to the outer city wall where it reluctantly ended, the tree branches scratching and scraping against the stone, as if trying to get in.

As the convoy neared the city gate that Nev and I had ridden under the night before, there was no sign of the sun breaking through the thick layer of clouds above us.

Tanrith and Canver's carriages had slowed down so that we could catch up with them, and we made our way through the busy streets together, drawing plenty of attention as crowds formed alongside us.

"I'm sensing a lot of animosity," Arella murmured.

I nodded. The people didn't look happy to see us. In fact, I'd have gone as far as to say there was open hostility on many of their faces.

"There have been executions every morning here for a week," Austell said quietly. "Tanrith told me this morning. The people don't like it."

"They're blaming the regional lords, too, by the looks of things," Arella said.

I had been thinking the same thing. Something was simmering among the townsfolk, a restlessness and sense of anticipation that spoke of future violence and discord. There was an uprising on the horizon. Damen would very soon have his hands full if he didn't do something, but I supposed that was what the Nothori were here for. Around the carriage, the Esari guards had drawn in close, their hands hovering at their swords as we made our way slowly towards the lower gatehouse at the bottom of the hill. I caught Nev's eye briefly, seeing the tension in his shoulders as he scanned for imminent threats, and I strengthened the shield around my mind.

My shadows trembled uneasily, warning me of something unseen, and a moment later the oath line began to throb. I flinched, my eyes catching on a cloaked figure in the crowd, his face partially hidden by his hood. As the carriage passed, he lifted the hood and smiled, causing my blood to run cold even as I felt that familiar burning sensation start to prickle across my skin. Finn was here.

"What's that?" Arella said, pointing out of the window towards the gatehouse.

Finn smirked at me before seeming to vanish into the crowd, the burning sensation disappearing with him, and I reluctantly tore my eyes away. I shifted in my seat to lean across her to look out of the other side and breathed in sharply. Someone had scrawled words across the wall in large, red letters.

The true Queen is coming.

"Fuck. That's a statement."

"That wasn't there when we left last night," Arella said. "It must have happened early this morning. Are there Loyalists in the city?"

I looked to Austell for confirmation and he nodded.

"They're here to cause trouble, to try and cause a distraction while we are in the palace. The more attention Damen is giving to them, the less he has for you."

He smiled, peering round us both to look at the wall, the palace guards doing their best to wash it off.

"I'm not sure Nev told them to do that, though. It's a nice touch."

"Unless it just heralds my arrival," I said, nervously playing with my fingers, Finn's sudden appearance still playing on my mind.

"Unlikely," he replied. "Jory was in a town 15 miles south of here with Merryn last night. It places Aeva Penrose well away from here."

I looked back out of the window as the carriage made its way up the steep, winding track. Fortunately the rain had eased by the time we had reached the top of the cliff, but a squally wind blustered around us as we stepped out of the carriages to a frenzy of activity and a cacophony of noise from all of the horses on the cobblestones. To my right, Canver half stepped and half fell from his carriage, narrowly saved from humiliation by a pair of quick thinking footmen. Caja and her maid followed him out more gracefully, her gown blowing around her legs.

Eager to get out of the wind, Austell held out his hand to me and I took it, letting him lead me across the courtyard and towards the palace entrance with Arella close behind. A stable boy darted in front of me, almost tripping me up and earning himself a sharp rebuke from Austell, but as I glanced at him I felt a rush of familiarity, my eyes widening in surprise. Ando sketched a bow to me, apologising for getting in my way, but I noticed the way he casually held his thumb and middle finger together against his stomach as he held my gaze. It was the Nevedeno signal that meant he had news for me. My brow creased slightly.

I had briefly forgotten that Lore's Gifted nephew worked in the palace stables. The two Valtanan spies shared the same gift of glamoring, able to shift their features so as to go unnoticed. My mind raced. I hadn't been foolish enough to believe my arrival at Rostorrmel would go unnoticed; the Nevedeno always had an eye on the palace's comings and goings. But Finn's presence had thrown me, and I didn't know whom I could trust. A few weeks ago, I would have counted Lore's as someone I could rely on implicitly. Every single one of his spies, including Ando, would have followed my instructions without question. But since Theo's revelations back in Esari, that had all changed.

I studied Ando; desperately wanting to believe Theo had been lying about Lore's knowledge of the trafficking and new Faelock. I could do with his help, but who knew what influence Finn had over him and what lies he had been spinning. Austell tugged on my hand gently and I looked away from the young spy, following him inside with a new feeling of apprehension unfurling in my stomach.

"We'll go straight to our rooms now," Austell said. "We won't see Damen until he receives us at court tonight."

We walked through the heavy oak doors where a footman dressed in the blue and gold livery of House Treforno bowed to Austell and completely ignored me. Arella pulled a face and I grinned, taking in my surroundings and noting the four Order priests that flanked the entrance. We walked swiftly down into the heart of the palace, and I felt like I had been transported back in time. Nev had been right; nothing had changed. Everything was exactly as it had been when my father ruled here. The same magnificent oil paintings hung on the corridor walls. The same suits of armour stood to attention. Even the richly patterned carpet beneath our feet was the same. The only new additions were the vases of flowers everywhere; their sickeningly sweet smell so powerful that they began to give me a headache.

At the end of the corridor stood a great imperial staircase, and I raised my eyes to where the large portrait of my parents used to hang, finding instead Damen's stern, unyielding face staring back down at me. My shadows twitched and my fingers tightened around Austell's hand as we climbed the stairs. He turned his head to look at me, his eyes silently asking if everything was all right. I gave a small nod and he squeezed my hand, pulling me forward so that I walked next to him.

He seemed to know where we were heading, and as we climbed another set of stairs up to the second floor I suddenly recognized where we were. For decades, each of the lords had their own suites at the palace, but it was only as I stepped into the large sitting room, decorated in the

Esari colors of sage and copper, that I realized I had never been inside any of them. As more footmen appeared and began to bring in our trunks and cases, Austell walked straight over to a side table and poured himself a large glass of brandy. Arella sidled up beside me.

"It's funny seeing the rooms from the inside, and not through a spy hole," she whispered to me, her thoughts echoing mine.

"Have whichever rooms you prefer," Austell said, taking a sip and gesturing at the doors leading off of the sitting room. "The room on the left has the better views in my opinion. There are four rooms so Arella you'll have your own room, too. Nev and I will take whichever rooms are left."

I pushed open the door furthest away and walked into one of the bedrooms. It was another big room, the dated décor tasteful at least, with a four-poster bed made up in soft green linens, and floral watercolor paintings in ornate frames hanging on the walls. I slipped my shoes off and padded across the thick carpet to the large bay windows, taking in the breathtaking views and the black storm clouds hanging ominously over the sea. I stepped closer to the glass where I could see down to the harbor and found the *Panacea* and *Halcyon* docked next to each other on the far side. Thunder rumbled in the distance, and I remembered the odd way that Arella's eyes had glazed over in Serenfell as she came to stand next to me.

"A storm is coming," I murmured, repeating her words from weeks ago as I pulled my fur around me, feeling suddenly cold.

"Oh, it's coming alright," she said. "About to make landfall and promising unspeakable damage and destruction. And here we are, too. Right in its midst."

CHAPTER 31
EFA

The stables were a lively affair. They now housed all of the horses from our convoy, and, from the looks of the liveries, Lord Hollis and Lord Montavis had also arrived in the last hour or so, leaving only Lord Denfor to make an appearance. I found the chestnut mare I'd taken to riding in a stall next to Nev's and made a show of loudly giving her plenty of attention since, should anyone be watching, Arella and I needed a legitimate reason to be in the stables. We'd only been there perhaps fifteen minutes when I heard a noise behind me, and I turned to find Ando coming into the stall. He bowed quickly.

"Apologies, Lady Esari," he said without meeting my eyes. "I came to see whether your horse requires anything."

I raised an eyebrow, giving him a sidelong glance.

"It's not Lady Esari yet, and no, thank you. She seems well taken care of."

Ando came forward, standing next to me. His hand

moved slowly over the mare's flank in calm, steady strokes.

"My uncle is here in the city," he murmured, his voice barely audible. "He wants to meet with you. I can take you now, but I can only glamor one of you."

Arella glanced at me, and then back at Ando. I knew she was trying to work out whether we could trust him, too. I'd told no one about seeing Finn on the way into the city. I wasn't sure why. Maybe because some part of me hoped that if I didn't say anything, I could pretend that he hadn't been there at all. That he was no threat if I refused to acknowledge his presence. I was only lying to myself, though. Of course he was a threat, and every instinct in me was trying to decide if Ando was about to walk me into a trap.

"Look at me," I commanded him, my voice sharper than I intended.

He obeyed, his gaze locking with mine, steady and unflinching. I searched his eyes, willing myself to see past whatever mask he might be wearing. But I saw nothing, and in the end I broke eye contact and shook my head. If Lore meant me harm, he could probably have done it already.

"All right. I'll come."

I glanced over at Arella.

"You'll be fine here?"

"Of course," she said. "What Lady's Companion wouldn't be happy to wile away an hour or so in the company of some very handsome stable hands?"

I snorted, turning back to Ando.

"You'll glamor me?"

It was a risk, especially with Order guards posted around the palace, but it was the only way to easily get me out of the palace in the middle of the afternoon. Ando nodded quickly.

"They'll only see what I want them to see. No one will know you. Put your hood up, and follow me out."

So, I put my life in his hands and did just that, walking side by side with him through the gardens and down about fifty treacherously slippery stone steps to the lower level. Twice I almost lost my footing, cursing under my breath as I regained my balance, and I held my breath as we neared the gatehouse, waiting to see if I was recognized. The guards might not know my face as Austell's fiancé, but the fine clothing I wore would probably give them cause for closer inspection. But when I glanced at Ando I was surprised to find a complete stranger next to me, and I assumed that whatever he was doing to his own appearance he was also doing to mine since we passed through the gatehouse with no trouble at all.

Out of the palace, we slipped down into the side streets, walking for a few minutes until we came to a small bakery on a busy corner. Ando pushed open a side door, glancing back to make sure I was still following. Inside, the place smelled of warm bread and sweet cakes, but I wasn't fooled. I squeezed the handle of my knife beneath my coat sleeve. Scents could lie as easily as people, and just because it smelled safe and welcoming, it didn't mean danger wasn't waiting for me.

The room Ando took me to was bigger than expected. It was decorated simply with nothing more than a few chairs and a desk by the window where Lore was currently sitting writing a letter. A petite girl of about nineteen stood next to him picking idly at her nails. It was the girl who had reported to us back at the camp about the Seer in the dungeons, the one who had become part of Damen's harem. I'd forgotten her name. At the sound of our footsteps, Lore looked up and smiled, putting down his quill.

"Efa Rescorla. The Smuggler Queen," he said, his eyes dancing as he stood up. "You've been causing a fair bit of trouble recently."

I watched him closely, searching for any hint of threat, but I found nothing.

"Would you expect anything less?"

His smile grew, and as he took a step toward me I felt myself tense. Then Lore pulled me into an unexpected embrace. I stiffened, suspicion still clawing at my chest, before a smile broke through and a small laugh escaped my lips. Before I could stop myself, I was hugging him back, warmed by our easy familiarity. Trusting the spymaster might cost me my life, but somehow I didn't think it would. It felt good to be around him, almost like home, but when I lifted my eyes over his shoulder to the girl, I found her eyeing me with a look I couldn't read. As Lore let me go and stepped back he gestured to her.

"You remember Roda?"

Roda. Yes, that was her name. I swept my eyes over her, smiling insincerely. Unease stirred within me. There was something in the girl's eyes—a guarded, calculating sharpness that made her seemed closed off. It wasn't outright hostility, but whatever it was it was enough to make me dislike her.

"Ah yes. One of Damen's whores, right?" I said.

She bristled at the insult and I heard a small noise behind me that might have been Ando stifling a laugh. Lore gave me a pointed but slightly amused look. It was a cheap shot, but I couldn't help myself.

"I'm a spy in his harem, if that's what you mean," she snapped.

I'd definitely hit a nerve. I nodded slowly, unbothered

by her attitude, and walked over to the window to look out, checking to see if we'd been followed and half expecting to see Finn lurking out on the street.

"Why am I here, Lore?" I asked. "You've presumably heard that I've left the Nevedeno, despite what Finn may think. You've probably also heard that Theo is dead."

He leaned casually against the wall and crossed his arms.

"I have. But then I've also heard that you accompanied Lord Mirle into the palace this morning as his future wife. An interesting turn of events."

I said nothing, only turned my head from the window to watch him. The amusement left his face and he took a deep breath.

"I didn't know about the arrangement with the Nothori, Efa. Nor did I know about Cai's experiments with Faelock. If I had, I would have spoken against it. We have *never* smuggled people, and I certainly don't condone creating a lethal version of a drug that works against my people. *Our* people, Efa. It puts us all at risk."

"Finn told you then?"

He frowned, bobbing his head.

"He's here in the city, you know."

"I know. I saw him earlier."

"I left him very little choice but to tell me everything, though he didn't want to. The girls…" he sighed. "I don't like that, although Theo's death has put a stop to it for now, thankfully. But the new Faelock… well, that's something altogether much more dangerous. What do you know about it?"

"Only that it almost killed me a few weeks ago. Theo coated his knife in it."

Lore let out a low whistle.

"Then he deserved to die. I'm surprised you're still

standing, to be honest. Faelock is bad enough, as you know, but the new variety is so much stronger. It can knock out abilities for *days*, not just hours, and depending on the way it's made it's a lethal poison once in your bloodstream, as you almost found out. It attacks the essence in your blood. It's what the Order has been using on Valtanans. Somehow they've figured out how to use it to take our abilities and kill us in the process."

None of this surprised me particularly. I had suspected as much. If Bran, an immensely powerful Fae male, had struggled to heal the wound Theo had inflicted on me, then it had to be bad. And deep down I had known that it had to be linked to what the Order was doing. I thought back to the High Priestess's final words. Blood magic. It had to be. Blood magic, Faelock, and the Amberstone. They were all connected. I knew it in my bones. I dug my nail into the pad of my thumb as I bit the inside of my lip and turned to face him.

"You didn't answer my question, Lore. Why did you ask me here?"

"Because I no longer recognize Finn as the head of the Nevedeno, Efa."

I raised my eyebrows, frowning. I hadn't been expecting that.

"Finn doesn't know that, of course. He believes he has my full support because that's what I told him this morning. But when I learned that you were to become Lady Mirle, just weeks after you were seen in the company of a certain Fae prince… well, I started to wonder if you might be up to something."

I said nothing, and he pushed away from the wall and came to stand next to me by the window.

"What I'm saying, Efa, is that *I* no longer recognize Finn Yadari, nor do the rest of the Nevedeno. Most of us have been unhappy with him for some time, especially the Valtanans amongst us. And *if* you are planning, and I very much hope that you are, to take him out along with Damen, then we're all behind you."

I flicked my eyes up at Roda. She stared sullenly back at me and I jerked my chin in her direction.

"She doesn't look like she's behind me. In fact, I don't trust her not to sell me out to Finn or Damen the first chance she gets."

"Roda reports to me. She knows her role, and how perilous her position is." He gave her a sideways look. "And she knows what will happen to her should anyone find out that she's a Nevedeno spy."

I stared at her coldly until she dropped her gaze. She'd be dead by my own hand if I thought that she was at risk of betraying me, but I decided to keep that thought to myself.

"It's complicated," I said, in response to his earlier comment. "The oath line makes things difficult. And Finn seems to have acquired himself a new Gift…"

"Yeah," he said, nodding thoughtfully. "I'd heard about that, too. It's why we haven't just killed him in his sleep. We need to know who he's in bed with first. Well, anything you need to help you, just get word to Roda or Ando."

I glanced at Ando who was nodding emphatically. I knew I could count on him. But Roda… we'd have to see. I took a breath and turned to face Lore again, my heart suddenly feeling heavy.

"Noa is missing," I said quietly. "Have you heard anything?"

Lore frowned, shaking his head.

"No. We assumed he was with you. Finn was complaining about the shit that went down with the Elraith and that neither of you were there to sort it. He seems unusually irritated about our Silvermist supplies being compromised."

"Was it an act, or do you think he really didn't know where Noa was?"

"I don't know, Efa. He was pissed off. He seemed pretty genuine to me."

I sighed heavily.

"Well, I guess that's a good thing if it's not Finn behind his disappearance."

"Let me see what we can find out. We'll ask around, and I'll try and make contact with Owen, since those two are usually tight. You'll hear from us within the next few days."

I nodded slowly, embracing him again and following Ando as he led me from the house and back towards the palace. Only one thought consumed my mind and we crossed back through the gate and back up the steps. Where the fuck was Noa?

CHAPTER 32
EFA

I was silent as Ando and I went through the gatehouse and retraced our steps back to the stables, finding Arella in deep conversation with a stable hand. One look at my face and she immediately stopped talking, coming to join me as Ando slipped away surreptitiously.

"What's the news?" she asked when we were half way across the deserted courtyard.

"The Nevedeno are turning on Finn. They're looking for a new leader."

"And Noa?"

"Still missing," I said darkly. "Lore didn't think it had anything to do with Finn, though."

Arella pulled a face and gave an exasperated sigh. Up ahead, there was a flash of cobalt as an Order priest patrolled the side of the palace, and I forced my face into an easy smile as Arella did the same. To anyone watching, we were simply out for an afternoon stroll, our conversation light and easy.

"Fuck," she whispered. "So, where is he?"

"I don't know. Lore said he'd look into it and see what

he can find out. I figure if anyone can find him, it's probably him. He's got eyes everywhere."

I bit my lip, feeling my shadows simmering under the surface. They were just as anxious as I was. I lifted my chin, taking a deep breath, and noticing a man standing on one of the balconies like a figure carved from the very stone of the palace. He was tall and lean, his posture rigid and commanding. The heavy fur coat draped over his shoulders gave him the look of a predator at rest, one that did not need to move to assert dominance. He dark hair was neatly shorn, his expression impassive yet edged with disdain, as though the world below existed merely for his scrutiny. And his cold eyes followed our every move.

"Who is that?" I asked, the hairs on my arms standing on end.

"General Brayson," she said quietly.

The name alone was enough to chill the air around us. General Brayson, the head of Melrith's armies. A man whose reputation for violence was spoken of in whispers.

"According to the rumors, we don't want to draw his attention."

"I think it's too late for that," I said dryly.

I could feel his eyes on us as we walked through the gardens. We kept our eyes down, walking casually, as if we couldn't feel the weight of his gaze upon us. But as I reached the palace, I remembered my father's words, the ones I had repeated to Nev on the journey here about not being afraid to meet my enemy's eye. Raising my head, I met his cold, arrogant gaze and smiled politely, inclining my head in greeting. He made no acknowledgement, but turned abruptly and left the balcony.

Nev and Austell hadn't been in our rooms when we returned but a note had been left to say that they had gone down to the palace barracks to train. When they arrived back sometime later, Nev looked like he had gone to battle, but Austell had his usual composed serenity, the only sign that he had exerted himself a slight flush to his cheeks. The four of us sat in the sitting room and I updated them quietly, unsure whether Damen's spies knew about the secret passageways and whether there might be eyes and ears on us, and advising them to be careful with what they said just in case. I pushed my hair back from my face and got up to pour myself a brandy. Usually I hated the stuff, but I was restless and fidgety.

"Any news from you both?" Arella asked.

"Nothing much. Denfor was arriving just as we were coming back upstairs, so that's everyone here. Tomorrow we'll sit down with Damen for the usual reports. For about three days we'll all meet in his council room to go through our regional updates. It's never usually particularly interesting but I'm expecting some additional tension this time round."

"Exciting," she said sarcastically. "What should we expect from tonight?"

"Oh, something gaudy and loud, I expect. Damen likes to make a bit of a statement. His whole court will be there, every one of them no doubt doing their best to improve their own situation and gain his favour. He'll want to be meet you, too, but I doubt it'll be anything particularly formal."

"Looking forward to it," I said.

I twisted a piece of hair and chewed on my lip.

"What if he recognizes me?"

"Is that likely?" Arella asked. "It's not like you really look much like either of your parents, and you've never been recognized before. The only people who have were Seers who'd seen you in visions, and Austell."

"And Austell never forgets a face," Nev said, as if to reassure me.

"It's true. Don't overthink it, Efa," Austell said. "It's been years since Damen last saw you, and you look a lot different."

I sighed. It was too late now anyway. We'd find out if he recognized me soon enough and deal with the consequences then. I stood up abruptly, excusing myself to go and take a long, hot bath since I was desperate to take some time to myself. Afterwards, I stood at the window looking out at the sea, my wet hair slowly soaking the back of the silk gown I was wearing and making me cold. Arella came in a few moments later, pausing to build the fire up in the hearth and then coming to stand next to me.

"Where is the *Panacea* going?" I murmured, nodding my head in the direction of the ship currently leaving the harbor. It seemed to be heading north. "I thought Torr was staying here."

"He'll be back. I expect that he wants to see the Nothori ships for himself."

I nodded absentmindedly, twisting Austell's engagement ring on my finger. Arella walked over to the wardrobe, opening it and surveying the clothing hanging inside. She took out the gray dress she had hung up earlier in the day, running her hands across the fabric and then turned to look at me, her face serious.

"Time to join the vipers in their nest, Efa. I hope you're ready."

I stared out over the ocean, watching the ship battle the waves.

"So do I."

CHAPTER 33
EFA

The sound of music and laughter echoed along the hallway as we walked toward the ballroom, my hand firmly in Austell's. As the doors opened on the evening's extravagant display, I checked and rechecked the shield around my mind and stood up tall, taking a deep breath as Austell squeezed my hand. I glanced up at him, seeing the tightness in his jaw and the frown between his eyebrows, but he gave me a small, reassuring smile.

The room was exactly how I remembered it, soaring high ceilings and beautifully carved beams that gleamed in the lamplight. On one side, tall glass doors stood open to the night, letting in a cool breath of air from the wide terrace beyond. From there, the cliff gave way sharply, plunging into a sudden drop that tumbled down to the rugged black waters below. The sea was beautiful in its violence, restless waves flashing silver beneath the moon, their roar faint but unyielding.

Inside, music and laughter spilled against the polished stone, mingling with the scents of beeswax, rich perfume, and the faint tang of sea salt carried in on the breeze. For a heartbeat I was transported back to my father's reign, remembering how I used to steal down to watch the glittering balls that I was too young to join. The only difference now was the sea of colours that dressed the hall—not the maroon and white of House Penrose, but the deep sapphire blue and gilded gold of House Treforno, glinting in banners, gowns, and jewels, as though the whole chamber had been dipped in twilight.

The first person I saw was Caja, dressed in a stunning cornflower blue gown and a glittering diamond choker. Stood between Canver and Tanrith, the petite girl looked even smaller than usual. She held a glass of wine that was almost empty and I watched as Tanrith clicked his fingers and beckoned a servant over to refill it for her. He was standing closer to her than was really proper, rubbing himself against the bare skin of her arm, and my fingers twitched as I watched him darkly, fantasising about all of the things I could do to him with my knife.

"That's Kitto and Kenwyn over there," Austell murmured, nodding at the two men that stood with them.

I dragged my eyes away from Tanrith to look at them, finding that the two men really did look very much alike. As we approached, the older of the two stepped forward quickly to shake Austell's hand and grasped him enthusiastically by the shoulder. He smiled broadly, and I felt a glimmer of recognition.

"Austell! It's been an age," Montavis said. "I've been most looking forward to seeing you again."

Kitto Montavis was well into his seventies, yet he carried himself with the easy energy of a man twenty years younger. His gray hair and beard were thick and unruly, and though his clothes were of a fine quality, they were far more informal than most in the hall—comfortable and lived-in, as though pomp had never interested him. There was a lilt to his movements, a lightness that made you forget his age, and an openness in his fine, friendly face that drew you in at once. When he turned to me, his eyes crinkling with warmth, I understood why my father had liked him so instinctively. Kitto had a way of putting you at ease, as though you had known him all your life. He took my hand firmly, moustache brushing the back of my fingers as he raised it to his lips with old-fashioned gallantry.

"And this must be Efa," he said as he beamed at me. "It is a pleasure to meet you. Please… please, you must meet my wife, Kerensa…"

He half turned to the woman standing next to him, an attractive woman with silvery blonde hair and pale blue eyes. She looked considerably younger than him, closer in age to Kenwyn, and as she took a step towards me she clasped both of my hands in hers.

"It's wonderful to meet you," she said kindly, her voice soft and melodic. "I am dying to hear more about the young woman who has finally stolen Austell's heart. You make a beautiful pair."

I laughed, glancing at Austell to find him looking at me in a way that made me blush.

"It's so lovely to meet you, Lady Rael."

"Oh, none of that here. Call me Kerensa."

Montavis gestured to the other couple standing beside him.

"I'm sure you've noticed my similarity with this fine young man here. This is Kenwyn, my cousin on my father's side, and his wife, Elestren."

Up close, the resemblance between the two men was uncanny, stronger even than I'd first noticed. Hollis was at least fifteen years younger, his hair longer and less gray, and his frame carried the extra weight of someone who clearly enjoyed his food and drink. Yet the similarities were undeniable. They shared the same easy smile, the same openness in their faces, and the same roguish glimmer in their eyes. And where Montavis's charm came tempered with age and grandfatherly warmth, Hollis's was sharper and livelier, the kind of mischief that belonged to a man still hungry for life.

The younger man's arm was casually slung around the waist of the woman standing next to him. Elestren had the tanned, golden skin of The Azuls and deep brown eyes. Her long, black hair hung in loose waves, and her green dress hugged a full, voluptuous figure. She inclined her head at me as Montavis introduced her but otherwise said nothing. Austell had told me that she was a shy, quiet woman but that he had always enjoyed her company, finding her to have a quick wit and a sharp mind. A servant walked past with a tray of drinks and Austell took two glasses of wine, handing one of them to me.

"We were just talking about the rather stirring message left on the walls in the early hours of this morning," Tanrith drawled, waggling his eyebrows dramatically. "It certainly makes for interesting reading."

"Indeed," Austell said lightly. "I heard that it was written in blood, too. Quite gruesome."

"Yes… two Order priests were found slumped against the wall. Their bodies had been drained."

"Zennor, please," Hollis implored, his voice much deeper than I had expected. "There are ladies present."

Tanrith held his hands up in apology, his eyes dancing with amusement. I lifted my glass to my lips and took a sip.

"Do you know what I can't understand?" Canver said. "How there are so few of them and yet somehow they are able to defeat ten or fifteen Nothori so easily."

"I think that says more about the Nothori than it does the Loyalists," a new voice said from behind me. The hairs on the back of my neck rose.

The first thing I noticed was how slight Lord Polruen was; yet he carried himself as though he were a much larger man. Perran Denfor stood of average height, his thin, angular frame drawn tight beneath the silvery jacket he wore, as though the fabric itself strained against the sharpness of his bones. His face was all edges and shadows, with prominent cheekbones and a pale, bloodless complexion that spoke of a man who avoided the sun. Permanent frown lines cut deep into his forehead, dragged down by the stern set of his brows. His eyes were the color of steel, and when they glanced to me it was as if they were already calculating, already measuring what I was worth. There was no softness in him, no humanity. He smiled, but it was the sort of smile that made you colder for having seen it.

His wife, Anneth, stood very close by, her presence as forbidding as his. She had dark features that might once have been considered beautiful, with arched brows, sculpted cheekbones, and eyes like shards of obsidian. But any warmth had long since bled out of them. Her hair, once black, was streaked heavily with gray, and was tied back in a severe knot that showed no softness or indulgence. One look at her and I knew Austell had been right that she was just as cunning as her husband. Born and raised in Tithra, she had come from a highly influential family linked to one of the Emirs. Their marriage had been a business arrangement rather than any sort of love match, their relationship one of ambition rather than romance.

"This must be our Lady-Designate Esari," Denfor said. It was the interim title to be used until I was married.

A less confident woman might have been thrown off by

the disdainful tone in which he spoke about me. But I was used to men trying to belittle and undermine me, and I was used to showing them what happened when they did, so I simply watched him indifferently. Next to me Austell smiled, clearly also used to the personalities in the room and choosing to find Denfor's aloof and superior attitude amusing.

"It is, Perran," was all he said.

"Tell me, Efa. What do *you* make of these Loyalists?"

I brought my glass to my lips and savoured the amber wine. It had a sweet, honeyed taste not unlike the wine Arella had introduced me to back in Serenfell. I took my time answering. I licked my lips before I spoke, aware of Tanrith's eye on my mouth.

"Oh, I don't know." I smiled coyly, looking at him from under my lashes. "I find that a little rebelliousness every now and then keeps things rather interesting, don't you think?"

Hollis chuckled, and Tanrith smiled deviously, but Denfor's expression didn't change. I winked at him, catching a dark look from his wife out of the corner of my eye. Laughing softly, I shook my head.

"Forgive me, Lord Denfor, I am teasing you. If you want to know what I really think… well, I believe them to be a reckless bunch of fools who have simply been very lucky so far. No doubt there is a handsome and equally foolish man coordinating things somewhere with fantasies of becoming the next Three Fingered Pell or Noa the Phantom."

Out of the corner of my eye I saw a smirk cross Austell's lips that he quickly hid with his wine glass.

"Their resistance is futile. It will be crushed soon enough. I'm sure of it."

"And what of the heir?" Tanrith asked. "What of Aeva Penrose? She is supposedly a rather dangerous threat."

"Oh, my Lord, how much damage can one woman really cause?"

Tanrith's teeth flashed as he laughed, and Denfor seemed to watch me with a newfound interest. He wife stared at me with open hostility.

"Austell, she certainly is a handful, this one," Tanrith said admiringly.

Austell lifted my hand to his mouth and kissed it slowly, his eyes roaming my face lustfully.

"Indeed, she is," his gaze heating as he smiled at me. "Luckily I have two hands."

"Oh ho!" Hollis laughed loudly. "Do you remember young love, Kitto?"

Suddenly, a hush fell over the room, and I turned my head, noticing Caja sway slightly on her feet, Tanrith steadying her with a hand on the small of her back. Behind us, the great doors of the ballroom swung open with a heavy groan, the sound echoing through the room like the forewarning of a storm, and there he was. The man I had thought about killing every day for the past two decades.

Damen strode in, the light from the chandeliers catching in his graying hair and glinting off the streaks of silver. My shadows pulsed violently as my breathing became quick and shallow, my hand trembling slightly in Austell's. The room had been filled with quiet murmurs and laughter, but now a silence had fallen, following him like a shadow. I wondered if everyone was thinking what I was thinking. About what he had done to sit upon his stolen throne. His eyes swept the room, dark and unreadable, weighing each face as though he were a predator searching for the weakest in the herd. A smirk, barely there, flickered at the corner of his mouth; just enough to remind everyone there that he did not need to command silence. It was given freely, out of fear and the unspoken knowledge that this man did not take defiance well.

His boots struck the floor with a steady, unhurried rhythm as he approached the dais. The golden glow of candlelight caught the fine embroidery on his sleeves—the black snake of House Treforno. When he stopped, he exhaled slowly, his gaze settling on those who dared to meet it. I released my own shuddering breath, staring at him from across the room. He looked exactly the same as the last time I had seen him. He had never been the kind of man that I would have described as handsome, but there had always been a charismatic and wicked charm about him, and according to the stories I had heard over the years he had been brave and daring, a fearless soldier. His beard was thick and dark with silver threading through it, framing a strong jaw, and his dark eyes had the steady, arrogant look of a man who had never questioned his own right to rule.

The sword at his hip swung as he climbed the dais and took a seat on the throne, no doubt the same one he had used at Nissae all those years ago, its hilt worn from years of use. The crown upon his head had been my father's, a sick feeling spreading through my stomach as I recognized it, and for the briefest of moments, as his eyes settled upon me in the crowd, I felt like a child again. He had always made me nervous, and I had endeavored to avoid being in the same room as him whenever I could help it. The same instinct was telling me to run now, to get far, far away from this place, but my feet were frozen in place, my fingers almost crushing Austell's where they held his hand so tightly.

For years I had learned to watch people from afar, learning as much about them as I could through their mannerisms and behavior, from the way they spoke to their friends or children, or more tellingly the people they thought to be beneath them. There was no denying that Damen had a certain energy about him. Much like Torr, he was the sort of man that you couldn't miss in a room full of people. But Damen was nothing like the sea captain, nothing genuine or unpretentious.

I saw the charming smiles he rewarded his courtiers with as they simpered and flattered, his jaw ticking when one took just a moment too long to bow. I noticed the way he ignored the servants completely, as though they weren't even there. Nothing had changed about Damen Treforno, my father's most illustrious General. He was as conceited and self-absorbed as ever, and no doubt blinded by his own sense of self-importance. But that might just be what would get me through the whole charade. It wouldn't even cross his mind that Aeva Penrose would have the audacity to enter his palace in plain sight.

My eyes moved to the woman who had entered the ballroom behind the king, walking with the confidence of someone who believed beyond a shadow of a doubt that she belonged there. The rich fabric of her gown clung to every curve with deliberate intent. The shimmering gold dress plunged at the neckline and was slit high at the thigh, leaving little to the imagination. Much like Elestren, Damen's mistress, Aleta, had the lustrous dark skin and feline eyes that suggested she had Azulian ancestry. But there was something else about her that I couldn't put my finger on. Something oddly familiar.

As she joined Damen on the dais, I dropped into a curtsey with those around me, lifting my eyes again in time to see him waft his hand around, letting his subjects know that we were free to stand at ease again just as another man took his place behind the thrones. General

Brayson stood tall, one hand on his sword as he searched the room for threats.

Damen sat lazily in his throne for the next forty minutes or so, and I continued to watch him discreetly from where I stood, hardly daring to breathe. He lifted his hand now and then in casual gestures, letting his courtiers simper and bow. Light conversation rippled around me—laughs, murmurs, and courtly exchanges that I barely followed, every word washing over me like meaningless noise while I kept my eyes fixed on him.

A huge buffet had been laid out for the court to enjoy, and there was plenty of ale and wine flowing, everything tasting like ash on my tongue. Eventually, Damen rose and offered his arm to Aleta, and they descended down the steps. The pair strolled around the room, greeting everyone and bowing their heads in mock humility, and smirking at the bows and curtseys they received in return. When he finally reached us, he smiled widely, silently waiting for us to bow and curtsey.

My pulse was a steady drumbeat in my ears as Damen stood in front of me, shadows straining to be released. I had thought about this moment over and over again, of what I would do to the man who took everything from me when I finally had the chance. But standing there, inches away from him, I felt something colder than rage. Instead, I felt only steady patience, sharp and tempered like a blade. His end would come soon enough.

"My Lords and Ladies. It's wonderful to see you all again and good of you to join me. I appreciate that it's quite the journey for some of you."

He nodded his head at Austell and Montavis and they smiled affably, as if it were no trouble at all. As if everyone here had a choice in attending. Well, I did, but that was by-the-by. A servant appeared and refilled our empty glasses, and I held my own out, drawing Damen's attention. His smile, more of a sneer than anything, fell on Austell.

"Ah, Austell the Gardener. Good of you to leave your rose garden to join us."

Austell chuckled and bowed his head good-naturedly, but I could tell that the nickname grated on him on this occasion. He'd once said to me that he prided himself on being a horticulturist, and that the nickname was a sign of friendship among those he respected and knew well. But the way that Damen said it, and the way I'd heard Tanrith use it on occasion, held a different undertone. It was patronising and disparaging.

"May I introduce you to my fiancée, Efa?" Austell said, taking my hand as I stepped forward a little.

Damen's eyes wandered over my face, and he licked his lips, looking me up and down. There was something unreadable and searching in his expression. I held my breath, waiting to be discovered, for the moment he saw my mother in the curve of my mouth, or my father in the shape of my eyes. But there was no spark of familiarity. To him I was just another woman to be admired. To be ignored.

"What a beautiful rose you have plucked yourself, Austell."

I smiled demurely at Damen's compliment, choosing to say nothing as my skin crawled.

"Thank you, Your Highness," Austell said, but Damen had already moved on.

"Caja," he purred. "Such a delight to see you again."

He drank her in hungrily, and she physically retreated into herself, the color draining from her face as the hand that held her glass trembled violently. I looked at Aleta just in time to see a dark look pass across her face. I'd seen that expression a hundred times on different faces and I knew exactly what it meant. Aleta was a jealous mistress.

Once the initial pleasantries were over, the conversation inevitably returned to the Loyalist's message on the wall, with Hollis remarking on the boldness of their actions.

"Oh, I admire their nerve," Damen said, grinning as he held his glass out to be refilled again. "But it was unwise. We have apprehended the three responsible for it already. They will, of course, face charges of treason."

I tucked my hair behind my ear and tried to look uninterested, but my stomach had roiled at his words. They had been caught? Already? I took another sip of my drink, barely tasting the wine. Montavis cleared his throat.

"Your Highness, I must ask... the Loyalist attacks grow more frequent, there is considerable unrest across Melrith, and there are reports of a large fleet of Nothori warships off the coast. Should we be concerned?"

Damen screwed up his face and waved his hand dismissively. He seemed irritated by the question.

"Let's not talk of unrest and rebellions tonight. All of this can wait until tomorrow. For now let's simply eat, drink and enjoy each other's company."

Montavis smiled awkwardly, clearly more perturbed than ever.

"Austell, your letter announcing your engagement certainly came as a surprise," Damen continued. "I must say, I hadn't thought that you intended to marry at all these days. Not since all of that business with Trystan and that *lovely* young country girl of yours."

My breath caught at the mention of his name, my heart leaping before I could stop it. For an instant, my shadows stirred, reaching instinctively for him before I dragged them back under control. I fought to steady myself, forcing a bland, practiced smile onto my lips and praying that no one had noticed my reaction. As it happened, they were all too focused on Austell. Sniggers ran around the group, predominantly from Tanrith and Canver, and though Austell smiled at the comment, a muscle in his jaw twitched.

"I confess I had thought that, too. Until fate brought me to Efa."

Damen stared at us for a moment, an odd smile on his face as he stroked his beard. Austell's hand tightened around mine slightly, but I didn't look away. Instead I daringly reached out for Damen's mind, testing to see what would happen. A cold, solid wall met me. I'd experienced the same with Morai in the forest. What the fuck was that? Was that what the mental shield Negan had taught me to create felt like? Was that what it was? Disappointment and frustration flooded through me when I realized I couldn't just shatter his mind. There was every chance that my shadows would have no impact on him at all, and that killing him might be more complicated than I'd thought.

"A beautiful love story, it seems," Aleta said.

It was the first time she had spoken, her sultry voice carrying the melodic undertone of the islands. I didn't think she could have sounded less sincere if she tried, and her voice tugged at a memory somewhere in the back of my mind, just out of reach. There was something familiar about her, something spiteful and devious in the way she looked at me.

"Indeed," Damen said musingly. "Well, you are most welcome at my court, Efa. I hope you shall enjoy your time with us. Perhaps one evening you might even honour me with a dance."

Austell's hand tightened even further around mine.

"Of course, if my fiancé permits it."

I had said it playfully, but Damen's face darkened. The atmosphere immediately changed and I knew that I had insulted him by suggesting he didn't have complete control over everything that happened in the palace. My shadows hummed in amusement and I fought the smile that threatened to pull at my lips. Damen stroked his beard and my eyes caught on something that twinkled in the light. The bastard even wore my father's ring.

"It is not for Austell to deny me anything," he said. "Nor you, for that matter. That is the first lesson you must learn in my court, Efa, and you would do well to remember it."

I met his eye for a moment and then dropped my chin, bowing my head deferentially. I kept my eyes cast down until he had walked away and moved on to speak to other people, but when I looked up a few moments later, I found the king still watching me intently from across the room.

~

The drafty halls had me shivering in my thin, chiffon dress as we walked back to our rooms. Tiredness pulled at my eyes and I had a slight headache, but my shadows buzzed restlessly, desperate for their freedom. After embracing my gift so freely down in Esari, containing it since we'd Baern had been a whole different kind of challenge, but they would have to wait until I was safely in bed and could let them loose into the darkness.

"How are you?" Austell asked.

"Fine," I replied, staring straight ahead.

What else was there to say? I couldn't even begin to put into words right then how I was feeling. Seeing Damen had sent me into a spiral as I tried to temper my anger and manage my own feelings of inadequacy at the same time as I berated myself for even embarking on this ridiculous, suicidal mission. There had been times that I had felt calm and composed, and then suddenly desperately worried and impatient to find Noa, wherever he was. Sometimes I trusted the instinct that had told me back in Cryf's Gap to follow Emrys to Esari, but I also regretted it enormously, thinking that if I hadn't left with him, Noa would be safe and sound with me and none of this would have even happened. In turn, that only made me chide myself again for being weak minded and cowardly.

My emotions were all over the place, to the point that I felt slightly delirious and detached from reality, as though I was watching the events of the night happen to someone else and not me. I was fully aware that I was prickly and easily irritated all of the time, giving short, snappy answers to the most well intentioned of questions. I craved company, but I also desperately wanted to be alone so that I could be with my own thoughts. I had been like this for days.

I gaze Austell a quick glance, conflicted there, too. His touch made my pulse race and sent a thrill through me, but something always held me back, always pulling me in a different direction.

"Are we worried about the three captured Loyalists?" I asked.

We were walking quickly, the hallways empty, but we still spoke softly just in case. He shrugged, but he looked troubled.

"No more than usual. Very few know that it's actually me that oversees and finances the resistance, and it's with my own money, not what Rostorrmel sends to the region. Nev only meets with a very small group of reliable men, like Jory, and we have to trust that they won't be broken should they be tortured. It's all we can do. Still, I won't sleep easily tonight."

We walked in silence for a few moments, and I thought about just how much of a risk we were taking by being here.

"How do you know about the passageways in the palace?" Austell asked, pulling me out of my thoughts.

"Because a long time ago I used to be the one listening. There are passages all over the palace."

"Where do they go?"

"The better question is where *don't* they go? Arella, Noa and I spent hours and hours in them as children, and I still don't think we explored them all."

"And of course, you being you, I imagine you'll be back in there tonight?"

I glanced at him mischievously.

"What if you meet someone unexpectedly in there?"

"Then whoever we meet will come to an abrupt end."

"So violent..." he said softly, his mouth curving into a smile. "You know you looked so beautiful tonight, Efa."

I laughed shyly, blushing as usual.

"You looked very handsome yourself."

"Ah yes, handsome and foolish... isn't that what you said?"

"I seem to remember that Three Fingered Pell was supposed to be *terribly* handsome," I laughed.

He held my gaze, eyes dancing, and like so many other times over the past few weeks, things suddenly became heated as his eyes dropped to my mouth. Our steps slowed and we came to a halt in the middle of the corridor, turning to face each other. He pulled me closer, his free hand coming up to stroke my cheek.

"You know that I would give you the stars and lasso the moon for you," he breathed.

I smiled and licked my lips, looking away nervously as I tried to ignore my shadows' remonstrations. He bent his head and I lifted my face to his. His eyes were a deep, mesmerizing blue in the soft, evening light, the color reminding me of the water out in Mira Bay. The sound of footsteps began to echo through the corridor and my head snapped round to see General Brayson appear from around a corner. His eyes were blazing and there was a sneer on his face as he stalked towards us. Austell inclined his head in greeting, but the General ignored us completely. Bemused, I watched him storm down the hallway, then looked back at Austell and shook my head with a smile.

"That guy," I muttered. "Where did Damen find him?"

Austell grinned, running a hand through his hair. The moment between us had been broken by the intrusion, and I had to admit that I felt a little relieved. Austell reached out for my hand.

"Come on," he said softly, pulling me in the direction of our rooms. "I've had enough of this place for one night."

CHAPTER 34

EMRYS

I watched the Order priest ride off, the dust rising into the air behind him as the horse bolted. I'd never seen a man move so fast. Once again, they had chosen the youngest of the Order priests to leave alive; a wise decision that I'd employed on a number of occasions. They often scared more easily, and there was nothing more infuriating to a commander than having a frightened, whimpering idiot sent back to you by your enemy. It made you appear weak and incompetent, and your men cowardly and spineless.

I had to admit that Merryn's theatrics lent a certain edge to the Loyalist attacks. The black smoke erupting around her hissed and coiled through the air, a poor copy of Efa's shadows, but convincing enough to rattle the Nothori and whip the villagers into a frenzy of whispers. Word of Novos and Aemylia's heir was spreading fast, carried on eager tongues, and for the first time the Loyalists were not dismissed as a hopeless rabble, but spoken of with awe. The townsfolk, never fond of the Nothori, were quick to believe, quick to cheer, and quicker still to side with us. With a shrug, I watched Merryn flick her braid over her shoulder as she wiped her blade clean on her pants.

"I guess she does kind of look like her," Morgan said from behind me.

I turned to look at him sharply, finding a frown on his face as he looked at the Loyalist woman. Dressed in black as she was right now, I supposed that you could be forgiven for thinking it was Efa standing in the middle of the square. If you didn't know any better. Her hair was the same color, and she was about the same age and height, but she had none of the captivating, hypnotizing energy and charisma that Efa seemed to naturally possess. There was no grace or elegance in the way she fought, and she lacked the beautiful, quiet violence that I found so mesmerizing to watch in Efa.

There was no rush of excitement through my body when Merryn smiled at me, no all-consuming urge to follow her wherever she went. My eyes didn't seek her out to know exactly where she was at all times on the killing field, and it wasn't her eyes that I saw in my dreams, full of hurt and anger when they looked at me. I didn't seek out her opinion when I tried to decide what to do next, or feel a sense of overwhelming calm and reassurance just by being near her. And it wasn't her small, delicate hand that I imagined holding in mine when I lay down to sleep at night, wishing she would be the first thing I saw when I opened my eyes.

"She's nothing like her," I snapped irritably.

I could feel Merryn's eyes on me later that night though as they sat round a fire, obscured somewhat from the road by a copse of trees somewhere on the border between Baern and Polruen. I was aware of her interest in me, but I pointedly ignored it. To be honest, I couldn't fathom the interest. I shouted too often, ordered too harshly, and left far too much blood in my wake. I was no charming lord or bright-eyed hero to fawn over. I was a blade, a shadow, good for killing and nothing else. Whatever she thought she saw, it wasn't worth the looking.

I was sat beside Bran, sharpening my blade on a whetstone while he whittled a chunk of wood silently. On my other side, Morgan was animatedly recounting how he had taken on three Nothori at once, his tale becoming increasingly fanciful with every sip of moonshine he took. More than once I caught Bran's eye as Morgan exaggerated the details. No doubt he'd be telling them about how he escaped the *Raeth's* clutches again next.

"There was plenty of talk about Lord Mirle's engagement in the last town," Nessa said, idly poking a stick into the fire. "It all seemed very quick. Do you think it's really love?"

"No, it's just an act, idiot." Merryn nudged the other girl good-naturedly. "It's so she can get into the palace."

"Has anyone told Austell that?" Treave laughed. "From what I've heard, he's completely smitten. Either that or he's a very good actor."

My hand tightened involuntarily around my knife and I clenched my jaw, my jealousy threatening to become violent. Bran shook his head at me, a silent reminder not to rise to it. In truth, I didn't really believe that their engagement was real. Efa was impulsive, but not that impulsive. But I knew Austell would probably give it his best shot with her, and it was that kind of thinking that made me so irrationally angry. The thought of him holding her hand or touching her waist while smugly introducing her as his fiancée was enough to send me into a blinding rage. I shifted on the ground, trying to get the image of the two of them together out of my mind.

"All I know is Damen's days are numbered with her around," Rumo said. "But what I don't understand is why you Fae lot haven't just killed Damen already."

Bran's knife stilled, and I felt him glance my way again as a hush fell over the group. I lifted my eyes from my blade slowly, looking at Rumo over the flickering flames.

"Is that a statement or a question?"

He smiled sheepishly, perhaps regretting his words now that I was paying him attention.

"A question, I suppose."

Jory took the opportunity to jump in, likely sensing that the conversation could go either way given my current mood.

"What I think he's asking is why the Northern Realm still seem to defer so much to Damen. You're here, fighting with us. Fighting against him. Why the pretense of being allies, when you clearly aren't? "

It was a fair question, and it was one that played on my mind all too often. It had completely consumed my thoughts for a time after what happened to Evyn. But of course, no one knew about that. We didn't talk about my younger brother, or the shame that had befallen the Northern Realm. No one knew what had changed for us, or what had been taken from us the night that Nissae fell. Just as no one knew why we continued to play our little game with Damen, pretending to be allies while we tolerantly waited for an opportunity to strike back. I reached out to Morgan and took the moonshine from him, taking a large mouthful of the stuff before going back to sharpening my knife.

"He stole from us," I grunted. "Something important. And he has threatened to destroy it should we move against him. We've thought about it, and discussed it over and over again. Opinions differ, but these are our orders for now. My brother feels that it isn't worth the risk, and we are a patient folk, so until we find it… until what was stolen is back on Fae soil, Damen lives."

My tone allowed no room for further conversation, and not long after I left the fire and tried to get some sleep. For a while I just stared up at the sky through the trees, but eventually I drifted off, waking sometime about an hour before dawn. I felt restless and needed to stretch my legs, so I rose quietly and wandered off towards the edge of the trees. It was a still, clear night, and the stars looked spectacular. I leaned against a tree and gazed up at them. All I could think about was her.

At the sound of leaves crunching behind me, I glanced back to find Cadoc walking towards me. He stood next to me companionably for a time, seeming content to stand in silence and look at the stars with me.

"You're awake early,"I said eventually.

"Ah, I never sleep well, you know that." He leaned against a tree and rested his head back.

"Bran thinks that I'm punishing myself," I said quietly.

Cadoc pushed away from the tree and placed a hand on my shoulder. Somewhere in the distance a fox shrieked.

"Emrys, I'm going to tell you what Morgan once told me in a rare moment of wisdom. Bad things happen no matter how hard we try to prevent them or if we think we're doing the right thing at the time. But to move forward, you have to be kind to yourself and accept that you aren't infallible. It is what you do after the bad thing that matters."

I nodded slowly. His words echoed Bran's, and I wondered if I would ever be able to truly forgive myself for losing my brother, and then losing Efa.

"We've had new orders, by the way."

I breathed out a laugh. Of course we did.

"Is he still angry?"

"I believe so. The messages are short but the uh... *tone* of the Citadel's messages are quite clear, not that I'm surprised. Aubrey has never taken defiance well, particularly yours. He won't be pleased that you have refused to return to the Realm, and that you have chosen to go against him. Again."

I snorted softly.

"What are my brother's new orders then?"

"Damen has requested the Realm's presence in Rostormel for a ball. In fact, he has specifically requested *your* presence."

"Why?"

Cadoc spread his hands wide and shrugged.

"If a reason was given, it was not passed on to me."

"So, Aubrey's orders are for me to go a ball?" I chuckled to myself. "So be it, Cad. We're heading that way anyway. I doubt they'd do something as stupid as keep the Amberstone in the palace, and then invite me in. But who knows, hey?"

I shook my head wearily and pretended to be annoyed at my brother for sending me off yet again to do his bidding. But the truth was the dark night hid the smile growing on my face. Because now I had a reason to see her again.

CHAPTER 35
EFA

The market square thrummed with restless silence. People shifted shoulder to shoulder, the murmur of their voices never rising about a hush. A cough broke out somewhere, and someone cursed under their breath. It was the uneasy stillness of an audience forced to watch what none of them wanted to see. But it was more than that, more than fear. Anger simmered beneath the surface, too frightened to break free.

The Nothori soldiers dragged the prisoners from the wagons, shoving them forwards like beasts to slaughter. Coarse hoods covered their heads, bodies stumbling blindly as boots and fists drove them toward the scaffold at the center of the square. The wood was already stacked high, tar-slick logs black and gleaming, kindling piled thick around the posts.

I crouched above on the sloped tiles of a roof, the chill of the stone seeping through the fabric of my pants as my fingers flexed nervously around the hilt of my knife. Across the square, I saw Jory, stood half-hidden behind a cart. His eyes found mine and I held his gaze, feeling his tension like a wire pulled tight. The soldiers bound the prisoners to the posts, jerking the knots until the ropes bit into bruised flesh, and the crowd rippled again, shifting like a restless tide. Then, one of the Order priests stepped forward, a torch blazing in his hand. The fire spat and crackled as he raised it for all to see. *Not yet,* I told myself, even as my body leaned forward. *Not yet*.

The priest lowered his torch slightly and gestured, and one of the Nothori yanked the hood from the first prisoner —a woman. Her hair fell tangled around her face, her lip split, both eyes swollen near shut. Her chest was heaving as she tried to draw breath past the ropes cutting into her ribs, and the crowd stirred again. Someone called out her name, quickly muffled by the hand of another. Anger rippled in the faces nearest the scaffold, but no one stepped forward.

The second hood was torn away. A man this time, his temple caked with blood. His face was gray with exhaustion, but his jaw was set, teeth clenched against the pain as his eyes blinked furiously against the light. My heart hammered in my chest as I glanced at Jory again. And then the last hood was pulled off.

My heart stopped.

Noa.

His face was pale beneath the grime and blood, his nose crooked and broken, but it was him. For a heartbeat I couldn't breathe. Panic threatened to overwhelm me, clawing up my throat as a raw, animal instinct surged inside me, desperate to break free. Every part of me screamed to move, to tear the Nothori apart and kill anyone who had dared to lay a hand on him. But across the square, Jory caught my eye, steady as stone, and shook his head the smallest fraction. I forced myself still, every muscle trembling with the effort, my nails biting into my palms as I hung on to control by a thread. One wrong move, one second too soon, and Noa would burn before my eyes.

Not yet. Gods, not yet.

The order priest took another step forward, torch lifted high, ready to proclaim the sentence. But before he could speak, a shout cut through he square. My stomach dropped as Damen appeared. He strode forward with effortless authority, the press of soldiers and villagers parting around him. Cloak trailing, and eyes alight with cruel purpose; he mounted the steps of the scaffold without pause. The priest faltered, then bowed low, offering no resistance as Damen extended his hand for the torch. The flames painted his face in shades of gold and shadow, and my panic surged. Against him, my shadows were useless. They wouldn't even touch him. A small, desperate sound left my lips as my eyes darted between Noa and Jory. I tried to calculate the distance, knowing that I was too far away to throw my knife, knowing that the pyre would be lit before I could get there. Even if I moved right then, even if my shadows tore through every Nothori between me and the scaffold, it wouldn't save him.

Suddenly, through the roar of my panic, Jory gave the signal. I didn't think. I reached for my shadows and sprang into action. But nothing came. My breath hitched, my body jerking as if I'd leapt into a void. But where the shadows should have surged, there was only emptiness, cold and bottomless, like reaching for a heartbeat that wasn't there. I stared at my hands in terror, fingers trembling. My mind raced—Faelock. It had to be. I dragged my gaze over my skin, searching frantically for cuts or grazes, any place the poison might have touched me without noticing.

Nothing. Only the hollow, suffocating absence where my gift should have been. My head snapped up, finding

Jory staring up at me with bewilderment as the crowd erupted around him, wondering why I wasn't doing anything. Damen had lowered the torch. The tar-soaked pyres caught with a roar, flames racing up the kindling in a rush of heat and smoke. As my head snapped up, my breath tore from my lungs, and I watched in horror as Noa, bound and helpless, his face lit by the inferno, went up in flames before my eyes.

~

"Efa!"

I jolted awake to the sound of my own scream, drenched in sweat and tangled in the bed sheets. Smoke filled my nose, flames still dancing behind my eyelids. Someone was calling my name through the haze, but all I could see was Noa burning.

"It's just a nightmare," a voice cut through. "It's not real, Efa. It's not real."

I sat upright with a gasp, dragging air into my lungs in great, heaving sobs. My hands clutched my head as I forced myself to breathe until at last my heart slowed and some semblance of control returned. When I opened my eyes, Austell was there beside me on the bed, watching carefully. His presence was solid and grounding.

"It was only a dream," he said quietly, reaching to take my hand.

The warmth of his fingers spread through me and I let myself lean into it for just a moment.

"You're safe, Efa."

I let out a broken laugh and shook my head. Safe? There was nothing safe about this palace, nothing safe about being anywhere while Damen and Finn still lived. Austell reached for my hand and I lifted my eyes to take him in. He was shirtless and golden in the dying firelight, hair mussed from sleep. His touch was warm and steady, but inside my mind, the image of Noa's face still burned.

"I couldn't save him," I whispered. "I couldn't save Noa."

He shifted on the bed and opened his mouth to speak, and for a second I thought he was about to leave. I caught his hand and held it tightly.

"Don't go," I whispered, my voice rough with sleep and something more fragile. "Stay with me."

"I wasn't going anywhere," he said gently.

He stood only to move closer, slipping beneath the covers with me. His weight dipped the mattress and then his arm came around me, pulling me against him until my cheek rested against the solid warmth of his chest. The chill in the room faded beneath his embrace, and he tugged the blankets higher around us. I closed my eyes, a headache pressing at the edges of my skull, and let the rhythm of his breathing calm me.

"Gods," I muttered, a wry, exhausted laugh catching in my throat. "I feel like I haven't slept in days. What time is it?"

"Dawn's not far," he murmured, his chin brushing the top of my head as he spoke. "An hour, maybe two."

I nodded against him. It had been a late night. Arella and I had waited until the palace finally fell silent, the last footsteps fading from the hallways, before slipping from the Esari rooms and into the hush of the corridors. We'd always known there had to be more passages hidden in the walls, but we'd only ever found two doors. One opened through a panel in my father's study—now Damen's—and the other was tucked behind shelves of ancient, dust-laden books no one had touched for years in the ground-floor library.

We had headed to the library, Arella lifting a lamp so that I could scrabble around in the darkness as my fingers searched for the small catch I remembered. After a few tense moments, the hidden doorway gave way with a low groan. The passage within smelled of stone and damp, the air cool against my skin. We closed the false bookshelf behind us, sealing ourselves in, and the silence deepened as the tunnel stretched ahead, part of the familiar maze we had once explored for hours as children. It didn't take long to reach the familiar fork where the passage split, one side leading to the coves, and the other eventually emerging into the Nijem Forest.

"I saw my old bedroom," I said softly to Austell. "Where I had slept as a child. It was completely empty, as if I had never been in there at all."

"That must have been odd," he said. "Did you meet anyone in the passages?"

"Not a soul. In fact, we're almost certain that Damen and his spies don't know about them. There would have been signs everywhere—scuffs in the dust, stubs of candles, old lamps. But there was nothing. The door we entered through clearly hadn't been opened for years, and when we went up to the passage behind my father's study, it was exactly the same. If Damen knew, he'd have used it himself to spy on you all. No, I'd bet my life he doesn't know they exist. "

"Well, that's very reassuring."

He kissed me on the forehead and said nothing more. Eventually, his breathing slowed as he drifted back to sleep, and I turned my head toward the window. I hadn't shut the curtains before climbing into bed, and the moon was bright in the sky, silvering the room. Quietly, I pulled back the covers, slid out of bed and dragged a nearby chair to the window. Wrapping myself up in a blanket, I curled up and gazed out at the night. The moonlight danced across unusually calm seas, and the stars burned sharp and magnificent against the clear skies.

My shadows stirred restlessly in my veins, tugging, always tugging, as if reaching for something far away. *Quiet*, I whispered inwardly, trying to still their ceaseless searching as I stared up at the stars. Yet even in the silence, my thoughts betrayed me. I wondered where he was, if he too was awake beneath the same night sky, looking up at the same constellations. And I wondered if he was thinking of me.

CHAPTER 36
EFA

I stayed by the window until the sun began to rise, lost in my own thoughts as Austell slept peacefully. I envied him. Like me, he was apprehensive, aware of the risks we took, but he carried it differently. He chose only to worry about what he could immediately control, and let the rest slip away. I wished I could do the same.

Dressing quietly so as not to wake him, I slipped from the room and went to knock on Nev's door. It took him a moment to answer, and when he finally opened it he looked disheveled, rubbing at his eyes.

"Morning," he said, eyeing me with suspicion. "What do you want?"

I grinned at his choice of words. All formality had disappeared in recent weeks, and I liked it.

"I need to get out of here. Can we train?"

He ran a hand over his face, his pained expression telling me he'd rather not. But then he smiled faintly and nodded, and I waited patiently in the sitting room while he got ready. It turned out we weren't the only ones drawn to the training yard that early; by the time we reached the palace barracks, a small group of Montavis' and Hollis' men were already sparring together. Nev nodded at two men in Esari colors and led me into the centre of the training ring. If anyone thought it was odd that Lord Esari's fiancée was there, no one showed it.

I made Nev push me hard; releasing the tension I had been holding in every strike. I didn't hold back, and to his credit, neither did he. He met me with equal force, driving me back again and again. Sweat stung my eyes as he watched me stagger to my feet for the third time in five minutes.

"Do you want to take a break? We've been at this for a while now."

I wiped the sweat from my temple with my sleeves as a cool breeze swept in from the sea. It was startlingly refreshing.

"No," I said. "The more you sweat in training, the less you bleed in battle."

He burst into laughter, and I put my hands on my hips, frowning as I stood there panting.

"What's so funny?"

"Because Morgan's nonsense has rubbed off on you more than you know."

I smiled grudgingly, remembering how irritated I'd been when Morgan first said it to me. Nev was right though—they'd all rubbed off on me, shaping me in ways I hadn't wanted to admit. Gripping my sword, I stretched my neck from side to side and pushed the hair from my face, ready to start again. Before I got the chance, Arella swept into the yard, pulling her furs tight against the wind.

"I thought you were sleeping in," I called, watching her as she approached.

The night before, when we'd finally made it back to

our rooms, she'd told me rather firmly not to wake her unless it was an absolute emergency.

"So did I," she grumbled, green eyes flashing. "But you've been summoned by our glorious leader. He wants everyone there this morning before the lords convene for council."

She gave me a once-over, arching a brow.

"And let me tell you—you'll want to get ready. You look a mess."

I snorted at the insult, pushing the loose strands of hair from my face again. She wasn't wrong. I was covered in mud and sweat, hardly fit for an audience with a king. After handing my sword back to Nev, the three of us trudged back up to the palace where I went straight to the bath, scrubbing away the grime and rinsing my hair clean. When I came out, Arella was already waiting, gowns draped across the doorway of my wardrobe like offerings. She held one up with a flourish.

"Lavender," she said brightly.

I pulled a face, shaking my head.

"Absolutely not. I should never have let Eseld choose that fabric. Burn it."

She rolled her eyes.

"What about this one?" She lifted a forest-green gown trimmed with fur. "Apparently you should dress warmly."

I frowned.

"Do we know what Damen wants us for?"

"No, just that you have to attend, and that it would be outside. Austell said he had no idea what it was for and, I don't know why, but I have a really bad feeling about it."

I sighed heavily. I'd had a bad feeling since we'd arrived in this place.

"Fine. The green one."

I dried off quickly and padded across the room,

throwing a robe around me. Arella passed me a comb, and as I sat on the edge of the bed working it through my hair, she dropped beside me. I caught her gaze out of the corner of my eye.

"What is it? You're looking at me like you've got something to say."

"Nothing. I just... wondered what's going on between you and Austell, that's all. I heard you both talking in here last night."

"Oh, Gods, I don't know," I sighed, rubbing at my temple. "I like him. I really do. A lot. He's nothing like the man I first thought him to be."

"No, he's not, is he?" Arella said. "He's surprised me, too."

"He's kind. Reliable. Affectionate. He's open with his feelings and not afraid to admit when he's wrong." I shook my head, letting out another sigh. "And if I'd met him before all of this..."

"Anyway," Arella smiled gently, dropping the subject as if to save me from myself. "You should be getting ready, and I need to be doing something with your hair."

She fussed with my damp hair, twisting sections into intricate braids to keep them off of my neck. As her hands worked, I noticed the faraway look in her eyes.

"What is it?" I asked.

She bit her lip.

"I had a vision today."

My eyes flashed to hers. Arella had always relied overly on her instincts, but she had always denied being a Seer or having anything close to a Witnessing.

"You don't get visions," I said slowly.

"I know," she whispered. "But this was different to anything I've had before."

"What did you see?"

"Men hiding in the trees. Runes carved into stone. I could smell salt in the air."

"That's all?" I frowned, and when she nodded I let out a breath. "That's not much to go on."

She helped me into the warm woolen dress and wrapped a thick, fur-trimmed cloak around my shoulders. A crease lingered between her brows, and I suspected the vision had bothered her more than she was letting on.

"I know. I don't know what it means."

"Well, I'm sure we'll find out soon enough," I said, throwing her a crooked smile, though unease settled over me as I walked to the door.

Out into the sitting room, Austell was dressed as immaculately as ever in a navy jumper and fur coat. He sat poised in one of the chairs, papers in hand, and looked up with a smile as I entered. There was a knock at the door, and Austell rose smoothly to his feet, offering me his hand.

"We are to be escorted, apparently," he said.

"Oh. That sounds ominous," I murmured.

"Indeed."

An Order priest stood stiffly on the other side of the door, and it seemed to me an odd choice of escort—why send him instead of a servant or guard? Yet there he was, leading us down the staircase and through the palace corridors until we were shown into a small, windowless antechamber. Already gathered inside were the other lords and their wives, or mistress, in Canver's case. The air was thick with anticipation, an almost tangible sense that something was about to break. The tension prickled along my skin, a warning I couldn't ignore. Hollis sidled up to Austell.

"There's something off about this," he muttered quietly, eyes darting about the room. "I don't like it."

I made light conversation with Kerensa and Elestren

for a few minutes, keeping a watchful eye on the Order priests that were positioned around the room. Denfor, Canver and Tanrith were talking quietly amongst themselves, their heads together. Caja stood awkwardly beside them, silent and still as a shadow.

"Caja," I called softly.

Her eyes lifted to mine in surprise, and I gestured for her to join us. For a heartbeat, her usual vacant expression cleared, and a small smile touched her lips.

"Your dress is just beautiful," I said as she reached us. "You must let me know who your seamstress is."

She looked as though she was about to reply when the door opened. Conversation faltered, the air thinning as General Brayson stepped into the room. I took the opportunity to study him at last. From what Arella had picked up in the palace gossip, Brayson was a cold, peculiar man—one prone to unpredictable outbursts and sudden violence, often directed at women and servants. He wore his dark, wavy hair cropped just short of his shoulders, a neat beard accentuating the hard, unforgiving lines of his jaw. His eyes swept the chamber with icy detachment, not in search of allies, but to measure and dismiss.

As he moved further inside, I caught a glance at the other lords. Each of them was watching him, too, though carefully. As regional Lords, they were considered to be of equal rank to the General, and as such I might have expected him to form friendships with them, but he hadn't. Instead, he seemed aloof and remote, treating them not even with indifference but with disdain. The lords eyed him with interest and perhaps a touch of suspicion. They weren't afraid of him, but they were certainly keeping a close eye on him, that much was obvious, much like I used to keep an eye on Theo. Brayson strode over to another door at the back of the room and then turned to us all.

"If you'll follow me," he said, disappearing through the door without another word.

Tanrith let out a small chuckle and gestured at Denfor to go first. I waited for the others to file through the door ahead of me, and then followed Austell's waiting hand into another, much larger room. The shift was deliberate and almost theatrical. Everything about the way we'd been assembled, marched, and steered through these doors felt orchestrated, designed to put us on edge. And as we stepped out onto the balcony, I knew that was exactly what they had planned.

The south side of the palace looked out over the city. To my left, the harbor spread wide, the *Panacea* and *Halcyon* still tethered in the docks below. To the right, the forest rolled for miles, mountains rising like dark sentinels behind it. It should have been beautiful, but my stomach sank. Because in the courtyard beneath us, a scaffold had been raised. Three stakes stood stark against the stone, rough and brutal. My shadows stirred nervously, pulsing in warning, as if they could sense what was about to unfold.

The Order priests who had escorted us from our rooms lingered by the balcony, silent and watchful. I swallowed hard and lowered myself into one of the chairs set out, wondering if it was true that they could sense our gifts. Kerensa slipped into the chair beside me, her hand trembling slightly in her lap.

"Brace yourself, my love," I heard Montavis whisper to her.

I pulled my cloak around me, a shiver running down my spine as my dream from the early hours started to feel far too much like a premonition. Only once we were all seated did Damen make an appearance, Aleta following closely behind him with her black hair gleaming against the pure white fur draped around her shoulders. There was a look on her face that made me deeply uncomfortable, as if she not only knew what was about to happen, but was looking forward to it. Damen escorted her to a seat in the front row and then turned to address us.

"Yesterday," he began, his voice carrying easily across the balcony, "a group of rebels thought it wise to enter *my* city and threaten me. They seem to believe they can succeed in their pitiful, ill-advised mission to overthrow me. That this long-forgotten heir that nobody has heard a whisper of in over twenty years could somehow take my place."

He paused, letting the silence stretch, his gaze sliding slowly across the room, making deliberate eye contact with each of us.

"They are wrong. This afternoon, those traitors will face judgment, and swift punishment. Let that be a lesson to anyone who dares forget their place."

The words landed like stones in my stomach, every syllable laced with arrogance. His expression shifted suddenly, cruel and satisfied. It was the same face he'd worn when he had counseled my father to take me in hand all those years ago. The face of a man who took pleasure in punishing others.

"The same fate awaits anyone else that dares to disrespect or go against me. They will *burn*."

In the courtyard below, the Order priests led out three men. I prayed desperately to the Gods that I wouldn't see Noa among them, my dream replaying in my head. I fought the urge to crane my head forward, to look more closely. To *know*. Instead, I stayed still, waiting, holding my breath as the prisoners stumbled toward the scaffolding. When I didn't recognize them, I breathed out a small sigh of relief. It was short lived.

I did my best to keep my face neutral, but there was a

riot going on in my head. Could I really sit there and watch three of my own be murdered? Men who had fought in my name, who had given their lives for our cause? Out of the corner of my eye, I noticed Brayson watching me. His gaze was sharp and predatory. I forced myself to meet his eye, staring back with all the emptiness I could muster. This was a test. Damen was making it clear who was in control here. He was assessing our loyalty, reminding us exactly what happened to anyone found lacking.

I turned away from the General, losing interest in his cold indifference, and instead, scanned the faces of those around me. Tanrith was near delirious with excitement, and Denfor watched like a hound scenting blood. One of the Order priests shouted the charges, his voice booming against the stone walls. My fists clenched, nails biting into my palms, as Damen gave the signal. Torches touched the pyres.

I watched in open-mouthed horror as the flames caught. None of the men cried out or begged for mercy. They only stared upward, eyes fixed on Damen, silent and unflinching, and I knew then that none of them would have broken down in Rostorrmel's dungeons. My chest constricted, time slowing, every breath a battle. I couldn't save them. My helplessness was a familiar, bitter taste—the same impotence I had known watching Ana's husband die at Cryf's Gap. It was heartbreaking. Agonizing.

Beside me, Austell was rigid. He looked as though he was carved from stone, but his jaw was so tight I could see the muscle twitch. Smoke curled thinly into the air, taunting us, and the men below us began to cough. But there was too little smoke rising from the pyres. Austell leaned in close to me.

"The bastards have used dry wood."

Hatred rose within me. If you were lucky, your

executioners might use damp wood so that you succumbed to the smoke long before you felt the flames, and since damp wood was a given in Rostorrmel given the storms, it meant this was deliberate.

"Your Highness," Hollis said, his discomfort obvious. "Is this really necessary? Must the women be made to watch this?"

Elestren had looked away, her face grey, and Caja looked visibly upset. Even Anneth, who hadn't torn her eyes away, looked like she was having trouble watching the scene in front of us unfold.

"They will watch, Lord Hollis," Damen ordered coldly. "You will all watch justice being served."

My shadows were raging, threatening to burst from my hands. I trembled with fury, but even as I stared at the back of Damen's head, desperate to shatter his mind with darkness, a grim resignation settled over me. Whatever the risk, I couldn't stand idly by and watch this. I might not be able to save them, but I could help to ease their final moments. I knew what I had to do.

I drew a steadying breath, aware of Kerensa's attention at the edge of my vision, and reached out. The Order priests loomed close, but I ignored them, focusing instead on the Loyalists bound to the stakes. One by one, I brushed against their minds, swift as the fire catching at their clothes. Darkness wrapped around them at my command, soft and merciful, until I felt their life-force ebb, their heads sagging forward. It was as though they had simply laid down their burdens, slipping quietly into the next life, the smoke surrounding them masking what I had done.

A single tear traced down my cheek as the flames devoured their bodies, knowing at least they felt no pain. Only then did it strike me—I had dropped the shield around my own mind.

CHAPTER 37
EFA

Thunder rumbled far away in the distance as I sat down on the palace's private beach later that afternoon. In the distance, lightning split the sky as another storm made it's way towards us and the light started to fade. I knew that I should head back up and dress for dinner, but I couldn't bring myself to do it. I didn't want to go back there. What I actually *wanted* was to run far away and never look back. That or burn the place to the ground. Sadly, neither was an option available to me right then.

I'd walked straight out of the palace after Damen had released us, and down to the coves where I'd been sitting for hours, staring sightlessly out across the gray water. As the surf sprayed up into the air and settled on my skin, I tried to get the image of the three Loyalists out of my head. Despite knowing that there had been nothing I could do to save them, I still felt that I had failed them, and their deaths pressed down on me with a weight I couldn't shake.

As the afternoon light was just starting to fade and fresh rain clouds appeared on the horizon, moving at speed towards land, I attempted to rally myself, knowing that I couldn't delay my return any longer. But just as I made to stand, I heard voices coming down the cliff path, and a moment later, Hollis and Montavis appeared. Neither man seemed surprised to see me sitting there. I turned back to the sea as the shingle crunched beneath their feet, and they wandered over, silently taking seats on the jagged rocks beside me. I said nothing, and neither did they for a while. In the end, it was Hollis who broke the silence.

"You've had quite the introduction to Damen's court, haven't you?" he said, lips curving in a smile.

I laughed bitterly, keeping my eyes on the water.

"If what took place today happens on the regular, I'd rather not be part of it. That wasn't justice. That was pure, cruel, self-indulgence."

I snapped my mouth shut, realising too late what I had just said and who I'd said it to, but Montavis only nodded his head in agreement.

"It was more than that. It was a thinly veiled threat to us."

"Thinly veiled?" Hollis laughed. "There was nothing subtle about that display, Kitto."

I went silent again, lest I was being lured into a trap, and picked up a pebble to throw into the water. Montavis did the same, launching the stone high into the air as he spoke. They fell with a splash into the waves.

"A week or so before Nissae fell," Montavis said quietly, "Damen sent word to Ken and I that Nothori warships had been spotted off the coast of Rostorrmel, much like they are today. At the time, most of my men were garrisoned just across the border in Baern since Ciaran, the old Lord Baern, and I had always found it mutually beneficial for our soldiers in times of peace to train together. Anyway, long story short, Damen ordered us both to send everyone we had north to defend the capital."

I turned to look at him, wondering where he was going with his story.

"And Kenwyn did. He had no reason not to, of course. His troops were further east and ready to mobilise. We had known Damen for years. He was Novos's closest friend, and he was General of Melrith's armies. We trusted him, so Ken gave the order to begin making preparations to march to Rostorrmel. Now, at the time, I should have been in Rael overseeing the harvest, but as it happened, Kerensa and I had decided to take a last minute jaunt to Cayam."

He paused to throw another pebble into the surf. I shifted impatiently.

"Why are you telling me this?" I asked bluntly.

"Yes, get to the point," Hollis said, grinning.

"Alright, alright. The *point* is that I shouldn't have been in Cayam, and I shouldn't have seen that Damen had given Cayam's previous Lord, a man named Maxen, very different orders. Orders to march on Nissae."

"Why would he do that?" I asked, although I already knew why.

"To draw us away, Efa. After Polruen, Ken and I have the largest regional armies. He had been planning this coup for months, and he must have known we would never have turned on Novos. Damen wanted us elsewhere, out of the way. There never were any Nothori off the coast of Rostorrmel."

I stood up slowly and took a few steps down the beach, still wondering why Montavis was telling me all of this. What was his angle?

"I ordered my men to go to Nissae, quickly and discretely, in plain clothes and small groups so that we wouldn't be discovered, and once there we dressed in Valtanan colors."

I turned to face him, a deep crease in my brow. He smiled conspiratorially.

"You might have heard from Austell that over the years there have been many comments on how much younger my wife looks, despite her being born just the summer after me. Here I am looking every day of my seven decades, and Kerensa looks like she has only just entered her fifth. It has been a source of great amusement to us over the years, until recently, when people have been starting to ask questions. You see, my wife is Valtanan, Efa, and she seems to have been blessed with particularly slow aging."

My mouth dropped open and I shook my head slowly in disbelief. Lady Montavis was Valtanan. She had been hiding in plain sight all along, right in front of Damen.

"Just before Damen arrived in Nissae, Novos took me aside, begging me that if anything were to happen to him or Aemylia, that if Nissae was to fall, I was to find their daughter and nephew, and keep them safe. But when word reached me in the thick of the battle that they had both been killed… by the time I reached Haeddas the building was completely ablaze. I was too late, and I had failed my king. In twenty years I have never forgiven myself for not doing what I promised, and for not protecting them. Those children's deaths were on my hands. Until now."

I stared at him unblinking, holding my breath the entire time he spoke.

"The true queen is coming," Hollis murmured softly, his eyes shining.

"Do you know what my wife's gift is, Efa? She is an Empath."

Well, fuck. That stopped my heart for a second. Negan

and I had discussed the unlikely event that Damen might have another Empath working for him, even though the ability was so rare, but it had never crossed our minds that one of the *lord's* wives would be one. I remembered Kerensa giving me a strange look out on the balcony as I took the lives of the Loyalists. In the briefest time that my shield had been dropped, she would have been able to read me like a book. The realisation must have shown on my face.

"Kerensa said that she could hear your thoughts as if you were screaming them, and that your rage, and the pain that you felt was indescribable. And she told me what you did for those men. A brave, compassionate act."

I laughed silently, my fist clenching involuntarily.

"I *murdered* those men. That's what I did. I have their blood on *my* hands."

"Novos used to say that to be a real leader is to sometimes have blood on your hands," Hollis said quickly. "I remember once he said that to rule was to be judged for your actions, and not for the choices available to you. Their deaths were inevitable at that point, Efa. There was no stopping it."

Montavis nodded kindly.

"What you gave them was a quick, merciful end," he said, "without the pain that Damen intended to inflict upon them."

Tears began to fall from my eyes and I turned back to the water, feeling rain on the top of my head.

"So…what now?" I asked, wiping my eyes with my fingertips.

"For twenty years I have been the custodian of what remains of Valtana," Montavis said, his voice belying the weariness he must have felt. "We pledged our loyalty to Damen only so we could try and protect what Novos and

Aemylia had built. But recently, we had started to fear that we could no longer do that. Circumstances have been escalating faster than we could ever have anticipated, and Damen is keeping secrets. But now… now we dare to hope."

I glanced back over my shoulder as the rain grew heavier. The smile that Montavis gave me lit up his entire face.

"You have our allegiance, Aeva Penrose. Whatever you need, Rael and Portreth are yours to command."

I walked back up the cliff path alone and with my head spinning, their words still replaying in my head. As Austell had intimidated, they had not betrayed my parents, and had only sworn their loyalty to Damen to try and protect Melrith and what remained of Valtana. I was still trying to take it all in as I crossed the gardens. I jogged the final stretch towards the northern entrance, pushing back my hood once I was out of the heavy rain and tucking my wild hair behind my ears. It was early evening now and the palace was reasonably quiet. A few servants were running errands but most were busy preparing for another night of music, eating, and dancing, which apparently took place every night in Damen's court. It meant that the hallways were quiet as I made my way towards the staircase nearest the Esari rooms.

Not quiet enough, it seemed, because a door opened just ahead of me and Tanrith appeared, looking at first surprised, and then delighted to see me. I smiled politely without slowing my steps, having no intention of stopping to interact with him. But it seemed he had other ideas, walking directly into my path.

"Efa," he purred at me, teeth flashing below his

moustache. "How convenient that we should meet like this. I had been hoping to get you alone."

I stared at him coldly, dropping the polite act. After the day I'd had, I really wasn't in the mood for putting on a pretense and dealing with his taunts. His leering and smirking had grown tiresome; as had the way he skulked around after me. He was walking on thin ice with me. He stepped towards me and I automatically took a step back, starting a game that I didn't want to play. Impatiently, I kept trying to evade him, but every step I took he would block me, moving me closer and closer to the wall. When my back finally touched the hard stone, my irritation peaked and I reached under my coat for my blade.

"You are almost as elusive as our Loyalist friends, Efa, slipping out of the ballroom before we might dance or keeping to your rooms. I had hoped to speak privately to you, to come to some sort of… arrangement, perhaps."

His face was too close to mine, his breath hot on my cheek. I was dangerously close to losing my cool.

"Like the one you have with Caja?"

"Oh yes, she is a fine creature, although I think Sandy would be most unhappy if he knew he was sharing her with me. But you… you are much more titillating. I would very much enjoy discovering all that you have to offer."

"Then it's very unfortunate that you will not have the opportunity to, my Lord. Now, if you could please let me go on my way."

I went to push past him, but he didn't budge. His smile only widened, the look in his eyes calculated and determined. He meant to have me, and I would have no choice in the matter. This was the Tanrith that Austell had warned me about, that I had been waiting to see.

"I'm afraid that I must insist."

He took another step, this time trapping me against the

wall. For a man of his age he was surprisingly strong, and the feel of his body against me set my teeth on edge. I shifted my body and leaned forward so that my lips brushed against his ear.

"No, Lord Baern. It is *I* who must insist."

Alarm flashed in his eyes, just for a second, as he felt the tip of my blade pressing against his cock.

"Back away," I murmured quietly, "or lose it completely."

A slow grin spread across his face as he chuckled delightedly, and I had the feeling that my violence had only served to make him desire me even more. Tanrith stepped back and released me, bowing mockingly. I stared at him, adjusting the blade in my hand, and then marching off down the corridor. I didn't slow my stride and I didn't look back, even though I could feel his eyes burning into my back, but resolution built steadily in my mind. Zennor Tanrith was going to die very soon, and I would enjoy every moment of it. No one touched me like that and lived.

CHAPTER 38

EFA

The weak morning sun crept through the gap in the curtains, dragging me from uneasy dreams. For a moment I lay still, hoping the quiet voices from the sitting room would fade back into silence. Then the pain struck. It was sharp, blooming in my arm where the oath line throbbed beneath my sleeve as if someone had pressed a knife against my skin.

With a curse, I shoved the covers aside and staggered to the dressing table, rummaging through the clutter until I found the small flask of hathersage root I'd been eking out for the last few weeks. Pulling up my sleeve, I looked at the oath line. It had healed, or seemed as though it had, but the ache never left—a constant, dull reminder of what bound me still to Finn and the Nevedeno. The bitter taste of the tea clung to my tongue, but it steadied the hammering in my chest just enough for me to think again, and I hoped to the Gods that the pain wasn't heralding Finn's imminent arrival.

In the bathroom, I splashed water on my face and tidied my hair, returning to the bedroom to dress. I glanced up from tying my laces as someone knocked on my door, and Arella slipped inside before I could answer. She carried herself quietly, but the faint crease in her brow betrayed her apprehension.

"General Brayson is here. For you."

I raised an eyebrow and followed her silently into the sitting room, finding Brayson looming in the doorway. Austell and Nev were already there, both watching him closely. The General's attention, however, was fixed on me.

"The king requests your presence," he said without preamble, his tone stripped of even the most basic of courtesy. "Now."

I frowned, glancing down at the simple clothes I'd put on in anticipation of a walk down on the beach.

"My fiancée should be addressed as Lady-Designate Esari, Brayson," Austell said, voice cutting like a blade. "It is not only her right, as my betrothed, but a courtesy you will extend if you value my respect."

Brayson's mouth twitched, though whether it was amusement or disdain was impossible to tell. He dipped his head the barest fraction, the gesture so lacking in sincerity it was almost mocking.

"As you wish... *Lady-Designate*."

"When Efa is ready, I will accompany her to the king's rooms."

Brayson's cold gaze slid to Austell.

"Not you, Esari. You can wait here."

His words hung heavy in the air. The insult was plain, the dismissal deliberate. Austell stiffened, shoulders squaring as though he meant to step forward and challenge the slight head-on, but I quickly intervened.

"It's quite all right, my love," I said pleasantly, my tone calm even though my pulse had quickened. "I'm sure no harm will come to me while the General escorts me. And since it seems the king is in a rush, I'll go as I am."

I walked over to Austell and rose on my toes to kiss him on the cheek, my hand resting briefly on his arm. He didn't relax, but I felt the shift of tension in his body. I knew he was worried, especially after Tanrith's behavior the night before, but he needed to know that I could handle myself. He took my hand and squeezed it once reluctantly before letting me go.

Brayson turned on his heel without another word, expecting me to follow, and as I stepped out after him I had to remind myself that I wasn't supposed to have been in the palace before now, and I would have no reason to know where Damen's rooms would be located. I forced myself to play dumb even though the palace was so familiar—every twist and corner etched into my bones. I feigned curiosity, letting my questions spill out in a steady stream, idle and harmless, buying myself time while I watched him out of the corner of my eye. He answered none of them. In fact, he didn't even glance at me, as if he hadn't heard me speak at all.

My parents' old rooms had stretched across the entire north side of the palace, with wide windows looking out over the ocean. It was the grandest suite in the palace with multiple bedrooms, two large sitting rooms, and, once upon a time, my father's private study. I had braced myself before stepping through the familiar oak doors, but in hindsight, nothing could have prepared me for what lay beyond. Brayson pushed me forward and the sound hit me first: a cacophony of moaning and screaming that pressed in on every side. I looked around slowly, bemused and impressed in equal parts. I'd seen plenty of brothels over the years, but I'd never seen anything quite like Damen's harem in motion. No wonder Tanrith had been so taken with the idea.

The rooms had been redecorated since I'd last been in them. The muted silks in soft browns and grays were gone, replaced with vibrant colors and gaudy velvets. Daybeds and chairs crowded every corner, too many to count. And on every single one—bodies. Twisting, writhing, shameless. There must have been upwards of twenty women at least, and just as many men. Some were half-clothed, some fully nude, all lost in varying states of lust. Everywhere I looked was frenzy—limbs tangling against walls, on rugs, or sprawled openly across marble. The air reeked of sweat, incense, and sex.

And then I saw him. Damen lounged in the middle of it all, draped across a half-reclined chair. His dark eyes locked on mine as he crooked a finger, a slow, seductive smile spreading across his face. I let my gaze drift around the room, marveling at the positions being adopted by some couples.

"Do you know, Efa," Damen said as I approached, his tone deceptively smooth, "the very first night I met you, I posed a question to my lords. I asked them how you would react if I brought you here, to my rooms."

I said nothing, only tilting my head slightly, forcing my face into stillness.

In front of me two men were pleasuring a Tithran girl at the same time. She seemed to be enjoying herself immensely.

"Ken and Kitto defended your honor beautifully, as expected. 'She is a lady, Sire', they said. Perran thought that you might blush prettily, averting your gaze and counting down the seconds until I released you."

Well, Perran had got one part right at least; I *was* counting down the seconds.

"But you," Damen leaned closer, voice dropping, intimate and poisonous all at once, "you never blush, do you? Never tremble. Never yield. And Zennor—ah, Zennor said you were different. That nothing would shock you. That you'd look, and keep looking. And he was right."

His eyes raked over me, as if he could peel back my skin with his gaze.

"I can see it now. Curiosity. Interest. A spark of amusement, even. Do you know what else I see in you, Lady-Designate? Disdain. You are entertained by what you see, and yet you judge me for it."

I shrugged, feigning nonchalance, and turned my face toward the window, refusing him the satisfaction of my eyes.

"It isn't for me to judge you, Your Highness," I said smoothly. "Though I would say I am more perplexed than entertained."

He studied me idly, stroking his chin.

"You're quite something, aren't you?"

I shrugged again, leaning on my usual strategy: say as little as possible until I knew exactly what ground I stood on. The trick was to remain aloof and indifferent, using silence as its own kind of shield. Across the room I saw a familiar face I recognized: Roda, on her knees before one of Damen's courtiers.

"In his letter, Austell confessed that he had been mesmerized by you. Entranced, even. I certainly see why. Nothing ruffles those glorious feathers of yours, does it?"

"That's very kind of you to say, Your Highness."

A crease formed between his brows as he narrowed his gaze.

"You look familiar to me. Haven't we met before?"

"No, Your Highness. I don't believe we have."

My voice held steady but my hand betrayed me,

trembling faintly before I forced it still. I made myself breathe evenly. Despite Arella's assurances, I felt certain he was going to recognize me. My eyes flicked to my right as Brayson began circling me.

"Are you sure?" he pressed.

"I am, Your Highness. I think I would remember meeting my king."

Brayson kept circling, like a predator pacing its prey. Each step seemed designed to test the edge of my composure, but I held my ground until finally, the words tore out before I could stop them.

"Perhaps you could call your hound off, Your Highness," I said, my voice now could enough to bite. "Or does he only know how to sniff at women until they bare their teeth?"

The silence that followed was heavy and dangerous. Brayson stilled, his eyes flashing with something feral. Then Damen's laughter broke the silence.

"Easy, Brayson," he drawled, amusement dripping from every syllable. "She's not yours to hound. Stand down."

Brayson inclined his head, but his eyes still burned into me as he retreated toward the windows. There was a subtle shift in Damen's expression as he stood up from his chair and prowled toward me. He still smiled, but it no longer met his eyes. My shadows pulsed, letting me know they were ready if they needed to be, but I held them at bay, knowing they were likely to be useless against him anyway.

"I know who you are, Efa."

Icy fingers stroked down my spine at his words and turned my body cold. This was the risk we had always taken—that one slip, one look, would give me away. That he would see through me and know exactly who I was.

Perhaps he already had. Perhaps I'd betrayed myself with something too familiar—an expression or a turn of phrase.. Whatever it was, I felt exposed. He stood, straightening to his full height.

"You're bold," he said. "I must say that. And foolish. Did you truly believe you could walk among us unnoticed? That I wouldn't know who you were?"

I held my breath, every instinct screaming at me to recoil, to lower my gaze, but I didn't. I locked my eyes on his, refusing to flinch. If this were the end, then I would go down staring my enemy in the eye. He leaned closer.

"I am the King of Melrith, Efa. There is nothing that escapes me. Nothing I do not know. And you…" His gaze swept over me, "are not who you pretend to be. So tell me, Efa… who are you really?"

I remembered once hearing Theo say that the first rule of smuggling was to never reveal too much too early. One should always wait; always see what the other side knew, because more often than not, they knew very little. I forced a smile arrogantly, throwing caution to the wind.

"Why don't *you* tell me who I am?" I asked lightly, as though the game amused me.

For a second, I thought perhaps that I had gone too far, but he seemed to find my insolence entertaining. He took a step towards me, and then another, and I resisted the natural urge to step back, my hand moving slowly towards the knife in my pocket. His voice dropped low.

"They're calling you *Queen*."

He was close enough now that I had to tilt my chin back to meet his gaze. My heart slammed against my ribs, and his hand came up, fingers brushing down my arm until they closed around my wrist. With excruciating care, he pulled back the sleeve of my jumper revealing my tattoo. Two circles linked by a solid line.

"Or is Finn your master?" Damen whispered, his breath hot against my cheek. "Did he send you hear to spy, smuggler? To double cross me?"

My heart lurched, my breath stolen for a moment until the truth sank in. Relief hit me so hard my knees nearly gave way. Fucking Gods. Theo had been right. Damen knew nothing.

He didn't see me, not really. Not the truth of who I was. He had meant only the stupid nickname I'd picked up along the coast—the *Smuggler Queen*. A joke, an insult born from whispers and tavern tales. I let out the breath I'd been holding, forcing a thin smile to my lips. Let him think it was amusement. Let him think I wasn't rattled.

"I've never known Finn to play fair," I said, half expecting him to come strolling into the room at any moment. "He only serves himself, but if he intends to fuck you over it has nothing to do with me."

"Indeed," he said thoughtfully, eyes gleaming. "And what about you, Efa? Who do you serve? My sources say that you're his second in command, and that you share his bed."

"Once perhaps, but not now. I'm a reformed woman, Your Highness. Perhaps your sources are out of touch. I've left that life behind now that I am Lady-Designate."

"Lady Esari," he repeated softly, tasting the words. "An ambitious leap, for a smuggler by trade. I wasn't aware that people could just leave the Nevedeno. I understood there to be… consequences…"

I shrugged a shoulder. Technically he was correct. No one had ever voluntarily left the Nevedeno. Not successfully, anyway.

"You seemed particularly upset by yesterday's executions. I would have thought that a woman in your profession would be used to such things."

My mouth went dry but I met his stare.

"I don't like to witness the suffering of others."

His smile curved.

"No. But you don't mind causing it."

Finally he broke eye contact and looked around the room. Across the far side Roda was coming to a climax and she moaned loudly. I wondered if she enjoyed her role, or if she was as desperate to be away from the palace as I was.

"I must say, it's wonderful to see Austell so blissfully happy. I cannot deny that you seem to care deeply for each other."

"He is a good man," I replied.

Damen nodded pensively, though I could see the boredom creeping in. His gaze dipped to my mouth before sliding lower, lingering too long. I lifted my chin, growing weary of the conversation and whatever was going on with him.

"What would you say," he said suddenly, "if I commanded you, as my loyal subject, to join my harem?"

"I'd say that if you've heard anything about me, you'd agree that my talents would be wasted in the bedroom and better used elsewhere."

"Oh, I'm sure they wouldn't be wasted..." he purred, his thumb stroking the inside of my wrist.

I pulled my hand from his grasp and stepped back. Anger flashed in his eyes.

"I could have you arrested. You are, after all, a notorious criminal who killed a tavern owner and three Order priests recently in Cryf's Gap. I'm sure that doesn't even scratch the surface of the things you've done."

I almost laughed at the idea of Edvarr being thought of as a tavern owner, but instead I nodded thoughtfully, looking around the room with vacant eyes until I saw someone else I recognized. Caja. Her head was lolled back against the daybed, eyes half closed and another woman's head buried between her legs. As she moved, I noticed a scar just like mine on the inside of her thigh. I'd have sworn it was an oath line. I returned my attention to Damen, calling his bluff.

"Perhaps you should. Of course, that might upset a few people in the Nevedeno, people that are still loyal to *me*. And that might cause some supply issues, I suppose. But then, perhaps this new, highly toxic Faelock isn't that essential to whatever it is that you're planning?"

He stared at me, and I thought that this time I really had gone too far, but once again he threw back his head and laughed.

"You know, I like you, Efa. There is something about you… I feel like I have known you in another life." I smiled tightly. "Very well, we'll agree to a truce for the time being."

He signaled to Brayson who began to weave through the bodies toward us.

"My congratulations on your engagement, Lady-Designate. I look forward to having you in my court."

I was being dismissed. Dropping low into a curtsey, I spun on my heel, eager to put as much distance between myself and Damen as possible without tipping to insult. As I neared the great doors, I passed by one of the bedrooms. Aleta leaned stood just inside watching me, her expression unreadable. I inclined my head in brief acknowledgement, but she only scowled, turning her back as I passed, and a heartbeat later, the bedroom door slammed shut behind her.

CHAPTER 39
EFA

I stood at the edge of the room, the heat and noise pressing in on me until it felt almost suffocating. The air was thick with music and laughter, a frenzy of activity like the night before, though at least half the guests seemed more interested in slipping away into the darker alcoves. The women from Damen's harem spun and swayed across the floor, their jeweled bangles flashing in the candlelight, while others drifted into the shadows to whisper and scheme.

The music throbbed in my temples, deepening the tension headache that had dogged me all day. Damen's words from that morning still weighed on my mind. The conversation had unsettled me, mostly because whilst he might not have known the whole truth about me, him knowing that I was Nevedeno still carried plenty of risk. He could change his mind and mete out punishment on a whim.

I forced myself to move, skirting the edge of the crowd and glancing up toward the dais where my father's crown glimmered under the light atop his head. My pulse was loud in my ears as I walked slowly toward Elestren and Kerensa, but before I reached them, a hand brushed lightly against my elbow, and I turned, startled to find Anneth blocking my path. She wore a gown of burnished gold that caught the candlelight and turned her tawny eyes molten.

"Lady Denfor. How are you this evening?"

"Quite well, thank you."

Something about her smooth, unchanging tone put me instantly on edge. Anneth was being perfectly courteous, but there was steel under the civility. She had an official place at court, a title. I did not. That she hadn't asked me to call her by her given name suggested that she was reminding me of that fact.

"We haven't spoken much since you arrived," she said. "What do you make of our court?"

"It's… quite the experience," I replied pleasantly, as if we hadn't all sat together watching three men burn the day before.

She laughed lightly, her eyes going to the pendant at my throat.

"That's an interesting necklace," she said. "Daxholla flowers, if I'm not mistaken?"

"Are they? I'm not familiar with them, really," I lied. "The necklace was a gift from Lord Tanrith, to celebrate our engagement."

I held the pendant in my fingers, twisting it once. Arella had found the necklace in my trunk and had been as horrified as I had been when I'd told her how I'd come to have it before deciding that I should wear it. She had thought that it was fate, and that it had made it's way back to where it should be. She thought that by wearing it, I honored our people and remembered them, as they deserved to be remembered.

"Yes," Anneth said, nodding slowly. "I seem to recall

that they used to grow in the pastures around Nissae. Aemylia had a particular fondness for them."

"Oh?"

"She had the ugly things scattered around that house whenever we were called there. The smell gave me quite the headache."

I said nothing, casting my eyes around the room looking for Austell and finding him in deep conversation with Montavis and Hollis on the other side of the room. He must have felt me watching because he glanced up, raising an eyebrow at me in silent question. When he saw Anneth, he immediately made his excuses and started to weave through the crowd toward me.

"In truth, I never liked that house, or that woman. She was always too arrogant. When she married Novos it was as if she thought that it was her right to rule Melrith with him, as if *she* was our monarch, and not he. No, I can't say I was sorry when that city burned to the ground."

My shadows pushed at the tips of my fingers, begging to reach out and wrap around her throat.

"Children died that night," I said quietly. "Thousands of innocents died."

Her eyes widened fractionally, no doubt sensing the anger behind my words. I was saved from saying anything more incriminating by Austell arriving, his hand slipping comfortingly around my waist.

"My love, will you not dance with me?"

I turned a dazzling smile on him.

"I thought you'd never ask."

He took my hand and out on to the dance floor, sweeping me elegantly around the room. My body was pressed against his, our faces only inches apart.

"Everything all right?" he asked me.

"Yes," I sighed. "I think you may have got there at just the right time. Who knows what I'd have said to her."

"Ignore her. Are we worried about Damen knowing that you're Nevedeno?"

"I don't know. My instinct tells me that I've gotten away with it, because arresting me might interrupt the supply of his Faelock. When I mentioned that, he looked genuinely concerned, which tells me that the Faelock is important. Very important. So no, I don't think we need to worry, but he might well hand me back to Finn if he thinks I present a problem."

"I won't let that happen, I promise you."

Austell pulled me against him a little tighter and pressed his lips against my temple. I leaned in against him a little, suddenly feeling tired and content to let him lead the dancing. He was a confident partner, but I tried to imagine him in a hot, candlelit tavern, dancing wildly and losing control. Somehow I couldn't picture it.

"Why are you smiling?" he asked.

"No reason. I was just trying to picture you, I don't know... wild and passionate, lost in the moment."

He laughed softly, the sound low and intimate, his hand tightening at my waist as his lips brushed across my forehead again, lingering this time.

"Say the word," he murmured, voice husky, "and I'll lose myself in you."

My head snapped up, heat flooding my cheeks as my lips parted in a breath I couldn't quite catch. His eyes locked onto mine, and for a heartbeat the world narrowed to that single look.

"Forgive me, Lord Esari," a new voice said, interrupting the moment. "Might I take the opportunity to steal this exquisite woman for a dance or two?"

Irritation flashed across Austell's face at the intrusion,

but he inclined his head politely and let go of me, allowing the newcomer to step in front of me. I didn't recognize the man. He was a few inches taller than me, broad shouldered and with a thick head of fair hair. He was well dressed and I wondered what he did, whether he was a merchant or perhaps one of Damen's advisors. As his hand slid around my waist, his features shifted momentarily and I blinked. Then he was the stranger again, grinning at me mischievously.

"You know I think you've gotten better at doing that over the years," I said, rather impressed.

"It's easy if you know how. I just make you see what I want you to see."

"So you've always said. I just don't remember you ever being able to glamor yourself hair."

Lore snorted.

"That's a low blow, even for you." He winked at me, narrowly avoiding stepping on my toes. "Anyway, how are you, Lady-Designate?"

"I've been better. This place is fucked up. What are you doing in here? You know you're taking a big risk?"

"I think it's worth it on this occasion. We've found Noa, Efa. Or, at least, we know where he was most recently."

My heart skipped a beat. Lore placed both hands on my waist and lifted me into the air as part of the dance.

"Where?"

"He was here, at the castle. All of my people here have been tasked with finding out information since we learned he was missing. We finally found it."

"And?"

"Roda periodically visits one of the captains stationed in the dungeons. All we know is that Noa was there, but he isn't anymore. He left the dungeons alive."

A dark look crossed my face.

"I want to speak to this captain."

"I thought you might. It just happens to be his night off, and we know where he likes to drink. Meet Ando at the stables tonight and we'll have him ready to talk to you."

When the dance finished, Lore bowed in response to my curtsey. Austell had been watching from the side and immediately resumed his position opposite me, his tension palpable.

"No need to be jealous," I said quietly. "That was Lore. Noa was here. He's alive, but they've taken him somewhere, Aus. I'm meeting him and Ando later tonight to see what else I can find out."

Austell's brows knit together and then he recovered, the mask slipping back over his face. He drew me in against him as we danced, the music slower now.

"Are you serious? Gods, Efa." The dance took us past the dais and he fell silent until we had moved away again. "Do what you need to do, obviously, but please take care tonight."

I nodded absentmindedly, already thinking ahead to that evening.

"I don't know what I'd do if something happened to you," he murmured quietly.

His words brought me out of my thoughts and I looked up at him, the heat that had been building before Lore interrupted us rising once again. I took a deep breath, my heart pounding. Part of me wanted to kiss him, but part of me still felt unsure if it was the right thing. I knew that it was stupid, but somehow I felt unfaithful, as if I were still promised elsewhere.

Then, without warning my shadows screamed, racing through my veins with alarming ferocity. Confusion was written all over Austell's face as I stumbled and gasped, feeling an overwhelming sense of euphoria and urgency that took my breath away. My heart felt like it was about to burst out of my chest and my mind went blank. Everything around me faded away, all except for one single, all consuming thought.

He was here.

CHAPTER 40
EFA

I stumbled on the next step of the dance, clumsily treading on Austell's foot and nearly losing my balance as I spun towards the door.

"What is it? What's wrong?" Austell asked, his voice edged with alarm at my sudden change in disposition.

I barely heard him. My feet moved of their own accord as we danced across the polished floor, some part of my subconscious remembering the steps my mother had insisted I learn as a child. My eyes searched the crowd frantically, shadows pulsing in excited recognition. I couldn't see him, but I knew he was here. And then I saw him.

"Emrys," I breathed.

His name slipped from my lips, barely a breath. He stole the air from my lungs, striding into the ballroom as though he owned it. Beside me, Austell's body went rigid, and all around us conversation faltered. Guests whispered nervously as the crowd parted, allowing two imposing figures to step through. There was no mistaking them: Fae, unmistakable in their presence. They moved with effortless authority, the onlookers caught between fear and awe. Their clothes were impeccable now, not the worn, ripped shirts and muddied boots that I remembered. Fine jackets and well-fitted fabrics replaced their creased linen and leathers, yet their hair was still pulled back in the traditional warrior style—a sharp reminder of who they were beneath the elegance. And they were beautiful. Heart-achingly so.

Not a moment too soon, the dance ended and Austell and I retreated to the edge of the room to join Montavis and Kerensa again. Like everyone else, they couldn't take their eyes off of Emrys and Bran.

"I wasn't aware that the Dark Prince had been invited," Montavis said, his surprise evident in his expression. "There hasn't been a representative from the Northern Realm at Rostorrmel since… well, since Novos ruled."

"No, I had no idea either," Austell said quietly. "It's quite unexpected."

As the two males approached the dais, Damen stood and slowly descended the steps. He beamed at them, holding out his arms wide in delighted welcome, but there was no warmth in Emrys's expression. Oh, he was courteous and polite, but there was no mistaking his animosity. In fact, I wouldn't have been surprised if he'd used his own bare hands to kill the king there and then in front of everyone. Perhaps Damen didn't notice, or perhaps he just didn't care, for when he reached the bottom of the steps he made a show of embracing the Fae Prince as if he was greeting an old friend, and I strained my ears to hear their conversation over the music.

"Prince Trystan! I'm so glad that you were able to join us at such short notice. It has been far too long since the Northern Realm graced us with their presence. And Lord Brannock, a pleasure as always."

"Lord Brannock?" I murmured to myself, frowning.

The name sounded odd to me. I'd only ever thought of him as just Bran. It had never even occurred to me that he might be a Fae lord. Somehow the title didn't suit him.

"Yes, Lord Brannock Vannfod," Kerensa said, hearing me and probably assuming that I didn't know either male. "His family is Fae nobility. They have been close to the crown for generations. His father served King Dafydd until he died."

I was floored. This was the man who carved wood around the fire at night, who didn't dance, and who had taught me how to find herbs in the forest. The quiet, loyal friend of the Fae Prince who had saved my life. Finding out that he was nobility surprised me, because I had never met someone more humble or grounded.

"We are honoured to be invited," Emrys was saying. "My brother sends his warmest regards."

"How is Aubrey? And his lovely wife, Aneira?"

It was barely noticeable to anyone who didn't know Emrys well, but the signs were there. Behind him, Bran watched the conversation carefully. Something about the innocuous question had set them on edge.

"They are both well, thank you."

Up on the dais, Aleta rose from her chair and made her way down the steps to join them, the sequins on her maroon dress glittering as she moved. She held out a manicured hand to Emrys, smiling seductively as he bowed and kissed her knuckles.

"Prince Trystan," she purred. "You are most welcome here. Perhaps you would honour me with a dance? I seem to recall that you were such a beautiful dancer."

"It would be my pleasure, my Lady," he replied smoothly, taking her hand and leading her out.

As they joined the other couples dancing, Bran moved

to the edge of the room, and I slowly released the breath I had been holding. Their arrival had thrown me completely, and seeing Emrys again had brought back feelings that I had wanted to forget. I knew that for the last month I had lied to myself every morning, telling myself that he had meant nothing to me, but having him there in front of me forced me to admit the truth to myself: that I wasn't over him. Standing there in that ballroom, watching him begin to dance, I felt like I was back in the gardens at Totease in the pouring rain, feeling my heart break all over again.

My shadows twitching aggressively at the way Aleta pressed herself against him, smiling and laughing at every word he said and brazenly flirting with him in front of the entire court. I glanced at Damen, who had returned to his throne and was lounging with a glass of wine, seemingly unbothered by his mistress's interest in the Fae Prince. My cheeks were heating and my headache kicked up a notch, and then Austell's hand was suddenly warm on my waist. I glanced at him gratefully, moving in towards him and turning my back on the dancing to join in the conversation he was having with Montavis and Kerensa. But only a few minutes later, I felt my shadows begin to tremble again, more violently this time. I waited until he stood right behind me before I turned to face him.

"Austell," Emrys said, a little curtly. "Good to see you again."

Emrys bowed his head towards Montavis and Kerensa.

"Kitto, Lady Montavis. It has been some years since we last saw each other. You both look well."

"As do you, Emrys," Montavis said easily, while his wife eyed the Fae Prince curiously.

"I hope you don't mind the intrusion, but I was hoping to ask the Lady-Designate if she might honour me with a dance."

For the briefest of moments Austell's eyes flashed with something sharp—jealousy, maybe, or irritation with the mocking way he had used my title—and his jaw tightened, before he quickly reined it in. With all the gathered eyes on us, he forced a courteous smile, inclining his head as though giving permission. My chest constricted and I smiled tightly, unable to stop my hand from trembling slightly. As I took his hand, it was as if the world stopped turning.

Essence rushed through me and my shadows surged as that familiar sense of completeness settled over me like a haze. Warmth pooled in my core as he held me close against him, and I breathed him in, memories of dancing with him in Cayam filling my mind and setting my stomach fluttering. I thought about what had happened afterwards, when he had taken me back to the inn, and I breathed in sharply trying to forget the memory of how he had made me feel.

Emrys's eyes were on my hand, gaze lingering on the ring glinting against my skin. His mouth curved, but there was no warmth to in it.

"Congratulations," he said.

The word was dry as sand, his irritation wrapped in mock amusement.

I tried to avoid his gaze, looking anywhere but at him, but that was a mistake. It only made me realize that everyone was looking at *us*. Austell, Montavis, Tanrith, Denfor… they were all watching us dancing together. I wondered what they were all thinking.

"Thank you," I said shortly.

"And here I was thinking that you might have missed me."

I rolled my eyes.

"You thought wrong."

"I'm sure Austell is delighted," he muttered quietly. "Even if it is just a ruse to get you in here, he looks pretty enamoured with you. What did he say, that he'd give you the stars and lasso the moon? That's his usual line. I bet he's hoping that ring stays on your finger permanently."

"So what if he is?" I snapped, trying my utmost to keep my face neutral under the scrutiny of the room. "You're sounding a little jealous."

"I *am* jealous," he said, his voice sounding clipped. "Violently so."

"Austell is a good man. I'm sure he would make me very happy."

The hand around my waist squeezed a little tighter, pulling me even closer against him. His beard grazed my temple as he murmured into my ear.

"I'm sure that he would, but does he make you feel the way that I do? Do you go to bed at night and think of him touching you? Or is it still me that occupies your dreams?"

My body betrayed me as it reacted to him, but his words had me incensed. I couldn't believe the nerve of him, that he would have the absolute arrogance to just stroll in here and not even seem the least bit contrite.

"Don't flatter yourself. I might have fallen a little too fast and a little too hard, mistakenly believing your intentions to be genuine, but you can be certain that I won't be so easily fooled again."

He tensed slightly, and the teasing curve to his mouth disappeared along with some of his cockiness.

"Come on, Efa. After everything we've been through, you can't honestly believe that what we have, what we feel for each other, that it isn't real."

"That's exactly what I believe. I know your reputation, and I've had time to reflect on everything in your absence.

I see it for what it was now: lust, and nothing more than that."

He made a low, guttural noise, his fist trying to clench against the thin material of my dress.

"Don't you dare, Efa," he warned. "Don't you dare berate me for not being honest with you, and then lie to me about this."

I said nothing, looking over his shoulder as I continued to avoid his eyes.

"So what…you're just going to pretend that this thing between us isn't there?"

"There *is* nothing there," I retorted. "We'll just go back to being strangers again."

"Strangers?" he gasped incredulously. "You want me to pretend that I don't know you, that we never met?"

He laughed mirthlessly, his fingers gripping my waist even tighter, hard enough to leave a bruise.

"No, Efa. I can't unknow you, even if I want to. Even if I *tried* to. No, we'll never be strangers again."

This time I caught his eye, staring up at him as my body shook with rage, and we finished the dance in silence, both of us seemingly as angry as each other. When the music finally stopped, I curtseyed swiftly, and walked towards the terrace doors, stepping breathlessly out into the cold night air, pleased to be away from him. It was a clear night, the almost full moon shining brightly from where it was nestled amongst the stars. I took a moment to gather my thoughts, breathing in the fresh sea air while I tried to calm the shadows that relentlessly tried to pull me back into the ballroom. To him.

"Get a grip, Efa," I muttered to myself, closing my eyes.

The cold wind went straight through my gown and made me shiver. I was just as annoyed at myself as I was

Emrys. Barely half an hour ago Lore had told me that Noa had been close to death in Rostorrmel's dungeons and was now missing. Now I was getting distracted by the male that had betrayed my trust. I needed to sort out my priorities. I was still berating myself about it when the sound of feet shuffling on stone behind me made me jump, and I whirled around expecting to see Tanrith creeping up behind me. He had been watching me like a hawk all evening and I suspected he was primarily turned on by the way I had rather forcefully rebuffed him the previous night. But I was wrong. It wasn't him.

"I'm sorry. I didn't mean to startle you," Bran said. "I was already here when you came out and it looked like you needed a minute."

As he came towards me, the light from inside the ballroom illuminated his face and he stood next to me, lifting his face to the stars.

"Just you, me, and the moon," he said softly. "How are you, Efa?"

I stared out into the void, letting wisps of darkness escape my fingers. I sucked in a deep breath and released it in a rush.

"I'm angry, Bran," I said, voice shaking. "I'm sad. I'm disappointed. I'm a lot of things, really. Most of all I'm tired. I'm really fucking tired. How about you?"

He nodded slowly, putting his hands in his pockets.

"Yeah, I'm all of those things, too."

We stood in silence, the two of us, just looking at the sky, and I lost myself in its vastness just like my mother had always told me to when things felt too much. As usual, Bran's easy, reassuring presence calmed me despite everything, and I felt some of the rage subsiding. He drew his hand out of his pocket and held something out in the palm of his hand.

"Here," he said. "I never had the chance to give these to you before we left Esari."

In his hand he held a string of beads, all beautifully and perfectly carved. Each was made of a different kind of wood, with different symbols etched into them.

"They're worry beads, to stop you from hurting your fingers. I make them for my sister sometimes. She's prone to bouts of anxiety, too."

I took them from him, holding them up to the light as I ran my fingers over each one. This had been what he had been carving when we were in the forest or down in the dungeons interrogating Theo. He had noticed what I did with my fingers when I was nervous, and he had made them for me. It was the most thoughtful gift that anyone had ever given me.

"Thank you," I said, feeling unexpectedly emotional.

"My pleasure. I have also had some hathersage root tea sent up to your rooms. I thought that you might be running low, although I trust that your injury is healed now. You seemed to move easily enough when you were dancing."

I laughed quietly, and then turned my head to look at him miserably. For whatever reason, standing here with Bran, I felt the full weight of what I had lost when Emrys had lied to me. Tears filled my eyes and I blinked them away, looking back out in the direction of the sea.

"Are you going to counsel me to hear him out?" I asked quietly. "To tell me that I should forgive him?"

"If I did, would you listen to me?"

"No."

"Then I won't," he said simply.

"He seemed pretty cosy in there with Damen's mistress," I said irritably, annoyed at myself for sounding so jealous.

"He's only playing the game, Efa. Just like you are."

There were voices somewhere out in the palace grounds, the sound of guards greeting each other. The breeze picked up and I shivered, beginning to feel rather cold without a fur around my shoulders. I shifted restlessly next to Bran, feeling like something unsaid was hanging between us in the silence.

"You think I overreacted, back at Totease," I said, but he shook his head.

"No, I don't think that. I think you were perfectly entitled to be hurt and angry. Emrys should have been honest."

"What then? You want to say something."

He laughed softly, and smiled at me knowingly.

"Alright, I *will* say it. I *do* think you should hear him out. Anything you want to know, he'll tell you. Let him show you who he really is."

I bit my nail, scowling in to the darkness. I didn't want to listen to a word Emrys had to say. Bran gently touched my elbow.

"The choice is yours, Efa. But just remember that we're here if you need us. Always. That hasn't changed. It never will."

I closed my eyes, willing the tears not to fall.

"Goodnight, Efa," he said quietly, turning and leaving me alone with the moon.

CHAPTER 41
EFA

The moment I walked out of the palace doors later that night I wrapped myself in darkness and sprinted down to the stables. Ando waited outside, his hands deep in his coat pockets and collar turned up against the blustery wind. I dropped the shadows when I was only a few feet away, smiling slightly to myself when he nearly jumped out of his skin, but since I was cold and irritable I immediately wrapped us both up back up in them. I didn't have the patience for the rigmarole of glamoring our appearances and explaining our reasons to the guards at that hour.

"What do you know?" I asked once we were through the gatehouse.

"Noa arrived at Rostorrmel about four weeks ago according to the captain. Then ten days ago he was taken somewhere else. Alive and relatively well."

"That's it? That's all we know?"

"So far, but don't worry. The captain's primed and ready to talk."

"He fucking better be," I muttered, pulling my hood up against the cold.

As we walked through the town and headed towards the water, I breathed in deeply, the damp, salty air reminding me of Astraea. On the far side of the city, the Nijem Forest called to me. By the light of the moon I could just about see her dark mass in the distance, and I longed to go to her, craving the comfort and reassurance that I had felt the last few times she had taken me in. *Soon*, I whispered to my shadows. Tomorrow I would find a way to take the hidden passageway from the palace that led to the woods.

We walked towards the harbor, passing the rowdy tavern that Ando told me the captain liked to frequent and continuing on until we came to a small house on the sea front. It was nothing special to look at—white washed walls with a faded red front door. There were fishing nets and random bits of driftwood outside, and sand everywhere, blown up from the beach. Ando knocked on the door and a young girl opened it. She eyed us warily, relaxing when she saw Ando and opening the door wide to let us in. Lore stood in the hallway behind her, the fancy clothes of earlier discarded and replaced by the thick jumpers that were favoured by the local fishermen.

"Ready?" he asked, and I nodded.

I followed him into a small room at the back of the house, finding it devoid of any furniture except a rickety chair. The man sitting in it had his arms tied behind his back. He was a few years old than me, with reddish brown hair and a reasonably attractive face despite the split lip and the nasty black eye that was starting to form. He was the kind of man that I imagined usually thought he was a big deal, bragging to his friends and saying whatever he needed to in order to bed a girl, but right now he didn't look like such a big man. Leaning against the wall was another man I vaguely recognized as one of Lore's spies in Rostorrmel. As we entered, Lore jerked his chin and he left, leaving just the three of us with the captain. His eyes followed me as I paced slowly about the room.

"Captain Pasco, is that right?" I asked pleasantly, tossing my Valtanan blade up in the air and catching it.

"Wh-what do you want with me?" he stammered, eyes wide.

"Information. Nothing more than that. I want to know what's in that pretty little head of yours."

I smiled disarmingly, touching his mind with my shadows just enough for him to feel deeply unsettled. I could see the immediate panic on his face and he thrashed against the restraints.

"Calm down, Captain. Tell me what I want to know, and then we'll let you go. Agreed?"

He nodded warily, and I winked at him.

"Good. A man was brought to the palace recently. Blonde hair, twenties. I guess some girls might think he's good looking. He goes by the name of Noa, like the Phantom. You know him?" I waved my hand, not waiting for an answer. "I know you do, because while you were fucking one of the girls in Damen's harem, which I'm fairly sure would earn you, a *guard*, a pretty spectacular and painful punishment, you told her all about him. I want to know more."

I sat down on the floor in front of him and crossed my legs, trailing dark fingers across his mind while I coaxed him to tell me everything he knew.

"So, tell me, darling… what do you know?"

In all honesty, I hadn't expected a huge amount of resistance. You can just tell with some people. But this man didn't even try to give the impression he had any loyalty to his king. Just the suggestion of pain had words tumbling from his lips and I thought of the Loyalists who had died taking their secrets to the grave. That was true strength and honor.

"The Order brought him in," he said. "A tip off, they said, from someone called Theo."

Fucking Theo. Of course it had been him that had sold Noa out to the Order. My guess was he'd done it just before we'd kill him, too, before he'd had a chance to tell Finn what he'd done.

"Whoever it was, he'd told the Order that the guy was Gifted, but they didn't know what he could do. When they tried to detain him, he attacked them. They said it was the black terror."

I rolled my eyes at the term. That was what those in Melrith sometimes called my shadows, and what the Fae called the *noswaith*. I slowly released my own shadows, letting them drift around him playfully, gently caressing his face. The captain froze, the only movement the quivering of his lower lip.

"As you can see, I'm familiar with the black terror," I said sweetly. "Say more."

"Th-they used Faelock to subdue him, b-but it was the stronger stuff, the new poison. By the time he arrived in the dungeons he was unconscious and in a bad way, but we were told to keep him alive. So—"

"By who?" I interrupted. "Who told you to keep him alive?"

"Lady Aleta."

"Damen's mistress told you to keep him alive?"

"Y-yes."

I kissed my teeth, glancing at Lore and wondering what business Aleta had down in the dungeons inspecting

Gifted Valtanans. It seemed we had underestimated her. She was more than just a concubine.

"Continue," I ordered.

"We called in a healer."

"Let me guess," Lore said, smiling wryly. "A Valtanan healer. Probably one you already had in the dungeons. Am I right?"

Pasco nodded, his face pale and sweating. Lore chuckled darkly to himself.

"Funny how our gifts are so useful when they need them," I remarked.

"Oh, they love our gifts," he said. "They just don't like *us* having them."

I returned my attention to the man in the chair.

"Continue," I muttered again.

"It took almost a week but he eventually recovered, and then one day he was taken elsewhere."

"Where?"

"I don't know… they didn't say."

I tightened the hold I had on his mind, watching him screw up his face in pain.

"Where?" I demanded, louder this time.

"I don't know! They took him down to the coves in the middle of the night. Wherever they took him, it was by boat. That's all I know, I swear!"

I sat back on my hands and looked at him. I believed him. I'd interrogated enough people in my life to know when someone was telling the truth, and this one had spilled his secrets far too easily. He hadn't held back.

"If they took him from the coves and not the harbor, then they can't have taken him too far," Lore said.

"Unless they were just taking him out to a larger boat somewhere further out."

"Do you know?" Lore asked the captain.

"It wouldn't be far. They like to keep them close by, the ones with the unusual gifts. They said they were taking him to the Dreor."

"The dreor? What is that, a person? A place?"

He shook his head and I looked at Lore but by the look on his face it meant as much to him as it did me. I stood up, dusted off my pants and left the room feeling just as frustrated, if not more. Where the fuck was Noa, and what were they doing to him? I needed to speak to Torr. Outside in the narrow hallway I paused to slip my knife back into my boot. Lore and Ando had followed me out and I looked at them quizzically.

"Have you ever heard of a Valtanan who could deflect another gift?"

"What do you mean?" Lore frowned, and I tried again.

"Say, for example, I could wield fire or I was an Empath. Could someone have the ability to be impervious to it? As if they can just, I don't know...repel whatever you're trying to do to them?"

Lore looked thoughtful, running his hand across his head.

"There was a family... I'm trying to remember... yeah, there *was* a family. In Cayam, I think it was. This is going back a few years now, but I think that one of the children was Gifted. Not the parents, they had absolutely nothing, not even slow aging. But the boy was seemingly unaffected by other abilities."

"What happened to him?"

"He got into a fight one day, I seem to recall. Nothing serious, just lads being lads. One was a fire wielder, actually, and he used it against the other in the heat of the moment, no pun intended, but it just bounced right off." Lore pulled a face, searching his memory. "It was a few years ago, like I said, but I'm pretty sure that the Order found out about it. Why do you ask?"

"Because Damen seems to have acquired that ability from somewhere. As have some of the Nothori."

"Ah. That's not good news."

"No."

I could see the wheels turning in his head. If that were the case, it would probably mean that they'd be able to see right through his glamor, too, which had made his trip into the palace riskier than we'd first thought. I started moving towards the front door but when I turned back to face Lore he was grinning. He cocked his head at me.

"Are we going to talk about what you did in there, by the way?"

I breathed a laugh, pulling my fur coat tightly around me before I went back out into the wind.

"No, we're not."

"I've known you for what, fifteen years? I've never known that you could do that. Or Noa. I'm impressed that you managed to keep that hidden for so long."

"We all have secrets, Lore. I'm sure you have a few of your own tucked away."

He chuckled and I opened the front door, stepping out to the sound of waves lapping against the shore. Ando was close behind me.

"I need to talk to Torr Voss. If they took him somewhere by boat, Torr might know. The *Panacea* is docked in the harbor, although you probably already know that. Can you arrange for him to meet me? Tomorrow night, down by the coves."

"Yeah," he said, placing a hand on his nephew's shoulder. "Ando will let you know if there's a problem."

"Any word on what Finn is up to?"

"No, worryingly he seems to have gone to ground, but

I'd be willing to bet he's still in the city. Even my spies can't find him.

"All right," I said, sighing. "Thank you for arranging tonight. I appreciate it. We better get back anyway, before anyone notices we're missing. I'll see you tomorrow."

I had only taken two steps when I thought of something else. I stopped and turned back.

"Lore," I called, waiting for him to pop his head back out of the door. "Drown the captain."

CHAPTER 42

EFA

I left Ando at the stables and jogged the final stretch back toward the palace, Eseld's words about its beauty echoing in my mind. The different levels of the building rose like stacking tiers of light against the black sky, its walls glowing with sconces while above, a million stars glittered in the velvet dark. For a moment, it looked almost unreal, like something plucked out of the folktales my aunt used to tell us.

I waited for two Order priests to vanish from view before slipping back into the palace, my senses on full alert. Every step I took reminded me how vulnerable I was here. My shadows might hide me from most, but these days I couldn't rely on them to remain unseen. If I were caught, dressed in dark clothes and roaming unescorted through the corridors, I suspected there was no plausible explanation that could save me.

My boots were quiet against the stone as I tried to recall the quickest route back to the Esari rooms, but somewhere between half-remembered turns and sheer guesswork, I miscalculated and ended up taking a servant's staircase, emerging into one of the palace's grand galleries. It was lined with enormous gold-framed portraits and oil paintings, interspersed with relics of armor, swords, pottery, and ornaments. I vaguely remembered there being a pair of narwhal tusks at one time.

Halfway along the gallery I heard voices, and I cursed under my breath. It was the worst possible place to be caught. The gallery stretched wide and long, its alcoves spilling pools of shadows between the windows. No other staircase broke the monotony. No doors offered escape. With the voices growing closer, I had no choice: I started to run, pulling essence to me to make me faster. But even that wasn't enough. I wasn't going to make it. Then, just as the night before, my shadows burst into life, and out of nowhere large hands seized me, hauling me off the ground. The air left my lungs in a sharp gasp as I was lifted, carried, and then shoved into one of the alcoves, my back hitting the cold stone wall.

"Lucky I found you again, smuggler," Emrys murmured against my ear, his voice a low ripple that sent shivers down my spine.

He caged me in with his arms, body towering over mine. I was used to his size, but in his Fae form that was something more, something different, every line of him carrying a power that felt untamed and dangerous. He was intoxicating. I breathed in the smell of him before my head regained control, putting my hands on his chest to try and push him away. He didn't even budge, and I glared up at him.

"What are you doing?" I hissed.

"Saving your life."

The voices were close now, echoing down the gallery. In seconds they'd be upon us, and we'd be seen.

"How, exactly?" I demanded in a whisper.

Without warning, his mouth crashed down onto mine, and Gods, I wanted to resist him. But the moment his lips claimed me, the fight bled away. The completeness I felt in his arms was devastating, pure ecstasy that unraveled every ounce of resolve I had left. I lost myself in him. In the heat of his mouth, in the familiar taste of him that wiped away weeks of pain and fury, and that drowned out the betrayal and grief until all I could think was *fuck, I missed him*. My hands fisted into his shoulders, dragging him closer, desperate to breathe him in like air. Oblivious to the danger, to where we were, I clawed at his back, arching into him as his body pressed mine against the wall. A gasp broke from my throat as I felt him hardening, answering the urgency that roared through me.

"Well, well. What do we have here?"

The voice was enough to break the spell, and I forced myself away from Emrys, my breath tearing free, ragged and shaking. My face was flushed, my lips bruised, and I almost laughed at the sheer madness of it, caught between lust and peril. I'd been so caught up in him that I'd forgotten that I was even running from them in the first place. Emrys leaned back just enough to look at me, his hands still tight at my waist. His grin was slow, infuriatingly confident, his voice pitched low and husky. As the Order priests smirked, he lifted his head and winked at them roguishly.

"I'm afraid you've rather caught us out," he said without even the least bit of shame. "Do me a favour, lads, and don't let Lord Esari know about this. He'd be crushed."

I closed my eyes and hung my head, groaning inwardly. Whilst I had to admit that it was a good excuse for being out this late, the last thing I needed were wild rumors circulating the palace about my infidelity. It added a whole extra layer of complexity that I really didn't need, and it wouldn't do Austell's reputation any good either. But the Order priests just chuckled conspiratorially, and I was grateful that they didn't seem suspicious in any way.

"Your secret is safe with us, my Lord," said the taller of the two. "Apologies for the, uh… interruption."

I smiled tightly and turned away to look out of the window, watching the sea ripple in the moonlight. As they walked away I heard them muttering and laughing.

"The Dark Prince strikes again," one of them joked.

"Never could keep his hands off of Lord Mirle's girls, could he?"

Their voices faded out as they reached the end of the gallery, and I finally let out the frustrated breath I had been holding. My heart was still pounding, and I was irritated with myself both for getting caught in the first place, and then somehow ending up in Emrys's arms. Despite everything in me still pulling towards him, I pushed him away and ran a hand through my hair, my head firmly back in control of my heart.

"What are you doing out here?" I demanded.

"You're welcome, by the way," he said. I sighed crossly, rolling my eyes. "I couldn't sleep, so I came out to explore."

"Looking for the Amberstone?"

"On the off chance, yeah, but I'd bet my life on it not being here. Anyway, I could ask you the same thing."

"What I'm doing has nothing to do with you anymore."

He took a breath and stared at me for a second, then shrugged sadly, looking down at his hands. When he lifted his head back up there was something in his eyes—something so unguarded it caught me off balance. My heart ached despite myself. I needed to get away from him before I did something I'd regret.

"Efa, please—" he began, but I cut him off.

"Good night, Trystan," I said.

He flinched at the name, the faintest shadow of hurt crossing his features, but I didn't wait for him to respond. Without another glance, I turned away, and left the alcove in silence.

CHAPTER 43
EFA

The sound of waves crashing against the cliffs pulled me from a deep, dreamless sleep. I cracked my eyes and found the room filled with golden sunlight and closed them again, nuzzling into my pillow and savouring the warmth of my bed. Soft kisses were being trailed up the inside of my thighs and I sighed, feeling my blood heat. My shadows trembled and my breath quickened as I opened my legs wider, urging the kisses higher.

"I have always been yours, *elnaya*."

My eyes snapped open with a jolt. I was alone in the room. There was no sunshine, only the usual weak, gray light that I had grown used to since arriving. I shut my eyes and leaned my head back into my pillow, staring up at the ceiling. My heart was still racing and I pressed my palms into my eyes. I was almost starting to miss my usual nightmares. At least they were always been predictable.

"How did last night go?" Austell asked me when I finally dragged myself out of bed and into the sitting room.

I slumped down into the chair opposite him and Nev

brought me over a cup of mint tea. I wasn't sure where to even start with the previous night. So much had happened, but all I could think about was Emrys's lips on mine.

"The captain was helpful," I said as Arella emerged from her room. "He confirmed what we thought: that Noa was here and that it was Theo who sold him out to the Order. They brought him here three weeks ago after he used his shadows to try and evade capture, and to subdue him they used the new Faelock. It almost killed him."

Arella gasped quietly, covering her mouth with her hands.

"Luckily for him, someone wanted him kept alive, almost certainly because of his gifts. He was healed, and about a week ago he left the dungeons and was taken somewhere by boat."

"Do we know where?" Austell asked, leaning forward to rest his elbows on his knees.

"The captain was under the impression that it was close by. I need to speak to Torr and see if he's noticed anything unusual or out of place." I looked at Arella. "Is he back yet? I asked Lore to set up a meeting for tonight down in the coves."

"Yes," she said, nodding. "The *Panacea* arrived back yesterday. She's in the harbor."

I took a sip of my tea, willing the smell of mint to settle my nerves.

"Did you get back into the palace last night without any trouble?" Nev asked.

I paused, studying him and wondering if he was asking out of curiosity or because he knew something, but he looked innocent enough.

"A couple of close calls," I said casually, deciding not to mention my meeting with Emrys in the gallery. "What do we know about Aleta?"

Austell sat back in his chair and rubbed his beard.

"Not much, really. Her mother was Azulian, but I don't know about her father. She appeared at court some time during Novos's reign, an ambitious social climber by all accounts. She was sleeping with Damen long before he took the throne, but it was only when he made himself king that he officially made her his mistress and started letting her have more authority."

"According to the servants here," Arella added, "she's a power hungry, cold-hearted bitch. They say she'll back-stab and sell out her closest friends if she thinks it'll help elevate her status."

"Just Damen's type then," Nev said dryly.

"Exactly. So why hasn't he married her?" Arella asked. "If he's so fond of her, and it's been so long, why not make her queen?"

I shot her an amused look.

"Why aren't you and Torr married?"

"Fair point," she said, grinning.

"He'd never make her queen," Austell said, getting up to refill his own cup of tea. "To crown her would be to share his power, and Damen would never give anything he could keep for himself."

Nev gave a quiet, thoughtful shake of his head.

"I've always thought there was another reason," he said quietly, lifting his head to look at me. "Aemylia."

I took a long, deep breath, recalling my conversation with Negan back at Totease.

"You know, Negan said something to me back in Esari. She said that everything is always about love, or the absence of it. That everything happening is about my mother. I thought that she'd meant Damen hated her, and on some level I'm pretty sure he does. But Negan, she thought—"

"That he still loves her," Nev finished for me.

"Yeah."

"I suspect you're right," Austell said, taking a seat again. "Why do you ask about Aleta, anyway?"

"Because the captain said that it was Aleta who ordered for Noa to be kept alive. She's not just Damen's mistress, Aus. She's much more involved than we thought."

"That's interesting," he said. His fingers tapped once against the arm of his chair before stilling, the only sign of him turning my words over in his mind. "Perhaps we've misjudged her."

"I learned something interesting today, too," Arella said. "I had myself a little rendezvous with a very handsome footman last night. It turns out that our friend, the recently deceased High Priestess, Gods rest her, was here at Rostorrmel a few weeks ago along with all of the other High Priests and Priestesses."

"For what purpose?" I asked.

"A 'demonstration'. He said an unknown man arrived at the palace late in the evening and was taken up to the room they were gathered in. All of the servants were made to leave, and then a few hours later, the man left again by boat. And Efa, we got it wrong in the temple. She wasn't saying 'door', she was saying 'dreor'."

"The captain said that last night, too. He said that they were taking Noa to the 'dreor'."

"What or who is that?" Nev asked.

"Exactly what I asked. The answer is we've no idea. I've never heard it before in my life, and neither had Lore."

"You know who *would* know the answer to that?" Austell mused. "Cadoc."

I sighed. Didn't I know it? I picked up my cup of tea

and sipped it slowly, brooding silently. The man had left by boat. Was it possible that he and Noa had gone back to the same place? Austell nodded at Nev, stood up and stretched, putting his empty teacup down on the side and strolling to the door.

"Time for council again?" I asked.

"Unfortunately, yes. Today it's all about farming and agriculture. By the way, this was left for me this morning. Any idea what it is?"

He picked something up from the table and carried it over to me. It was a small bunch of herbs, tied together with black string. I breathed in sharply, feeling my jaw clench.

"Austell the Gardener," I said with a dry smile. "I'm surprised you don't know what this is. It's the herb that Faelock is derived from. It's a threat from Finn. He's in the city."

"Ah," he said, adjusting his collar. "Well, I can't say I haven't been expecting this. I am your fiancé after all. But as I said back in Esari, it's a risk I'm willing to take."

He took a few steps toward me, leaning down to brush his lips against my temple.

"Take care today, Efa," he murmured. "I'll see you later."

After they left, Arella eyed me curiously.

"What? What's that look for?"

"Why didn't you tell me Finn was here? Or anyone, for that matter?"

"You'd have only worried, I guess. What good would knowing he was here do anyone?"

"Well, he's making threats on us, so..."

"If he wanted us dead, we would be, Rell," I said shortly. "I don't recall my previous lovers being sent Faelock posies. They just turned up dead in their beds.

Besides, Finn would really have to have some balls to kill one of Damen's lords. No… this is Finn playing a game. He's teasing me. He knows there's nothing stopping one of you from taking him out, so he's keeping a low profile, but he's still letting us know that he's watching, waiting patiently. That he can get to me, or Austell, if he wants to."

Arella leaned forward on her knees, staring at me.

"Did anything happen last night?" she asked suddenly.

"No, why?"

"You just seem… off."

I averted my eyes and stood up. I felt bad about lying to her again, but I didn't have the energy to get into it with her when I could barely get my own thoughts together.

"I'm just tired. I think I'm going to take a walk down to the coves and clear my head for a bit. Get some fresh air. What will you do?"

"I'm going to take a long bath, and then go down to the kitchens with some excuse I'm yet to think of. Do you know how much gossip there is down there?"

I laughed and then went to get dressed. It was milder than the day before and the weak sun was trying it's best to break through the cloud, but there was still a chill in the air. The sea was relatively calm and I stood watching the waves once I reached the bottom of the cliff path. I was almost out of my mind with worry about Noa, but I was trying to put it to the back of my mind so I could continue to function since I needed my wits about me. I was also frustrated with myself, annoyed about my reaction to Emrys when I was supposed to be putting him behind me.

I dropped my hands to my sides and wandered along the water's edge, the sand damp and cold beneath my boots. At first, I thought I was alone, but then I saw her. Half-hidden by the jagged rocks at the end of the bay, Caja stood knee-deep in the surf, waves breaking against her legs. Her hair whipped around her face, dark and wet with spray, her thin frame trembling as though she were carved from grief itself. My chest tightened. She hadn't seen me yet. Or maybe she had and didn't care. I picked up my pace, looking around to see if anyone else was around, but the beach was deserted.

"Rough morning?" I called softly, the words barely carrying over the crash of the tide.

She laughed, the sound brittle and broken, but didn't turn around. The weight of it sat heavy in the air between us, pulling me awkwardly closer, unsure of what to say to someone so clearly at the edge. The only thing that stumbled from my lips was, "Tell me about the oath line."

For a long moment she was silent, just staring out at the endless water. Just when I thought she wasn't going to answer, another harsh laugh broke from her.

"It was her idea. The mistress. She said the rite would keep Talan alive."

"Aleta was involved?"

"Yes." Caja's voice cracked. "That was the deal I made to save my brother's life. Tie my life to Canver's, and keep him breathing in Rostorrmel's dungeons. That was the price."

This was it, then. This was why she had chosen Canver. Not greed, or ambition. Survival. Family. A bargain that had stripped her soul as surely as it bound her body. She had made a deal, just like I had.

"So, what's changed?" I asked gently.

Something had happened to bring her here, to this moment. She drew a ragged breath that seemed to hollow her out from the inside.

"My brother is dead," she whispered. "Executed in Cayam two days ago." Her words shattered against the waves, carried off into the vast, merciless sea. "They stole his gift, and then discarded him as if he meant nothing."

I closed my eyes, shaking my head sadly.

"What was your brother's gift?" I asked softly, though a part of me already knew.

"It wasn't a gift. At least, we never thought of it that way. But now I see it. It is one of the most dangerous things there could be."

"The power to remain unaffected by other gifts."

She nodded slowly, as if forcing the admission out, then turned her head just enough to glance at me over her shoulder. Her eyes were bright and focused, and I realized that for the first time I was seeing her sober and not under the influence of Silvermist. Tears cascaded down her cheeks. She was a woman who had reached her limits, and if I'd not found her when I did, I wondered if I'd have ever seen her again. Taking a step forward, I fumbled with the sleeve of my coat and pulled it up to reveal my own oath line. Her lips parted slightly as she stared at it, and then slowly she lifted her eyes to mine.

"Who is it?"

"Finn Yadari."

"The Nevedeno leader. I know him."

I took a step forward, the waves lapping at my boots and soaking through them.

"Listen to me, Caja. I might not be able to do anything about Finn, but I'm going to kill everyone else. Canver, Tanrith, Perran, Brayson, Damen… and anyone else that dares to hurt us. I *will* get you out of this, I promise, but I need you to be strong for just a few more days. Can you do that?"

Her lower lip trembled, and I could see the storm breaking inside her. She had nothing left to give. Killing Canver hadn't necessarily been high on my list of things to do, but now that I knew what he had done to her, what he had reduced her to, he had earned himself a swift death.

"Just a couple of days, Caja," I said. "And you'll be free of him. I give you my word. You can do this. I know you can."

She stood utterly still as I held out my hand to her. For what felt like eternity I waited for her to take it, thinking she would never move, and then finally she turned around, wading through the waves to place her hand in mine. It was cold and light, so fragile that I was afraid it might vanish if I held too tightly.

We walked in silence back to the palace, her skirts whispering in the sand, trailing like shadows behind her. At the top of the imperial staircase, I let her go, sighing heavily as I watched her small figure disappear. Turning away, I knew I couldn't go back to my own rooms. Not yet. I needed air, distance, something different. Without letting myself think too much, I spun on my heel and jogged back down the stairs toward the library.

CHAPTER 44
EMRYS

My finger idly drew a symbol in the dirt as I sat on the forest floor with my back against a fallen trunk. It was the symbol for life, or at least I thought it was. Maybe it was the symbol for death. I didn't really care, and as I traced it again and again I let my eyes glaze over. It was quiet in the Nijem. No wind blowing, no loud roar of the ocean, just the birds singing and the whispering trees above me. This far in I couldn't see the palace or the city, either. It was the solitude that I had been craving.

I started to draw another symbol, but I could barely remember my mother's teachings now. I'm not sure I'd ever really got the hang of them, not like Evyn had. I'd never had the patience to learn them, but he had just picked them up so quickly and easily, sitting for hours in the depths of the Citadel library in Cyfnos, poring over ancient tomes and scrolls to learn more. I'd never liked to be inside for too long, preferring to be out in the fresh air. That was one of the big differences between us. Evyn preferred to read about it, whereas I preferred to just live it. I still remembered the excitement on his face when he had told me how runes could strengthen our abilities if they were used in just the right way, and the unease settling in the pit of my stomach as I watched him draw the symbols onto his own skin

I pushed my hand through my hair and looked up at the sky. My worries hadn't mattered, in the end. My brother was gone and none of my fears had come to light, but I missed him more than I could put into words. I missed Efa, too. I hadn't realized just how much until I had seen her face again the night before, my jealousy flaring when I'd seen her in Austell's arms. But when I'd kissed her, I felt just for that brief, blissful moment, that everything was going to be all right. I'd felt like I was home, and when she walked away again it had hurt even worse than the first time. I had lain awake all night wondering if the Seer had been wrong. Maybe no amount of patience would ever bring her back to me.

I was so lost in my thoughts that it took me a while to notice that the sounds in the forest had changed. Only when my neck prickled did I realize that it had gone absolutely silent around me. Slowly, I reached for my sword, feeling the hairs on my arms start to rise, but when the temperature dropped suddenly, getting so cold that my breath misted in front of my face, I stopped reaching for it. I wouldn't need it. This was no soldier or assassin. This was something much more deadly.

Movement between the trees caught my eye but there was nothing there, a shadow perhaps, or a trick of the light. I waited patiently, knowing that she would take her time in appearing. I remembered the symbol for death and I drew it in the dirt. Minutes passed, and then suddenly she was there, standing a few meters in front of me.

"Hello, Emrys," the *Raeth* said, her voice light and breathy.

She was as beautiful as Morgan had said she was, with flawless, pale skin and long, dark hair. Runes were tattooed on her exposed skin, and she wore a flowing black dress and a heavy fur stole, her lips stained blood red. She was enchanting and wholly unnatural, an ancient creature merely presenting as a woman. She might have looked soft and delicate, her expression faintly seductive, but there was no doubt in my mind that she had come to claim me, and that I was powerless to do anything about it. I closed my eyes and let out a long breath. *Too soon*, I thought.

"You are not surprised to see me," she said.

"No," I said, opening my eyes again. "But I'd hoped I would have more time before I did."

"Doesn't everyone?" she replied, spreading her hands wide.

"I just need to make sure that she's safe. I need her to know that I…"

My words fell away and I hung my head, suddenly feeling so tired. How could this be the way that it all ended? What was the point of us being Gods Fated if I died without her ever knowing how I felt about her? Without her ever knowing the truth? The *Raeth's* eyes studied the crude symbols I had drawn in front of me, razor sharp teeth appearing as she smiled.

"The rune stones have been thrown. I have seen into the future. This is what must happen for her to live. For her to become who she needs to be. For balance to be restored."

For her to live. It was all the *Raeth* needed to say. I nodded my acceptance.

"Your fate has already been decided, Emrys."

I smiled wryly, dragging a hand across my face and closing my eyes.

"Then she is my fate after all," I said.

I heard her footsteps on the damp ground, and I opened my eyes expecting to find those otherworldly eyes burning into mine. Instead I found myself blinking and laughing in surprise. The Gods were playing with me. Clearly she hadn't expected to find me here either. It was written all over her face as she stalked towards me. The laughter died on my lips as quickly as it came and I just looked at her, drinking her in as if it was the last time I would ever look upon her face. Maybe it would be.

"Efa." I breathed her name like a prayer.

She had caught the sun in Esari, and there was a smattering of freckles sitting prettily across her nose and cheeks. She had lost weight, and there were dark circles under her eyes as if she hadn't been sleeping well, and the same frown that had been on her face the night before pulled at her forehead again as she stared at me. There was pain in her eyes, and I knew that had caused that. I couldn't forgive myself for how badly I had hurt her.

"What are you doing out here?" she asked, her voice harsh and abrupt.

"Having my fate decided for me, it seems."

I glanced around but the *Raeth* was nowhere to be seen. Perhaps I had only imagined her. Efa rolled her eyes, turning away from me. I sprung to my feet, desperate for her not to leave.

"Efa, please talk to me. Please let me explain."

"No, Trystan," she said loudly, walking faster. "I have nothing to say to you. I don't want to hear your excuses."

Hearing her call me that again was like a knife to my heart. The name symbolized everything that I wasn't; everything that I didn't want to be. It was the name my father had insisted on when I was born, and was synonymous with the fear and dread that people experienced when they thought of the Dark Prince. No one but my father and elder brother ever called me that. I couldn't bear for her to use that name, too.

"I don't want to give you excuses, Efa. I want to tell you the truth!"

She whirled to face me looking absolutely furious.

"The truth? You should have told me that a long time ago."

My own temper began to rise, exasperated by her hypocrisy and her unwillingness to even let me explain.

"Like you told me?"

Her face turned dark, and she almost ran towards me, jabbing a finger into my chest.

"Are you actually asking me that?" she hissed. "I haven't been that girl since I was eight years old, because if anyone knew who *I* was they'd have murdered me, or worse. But you... you chose to hide who you are because it suited your own selfish purpose. There's a big difference."

I took a step back from her, trying to get a grip on my own anger and frustration. I knew that I had fucked up, but her stubbornness and righteousness was starting to piss me off.

"Answer me this: if I'd told you who I was in the mountains... if I'd been upfront with you then, would you have come with me to Esari?"

She said nothing, her chest rising and falling with furious breaths. She didn't need to say anything though. I knew the answer.

"That's what I thought. You know that almost none of it is true, don't you? The Dark Prince is nothing more than a legend, a host of lies and fabrications. Gods, Morgan and Cadoc deliberately spread half of those rumors because if people feared me, it made it easier to do the things my brother ordered me to do, without having to resort to violence and destruction. But I'm not that person, Efa. It's not me."

"No? So you're telling me that you *didn't* seduce the woman Austell was courting and then refuse to marry her once you'd ruined her reputation?"

I blinked, caught off guard by her accusation, though I shouldn't have been surprised. I hadn't handled myself with much grace on that occasion, even though it was blown massively out of proportion, and Austell was still sore about it. I didn't doubt that he'd told Efa to twist the knife in and really turn her against me. I wouldn't lie to her though.

"Yes, I—"

"And you *didn't* slit a man's throat up in Cryf's Gap and hang him in the middle of the square for the whole town to see?"

"Yes," I growled. "And I'd fucking do it again to any man who touched you like that."

"And you *weren't* seen in Nissae the night that it burned?"

I sighed, pushing back my hair in exasperation.

"I was there, but—"

"Then I think you need to take a long, hard look at yourself, *Trystan*. Because right now to me, you look exactly like the Dark Prince."

I stood there speechless, opening and closing my mouth like some kind of idiot as she turned on her heel and set off again. I paced back and forth a few steps, clenching and unclenching my fists. I was frustrated and exasperated with myself more than anything, out of time, and with only myself to blame. But still I couldn't bear the thought of her not knowing the truth.

"Efa," I called after her, trying one last time to reach her. "I know you don't want to listen to me right now, and I understand that. You have every right to be angry with me, and never want to speak to me again. But please..."

She paused, but didn't turn around. I took a deep breath and sent a silent prayer to the Gods. *Please give me a chance to make this right. Give me just a bit more time.*

"When you're ready to hear me out, I'll tell you anything you want to know. No lies. No excuses."

She stood silently, and for the briefest moment I thought she was going to stay, but then she spoke into the quiet. I thought I heard her voice tremble.

"Do you know what I've learned from all this, Emrys? I've learned that the saddest thing about betrayal is that it hurts the most when it's the people you cared most about. The ones you thought would never hurt you."

She carried on walking.

~

I sat down heavily on the fallen tree, my head in my hands. I didn't know what else I could do.

"Tell me about the Amberstone."

I almost jumped out of my skin. I hadn't heard her come back.

"I don't want to know anything else. No excuses, no justifications. Nothing. Just tell me about this fucking stone."

"All right," I said, sitting upright, overjoyed to just have the chance to finally speak to her. "I'll try to put this simply, because the details are… put it this way, it can take some getting your head around it. The Amberstone is a big deal to us. It's critical to Fae powers. It's what keeps everything in balance, everything in careful equilibrium. Without it… well, I'll get to that.

"In the Northern Realm, we have a celebration for the spring equinox. *Forar*, it's called, in our tongue. It's traditionally the time when the ice melts in the fjords and everything begins to thaw. Most of the villages have their own way of celebrating, but my father and Aubrey always celebrated in Nosfell. The Amberstone would be brought from the Ro Temple just east of Nosfell to the city for a traditional, very formal ritual. It's the *only* time that the Amberstone ever leaves the Ro Temple, and it's been that way for centuries."

Efa took a few steps forward and sat down on the tree trunk. She was still keeping her distance, but I figured this was progress. At least, I hoped it was.

"Cad was responsible for bringing the Amberstone to Nosfell. He was escorting Aneira, my brother's wife, too. Bran and I had been dealing with something on the border of the Rhew Woods and we were on our way there with Evyn, my brother, when we were attacked. They had Faelock and the element of surprise, and whether they wanted me dead and were unsuccessful, I don't know, but one thing was for sure. They *had* come for Evyn."

A crease formed between her brows. Her eyes hadn't left my face while I'd been speaking and my hands were desperate to reach out to her.

"Why?"

"Leverage," I said. "It was only when we reached Nosfell the next morning that we learned about Damen's impending attack on Nissae. Aubrey's first response was to send aid, because why would we not? Your parents were our allies. They always had been. But that was before Aubrey knew about Evyn. Before Damen ambushed Cadoc's party, abducted Aneira, and stole the Amberstone."

CHAPTER 45
EFA

"That's how Cadoc came to be disgraced," I murmured to myself, slowly piecing everything together. "It wasn't just any lord's wife. He lost the Fae Queen."

Emrys nodded, his lips pressed together in a thin line. Yes, I could see now why that would be such a big deal.

"But that doesn't explain why you betrayed us," I snapped. "Surely what it meant is that we had a common enemy. Damen was preparing to obliterate Nissae, and he'd committed an act of war by abducting two members of the Fae royal family and stealing the Amberstone. I don't understand. Your forces were on the border. Why wouldn't you just come out fighting with everything that you had?"

"That's the thing, Efa. Our forces were decimated when we lost the Amberstone."

I blinked; not understanding, and then I remembered what Negan had said about feeling her abilities weaken around the time that Nissae had fallen. She'd said they had never recovered. Suddenly, realisation dawned.

"When he stole the Amberstone, you lost your power."

"Yes. Most of them, at least. Our armies weren't used to fighting without them. It was a fundamental weakness in our defensive position that, in our arrogance, we had never considered."

"You've never used the *noswaith*. I've never seen it."

He slowly raised his eyes to mine.

"I can't, Efa. I held onto it for as long as I could out of sheer desperation and determination, but by the morning after Nissae had fallen, it was gone."

I stared at him blankly.

"But the others, they still have their abilities..."

"Yes, but they aren't what they were. That's why Bran struggled so much to heal you, and why Morgan and Cadoc find it so difficult to pass messages to one another. I can still compel people, too, but it's harder to do, and it has its limits."

I stood up and started walking back and forth.

"But that just makes your army the same as any human army. They were still soldiers, still capable of fighting."

"I agree. In fact, I counseled my brother to send them anyway. Our army was built around our abilities, and losing them would throw us off, naturally, but we were still a phenomenal strength. I was overruled. Aubrey believed that if they went, the losses would be catastrophic, and he was unwilling to risk Aneira and Evyn's lives. Damen threatened to kill them if we went to Nissae's aid."

I stopped pacing and stared at him again.

"And?"

"I defied my brother. I pulled rank and gave orders for our forces to march down through Tywell's Pass anyway. That's when they killed Evyn. I had no choice but to pull them back if we wanted Aneira returned. And she was, but only after Nissae had fallen. But Damen never returned the

Amberstone, and that is why we have never fought back. Because he threatened to destroy it, and if that happened, we would lose everything, permanently. It would be devastating to the Fae."

I understood it, I really did. The rational part of my brain recognized the impossible situation that they had been placed in. Damen had forced them to choose between saving the people they loved more than anything, and sending aid to their allies across the border. And I understood how they must have felt. The Gods knew I was experiencing it right then with Noa. But if it were me, and I was faced with saving Noa or seeing an entire city burn to the ground… well, I knew what I would have done, as hard as the choice would have been.

"I tried, Efa. My brother died because of the choices I made that night."

"And my heart breaks for you, Emrys! But while you lost your brother that day, we lost *everything*. Thousands died. Children died. And hundreds more have been persecuted, imprisoned and murdered since then. Because of the choices *your* brother made."

I passed a hand over my face, pinching the bridge of my nose as I shut my eyes. A fresh headache was forming.

"It was an impossible situation," I said quietly. "I understand that. It doesn't mean that I can forgive it."

When I looked back at him he looked inconsolable, pain written all over his face. My shadows keened, pulling towards him, and a very small part of me wanted to go to him, to hold him and kiss him until it all went away. But nothing had ever been that simple.

"Trust me when I say that I understand some of how you felt that night," I said quietly. "He has Noa, Emrys."

His eyes widened and he muttered a curse.

"I guess now it's my turn to decide on what I'll do to get him back," I said quietly.

I began to walk away from him. I had come to the forest to try and find some kind of peace and clarity, but now I felt even more lost and confused. I heard him stand up as if he was going to come after me, and I held up my hand.

"Don't follow me, Emrys. I'm going to need some time to think all of this through."

And as I walked back into the trees, he didn't follow me. But even though I'd told him not to, I couldn't help but wish that he had.

CHAPTER 46

EFA

When I got back to our rooms, Nev and Austell were still gone, but Arella was practically bouncing off the walls. Since we'd arrived at the palace, when she wasn't out eavesdropping in the stables or kitchens, she had been in the passages out of curiosity more than necessity, and her excitement was because that morning she had discovered not one but two new entry points in to them.

"I wonder just how many there are in the palace," she said. "They must be everywhere. Do you really think Damen doesn't know that they exist?"

"I honestly think that we would have seen signs," I said, "or that we'd have met someone in there by now."

I sat down in one of the chairs in the sitting room and reached out for the blanket folded on the side table.

"My father was a cautious man. I don't think he'd have told anyone in case the information got into the wrong hands, and don't forget *we* only discovered them by chance because we were particularly inquisitive children with too much time on our hands."

I pulled the blanket around me and leaned my head back, feeling weary.

"Where did you go this morning?" she asked me.

"The beach, and then out into the forest via the passages. I thought that maybe I could sit on my own and actually hear myself think for a few minutes, but it seemed she had other plans. Emrys was there."

"Oh?"

I filled her in quickly on finding Caja down at the beach and then my heated conversation with Emrys. She listened quietly, brow furrowed as I told her what he'd said about Damen abducting Aneira and Evyn, and stealing the Amberstone.

"So Evyn is dead?" she said, looking confused. "But all these years they've been telling everyone, even their own people, that he was abroad. Why wouldn't they say anything?"

"Your guess is as good as mine, but I think that they were secretly humiliated and had their egos bruised. They think of themselves as this all-powerful Fae race, and yet somehow Damen, a mere human with no gifts or special abilities, has somehow outsmarted them. He took their queen, their prince, and their most sacred artifact, and then he threatened to destroy it all, holding it over them for *years*. Acknowledging what had happened would have made them look foolish, or worse, weak."

"But they could have made up some excuse at any time in the past two decades. They could have said he died at sea, or from an illness whilst he was abroad."

I shrugged my shoulders, just as puzzled as she was.

"People do odd things when they're grieving, and I suspect Aubrey has a large ego. What I'm wondering is how he explained the loss of power to his people. Surely they asked questions."

"Maybe you need to take Emrys up on his offer to tell you everything," Arella said, twisting a loose lock of hair in her fingers. "There are a lot of questions that we don't have answers to. And I bet that it's important to whatever Damen is planning, too."

I said nothing, staring down at my hands as I picked at my nails.

"Seeing him today in the forest has unsettled you," she said quietly. "You missed him, didn't you?"

"More than anything," I whispered, my voice quivering slightly. "But I don't trust him anymore. How can I really believe anything he says? And what about the claims that he was in Nissae murdering our people that night? He admitted to me that he was there..."

"That just doesn't really fit with what he told you earlier though, does it? About wanting to send aid to Valtana."

"But what if he's lying to me, Rell? Again."

She looked at me for an age, biting her lip as her eyes searched my face.

"I'm not even sure that you truly believe that."

I scowled, opening my mouth to protest but she held up a hand.

"I know you, Efa, sometimes better than you know yourself. If you honestly thought that was the person he was, that he had stood on Valtanan soil and murdered our people, and that after all this he would *still* lie to your face... well, I don't think we'd even be having this conversation right now. You'd have simply walked away. Or actually, more likely, you'd have shattered his mind and left him dead in the forest."

I dropped my head and closed my eyes, afraid to admit that she was right. Everything just felt so fucked up.

"You're hurt," she said gently. "He didn't tell you the

truth when he should have done and that takes time to get over, but I think this conflict that you're feeling is because deep down, you're trying to reconcile the male that you know and care about with the one in the rumors and stories, and if I'm honest, it just isn't quite adding up."

I reached over to grab a cushion, placing it under my head and burrowing down under the blanket while I brooded and sulked.

"Give it time," she said simply, sitting back in her chair. "Just think it over. Time heals most things. "

"Does it?" I asked, more to myself than her.

After a while, I must have dozed off, because I jolted awake at the sound of Austell and Nev returning. They both looked tired and drawn, and Austell immediately went to pour himself a drink.

"What happened?" I asked, sitting myself up slowly as they both slumped down into the chairs opposite.

"It was infuriating," Austell said, glowering into his glass. "We're all pussyfooting around in there pretending that there isn't something bigger going on, but Damen is toying with us rather than just telling us what it is."

"I thought today was about farming," Arella said.

"So did I. And it was, but it's all with a view to understanding our supply position and what reserves we have. The questions we're being asked... Gods, he's treating us like children. We're supposed to be his council, for fucks sake."

"Do the others feel the same? Montavis and Hollis?"

"They're just as frustrated, and you can tell that Zennor is losing his patience, even though he never shows it. Sandy doesn't know his arse from his elbow most days, but Perran... oh, Perran definitely knows something. His captain looked far too smug throughout the meeting."

He finished his drink and slammed his glass down on

the table, unbuttoning his shirtsleeves and rolling them up as Nev got up to get them both another.

"Was Emrys invited to join you all?"

"No, why?"

"No reason, I guess. I'm just trying to work out why he's been invited. Surely not just for the ball?"

"Who knows with Damen?" Austell said. "Maybe he just wants to get the measure of him."

I thought about what Emrys had said in the forest. I wouldn't put it past Damen to invite him here just to taunt him about Aneira and his brother. I could feel Austell looking at me.

"Are you all right?" he asked. "With seeing him here, I mean?"

I forced a smile on to my face.

"Yes, I'm fine. It was a shock seeing him, I suppose... but it's fine."

I looked down at my hands and he watched me for a moment. I clearly didn't want to talk about it so he changed the subject.

"How have both of your days been?" he asked.

"Uneventful," I lied.

At some point they would need to know about the Amberstone, but right then it didn't seem like the time to get into it. I couldn't trust myself not to give my feelings away, and the truth was that it felt kind of awkward talking about Emrys with Austell. Since he'd had arrived, something had shifted between Austell and me. He wasn't saying anything, but I knew Austell was feeling jealous and threatened by Emrys's presence, and now there was a tension between us that I wasn't quite sure how to navigate. In the end I settled for telling them about Caja.

"And Arella also found new ways into the passages, which might come in useful."

"That is useful." He huffed out a breath and then looked at me, really looked at me. "You look tired. I'm sorry we woke you when we came in."

"It's fine," I said again.

He leaned forward and took my hand in both of his, smiling at me gently.

"Why don't I make our apologies and we'll stay in our rooms this evening, have dinner brought up to us. You have enough on your mind without having to put on a display down there."

My shoulders sagged and I rested my head back down on the pillow, squeezing his hand.

"I would love that."

"Then it's done. What time are you meeting Torr?"

"Late, as usual. Arella will come with me," I said, nodding at her. "Gods, I hope there's some good news."

"Efa, you are weathering this storm phenomenally. I am in awe of your strength."

"How long can we keep doing this though?" I whispered. "We still don't know what he's planning."

"Be patient, and we will get to the bottom of this. Things are happening, and he can't keep us in the dark forever. Focus on Noa for now, and then we'll figure out our next move."

I nodded; feeling absolutely exhausted all of a sudden. Exhausted, and utterly terrified of what was to come.

"Let me sort you a bath," Arella said, standing up. "And then I'll be a dutiful Lady's Companion and run downstairs to get our dinner brought up here."

I did as she suggested, even though the scalding hot water and glass of brandy she convinced me to have did nothing to help quiet my mind. When I wasn't thinking about Emrys, I was thinking about Noa. Was he all right? Was he in pain? And where even was he? Suddenly I thought of something and sat up sharply, sending water sloshing over the sides. I couldn't believe that it had slipped my mind—that I hadn't thought of it sooner.

"Arella!" I yelled, hoping she'd hear me from the other room.

I waited a few seconds, and then called her again, louder this time. I heard her footsteps hurrying through to my room, and then her worried face appeared at the bathroom door.

"Rell, we need to get a message to Ando. Tell him he needs to find Morgan."

CHAPTER 47
EFA

Of the entrances that we knew about, the library door was still the closest to our rooms. It creaked quietly as we pushed it open and lit the lamp Arella had left in there earlier in the afternoon with one of the library candles. It was cold and dusty, but as we left the confines of the palace, the floor began to slope toward the coves and the air turned damp, water dripping down onto our heads. The sound of waves crashing against the cliffs grew louder as we neared the beach, and my shadows began to tremble, urging me on desperately.

"Emrys is with them," I said tersely.

Arella glanced over her shoulder at me as we emerged into a deep cave, but she said nothing, not asking me how I knew. I was hardly surprised that he would have come. He had a habit of turning up unexpectedly, and clearly my message to Morgan had made its way back to him. My feet sank into the loose shingle as we left the cave, and I could just about make out the four shapes standing a little way off, illuminated by the moonlight. Morgan was bouncing around on his toes when we reached them, as usual seeming to have more energy than he knew what to do with. He grinned mischievously at me.

"Rescorla. Its good to see you again."

I nodded at him brusquely. Seeing him again made me realize that I'd missed him, too, but I was still pissed at him and I wasn't feeling in a particularly forgiving mood right them. I looked past him to where Emrys was perched on a large rock. Even in the darkness I could feel his eyes on me and my shadows longed for him. The pull to go to him was almost overwhelming, but I turned my head and focused on the other two instead. Since Arella hadn't met Lore or the two Fae before I quickly introduced them all.

"Right then," I said, skipping the niceties and getting straight down to business. "Here's what we know: four weeks ago the Order brought Noa to Rostorrmel. He was poisoned by lethal Faelock and was close to death when he arrived. Damen's mistress was the one who made sure he was kept alive."

Morgan snorted and I snapped my head round to look at him.

"What?"

"I'm just not at all surprised Aleta's involved."

"You know her?" Arella asked.

"Yeah. Well, Emrys does," he said with a wink in Emrys's direction.

Emrys shifted uncomfortably. In the silvery light I thought he wore a pained expression, and I remembered the way Aleta had been all over him the night he'd arrived.

"It was nothing," he said quickly. "A flirtation, over before it even started."

Jealousy flared unexpectedly and shadows burst from my fingertips before I could reign them back in but luckily they went unnoticed in the darkness.

"It looked like she might like to rekindle things," I muttered.

"Well, she won't be. I'm not interested in her, and we're talking forty or fifty years ago. It's hardly recent."

"Fifty years?" Arella spluttered. "How is that possible? She's not old enough."

"She's half-Fae," Emrys said, frowning. "You didn't know?"

There was a stunned silence as Arella and I looked at each other.

"From the looks on their faces I'm going to say they didn't know," Torr said with a chuckle.

"Hold on," Arella said. "Let's pause. You're telling me Aleta is half-Fae? Why would Damen choose *her* as his mistress? And why would she choose *him*? I thought you guys hated each other?"

"No, no, no... she hates the *Fae*," Emrys said shaking his head. "Her Fae father wanted nothing to do with her or her mother, and neither did his family, so now she hates us all. I'm not sure why Damen tolerates her, other than the fact she's easy on the eyes, but she's power-hungry so it explains why she is where she is."

"And her powers? She must have some, if she's half Fae?"

He looked thoughtful for a minute.

"I'm not sure I know. Cadoc would be able to confirm. Morg, ask him quickly, will you?"

Lore frowned at their exchange, watching Morgan turn his gaze out to the water while he concentrated briefly. Lore suddenly snapped his fingers.

"You're a fucking Messenger!" he said, grinning like a child who'd just seen a street performer's act. "Gods, what I wouldn't give to have a couple of you in my ranks."

"Yes, yes, it's very exciting," I said impatiently. "Can

we get back to the matter at hand, please? *Two* weeks ago, Noa was removed from the dungeons and taken somewhere by boat. That's all we know. So, Morgan… please, I'm coming to you first. I need to know if you can find him."

He nodded and walked over to me.

"I'll try. Give me your hand. It'll be easier that way."

"Don't tell me you're a Tracker, too?" Lore exclaimed. "Gods, if you ever want to join a spy network, you let me know."

Morgan grinned, his hand feeling warm around mine, and we stood like that for what felt like eternity. There was a slight crease in Morgan's brow as he stared down at the ground, and eventually he shook his head, his eyes darting to Emrys.

"I can't find him."

"What do you mean you *can't find him*?" I said.

Panic was beginning to rise. What did that even mean? Morgan turned to Emrys.

"It's the same as the Amberstone. Exactly the same. Shrouded. He's there and I can sense him, but I don't know where 'there' is."

"What does that mean?" Arella asked softly, voice laced with concern.

Morgan and Emrys were still looking at each other, obviously thinking something through. Emrys scratched at his beard thoughtfully.

"If I had to guess, I'd say that it means that the Amberstone and Noa are in the same place, and that wherever they are, it's warded. That's what is shrouding them."

"Can you find Finn, too?" Lore asked.

Morgan rolled his eyes good-naturedly and tried again, shaking his head again.

"No, but this one is different. I can't find him at all."

"Try Damen, too."

"We know where he is—"

"Just try him," I snapped a little impatiently.

"Same thing," Morgan said with a shrug. "Not shrouded, just not there."

"It's the stolen gift."

Emrys looked at me quizzically and I told them what Caja had told me, about what her brother's gift allowed him to do.

"*Skold*," he said simply. "That's what that power is. It means 'shield' in our language. Morgan's ability to track him won't work on anyone with that. It's like being completely invisible. We have a fair few of them in the Fae armies."

I took a deep breath and tilted my head back to look at the stars. So Finn was impervious to any gifts, too. Torr had been sitting quietly throughout, which was rather unusual for him. I knew from experience that he struggled to keep up with conversations related to gifts and powers, even though he had plenty of Valtanans in his crew, and he was probably trying to make sense of it all. I turned to him now, my fingers playing with the worry beads in my pocket.

"Torr, did you see anything suspicious or unusual when you went out to observe the Nothori?"

"Well, there are plenty of small islets out on the archipelago. They're all uninhabited, mostly just breeding grounds for petrels. It could be any one of those."

"I know, Torr, but—"

"But tell me this, Efa," he said, cutting me off. "If those islands *are* uninhabited, why would one of them have Order priests lurking in the trees?"

My mouth dropped open at the same time my shadows

murmured their agreement and I felt the hairs on my arms stand on end.

"You saw them?"

"Two of them. No cloaks, but still recognizable as the Order."

I glanced at Arella to find her eyes wide. *Men hiding in the trees. Runes carved into stone. Salt in the air.*

"That's where he is," she said. "The Amberstone, too. I can feel it in my bones, E."

Emrys slowly stood up, his eyes glinting in the moonlight. I could see the excitement on his face. He looked genuinely hopeful as he and Morgan looked at each other. After all these years, had they finally found the location of the Amberstone?

"Can we get there tonight?" I asked.

Torr shook his head, gesturing out to sea.

"By the time we get a boat round here the tide will have turned. Besides, that moon is too bright. They'll see you coming a mile off."

"Don't worry about that," I said, knowing that my shadows would take care of that, hopefully. "We just need to get there."

"Tomorrow then, early evening just after dark. I can have a boat ready to leave from here."

Morgan cleared his throat and we all turned to look at him.

"Cadoc has replied. He doesn't know what powers she has, but he knew her father. He was a *dreor*."

My head whipped to find Arella. *They were taking him to the dreor*. When I looked back, Emrys was giving Morgan a worried look. Icy cold fingers trailed down my spine.

"What exactly is a *dreor*?" I asked nervously.

Emrys licked his lips and pushed a hand through his hair.

"It's the name given to someone with a particular ability. A rare one."

"*What* ability, Emrys?" I asked impatiently.

"Blood magic."

CHAPTER 48
EFA

"It was her," I whispered to myself as we traipsed back through the tunnels.

"What?" Emrys said from behind me.

It was just the two of us going back to the palace, something I wasn't particularly overjoyed about. Arella was staying on board the *Panacea* for the night to help Torr with his accounts, and would make her way back in the morning, leaving me alone with him in a very confined space. I had more or less ignored him for most of the climb back up, except for the brief few minutes where we couldn't find the cave entrance to the tunnels in the dark. And as we walked silently through the passages, I started to work through everything in my mind.

It all made sense, that feeling that I hadn't been able to put my finger on with Aleta. She'd had that ethereal quality about her that I couldn't work out. Now I knew it was down to her being half Fae. More than that, I'd had that feeling of familiarity, as if I'd seen her before. I could remember clearly now, those feline eyes of hers underneath the heavy hood of her black, fur cloak; the smooth, sultry voice that flirted with Finn and spoke the ancient words.

"Aleta performed the ritual," I said suddenly. "The one that bound me to Finn."

He stopped in the middle of the tunnel and I turned to look at him, grateful for the chance to catch my breath. His breathing laboured slightly, but not as bad as mine. It was an unforgiving climb back up from the coves, longer and steeper even than the cliff path up to Totease.

"You're sure?" he asked, and I nodded.

"Positive. It was Aleta, and she remembers me, too. I'd be willing to bet that it was her that told Damen that I was Nevedeno."

"He knows about that?"

I nodded again, forgetting that there were developments that he didn't know about. He stared at me and I met his eyes, trying to decide who I thought he was. Did I really believe that he was as terrible as the stories said? Did I believe that he was lying to me? He had been in Valtana that night; he'd never denied that. So what was he doing there? I could have just asked him outright then and there, but the truth was, I was scared of his answer. I felt that familiar tug between us and I quickly turned away and started walking again, hearing him following behind me.

"So, you and Austell..."

His question hung in the air between us, tension simmering.

"What about it?"

"Are you two...?"

I looked back at him, glaring at him murderously, and then sighed heavily.

"No."

I could feel him smiling even with my back to him, and I walked a little faster. Back in the palace, the hallways were fairly quiet, but twice we heard the sound of guards up ahead, and we had to adjust our route, taking a narrow, winding staircase up to the first floor. I hesitated at the top, trying to get my bearings.

"This way," Emrys said, nudging me forward.

But half way down the corridor we heard voices again, closer this time and coming towards us. Before I could even react, Emrys had grabbed my hand and pulled me round a corner. He opened a door, pushed me inside and shut it just as a flash of blue appeared. He moved quietly around the room lighting candles, and as my eyes adjusted to the dark I saw that we were in a large bedroom, one of the many standard guest rooms in the palace. It was furnished with heavy, mahogany furniture and dark green fabrics, and there were clothes hanging on the back of the wardrobe.

"It's my room," Emrys said softly. "It seemed the easiest option, since I didn't think you'd appreciate me pulling you into an alcove again."

"Oh," I said, glancing around again.

There were very few of Emrys's things in the room. His fur coat, the one I had slept under in the forest, hung on the back of the door, and the shirt I had worn to sleep in was strewn across the bed. He leaned against the wall saying nothing and looking uncharacteristically nervous as he swallowed hard and looked down at the floor.

"Efa," he began, but I cut him off.

"Don't, Emrys. Don't say anything, please. Things have changed between us, and I don't know… I can't make sense of what I'm feeling right now. What with Noa, and being here in this place with Da—." My breath caught and I could hear my voice trembling as my emotions threatened to overwhelm me. "It's too much. I can't…"

He looked up at me sadly, and I felt my shadows pleading with me.

"I just…" My voice was barely a whisper. "I just need…"

He pushed away from the wall and stood in front of me. His hand came up to cup my cheek. This time I didn't push it away. He gazed down at me with raw emotion.

"What do you need, Efa?"

I stared up into those amber eyes, thinking that I still didn't know what they looked like in the dawn light.

"What do you need, Efa?" he asked me again, and I took a shallow breath.

Him. I needed him. My shadows were begging me to give in to him, to go to him. So I did. I lifted up onto my tiptoes and kissed him as if it was the only thing I had ever been born to do, sighing as he responded with a groan that had me instantly turned on. Gods, I wanted him. His hands were in my hair as he kissed me passionately, his tongue plunging into my mouth. I breathed in the smell of him, overwhelmed by how right it felt to be in his arms. How everything else just ceased to matter. My skin tingled and my shadows sang, his touch chasing away that soul-destroying, perpetual loneliness that I had felt since he'd left Totease.

"Fuck Efa," he breathed. "I feel *nothing* without you."

I tore at his clothing, pulling his jacket from his shoulders. Lifting his mouth from mine, he stepped back from me and I smiled as we frantically fumbled with our clothing until he stood gloriously, beautifully naked in front of me, and when he grinned he revealed the dimple that made my heart skip a beat. Then he lifted me up and carried me to the bed, and I couldn't help myself. I was completely feral. Everything about him had me acting wild and out of control. I moaned and screamed, not caring whether anyone could hear us, consumed with my need to touch him, to taste him. I needed his hands on me and inside of me.

All I could think about was having more of him. Harder, faster, deeper, and when eventually he flipped me onto my knees and pushed into me from behind, my eyes rolled back in my head as pleasure spread throughout my body. The feel of him filling me up was absolutely exquisite. Cold, glittering shadows filled the room as I threw caution to the wind and released my shadows, letting them dance around and caress our damp, bare skin. And when he finally took me over the edge, I whispered his name against the pillow, over and over again as waves of pleasure rippled through me and stars filled my vision.

~

Afterwards, I lay there in the darkness staring at his face as he slept peacefully. He was still the most beautiful thing I'd ever laid eyes on, so much so that it made my heart ache just looking at him. Once, there had been a time when I'd imagined a whole future with him. Now, I hardly knew what kind of future I would even have, or if I would even make it out of this palace alive. My fingers played with the wolf medallion around his neck as his chest gently rose and fell with each breath, and I remembered him telling me about what his mother had seen in the wolf: loyalty and freedom. In Valtanan culture, the wolf represented untamed wildness. Some people said that hearing the howl of a wolf stirred something deep within us all, and that seeing one meant that you were truly in alignment with your destiny. I honestly wasn't sure what I believed anymore.

I let the medallion drop gently onto his chest, resting

my head back and squeezing my eyes shut, feeling tears begin to form behind my eyelids. I peeled the covers off of me and slipped silently from the bed, trying to find my clothes and get dressed by the light of the single candle still burning. My blade had fallen under the bed in the earlier frenzy, and I crouched to retrieve it before tucking it into the back of my pants. Before I left, I glanced back at his sleeping form one final time, and then risked it all by wrapping myself in shadows as I ran through the hallways back to the Esari suite. Only when I was safely back in my own cold bed did I finally let the tears fall.

CHAPTER 49
EFA

I tossed and turned all night, dreaming of a wolf stalking me through the forest and Noa burning in flames, screaming my name. When I looked in the mirror, my thin face looked pale and there were dark circles under my eyes. I hardly recognized myself, and I wondered how long I could physically withstand this storm. I barely slept, I barely ate, and I was just about holding my emotions together. I wondered at what point I would finally break. When I went out into the sitting room after dressing the servants had built a fire and were laying out breakfast on the table. I sat watching the flames on my own for a while and then helped myself to a cup of tea just as the suite door creaked open and Arella came in.

"Is it just me, or are there are lot of guards around at the moment?" she said quietly.

"The palace is inundated. Emrys and I were almost caught three times last night by Order priests."

"Something bad is going to happen, I can feel it in my bones."

"Don't say that," I said with a grimace.

"Not with Noa. I'm certain we'll get him back safely. This is something else… something niggling at the back of my mind…"

I stared at her while I picked at my fingers. After the recent change in her abilities and the vision she'd had, her comments made me deeply uneasy, but I didn't get the chance to ask her more because Nev and Austell simultaneously appeared from their own rooms. While Arella disappeared to freshen up and change, I filled them both in on the conversation from the night before, or at least I told them about the part on the beach. Since I was telling them that Emrys had also turned up I figured it was a good time to tell them about the Amberstone and Evyn, too."

"I always had a feeling something like that had happened," Austell murmured when I finished. "But for Damen to kill Evyn? Gods, I'm surprised that they didn't declare all out war."

"I know, me too," I said. "The Amberstone must be incredibly important to them for them not to want to risk it."

"So, let me get all of this straight." Nev was clearly trying to work through everything I'd told them. "Damen abducted Evyn and Aneira, stole the Amberstone, and said that he would kill them both if the Fae sent aid to Valtana. When Emrys defied him, they killed Evyn, which the Fae have never made public in twenty years. Aneira was returned, but the reason that the Fae have never moved against Damen in retaliation is because he holds the Amberstone, which somehow controls their powers."

"That's about the size of it," Arella said, breezing out of her room in a clean dress and with her hair braided up. "Confusing, isn't it?"

"And you believe Noa is on this island out on the

archipelago?" Nev said. "So, what's the plan for tonight? What do you need from us?"

My shadows began to vibrate and I sat up. A moment later there was a knock on the door and they all looked towards it. Nev rose to open it and I went back to my tea, already knowing who would be standing the other side of the door. I shifted in my chair as the two males stalked into the room, letting Arella perch on the arm as they all sat down. I noticed her eyes tracking Bran with interest as he followed Emrys across the room and took a seat, and then there was an awkward moment where no one said anything. I could feel Emrys watching me. I wondered how he'd felt when he'd woken this morning to find me gone. My fingers were twitching nervously, the pad of my thumb raw from all my worrying the past few days. I'd left the worry beads in my rooms, but Bran reached into his pocket and drew out another set, leaning over and passing them to me.

"Here," he said with a kind smile. "I made an extra."

I laughed quietly as I took them, disarmed as always by his thoughtfulness.

"I don't believe we've met properly," Arella said, turning a dazzling smile on him. "I'm Arella."

A slow, easy smile split his handsome face.

"Bran."

I flicked my eyes between them both, noticing the way their eyes seemed to linger on each other.

"All right..." I said slowly, amused by their little interaction. "Shall we talk about why we're all sitting here? Emrys, is there something you'd like to say?"

Emrys hadn't taken his eyes off of me since he'd come in, and now he cleared his throat.

"I'm coming with you tonight," he said. "If the Amberstone is on the island, then I'm getting it back."

"All right," I said again.

I supposed that was fair enough. Who was I to deny them the opportunity to finally retrieve it?

"And Bran and I have discussed it at length. We think that it would be wise to orchestrate some kind of distraction here at the palace."

"I agree," Nev said. "I was thinking the same thing. We need something that means that your absence in the palace won't be noticeable."

Emrys nodded, clearly relieved to have Nev's support.

"The last I heard, Jory was just outside the city. If we could get a message to them in time, could they get inside the palace?"

"I could bring them in through the coves," Arella said. "I could meet them down there and show them the way."

"It's a big risk for them," Austell said, deep frown lines etched into his forehead. "If they're caught, and it's a pretty high likelihood given the amount of Order priests around here, they'll face torture and a painful death. I don't know about you, but I don't particularly want to watch my men burn at the stake again any time soon."

I remembered the looks on the Loyalist's faces as the flames grew around them.

"He's right," I said. "I don't know if I could ask them to risk that."

"It's the risk that they take every day," Emrys said. "We know that Damen doesn't consider the Loyalists to be a threat. Not a serious one, anyway, but if they breached the palace, now that would get their attention. Besides, it's for their queen, and the only other heir to Valtana's throne."

"No," Austell said firmly. "I won't give that order. They can cause havoc in the city, absolutely, but I won't order them in here. The risk is too high right now."

I looked at him, seeing his fists clenched tightly in his lap. I wondered how much of this resistance was because it was Emrys asking. I shot a look at Nev who shrugged slightly, probably thinking the same. I sighed inwardly. I agreed with Austell; the risk was great and I didn't want to ask Jory either, but if we were to get Noa back, then we did need a distraction. I placed a hand on Austell's arm and spoke gently but assertively.

"Austell, whatever is going on here, I think it's safe to say that the Amberstone plays a pretty big role in it. If they know that Noa is Prince Aeden, and I'm pretty sure they will do since they know about his shadows, then when we go to the island, we can't fail. We need to ensure their attention is here, and breaching the palace sends a big message."

Austell's eyes darted between Emrys and me. I could see the tension in shoulders, his jaw clenched. I reached for his hand, seeing Emrys shift in his seat out of the corner of my eye.

"Austell, *this* is what they're fighting for. *This* is what it's all about."

He turned to look at me, and I saw the weight of what he carried on his face. The risk he had taken on since he took on the Loyalists after his father died, not just with his own life, but also with theirs.

"I don't want to watch more of my men burn, Efa."

I nodded sadly, thinking about what Hollis had told me my father used to say, that sometimes leaders had to have blood on their hands. This was a war, and there were never any easy decisions in war. I raised my chin and looked him squarely in the face.

"Then don't command them to risk their lives, but give them the choice. It's up to them if they'll do it, and I'd hold nothing against them if they don't." I hesitated, looking at Emrys and Bran. "What about Morgan? Would he come?"

"No question," Emrys said, looking pointedly at Austell. "We all would."

Austell scoffed, leaning back in his chair and shaking his head.

"Maybe we value our men's lives a little differently."

Emrys's face turned dark and I could see him getting angrier. The tension between the two was building by the second and I knew I was in the middle of it all. Bran held out a placatory hand.

"Look, this isn't helping. I think we all value the lives of our soldiers highly, there's no question of that. But I think we also recognize that drawing attention away from Efa and Emrys is the sensible option, and penetrating the castle should unsettle Damen considerably. It lets him know that the Loyalists *are* a real threat, and he's not as safe as he thinks. "

"Precisely," I said. "And I'm not talking about an assassination here."

"Why not?" Arella asked. "Tell me again why we aren't just killing Damen?"

"Because," I said, "aside from the fact that we don't know what gifts he has stolen and how he might defend himself, it's bigger than him. There is so much more at play here. The Nothori are here in their thousands, and I'd put money on Denfor being poised to take over and continue whatever plans Damen has put into motion if he died. Or Brayson. No, if we simply killed him in his sleep it would be short sighted. The roots of his plans go deep, and we need to know exactly what we're dealing with and what arrangements he's made. And besides, he's not the only one that needs to die. If we kill him now, the others might scatter."

Nev and Bran were nodding along in agreement. In my lap, my fingers were furiously moving the worry beads around in my hands.

"So, right now what we need is chaos and confusion in the palace, just like we have been causing in the villages."

"Shadows and fury," Nev grinned, and I smiled back.

"Exactly."

I fixed Austell with a look.

"Austell, are we agreed? We'll ask them to volunteer?"

I saw him take a deep breath and he nodded grudgingly.

"Good, that's settled. Emrys, there is one additional assignment for Morgan, if he's up to it." I smiled. "It might not be Damen, but there is one man who does have to die tonight."

CHAPTER 50

EFA

All in all, it was a tense morning. By some miracle, we managed to finish making plans for that night without Austell and Emrys killing each other. But after the two Fae left, Austell sat brooding in his chair, saying very little. I knew he was upset. I also knew he wasn't really trying to obstruct our plans to save Noa. He was just frustrated, jealous even, and I was certain he was now berating himself for his behavior.

He was clearly disappointed, too. We had been circling one another for weeks now—shared looks, brushes of hand, almost-kisses—but nothing had ever crossed that fragile line. And now, with Emrys's sudden reappearance, I had pulled back. Austell wasn't stupid. He could feel the distance. He knew something had shifted between us, and the knowledge sat between us like an open wound. I couldn't look at him for long. Every time I did, I caught the questions in his eyes, the hurt he tried to swallow down, and the quiet plea for something I couldn't give. And so I kept to silence, adding guilt to the list of emotions I was also experiencing.

He left around mid-morning with Nev to Damen's final council meeting, and Arella and I took a walk out into the grounds and down to the coves while we discussed the finer details. The day passed with excruciating slowness, every minute stretching long and heavy. I bathed, scrubbed until my skin was raw, and carefully chose a sea-green gown with billowing sleeves and a soft, layered skirt that whispered against the floor when I moved, the simple swish of the fabric seeming deafening in the silence of the room. Arella pinned half of my hair back with deft fingers, lined my eyes and rouged my cheeks, and I slipped on the delicate slippers to match the gown, lingering in front of the mirror, my fingers toying with the gold pendant at my neck. For the time in my life, I reminded myself of my mother.

I stood by the window, watching the harbor bathed in the shifting light, and waiting for the inevitable. Behind me, Arella packed quietly, her movements brisk and efficient. She tucked away my boots, my knives, and my usual jumper and pants into a bag by the door, ready to be left inside the passages for later that night. Outside in the sitting room, Austell was waiting for us, dressed in a deep, sapphire blue jacket embroidered with silver thread. It made his eyes look even more vibrant than usual, even more luminous, and yet there was a sadness in his gaze as he crossed the room toward me. He fastened the last button on his sleeve, then reached for me, kissing me softly on the cheek. His lips were warm and fleeting against my skin. Not demanding, not desperate, just gentle. A sad sort of kiss, but not one of blame, and beneath it there was still that hope, fragile but unbroken.

For a second, I let myself lean into him, as if I could hold on to that fleeting softness, and the safety that came with him. But when his lips pulled away, I kept my eyes down, afraid of what he might see in them. My throat tightened. I wanted to say something—thank you, I'm sorry, don't hope for more—but the words tangled in my mouth, heavy and impossible. Instead, I touched his sleeve lightly, a small, useless gesture that wasn't quite an embrace. Then I stepped back, forcing a faint smile.

"I have never seen you look more beautiful, Efa," he said quietly. "Are you ready to go?"

I touched the pendant around my neck again and then turned to hug Arella goodbye.

"Time to get this over with," I whispered to her. "I'll see you later tonight."

As usual, I took Austell's hand, ever the dutiful fiancée, and let him lead me from the room, ignoring the way my shadows protested and tugged me impatiently towards the stairs. When we reached the first floor, they jumped delightedly, and I scanned the hallway, waiting for Emrys to appear. Sure enough, he and Bran came round the corner just a moment later and Austell tensed beside me, his hand tightening almost possessively around mine. From the way Emrys's eyes narrowed slightly, I knew that he'd noticed.

"Efa..." he said gently, indicating that he wanted to speak to me.

My mouth had gone dry and I licked my lips, my pulse racing as I remembered the feel of his mouth against my skin the night before. The way I had moaned his name into the darkness. Austell hesitated, and I smiled reassuringly up at him.

"Go ahead. We'll be right behind you."

Reluctantly he let go of my hand and moved away, continuing down the stairs with Bran, Nev and Arella, and glancing back over his shoulder as he went. Emrys watched them go, but when he looked back at me he looked so desolate, as if a great weight sat on his shoulders. He walked over to the staircase and leaned against the balustrade with his back to me.

"You know, I don't live in Cyfnos's Citadel anymore, not since I was fifteen and my father sent me away to train as a soldier. The village that I think of as my home, and where my mother and her brother are buried sits on the edge of a great fjord. In a few weeks it'll be completely frozen over and everything will be pure, unblemished ice and snow as far as the eye can see.

"Some nights," he said, turning back to face me, "when I can't sleep, or dreams of my own brother haunt me, I sit outside and watch the way everything glitters silently under the moon. Sometimes the northern lights dance above me, and it takes my breath away. It's not just that it's beautiful, though it is. It's the peace. The quiet."

He exhaled, a weary sound, his eyes clouded with something I couldn't name.

"It's the only time the noise inside me stops. The fears, the guilt, the regrets... they all fall away. For a moment, I almost feel whole again."

He took a few steps towards me until there were only inches between us, and I held my breath, staring up into his face.

"I used to think that I would never find anything that could make me feel that way," he murmured, voice rough with honesty. "Not until I met you."

I looked away, blinking hard, trying to stop the tears burning at the corners of my eyes.

"Whatever happens tonight… nothing has changed for me, Efa. I meant what I said before. I'm all yours, for as long as I'm breathing. I just… I need you to know that."

The words undid me. I lost the fight, a hot tear spilling down my cheek before I could stop it. Emrys reached up gently, his thumb brushing it away as if had wounded him to see it fall.

"We should go," he whispered, softer now, though his hand lingered against my skin.

I nodded, unable to speak, my emotions fraying and spilling everywhere. He held out his arm, and after a moment's hesitation, I slipped my hand into the crook of his elbow, and together we walked down the stairs.

CHAPTER 51
EFA

The palace had been a hive of activity all day, and by nightfall it had transformed into something gaudy and suffocating. The ballroom blazed with light, its high beams draped in swathes of blue and gold banners bearing the Treforno crest, and flowers crowded every surface, spilling from gilded vases in sweet, cloying abundance until the air felt too heavy to breathe. At one end of the hall, a banquet table bowed under the weight of roasted meats, sugared fruits, and glittering decanters of wine, while servants in pressed uniforms flitted at the edges, arms already laden with brimming glasses.

The music was deafening, a crashing swell of strings and pipes that tangled with the thrum of voices and the stomp of dancers' feet. Heat rolled off the crowd in waves, a heady mixture of perfume, wine, and sweat. Couples spun and laughed, their silks flashing like jewels in the candlelight, while courtiers and dignitaries clustered at the edges of the dance floor, shouting to be heard over the din.

It was louder, brighter, and far more crowded than any of the evenings I had endured before. This was no casual night of indulgence or empty entertainment; this was a spectacle. The usual courtiers who hung about the palace sucking up to Damen trying to better their positions were there as was expected, but this time they were joined by wealthy landowners, merchants, and aristocracy who had been invited from across Melrith, Tithra and even continents further afield. I even spied one or two senior members of the Fraternity, and quickly turned away before they recognized me, wondering how they'd managed to get an invitation.

Beside me, Emrys cut a striking figure, commanding space even without a word, and I felt the familiar burn of eyes following us as we moved deeper into the room. His hand was warm on my lower back as he leaned down to speak quietly against my ear.

"I'll see you when it's time, smuggler."

He strolled away, slipping effortlessly into conversation with Bran, who was chuckling at something Hollis had said. My shadows urged me to follow him, but I stayed rooted, scanning the crowd with restless eyes. Across the room, Austell was deep in discussion with Nev, Arella, and Kerensa, but periodically his eyes lifted to Emrys, his expression sharp and unreadable.

I forced myself to breathe, to still the twitch of my hands against my skirts. My stomach churned with unease, my shadows dancing restlessly, eager to get on with the evening's plans, but I smiled and nodded as if I belonged there. Restlessness was always a giveaway that something wasn't right, so I took a glass of wine from a nearby footman, unclenched my jaw, and forced myself to relax, pushing Noa temporarily out of my mind. I let out a light laugh at some half-heard jest from a merchant nearby, and pretended I was having a wonderful time. I even went so far as to send Damen a dazzling smile, sinking into a low curtsey when he entered the room and climbed the dais, my instincts recoiling at the smile he gave me in return. But always, beneath it all, I was waiting.

I let my gaze drift around the ballroom. Denfor and Anneth stood near the terrace, their laughter brittle as they entertained a cluster of Tithran nobles. One of the men—an Emir, by the look of the heavy gold rings crowding his fingers and the ropes of jewels spilling down his chest—gestured broadly as though the room belonged to him. Further along, Tanrith leaned against a column, his posture deceptively casual as he bent close to a girl I recognized from Damen's harem. She laughed at something he said, though the sound was too high, too sharp, to be real. I swept the room again, but there was still no sign of Caja, and I prayed it was because she had simply slipped away to some quiet corner of the palace.

An hour passed, perhaps more. Austell asked me to dance, as did Montavis and Hollis, and by the time I returned to the side to catch my breath, Aleta was descending regally from the dais, coaxing Emrys onto the dance floor. She was radiant, as always, in a scarlet gown that clung to her and left most of her back exposed. Emrys caught my eye as they moved together, Aleta pressed flush against him, laughing too sweetly at every word he said. Heat flared in my chest and I turned away, angry with myself for caring, until Bran appeared at my shoulder.

"Would you dance with me, Efa?" he asked, seeming shy as he made his request.

"I thought you didn't dance," I said as I placed my hand in his.

"I don't, usually," he admitted, "but I owe you a formal apology, and I'm hoping that by this grand show of suffering and discomfort on my part, you might accept it more readily."

A laugh escaped my lips. To my surprise, he moved with skill, leading us smoothly and confidently through the step. Whatever his personal feelings were towards dancing, there was no denying he'd been well trained. He guided us easily across the floor, always careful to keep a deliberate distance from Emrys and Aleta.

"I'm sorry, Efa," he said at last. "For my part in deceiving you. There are things we all keep hidden, naturally. Our orders demand it. But I think we had gone beyond that point. We should have been more honest with each other.

It was neatly done—skillful, in fact. A reminder that I had hidden my own secrets as much as they had, albeit for very different reasons. But, as was typical with Bran, his words were delivered in a way that didn't immediately get my back up.

"You're right, but you shouldn't apologize for your loyalty, Bran. He is your commander, and it was him alone who was responsible for telling me the truth."

"Be that as it may, I should have counseled him harder. Encouraged him to be brave."

"Brave?"

"It was never intentional to deceive you, you must know that. Emrys wanted to tell you, but he was afraid."

"Afraid? Of what?"

"Of what you would do when you learned who he is, or at least who he is painted to be. Of course we told him, the longer he waited, the worse it would be. Even Morgan told him that. But the longer it went on, the more he feared losing you."

I dropped my gaze, tracing the stitching on his jacket, forcing myself to focus on the pattern rather than his words. Across the room, I caught Aleta's laugh and felt it twist like a knife. My chest ached and fingers tightened around Bran's hand.

"What was Emrys's brother like?" I asked softly, my voice betraying the strain.

Bran's smile was gentle, almost wistful.

"Optimistic. Good-natured. Talkative. In many ways, the complete opposite of Emrys. He was young, inexperienced, and too clever for his own good. A visionary, always talking about changing things for the better. He believed that he could."

"Isn't that just youthfulness? Then life changes you, hardens you up."

Bran shook his head.

"No… I don't think that was it. He and Morgan were the same age, but Morgan was always grounded and realistic. He sees the world for what it is. Not Evyn. Sometimes he was too trusting, but he always wanted to see the good in people. In many ways, that was one of his best qualities, but it would get him into trouble sometimes."

"Emrys must miss him a lot," I said quietly.

"He does. So do I. He was as much a brother to me as Emrys is." Bran cleared his throat, and pulled me in a little closer so he could lower his voice. "Everything is in place for tonight. Jory, Treave and Rumo were more than willing to get inside the palace, and Morgan, too, obviously. And there are plenty of others who will remain out in the city causing havoc outside the palace walls. Just… take care of each other tonight."

I nodded slowly as the dance came to an end.

"You know, you dance beautifully, Lord Brannock." I said, curtseying. "And I accept your apology."

He grinned as he bowed to me, and we moved to the side of the room as another dance began. We were at the bottom of the dais when I noticed Tanrith, Denfor and

Canver leaving the room together. Austell appeared next to me, his hand on my elbow, concern in his eyes.

"Damen has requested that the lords join him separately," he said. "I'll find you after."

Montavis and Hollis hovered just behind him, both looking similarly apprehensive.

"Prince Trystan," a voice rang out across the music.

Brayson stood on the dais, glaring down at Emrys who was still standing with Aleta. Emrys lazily dragged his eyes away from Damen's mistress and up to the General, and I had to admit that I found his insolence mildly amusing.

"The king has requested that you join him. Lord Brannock, too."

Damen had risen from his chair and was draining the glass of deep, burgundy wine that he held. He placed it down on the table and then stood up, scanning the room. When he found me next to Bran his face lit up.

"Efa. Why don't you join us, too?"

I hesitated for the briefest of moments. None of the wives had been invited to join them, so why me? His jaw twitched, and I quickly inclined my head, not wanting to incur his wrath. As we left the room, I caught Arella's eye across the crowd and remembered her earlier warning. The dread in my stomach only deepened.

We followed Brayson into the adjoining hall, where a long table waited. Damen strode in a moment later and took his place at the head of the table, lowering himself into the high-backed chair like a king returning to his throne, and the rest of us took our seats. A row of wine bottles gleamed in front of him, and he leaned forward to pour himself a glass while Brayson positioned himself just behind, the guard dog as always.

"I hope you are all enjoying the ball," Damen said brightly, wiping the wine from his lips with his thumb.

His tone was cheerful, but his eyes gleamed like a predator's. He looked around the table, gaze lingering on each of us in turn, before settling on Emrys.

"Prince Trystan, you have been quiet since you arrived."

Emrys raised an eyebrow, his expression cool, almost bored. He spread his hands open on the table.

"I confess I have been wondering why you have asked us here. The Northern Realm has not been invited to Rostorrmel for more than twenty years."

Damen leaned forward slightly, smile sharp.

"Well, we are allies, are we not? It is time that we started acting like friends, no?"

From across the table, I noticed Denfor smothering a smirk behind his hand, and something shifted in Emrys's face, just for a second. His composure cracked, just enough for me to glimpse the steel beneath, and I was sure that his eyes flashed black. His voice dropped an octave as he replied.

"Circumstances have dictated that we be civil with each other, as you well know. But make no mistake—the Northern Realm and Melrith are not allies. We are not friends."

The atmosphere turned frosty, and I held my breath, knowing that this was exactly what Damen had wanted to happen. He was baiting Emrys, and Emrys knew it.

"Then why *are* you here, Trystan? Why accept my invitation at all?"

"It presents a good opportunity to discuss a cause for concern that I'm sure we all have. That of the increasing threat from Nothori slavers."

"Ah yes, I'm well aware that the Nothori have been

abducting women and girls along the border. Until recently they had an arrangement in place with the Nevedeno gang, but I am told that arrangement has come to an abrupt end."

He turned to look at me, grinning knowingly. I lifted my chin, meeting his eyes and staring him down defiantly as everyone's attention slowly shifted to me. I wondered exactly what Damen knew. What had Finn and Aleta told him, if anything? Did he know about Emrys and me? Did he know that we had killed Theo? Had Finn told him that I was Valtanan, or about my oath line? His smile didn't waver.

"We no longer need to concern ourselves with the Nothori slavers anymore," Damen said lightly, as if delivering news of no consequence. "That problem has been... taken care of."

A cold prickle raced up my spine.

"What does that mean?" Emrys growled.

He wasn't the only one unsettled. I caught the briefest exchange of looks between Hollis and Montavis, and even Canver's fat face was a picture of confusion. Hollis moved uneasily in his chair, his voice cutting through the silence.

"Your Highness," he said, "I fear that we cannot be put off any longer. We, too, are concerned about the increasing Nothori presence in Melrith. I must ask—what arrangement have you entered into with them, and to what end?"

Damen sighed dramatically and leaned back in his chair, taking a large mouthful of wine.

"You're right, Kenwyn. I do owe you an explanation," he placed his glass down and stood up abruptly. "There is a threat against this throne. One that has been steadily growing these last few years. Despite our hopes that these so-called 'Loyalists' would tire themselves out when they realized their efforts were fruitless, they appear to be gaining more traction, their popularity with the common folk growing by the day."

I shot a sidelong look at Austell. His face was neutral, but I knew he'd be pleased at how irritated Damen was with the Loyalists.

"The revelation that the heir lives has only served to inspire them further, so it's time that we nipped this rebellion in the bud once and for all. You asked to what end we have allied with the Nothori. From tomorrow, they will deploy to each of your regions."

Tanrith was the first to react, his face flushing with indignation, though he said nothing, knowing it would be unwise to question the king. In contrast, Montavis sat perfectly still, fingers steepled, his expression carved from stone. Only the taut line of his jaw betrayed his anger. Canver blinked, as if struggling to catch the thread of the conversation.

"Sire," Hollis began quietly, "is that wise?"

"It is for the protection of our people, Ken," Damen said evenly, but there was a look in his eyes that dared Portreth's lord to challenge him.

"Sire, we might call it protection," Montavis said, "but my people will see it as an occupation. They will not welcome foreign boots on their soil."

"Oh, be quiet, Kit," Damen snapped, all lightness gone from his expression. "The Nothori will join my Order priests in putting down this rebellion for good. They will root out these Loyalists, dragging them from the shadows in which they hide, and they won't stop there. They will also root out every Gifted Valtanan left in this land and eradicate them."

"And Aeva Penrose?" Denfor asked quietly, eyes sparkling. "What of the girl? The heir?"

A slow, cruel smile split Damen's face.

"I'm glad you asked, Perran. Aeva Penrose will burn with the rest of them."

CHAPTER 52
EFA

There was a stunned stillness in the room. Only Tanrith and Denfor moved, watching on with sharp, measuring eyes. Tanrith's irritation from a moment ago seemed forgotten now that there was the promise of cruelty hanging in the air. Everyone else looked horrified. My own breathing had slowed right down, coming shallow and tight as I fought to keep my shadows leashed, the rage boiling in my blood threatening to burst from my fingertips. My eyes found Emrys's where he was sitting across from me. This time they really were black, his clenched fists resting on the table in front of him.

"The Northern Realm will not stand by and watch you massacre innocents," he growled, his voice low and thick with threat.

Damen tilted his head, feigning surprise, and then laughed softly.

"But you already have, Trystan. Isn't that what you and your brother did, all those years ago? Stood by. Watched as Nissae burned."

Emrys's entire body trembled with barely checked

rage. His chair creaked as though it might splinter beneath him. I held myself perfectly still, forcing calm into my expression, whispering to myself that there would be time later—a time to act, a time to seek vengeance. But right then, I had to prioritize Noa. But Emrys… Emrys looked as though he might leap from his chair to strangle Damen with his bare hands. Brayson shifted beside Damen, his hand falling casually to the hilt of his sword.

"Careful, Trystan," Damen murmured. "I would hate for our newfound friendship to falter so soon."

Emrys's eyes flicked to mine, and I gave the slightest shake of my head, silently begging him to hold. To wait. To let it go for the time being. And as he smiled tightly, unclenching his fists, I knew that it was taking everything in him to restrain himself.

"The Gifted have out whiled us for years, Your Highness," Tanrith said carefully. "They have used their abilities against us. Just because we have the Nothori on our side, it doesn't mean they are immune to Valtanan abilities."

"Ah, I'm so glad you said that, Zennor," Damen replied. "Because things have changed."

He paused to take a deliberate sip of wine, and then clicked his fingers.

"Let me demonstrate."

Two servants came scampering forward at his signal, extinguishing the lamps until the chamber was lit only by the guttering glow of a few scattered candles. They set two chairs in the centre of the room before hurrying back, heads bowed. Austell and Hollis exchanged a glance. Tanrith poured himself a glass of wine, settling himself as though preparing to be entertained. Then came the sound. Something heavy was being dragged across the floor in the corridor outside. My stomach dropped as two Order priests appeared, hauling a man into the room.

He was conscious, but barely, dressed in only a loose pair of pants. Thin and malnourished, he slumped between them, his head lolling forward, dark hair falling across his face. The priests shoved him onto one of the waiting chairs where he sagged limply, breathing slow and shallow. His eyes fluttered closed. I searched his face, and then checked his arms. The veins on his arms had taken on a silvery hue. Silvermist.

The Order priests stepped back and took up positions against the wall, their faces hidden beneath their hoods. My shadows were pounding in my veins. *This is it*, they screamed. This was what we've been waiting to discover all this time. Something terrible was about to happen, and I was going to be powerless to stop it. I couldn't save this man. I couldn't use my Gift, not now when we were so close. Not without signing my own death warrant.

"For years," Damen said, his voice carrying easily through the hall, "my High Priests and Priestesses believed the key to understanding and unlocking the mysteries of essence lay in the ancient texts—in the runes and symbols long forgotten. We have asked ourselves the questions: why should only some wield such power? Why should Gifts not be shared?"

He stood, moving slowly, circling the Valtanan prisoner as though he were a vulture testing the strength of his prey.

"And so we hunted. We searched every book, every scroll, every whisper of knowledge, for a way to transfer power from one person to another. At first, it was only possible to borrow Gifts. A brief spark, fleeting, short-lived... gone as quickly as it came." Damen's mouth curled into a smile, his voice almost gleeful. "But then at last, my darling Aleta found it."

He paused, letting the silence draw out before he continued, softly, almost with reverence.

"Now... we can take their Gifts entirely, use them against them. Eradicate them."

I had to resist the urge to shake my head, disbelief threatening to spill over. For the barest moment I felt almost sorry for him—for the grief that had eaten him alive, for the jealousy that had turned to hatred. But pity curdled quickly into dread. He was so consumed by it that he had lost all sense of reality. Nor could he see the irony in his actions. I could only think that his lust for power had made him jealous of Valtanans. Our gifts made us stronger than him, and that made us a threat, even when we had never sought to be one.

Valtana had only ever been a peaceful nation. Its people used their gifts for the better of their communities. But now we challenged his ego, his power and authority. Taking my father's throne had never been enough. He wanted *all* power, *all* control. But surely that would mean he wouldn't just stop with Valtana. The Fae were even more dangerous. Surely he didn't mean to go after them, too?

"How?" Canver asked hoarsely, breaking the silence. "How is this possible?"

Damen fixed his eyes on Emrys and Bran. Bran had lifted his chin, a cold, lethal expression hardening his face. It was one I couldn't remember ever having seen there before.

"In the end," Damen said softly, almost with satisfaction, "the answer lay with our allies."

"How so?" Emrys pressed, fists curling again.

"Blood magic," Damen replied simply. He let the

words hang, enjoying their weight. Then he called," Aleta."

Denfor sat forward in his chair and leaned his elbows on the table, a rare smile on his face as the mistress came striding back into the room. She had abandoned the red dress from earlier and now wore a sleeveless black gown that trailed along the floor behind her. The neckline plunged low, exposing most of her breasts, her shoulders her arms—all of it painted with runes. Dark, jagged symbols snaked across her skin, and every line shimmered as though it were alive. My breath caught. A small gasp escaped me before I could stop it. Blood. The runes were drawn in blood.

Aleta's eyes glittered as she crossed the room without hesitation. She stopped before one of the Order priests and, with ritualistic precision, held out her hand. He placed his long, thin blade across her palm, and she carried it back to Damen as though it were an offering. Without hesitation, she seized the Valtanan man by the wrist and drew the blade along the inside of his arm. Blood welled, dark and sluggish, tinted with silver. He didn't even flinch.

"The key," Damen said smoothly, " is Faelock, a particularly lethal variant that is combined with Silvermist. For that, we must convey our gratitude to the Nevedeno."

He glanced at me knowingly, and I caught Tanrith's face turning toward mine, heavy with interest.

"Beautifully lethal," he continued, almost in admiration, "it helps to break the bond between the essence and the host. The body weakens, drifting in that exquisite space where they hover between life and death. And it is in that state, when they hover closest to the veil, that the power can be transferred."

Aleta dipped her finger into the man's blood and began to draw symbols over his chest and shoulders. The runes bled crimson across his skin, grotesque and mesmerizing all at once. Nausea clawed at my stomach. This was what Finn and Cai had been working on. It wasn't just a new variant of Faelock. They had spliced it with Silvermist, too. The thought made my stomach turn. How could Cai have done this? To his own kind? I suspected I'd never know, but I silently added him to the growing list of people I was going to kill. Sitting up straight, I tried to look fascinated, but my knee bounced up and down and Austell placed his hand firmly against it to still it.

"Impressive," I breathed, masking revulsion with forced awe. "I can't tell you how excited I am to finally see it in action after all this time. I have heard whispers of people who could such things, of *Dreors*... I didn't realize that your own mistress was one."

Aleta's head snapped toward me, her eyes flashing venom. She didn't like me openly referring to her as his mistress.

"Oh no, no, my dear," Damen corrected, amusement curling in his voice. "Aleta is merely an acolyte. She might have had the vision, but it took someone much more special to bring this to life."

Aleta closed her eyes, her lashes lowering in mock humility, and when she spoke, her voice dipped into a low, sensual murmur. Ancient words carried from her lips in another language. Only when I saw Bran's brow furrow and his exchanged look with Emrys did I realize it was the old Fae tongue. Her words curled around us in smoke, growing louder and louder, and the air around us became charged with energy. The runes on the man's skin began to glow in response to her words, and Damen sat down in the chair next to him. He removed his waistcoat and unbuttoned his shirt, allowing Aleta to paint the same symbols onto her lover's chest with the Valtanan man's blood as she continued to chant.

"This man's gift is fire," Damen said. "In the aftermath of Nissae there were rumors circulating. Some said that they had seen me wielding fire with my bare hands, and how I *wished* that had been the case. But today, it will become a reality."

Aleta's voice grew louder still and the atmosphere in the room became almost unbearable. Montavis was watching with barely concealed horror, and I could hear Austell's foot tapping nervously against the leg of his chair. The mistress uttered a bone chilling, guttural sound and then went silent, and the Valtanan's head slumped suddenly forward. Damen smiled and held out his hands in front of him, gazing wondrously on the sparks that flared from his fingers.

In an instant, flames consumed my vision, and I was no longer sitting in the throne room. I was back in my bedroom in Haeddas, the beams above my head cracking and creaking as the house burned furiously. Noa's hand was gripping mine tightly and all I could hear was the sound of screaming from outside. My breathing turned shallow, and darkness pulled at the edge of my vision as I began to lose the tenuous hold I had on my emotions. Panic threatened to overwhelm me.

Look at me.

The command came abruptly, the voice thundering not from across the room but inside my own head, reverberating through me until I had no choice but to obey. My eyes snapped up, colliding with Emrys's gaze like a blow.

Breathe. You will be calm.

When the second command came I realized what he was doing. For the first time since I'd known him, he was using his own abilities on me, compulsion, curling around my thoughts and holding them steady. Without hesitation, I took a deep breath. The noise of the hall receded, and the smell of blood and smoke disappeared until there was nothing left but him, his voice, low and steady within me.

Breathe.

I took another shuddering inhale. Then another. My vision cleared, edges sharpening again. And just as suddenly as it had seized me, the grip loosened. My thoughts were my own again. I blinked, glancing around me. Had anyone noticed? No. Damen was still speaking. Tanrith was still watching with that gleam in his eye. But Emrys's eyes remained locked on mine. He arched a brow in silent question. I dipped my chin, the smallest acknowledgement. I was back in control, at least outwardly. Inside, my heart was hammering.

"Incredible," I heard Tanrith murmur as Damen made the flames grow higher in his hands.

"*This* is how we will defeat them," he said.

"And the heir?" Canver asked. "What will you do with her, Your Highness? How will you find her?"

Damen turned his head to look at Aleta and she smiled, revealing her perfectly white teeth. She still stood beside the Valtanan man but he had gone completely motionless, and I knew that he was close to death, the Faelock slowly but surely killing him. My heart wept for him. When I returned my attention to Damen, I noticed something I hadn't seen before—a familiar mark on his collarbone.

"Oh, we don't need to find Aeva Penrose," Aleta said with a smirk. "She will come to us."

"You're so sure?" I asked, unable to help myself.

She turned her intense gaze on me and I held her eye, smiling slightly as she raised her chin defiantly at me.

"Certain."

"Why would she do that?" Montavis asked, throwing me a quick sideways look.

"The Order brought a man to the palace a few weeks ago, one who tried to use what the men are calling the black terror, but what the Fae call the *noswaith*. Very few have the gift, as Prince Trystan here can testify."

She glanced at him, biting her lip seductively. His jaw tightened fractionally in response.

"The *noswaith* runs through the Ashae family line, passed on through Aemylia and her brother, Arlo, to their children. Which means that the man in our dungeons is none other than Aeva's beloved cousin, Prince Aeden. I believe that she will come for him, and so does he, apparently, according to his ardent threats."

My blood ran cold. I had been hoping fervently that they hadn't, but of course they would have made the connection. They knew who he was, and what he meant to me, to Aeva. A million questions ran through my mind. Did they know he was Nevedeno? If they'd found his tattoo, then maybe. Luckily, his wasn't as obvious as mine. For a laugh he'd had his inked on one of his ass cheeks, so there was high chance it hadn't been discovered. And, since I wasn't currently in the dungeons being interrogated, my instinct told me that they didn't know about that. Yet.

"What a stroke of luck," Tanrith said with a grin. "And quite the gift, too."

"Indeed," Damen said. "This one is proving… troublesome to extract. The *Dreor* has to work a little harder with this gift. But he *will* succeed. And when he does, we will strip the Valtanan prince bare, tear the gift from his bones, and silence their so-called queen. With the Nothori at our side, we will hunt down the rest of the Gifted, every last one of them. We will take everything—every shred of power, every drop of blood—and just like their queen, they will beg for mercy, and die screaming."

CHAPTER 53
EFA

Back in the ballroom, I drifted through the press of silk and jewels like a ghost, the music and laughter clashing harshly against the image burned into my mind. All I could see was the Valtanan man, slumped forward in the chair, the life draining out of him. It was the worst thing I had ever witnessed. I wondered who he was. Did he have a family waiting for him, children who would never know what became of their father? Did he believe, right up until the end, that someone might save him? Or had he given up hope a long time ago?

Around me, the guests danced and smiled, oblivious. Laughter spread like spilled wine, while I felt as though the walls were closing in. I leant a trembling hand to the nearest table, forcing myself to breathe. This wasn't the time to fall apart. Not now. Not when Noa needed me so badly. Not when there was so much to fight for. This—this horror—it was the proof of what we were fighting against.

Emrys had been the first to stand after the demonstration, standing so fast that his chair screeched and fell over. He had stormed from the room with Bran following in his wake without a single word, clearly done with any semblance of diplomacy. I had wanted to do the exact same thing myself, but I left the room gracefully with Austell just behind Montavis and Hollis, who quickly gathered up their wives and slipped away, presumably to debrief them on what had just happened. Outside in the ballroom, I rallied myself and walked slowly over to where Austell and Nev stood by the terrace doors.

"I'm assuming from the looks on your faces that whatever happened in there wasn't good," Nev said, quietly. "Austell will undoubtedly fill me in, but it's time to go, Efa. Arella has already gone to meet Jory and the others."

I nodded, a sudden desperation clawing at me to escape the suffocating room and breathe in the fresh, salt-laden air of the coves. My gaze swept the crowd until I found Emrys across the room, his eyes already fixed on me. I gave a small nod to show I was ready, feeling Austell's hand close gently around mine. When I lifted my face to his, his clear blue eyes looked anxious.

"Promise me that you will take care, Efa," he said, his eyes darting up to where Emrys waited. "Both of you."

"I will. And so must you. Be ready to leave at any moment, and if you think they suspect you, get out."

I pushed up onto my tiptoes and kissed him softly on the cheek, squeezing his hand before I let go, and then I made my way through the increasingly rowdy crowd, leaving the ballroom alone. Emrys and I were to meet in the library and I walked in that direction unhurriedly, admiring the paintings on the walls and smiling politely at the other guests that I passed on the way. When the library came into view, I picked up my pace, but then a voice called my name behind me, and my stomach dropped. Cursing softly, I turned to find Damen and Brayson standing just a few meters away.

"Surely you aren't leaving the ball already?" Damen asked, closing the distance between us. "The night is so young."

I laughed and shook my head, pointing down to the hem of my dress.

"No, Your Highness. I'm sure you'll laugh at me, but I'm wearing new shoes for the occasion and they are quite uncomfortable. I was returning to my room to change them."

"What an inconvenience! Women and their fashion."

I smiled slightly at the joke, praying that he would release me quickly so I could be on my way, but he had other ideas.

"It is fortuitous that we found you here," he continued. "I was hoping to speak with you. Perhaps I could trouble you to join me for a short time in my rooms before you change your shoes?"

I hesitated, tilting my head and licking my lips nervously. This was unexpected. My shadows moved restlessly, thrumming a warning and reminding me that I needed to go. Instinct told me that danger lay ahead if I followed him to his rooms, but I could hardly say no.

"Of course," I said, smiling pleasantly.

Damen gestured for me to walk beside him and we began to stroll back in the direction I had just come towards the ballroom, Brayson following us silently like some kind of death spirit. The king made light conversation, pointing out portraits and telling me who each subject was and their role in Melrith's history, completely unaware that they were my own ancestors hanging on the walls, or so I hoped. I nodded along amiably as he spoke while I imagined all of the different ways that I could kill him when the time came, but the truth was I was nervous.

What did he want from me now? Had I misjudged how

much he knew? Had Finn told him something—anything—about me? Perhaps he had finally learned that I was Gifted, or spoken of my relationship with Emrys. My thoughts spiraled through every possibility, but the more I turned them over, the more I convinced myself that Finn wouldn't expose me. He wouldn't risk jeopardizing me, since what he wanted above all else was me returned to him. Which meant something else was afoot. I just didn't know what.

When we reached them, we found Damen's chambers quieter than before. Most were likely down at the ball, but there were still several couples in there, moaning and panting breathlessly. I briefly wondered if Damen ever got bored of the constant noise, or if he ever got any sleep, since it appeared to be a constant hum of activity in there. I would have found it immensely tiring, but then I wasn't a crazed tyrant.

Damen poured two glasses of brandy and handed one to me, his fingers grazing mine as I took it. I waited for him to take a sip and then did the same, grimacing as the liquid burned my throat. I ignored the people around me and looked out of the windows into the darkness beyond, just about making out the twinkling lights down in the harbor.

"So, Efa, what did you think of our little... display."

What did I think? I thought the whole thing was fucked up, twisted beyond belief. I had witnessed and done some terrible things in my life, but nothing compared to the malice I had seen play out in that room. And the worst of it was that I now understood just how formidable an enemy Damen was. Even if he didn't know how to fully wield his stolen gift, the potential was there, and it terrified me.

I took a breath. Defeating him would not be simple. It wouldn't be brute strength or reckless courage that brought him down. It would take strategy, patience and something meticulous, something extraordinary. Because when the time came, we'd likely only get once chance. And only the Gods knew what other abilities he might steal before then, or how long it would be before he mastered them all.

I swallowed, trying to think of the right thing to say, ignoring the pull toward the ocean. To Noa.

"I… well, I'm speechless, Your Highness. I'm honoured that the Nevedeno has played a role in making all of this possible, even if I'm no longer a part of it."

"Indeed. It really is such a shame that you are no longer affiliated with them, don't you think?"

I smiled and shrugged good-naturedly, but then the sound that drifted across the room made my blood freeze. A low grunt, rough and familiar. My smile faltered as I turned my head, finding him. He was turned away, broad back to me, shoulders flexing, his head tipped down looking at the woman beneath him. I couldn't see his face, but I didn't need to.

I knew that sound.

The hair at the nape of my neck prickled as I took in the thick, dark hair, the strong line of his frame, and the large tattoo that covered his tanned, flawless skin, stretching from shoulder to shoulder. I would have recognized him anywhere. The oath line stung sharply as I relived the pain he had caused me on the cliffs. The way that I had *burned*.

With a final, loud groan Finn stilled and then abruptly stood up, buttoning up his pants and pulling on the shirt that had been draped across the chair next to him. He ran a hand through his hair while I stared murderously at his back, and then turned slowly, his eyes widening with delight as he saw me. The girl he was with sat up and reached for a glass of wine as she adjusted her dress. With her hair disheveled and her cheeks flushed, Caja looked more beautiful than ever.

Damen was watching me watch Finn, his calculating eyes drinking in my reaction to the man who had controlled me for years. He lifted a hand and beckoned Finn over to join us, and I shifted on my feet and flexed my fingers, widening my stance and feeling the weight of the blades strapped at my thighs. Brayson strolled around the room as if this was all a game, but I could sense the threat growing with every passing moment.

"I told you I'd be seeing you again soon, didn't I?" Finn drawled, his voice as familiar as the scar he'd left on my body.

I stared at him. I knew Finn; I knew his tells. I knew the way his mouth tightened when he lied, and the faint tic at his jaw when he was angry. But here, now, I couldn't get a read on him. I wondered if he had been somewhere in the palace all this time, watching and waiting. Maybe he'd delivered the Faelock to the Esari suite himself. I supposed it didn't really matter at this point. I'd always known I'd have to face Finn again, I just hadn't expect it to be there in the palace with Damen pulling the strings. How much had Aleta told him? Did he know about the oath? About the rite? About the hold Finn still had on me?

"It's funny," Damen started, stroking his beard, "Finn has often spoken about how the woman he loved had gone astray."

The woman he loved? Please.

"He missed her terribly. At times he seemed quite inconsolable. Only recently did I find out that the talented smuggler he has talked about so much was none other than our dear Lord Esari's new fiancée. Our Lady-Designate. Quite the coincidence, isn't it? Of course, it was a bitter blow for Finn, seeing you with another man."

"It looks like he's rather gotten over it already," I said smoothly, nodding my head at Caja. "We have both moved on, I think that's for the best."

Finn's expression darkened and he took a step towards me, the look in his eyes becoming dangerous.

"Perhaps," Damen said musingly. "In any event, Finn has certainly played an instrumental role in getting us to where we are. It was he who offered up his extraordinarily talented gardener to create the new hybrid, and he who helped to negotiate our new alliance with Nothore."

I kept my face neutral, but underneath the calm exterior my shadows were simmering with rage.

"And, of course, he was one of the first, brave volunteers to have the rite performed on him."

"Is that so?"

Damen smiled smugly, letting a small flame appear in his hand as he talked.

"Like me, he seems to have an affinity with fire."

I grit my teeth, refusing to rise. As Damen took a seat in a nearby armchair, Finn turned away and arrogantly helped himself to a glass of brandy.

"Of course," Damen said casually, "as invaluable as he has been, he is a *complete* liability."

Well, that caught my interest. I snapped my eyes back to Damen, noticing the way Finn's body had gone completely still.

"I've heard him be called unhinged, fixated, even neurotic. You, yourself, have told me that he cannot be trusted, and that he would betray me in a heartbeat if it suited him."

Well, that was certainly awkward.

"Oh, Efa… that's both unkind and unfair," Finn said, turning to look at me with his hand on heart in mock injury. "And this coming from a woman with no loyalty or fidelity. You have, after all, betrayed not only me, but the rest of the Nevedeno, and that is an unforgivable offence."

I sighed heavily and rolled my eyes, growing tired of the game we were playing. I placed my glass down on a nearby table and put my hands on my hips, smiling tightly.

"Forgive me, Your Highness, but perhaps we could get to the point. What are we all doing here?"

Damen's eyes flashed with amusement and he leaned forward, resting his elbows on his knees.

"You really are quite something, aren't you? You are truly captivating... quite enchanting. Yes, I understand *exactly* what they see in you."

He held his empty wine glass up to Brayson in a silent command for the General to refill it for him. For a moment, I took my eyes off of the king and watched Brayson, bemused by the relationship between the two men. Perhaps it was because I had been too young and naïve to really understand, but I'd always thought that my father had seen Damen, his most senior General, as his equal, or at the very least a trusted advisor. But Damen treated his General like a servant. I couldn't understand why Brayson would put up with that.

"Let me be blunt then, too," Damen said. "I'm afraid I cannot allow your marriage to Austell to take place."

My heart skipped a beat.

"I see," I asked slowly. "May I ask why?"

"Well, I simply cannot have you squirreled away down at Totease, lost amongst the roses."

He loosened his collar and I caught a glimpse of the runes Aleta had drawn, the blood now smeared across his chest. Brayson returned with a fresh glass of wine and then resumed his position between Finn and the king.

"Oh, I know that Austell will be deeply disappointed,

but I'm sure he'll understand that I have a much greater need for you."

"If this is your way of asking me to join your harem again, then I'm afraid that I must *again* respectfully decline. Or, indeed, if you think to force me to return to the Nevedeno with Finn Yadari again, you should know that I have no intention of going anywhere with him."

A look passed between them, and I knew with absolute certainty that Finn had struck a deal. He'd bargained his way into Damen's graces, and whatever promises he'd made, I was sure that the matter of my returning to him was non-negotiable. He would stop at nothing until I was his again, and the thought chilled me more than death. Finn's eyes were on me, a smile tugging at his mouth as if I were already his prize reclaimed. He took a step forward, and it took everything in me to stand still, resisting the urge to move back.

"No," Damen almost sang, swirling the wine with mock delight. "No, I won't make you go with him."

Finn's body tensed, his eyes narrowing as they focused in on Damen.

"Of, course, I understand his desire," Damen continued silkily. "To own you as Finn has must feel... *extraordinary*. In fact, I'd very much like to feel it for myself. To have you as part of my harem... "

He smiled dreamily, no doubt imagining it. My skin crawled. He knew about the oath line then, and the way that it bound me to Finn.

"But no," Damen continued, taking another sip of his wine. "I don't think I shall put you through that."

Finn's expression had gone absolutely savage, and this time I knew that look. I had seen it far too many times before, and I knew exactly what it meant. Damen had made an agreement with Finn, and now he was going back on it. Had his arrogance made him reckless and stupid, or did he have another play here? Surely he didn't expect to cross a man like Finn and not suffer some kind of backlash.

"*What*?"

Finn's voice was barely above a whisper, but it promised so much blood and violence. I wondered if Damen had any idea what he had just done, but I suspect that Brayson did. His hand moved to rest on his sword.

"You have been an integral part of our planning, Finn, but I'm afraid you have become too much of a risk. It's time for change. I've decided that I want Efa to take command of the Nevedeno. With immediate effect."

His statement hung in the air between us and I blinked once. Twice. What the fuck was going on? I held my breath, as I looked between the two men.

"You must be mistaken," Finn said slowly. "It is not for you to decide who leads the Nevedeno. We have never been controlled by anyone except ourselves, and that isn't about to change simply because you have been enchanted by *my* whore that *I* raised from the streets."

I frowned, bristling at the insult and holding myself up a little straighter. He gave himself too much credit. I had fought every day to get to where I was now, and it had very little to do with him. Damen simply laughed, clearly growing tired of the conversation and seeming impervious to Finn's threats. That was a mistake. Finn's ability to wield fire might mean nothing to the king since he had stolen Ross's gift, but that didn't mean that Finn wasn't still an exceptionally violent man armed with just a blade, or his bare hands if that was all he had. If he didn't try to kill Damen there and then, he would stop at nothing until he had his revenge. The king had to know that, but it didn't seem to bother him in the slightest. Instead, he smirked, turning his head my way.

"Kill him, Efa."

The silence felt too loud. For a heartbeat, I thought Damen was joking. He *had* to be joking. But then I met his eyes. They were cold and merciless, and the trust landed like a blade between my ribs. He was deadly serious.

"What?" I said dumbly.

"Kill him. *Now*."

My breath caught. *Kill Finn*? He knew. He had to know I couldn't, that the oath line bound me tighter than chains. Surely someone had told him what it meant. So why would he command me to do the one thing I couldn't do? My gaze flicked to Finn, searching his face for some clue, some explanation, but I could see the shadow of surprise on his face, too. This was unexpected.

My mind raced. Was this a test? A game? A way to see what I was truly capable of? To prove my loyalty? Around us, the room had gone deathly quiet. Even the usual moaning from Damen's pets had stilled, every breath held, every gaze fixed on me. Waiting.

"Come on then, Efa. Kill me," Finn said mockingly. "Perhaps just this once you can follow an order."

I hesitated, paralysed by indecision. My shadows fought to get loose but it would have been futile. Instead, I tried to calm them. To still the screaming.

"Kill me, Efa," Finn said again. "Slit my throat like you did Edvarr's and Theo's. Kill me, and take the position you've desired for so long. Do it, if you can, my little Smuggler Queen."

There was movement behind the three men, but none of them noticed. Only I saw the petite woman in the silk dress, gliding closer. Finn's sharp, intricately carved blade was clutched in her hand, lifted from where it had fallen on the floor. She moved slowly, and deliberately, her footsteps muffled by the thick, bearskin rugs. I didn't move. I kept my eyes on Finn, willing him to focus on me as I feigned helplessness and indecision, desperate to keep his attention away from what was coming. Somehow, it worked. Finn laughed arrogantly, certain he'd already won.

"That's what I thought," he said triumphantly. "It seems you've learned your lesson after that day on the cliffs. You remember your place, and what I can do to you should you ever defy me again."

Without warning, hot, searing pain shot through me, and a scream burst from my mouth. Tears filled my eyes as my skin began to burn and I closed my eyes, bowing my head submissively, forcing myself to take deep, shuddering breaths as I waited for the torment to be over. He laughed again, and the pain suddenly eased, a sob escaping my lips as I tried to steady myself. Slowly, I raised my head, eyes locking on to his as I drew in another breath, stealing myself.

"The thing is, Finn," I said quietly, my voice trembling, "you've got it all wrong. I never wanted to lead the Nevedeno; I only ever wanted to be free of it, and free of you. And I didn't kill Edvarr, or Theo, even though I was there. Watching. I had someone else kill them." Now it was my turn to smile. "On my orders."

Too late he realized what I was trying to tell him. Too late he twisted his head, perhaps just catching a glimpse of Caja standing behind him. The blade glinted in the lamplight as she drew back her arm, and then, before he could even react, hot blood sprayed across my face as she plunged it into his neck.

CHAPTER 54
EFA

I must have dreamed about the day Finn Yadari would die a hundred times, but never had I imagined that it would be like this, with Canver's mistress standing in front of me, her soft silk gown splattered with blood. Nor had I expected to feel so little when the oath was finally broken. There was no rush of essence through my veins, no searing pain—or sensation of *any* kind—on my arm. Finn lay on the floor, his blood seeping slowly into the bearskin rug beneath him, and in the end, it was almost anticlimactic. The constant burning and throbbing I had lived with for so long was simply gone in an instant, and I knew that if I pulled back my sleeve, the oath line would no longer be there.

Caja's beautiful face remained composed, but her chest rose and fell in sharp bursts, the hand clutching Finn's knife trembling violently. She stared at me without blinking, something unspoken passing in the silence between us. The sound of Damen's slow and deliberate clapping drew my attention away from her. He leaned back in his chair, a look of delight etched on his aging face as his eyes moved between Caja and me. No doubt he was seeing her in a new light, admiring her more than ever. Little did he know that before the night was out, Morgan would have completed his task, and Caja, too, would be free of her oath. I intended to make certain no one ever forced her consent again. I cleared my throat and reached up to wipe Finn's blood from my face.

"Thank you, Caja. You may leave us now. I suggest that you go and find Captain Bairstow or Lord Esari."

She nodded quickly, dropping the knife unceremoniously on to Finn's body before slipping from the room; her movements hurried but graceful, as if afraid to look back.

"It seems I have underestimated you, Efa Rescorla," Damen said, his eyes dancing with something unreadable.

I knew then for certain that he'd known I couldn't kill Finn. There was something in his tone of voice and expression. It *had* been a test. He'd wanted to see what I would do and how I handled myself. No doubt if I had done nothing, or if Caja hadn't done what she had, he would have given me back to Finn after all. But that was a very dangerous game to play. Had Finn still been alive, he would have never forgiven Damen for going back on a deal, test or no test.

"I accept your offer," I said much more confidently that I felt. "I will lead the Nevedeno. They have long been in need of a fresh direction."

"I couldn't agree more," he said, smiling like the predator who had finally caught his prey.

Despite the precarious position I found myself in, I could hardly believe my luck. Twice I had been summoned to Damen's rooms, and twice I had been certain my end was near. Yet here I stood. Finn lay dead at my feet, and Damen was still none the wiser to my true identity. Now, with Finn gone, I could ensure the Nevedeno ceased supplying him with the drug he craved so desperately. I was close—so close—to finding Noa and the Amberstone, to walking out of the palace with everything I needed to bring Damen down. To destroying the man who had murdered my parents, and all those who aided him. The thought left me almost giddy, a dangerous strand of euphoria threading through the fear. But it was short lived.

Only a moment later, my shadows pulsed in sudden warning. Damen opened his mouth to speak, but the main doors to the suite swung wide, and Emrys strolled in, flanked by two Order priests. My breath caught. Arella's warning rang in my head. He shouldn't have been here. He should have been waiting for me in the passages. His eyes skimmed over Finn's corpse, the blood staining my dress, and no doubt the feral edge in my eyes as adrenaline still coursed hot through my veins. He gave me the look I knew so well—the silent question. *Are you all right?* I forced a small nod.

"Ah Trystan," Damen said, rising smoothly to his feet. "We've just been taking care of some long overdue business."

Emrys's gaze dipped to Finn again, and then returned to the king. He smiled lazily.

"I can see that."

My attention shifted to the Order priests. Both looked like hardened soldiers, their scarred knuckles and wide, grounded stances showing their training and experience, their eyes cold and merciless. Emrys tilted his head fractionally, checking their positions, but otherwise appeared unfazed. The fury I'd seen in him before was gone, replaced by a detached indifference that unsettled me even more. I wished I could mirror his composure, but my shadows betrayed me, trembling at the edges of my vision. Deep-rooted fear was unfurling in my stomach, as Damen stood motionless, watching Emrys with quiet calculation. Behind him, Brayson lingered, ever watchful.

"Everyone out!" Damen bellowed so suddenly that I flinched.

The room erupted into frantic motion. Men and women scrambled, fumbling with clothing, shoving past each other in their rush to obey. I took a step toward the door, hesitating for a second in my unwillingness to leave Emrys, but Damen held out a finger to me.

"Not you, Efa. You stay."

Cold dread slid down my spine. My pulse hammered as the last half-dressed girl left, shutting the door behind her. Only then did I realize I'd been holding my breath. I exhaled slowly, forcing myself to keep still as Damen lifted his glass, his eyes fixed on Emrys over the rim.

"Trystan," he said smoothly, setting the glass down with a deliberate clink. "Thank you for joining us. As I was saying, there is one final matter to address."

Emrys spread his hands wide, looking thoroughly bored by the conversation.

"I'm all ears."

A muscle ticked in Damen's jaw, the only betrayal of irritation. He smirked, looking between us.

"You know… I've heard rumors. Whispers of a romantic interest between you both."

Emrys let out a low chuckle, grinning roguishly.

"A flirtation, perhaps, nothing more. It's always entertaining to watch Austell lose his composure, and the Lady-Designate *is* pretty."

Damen's eyes gleamed with amusement, his lips curving into something between a smirk and a sneer. He loathed Emrys, I could see it in the tightening of his jaw, and the way his fingers tapped against his leg. But the notion of Austell—dutiful, self-righteous Austell—being provoked made him laugh. He savored the thought, even as his hatred simmered beneath the surface.

"Ah," he said, almost indulgently. "If it unsettles Austell, then perhaps there *is* some merit in it."

Emrys only shrugged again. I kept my mouth shut, unwilling to add fuel to the fire.

"Anyway," Damen continued. "As you will see, there is to be a change in the Nevedeno's leadership. I believe you and Finn were… acquainted. It seems Austell's fiancée was a little more than she appeared. She will succeed him."

Emrys raised an eyebrow as if only slightly surprised by the news.

"Efa," Damen said, turning to me. "I expect a smooth transition of power to you. Delays to my shipments will not be tolerated, and we will be requiring more than originally anticipated. Our plans are expanding."

"Oh," I said. "How so?"

Out of the corner of my eye I saw Brayson move away from us toward the window, his brow creased in consternation. Out towards the harbor, a bright orange glow was flickering amongst the houses as the flames spread. The Loyalists were in the city.

Damen took a step toward us, and my hands itched for my knife. I almost abandoned my plan not to kill him there and then. On impulse, I reached out toward Brayson and the two Order priests, testing if my shadows could slip past their defenses. My stomach sank. They all had the *skold*, too. All three of them were shielded, untouchable, and impervious to me. I clenched my fist in frustration.

From the corridor came the thunder of boots, men running hard. Shouts echoed faintly from outside, sounds of panic and chaos, and Brayson's head snapped around. He strode to the door, yanked it open, and seized one of the sprinting guards by the collar, demanding to know what had happened. The soldier stammered something in response that made the color drain from Brayson's face. He shoved the man aside and hurried back in, leaning close to Damen to whisper in his ear. I didn't need to hear the words. I already knew. The Loyalists were here. My certainty sharpened when I caught the ghost of a smile on Emrys's face. Jory and the others had made it into the palace. Damen's mouth thinned to a hard line, and he gave a curt nod.

"There is something I need to attend to," he said, "so I'll make this brief. I know what you seek, Trystan. I know that you travel my country in disguise, defiling my temples and killing my acolytes as you search for the Amberstone."

The indifferent expression had left Emrys's face. Now, we saw him for exactly what he was. Powerful. Terrifying. Undeniably lethal.

"We will *never* stop searching for what you stole from us," he said darkly.

"I know that," Damen said lightly. "But what you might not know is this: you were recognized recently by a Nothori soldier who escaped one of the Loyalist's slaughtering. A rare thing really—I've never known a Nothori coward before. He was quick to die after confessing, but not before he told us what he saw."

Damen stepped forward, his smile razor sharp.

"That Prince Trystan was fighting with the Loyalists."

Emrys's teeth flashed white, but he said nothing. Outside, the shouting in the palace swelled, closer and louder than it had been before.

"So you see," Damen went on, voice hardening, "we really aren't allies, are we? There is no pact between the Northern Realm and Melrith. Despite the position the Fae find themself in, Aubrey still sends his own brother to work against us."

A slow, insolent smile pulled at Emrys's lips, and my shadows surged in warning, tasting danger. Without thought my hand went to my blade.

Don't fight.

The command slammed into my mind, and my fingers froze, bound by an invisible leash. Breath caught in my chest as I stared at him, begging him silently to let me move, to let me *do* something.

"That just won't do, Trystan," Damen murmured, his words low and final. A death sentence.

I fought against Emrys's will, begging my fingers to twitch, to reach, to fight.

Don't fight, Efa.

The words pressed down on me again, not spoken, but swirling through my veins.

You will not fight to defend me. You will not reveal yourself. You will endure, no matter what.

His command wound through me like iron chains, binding me into stillness. My chest rose shallowly, and I knew my eyes were wild as I pleaded silently for him to let me go, shadows repeating their warnings, but he didn't look at me. Not once. His eyes stayed locked on Damen, his face grim with resignation.

Then cobalt flared. My shadows shrieked inside me, and agony ripped through my chest as if my heart itself had been torn. The Order priests had struck. Their blades, long and gleaming, drove into him, and Emrys staggered, the sound of his knees cracking on the wooden floor searing into me like a brand. His blood spread fast, soaking his shirt, and spilling dark across the boards where they mixed with Finn's. I screamed without sound, my mouth opening useless as time fractured, slowed, stopped.

I fought him. I fought the invisible compulsion, clawed at the edges of my own mind, desperate to move. But he held me fast, even as his life poured onto the floor. His power ebbed, Faelock coursing through him, the poison already dancing through his veins. And still he held me. Still, he kept me from reaching him. Tears blurred my vision as Damen strode forward, each step echoing like a death knell. He caught a fistful of Emrys's hair, wrenching his head back and forcing him to meet his eyes. And I could do nothing. Nothing but watch.

"I have looked forward to this moment for a long time," Damen hissed. "Mark my words: first Valtana will fall, and then, so too will the Northern Realm."

He let go of Emrys roughly, pushing his head down towards the floor before straightening up and turning to me. He cleared his throat, adjusting his waistcoat as if nothing had happened. I didn't bother trying to hide my horror as he looked at me. His voice cut through the ringing in my ears. It was casual and cruel.

"I do hope you weren't fond of him, Efa."

My mouth opened, and then closed gain, no sound escaping. Words wouldn't come. My throat was tight, my chest hollowed out, the pain so absolute it felt as though something inside of me had split apart. My heart was breaking, shattering, and still I could do nothing but stand there, silent and undone, while Damen smiled at me.

"It's time to leave, sire," I heard Brayson say, his hand on his king's back.

Damen ignored him, still smiling at me as he nudged Emrys with his boot.

"You will need to learn this quickly now that you control the Nevedeno, Efa. To be a true leader, one must be bold, ruthless, and unflinching, something that my own predecessor never managed."

My fists clenched tighter at my side.

"*This* is what will happen to you if you betray me, Efa," he continued. "I expect your complete discretion and your unwavering loyalty, or you will meet the same fate."

Red pulled at the edge of my vision. I felt consumed by hatred, my hands desperate to wrap around his throat and watch the life leave his dead, soulless eyes.

"What about Aubrey?" I asked tightly. "The Fae won't stand for this."

"Oh, Trystan's death will be easy to explain," he said, dismissively. "We'll say that it was the Loyalists currently infiltrating the castle. Perhaps they were hoping to turn the Fae against me, or perhaps they blamed the Fae for not sending aid to Valtana all those years ago." He spread his hands and smirked. "It doesn't matter. The Fae know their place. They will mourn their prince, and stay quietly and obediently on their side of the mountains while we finish what we started and eradicate the Gifted. And then, with your help, we will look north of the mountains. And we will destroy the Northern Realm, too."

CHAPTER 55
EFA

The screaming in the palace had grown louder as chaos spread, but I held myself utterly still, caught in the invisible grip of Emrys's compulsion. Only when Brayson had half-dragged Damen from the room, the Order priests following close behind, did the hold on me vanish. They were so certain the poison would finish him, so certain of my silence and loyalty, that they hadn't even spared Emrys a second thought. The door slammed shut, and I collapsed to my knees beside him. I cradled his head in my lap, my lip trembling as I traced the silvery hue beneath his skin, the telltale mark of the poison that *was* slowly and surely killing him. My shadows screamed at me, desperate to do something, anything, but I was powerless.

"Why didn't you fight?" I choked, clutching his hand and holding on to it tightly. "Why didn't you let me do something?"

"Oh, Efa," he whispered, so gently it broke me further, "the *Raeth*… you can't outrun your fate."

"Fuck fate, Emrys! I could have *saved* you. Gods, you could have saved *yourself*! You're the Dark Prince!"

"No," he said. His eyes found mine, heavy with sorrow and finality "It had to be like this."

Tears blurred my vision as I bent over him, sobs shaking my chest.

"Emrys… I can't… I won't…"

The doors crashed open and I startled, hand going for my blade. But it was only Bran and Morgan, swords drawn and faces hard. Relief flooded me for a heartbeat, but it couldn't touch the desolation I felt inside. Emrys lay bleeding in my arms, and no power in the world could stop what was coming.

"It's the poison…" I gasped breathlessly, looking up beseechingly at them.

"We need to get him out of here," Bran said, his voice low and urgent.

Bran and Morgan bent to lift him, and when their eyes met over his slumped body, I saw the horror there. They had seen him bleed before, had fought beside him in battles, but never like this. His weight sagged between them, his breaths ragged, blood staining their hands as they tried to steady him. Bran's jaw clenched, a flash of panic breaking through his usual calm, and Morgan's face had gone stark white. For a moment, they just stared at him, as if unable to reconcile the Emrys they knew with the broken body in their arms.

"Move," I urged, shoving myself to my feet. My voice cracked with desperation. "There's an entrance into the tunnels from Damen's study. This way."

I snatched a lamp from a nearby table and hurried towards the closed doors at the far side of the suite. When I flung them open, the familiar gloom of my father's study met me. It was like stepping into the past. The same desk.

The same worn armchair. And above it, the same painting. I froze.

Her face stared down at me, captured in soft oils. I took in the loose hair, the muslin dress, the way her eyes seemed almost alive with warmth. Not a queen here, not adorned or distant, but a woman, young and unguarded. My mother. For a moment, it stole my breath, because it was so wrong, so out of place in Damen's chambers, and yet… here it was untouched. Preserved. Still hanging where he could see it every day. The realization struck cold. Negan had been right. Damen hadn't just coveted the throne. He had loved her. And he had kept her here with him.

I shook my head. I had no time to dwell on ghosts. Tearing my gaze away, I forced myself to move, my hands scrabbling around on the wood paneling behind the desk, feeling for the concealed catch that would release the door. When I found it, it swung open with a creak.

"Efa!"

I heard Austell's voice out in the main rooms and I handed the lamp to Morgan, ushering them inside.

"Take the left hand passage when it forks. I'll be right behind you."

Austell's footsteps were loud on the wooden floor and I rushed towards him as he entered the study, my hands finding his.

"Did Caja find you?"

"Yes, she told me about Finn. Are you all right? What's happened to Emrys?"

"I'm fine, but Emrys… the Order… fuck, Aus. The poison is killing him. I have to get them out of here."

"Tell me what you need me to do."

I stared up at him wildly, my breathing fast and erratic

as I tried to sort through the thoughts in my head. My hands gripped his so tightly my knuckles ached.

"Stay here tonight and don't do anything suspicious. Damen has forbidden our marriage and made me leader of the Nevedeno. You'll need to look shocked, upset—believable. Leave first thing, and take Caja with you. Get her somewhere safe."

His eyes held mine, steady and searching, though I could see the fear there.

"Of course. Be safe, Efa."

There was no time for more. I leaned up and brushed my lips against his cheek, and then pulled my hands from his, running blindly into the passages as the hidden door shut heavily behind me. I caught up with them quickly. They were moving at a glacial pace, the narrow, winding passages far too tight for their Fae height and broad shoulders. In some places, it was almost impossible for even one of them to support Emrys, let alone two.

I went ahead with the lamp to lead the way, praying that I didn't take a wrong turn through the hazy passages. Smoke was trickling in through the spy holes from the fires within the palace, and the three of us were struggling to suppress our coughs, trying not to be heard. Not that it mattered much. I doubt anyone would have heard us over the sound of the guards on the other side of the wall shouting and yelling as they tried to put the fires out and regain order. I glanced back over my shoulder and immediately wished I hadn't when I saw Emrys's pale, gray face in the half-light.

"What happened to Jory and the others?" I asked breathlessly.

"They were back in the passages before the bastards even knew we were there," Morgan grunted, repositioning Emrys after navigating a particularly tight corner.

"And Canver?"

"Easiest kill I've ever made. It'll look like he just died in his sleep."

I nodded. At least I had made good on my promise to Caja. We turned the next corner and went down the steps that had been crudely carved into the stone, leaving the confines of the palace and entering the tunnels that would eventually lead out into the forest. The temperature dropped with every step, and the air turned damp.

"Watch your footing," I said. "The moss here makes it slippery."

The ground began to slope as we moved deeper into the cliff, the tunnels widening just enough for Bran and Morgan to better support Emrys. But I could see the strain on their faces, the way their steps grew heavier with every yard.

"How much further?" Bran asked, breath tight.

"About half a mile. Maybe less," I said, though the words felt like a curse.

It was the longest half-mile of my life. Only Emrys's pained groans and our labored breathing broke the silence, and each time I glanced back, he looked worse, his body shuddering with tremors he could no longer control. Fear iced my veins and left me shivering as if the cold had seeped into my bones. I was certain I was watching him slip away. Even when we finally emerged into a shallow cave that opened into the Nijem Forest, the rush of fresh air on my face gave me no relief. The bare branches pierced the dark sky above us, stark and unfeeling.

"Help him," I whispered to the trees, to the Gods, to anyone who might listen, as Bran and Morgan lowered his limp body onto the ground. My voice broke as I begged, "Please, just help him."

I stood useless as Bran set to work, his knife ripping

through Emrys's shirt with practiced ease. Morgan dug frantically through the canvas bag slung over his shoulder, pulling free a battered bottle of his moonshine. In any other moment I might have laughed at the absurdity of it, but now the acrid stench of the liquid as Bran poured it over Emrys's wounds nearly undid me. A strangled sound tore from his throat, his body arching with pain, and I flinched as if the blade had cut into me instead. Another prayer found its way onto my lips, though I knew it was hopeless. The Gods had stopped listening a long time ago.

"What happened?" Morgan asked, leaning back on his knees and holding up the lamp to give Bran space to work.

Bran placed his hands on either side of Emrys's stomach, assessing the damage. My shadows began to vibrate and the hairs on my arms prickled, the air around us seeming to hum with energy, as if the forest was watching. I opened my mouth to speak, reliving the moment that I had seen him collapse, and before I knew it tears were streaming down my cheeks. I dropped to my knees beside them, taking Emrys's hand in my own and bringing it to my lips. I must have been shivering again because without a word Morgan took of his coat and placed it around my shoulders.

"Damen knew that you had been fighting with the Loyalists," I said. "A Nothori soldier recognized him in one of the villages."

"Bastard," Morgan muttered. "I know the one it was. Saw him running off into the fields."

"Damen wants to eradicate the Gifted, and then he said he's coming for the Northern Realm. But this… this was personal. I think he's waited a long time to do this to Emrys. And Emrys…" I paused, a fresh wave of tears filling my eyes. "He didn't even fight. He stopped me from fighting, too, and he… he just let it happen."

Morgan reached out to place his hand on my shoulder and I looked at him, shaking my head miserably.

"Why didn't he *fight*?" I whispered.

"He saw the *Raeth*," Bran said quietly. "Here in the forest. On the day you saw him. He believed his death was inevitable, that it had to be this way for you to become who you needed to be. For you to live."

"Shit," Morgan breathed, echoing my thoughts exactly.

Emrys's eyes opened slowly, and he dragged in a breath.

"Finally one you can't heal, brother," he said, his murmured voice full of pain.

"You're not dead yet, Em," Bran said.

Emrys lifted his chin to gaze up at me, the look in his eyes breaking my heart all over again. Somehow, despite it all, he smiled at me.

"Efa… my heart talks of nothing but you."

His voice was hoarse and rasping, and his breathing was becoming more labored, as if he was fighting for every breath. I glanced at Bran, seeing the sweat running down his temples as he worked. He furrowed his brow in concentration and sighed, using his forearm to wipe his forehead as he shook his head.

"You know," Emrys said softly, "I can still remember the first time I saw you, that night in Nissae."

"Astraea, you mean."

Emrys chuckled weakly, wincing as he did so.

"Astraea… right. Even then, I knew that you would be the one to change everything. The white stag. The light within my darkness."

His voice faded out and I looked helplessly at the others as his eyes shuttered closed. Bran's face was full of raw emotion. Shadows danced across his face as the breeze picked up and made the lamplight flicker.

"I'm only just keeping him alive, Efa. The wounds themselves are bad, and the poison is everywhere. It's weakening him by the minute. I'm giving everything I have, but its only just keeping death at bay."

He paused, staring down at his bloodstained hands where they were pressed against Emrys's skin. When he looked up at me, I felt the world tilt. Panic filled his eyes. For the first time, Bran, always steady and unshakeable, looked terrified. He was afraid.

"I'm not healing him, Efa. Do you understand what I'm saying? What I'm doing just isn't enough this time."

Fear gripped me, my own panic rising up as I raised my head and looked wildly around the forest.

"What do I do?" I shouted. "Tell me what to do to save him!"

My words echoed into the forest. I was sobbing now, my tears hot on my cheeks as I screamed into the cold darkness.

"You told me he was my fate. You told me he was mine! This—" my voice cracked as I looked down at his pale face, "—this can't be it. This *cannot* be it!"

But it was Morgan, not the Nijem, who answered me, his voice steadier and more serious than I had ever heard.

"We need the Amberstone. It's the only way you'll be strong enough to heal him, Bran."

"Would that work?" I asked, desperate. "Would it be enough?"

"It might be," Morgan said quickly. "Without his full strength, he can't do anymore than he's already doing. But with it..."

Bran pushed his damp hair back from his face, leaving a dark smear across his forehead. He nodded once.

"I think it's the only chance we have," he said. "We need to get the Amberstone back."

The breeze dropped suddenly, and all I could hear was the sound of Emrys's ragged breathing. I stared at Bran, my heart clenching.

"My uncle is on his way," Morgan said. "He'll be here in a few minutes with horses. If you start making for Tywell's Pass, Efa and I can meet you there."

"To the Pass?" I asked with alarm. "Will he make it? Surely we can't move him like this."

"We'll have to try," Bran said. "The Amberstone needs to be on Realm soil. We need to get them both across the border."

On impulse, I seized the flask of moonshine and lifted it to my lips, wincing as the liquid fire scorched down my throat. The burn steadied me.

"All right," I said.

I bent over Emrys, pressing a kiss to his clammy forehead. His skin was cold beneath my lips, and fear clawed at my stomach. I couldn't shake the feeling that this might be the last time I would ever see him alive. Morgan stood and offered me his hand, and I took it, letting him haul me upright. My legs were numb, but I forced myself to stand tall and handed his coat back to him.

"We'll wait for you at the Pass unless we hear otherwise," Bran said. "Though in truth, you'll likely catch us long before then. I doubt we'll be moving very quickly."

I nodded, laid a hand on his shoulder, and gave it a firm squeeze. Then, after one last lingering glance at Emrys, I turned and ran for the entrance to the caves, Morgan close behind me. It was time. Time to do what we had set out to do. Time to find the Amberstone. Time to save Noa. And may the Gods grant that it would be enough to save Emrys, too.

CHARACTER LIST

Character: Aemylia Ashae
Pronunciation: AY-MEE-lee-uh a-SHAY
Description: Former Queen of Valtana, wife of Novos, deceased

Character: Aleta
Pronunciation: ah-LEE-ta
Description: Damen's mistress

Character: Ando
Pronunciation: AN-doh
Description: A Gifted Nevedeno spy, Lore's nephew

Character: Androw
Pronunciation: ANN-droh
Description: An Esari soldier

Character: Aneira Danascalon
Pronunciation: ann-EAR-ruh dan-ASS-cuh-lon
Description: Queen of the Fae, Aubrey's wife

Character: Arella Raenord
Pronunciation: uh-RELL-uh RAY-nord
Description: A Gifted Valtanan woman

Character: Aric Mirle
Pronunciation: AIR-ik MER-uhl
Description: Austell's older brother, deceased

Character: Arlo Ashae
Pronunciation: AR-lo a-SHAY
Description: Prince of Valtana, Aemylia's younger brother, deceased

Character: Aubrey Danascalon
Pronunciation:: AW-bree dan-ASS-cuh-lon
Description: King of the Fae, older brother of Trystan and Evyn

Character: Bran, Lord Brannock Vannfodd
Pronunciation: BRAN, bran-OCK VAN-fod
Description: Emrys's friend

Character: Cadoc Angove
Pronunciation: CAD-ock AN-gove
Description: Emrys's friend

Character: Cai
Pronunciation: KYE
Description: The Nevedeno's poison specialist

Character: Caja
Pronunciation: KYE-ya
Description: Lord Cayam's mistress

Character: Caydan
Pronunciation: KAY-dan
Description: A Loyalist

Character: Dafydd Danascalon
Pronunciation: DAH-fid dan-ASS-cuh-lon
Description: Former King of the Fae, Aubrey, Trystan and Evyn's Father, deceased

Character: Damen Treforno
Pronunciation: DAY-men tray-FOR-noh
Description: King of Melrith

Character: Edvarr
Pronunciation: ED-var
Description: Leader of the Elraith gang

Character: Efa Rescorla/ Aeva Penrose
Pronunciation: *EE-fa res-COR-la* / AY-vuh pen-ROSE
Description: A Nevedeno smuggler, Princess of Valtana, daughter of Aemylia and Novos

Character: Emrys / Trystan Danascalon
Pronunciation: EM-riss / triss-TAN dan-ASS-cuh-lon
Description: Prince of the Northern Realm, Aubrey's younger brother, the Dark Prince

Character: Eseld Mirle
Pronunciation: EH-seld MER-uhl
Description: Austell's illegitimate niece and ward

Character: Evyn Danascalon
Pronunciation: EV-in dan-ASS-cuh-lon
Description: Prince of the Northern Realm, Aubrey's youngest brother

Character: Finn Yadari
Pronunciation: FIN ya-DAR-ee
Description: Leader of the Nevedeno

Character: General Brayson
Pronunciation: BRAY-son
Description: Damen's General, Head of the Melrithian army

Character: Iona
Pronunciation: eye-OH-nuh
Description: A Seer

Character: Jato
Pronunciation: JAY-toe
Description: Captain of the *Zephyr,* one of Torr Voss's ships

Character: Jory Marrak
Pronunciation: JOR-ee MAR-ak
Description: A senior member of the Loyalists

Character: Lady Anneth Denfor
Pronunciation: ANN-eth DEN-for
Description: Lord Denfor's wife, known as Lady Polruen

Character: Lady Elestren Hollis
Pronunciation: el-LES-tren HOL-liss
Description: Lord Hollis's wife, known as Lady Portreth

Character: Lady Kerensa Montavis
Pronunciation: keh-REN-sah mon-TAV-is
Description: Lord Montavis's wife, known as Lady Montavis

Character: Lady Tiva Mirle
Pronunciation: TEE-vah MER-uhl
Description: Austell's mother, deceased

Character: Lassa
Pronunciation: LASS-a
Description: Austell's estate manager

Character: Lord Austell Mirle
Pronunciation: AW-stell MER-uhl
Description: Esari's regional Lord, known as Lord Esari

Character: Lord Kenwyn Hollis
Pronunciation: KEN-win HOL-liss
Description: Portreth's regional Lord, known as Lord Portreth

Character: Lord Kitto Montavis
Pronunciation: KIT-oh mon-TAV-is
Description: Rael's regional Lord, known as Lord Rael

Character: Lord Perran Denfor
Pronunciation: PER-an DEN-for
Description: Polruen's regional Lord, known as Lord Polruen

Character: Lord Sandow Canver
Pronunciation: SAN-doh CAN-ver
Description: Cayam's regional Lord, known as Lord Cayam

Character: Lord Zennor Tanrith
Pronunciation: ZEN-or TAN-rith
Description: Baern's regional Lord, known as Lord Baern

Character: Lore
Pronunciation: LOHR
Description: Head of the Nevedeno's spy network

Character: Merryn
Pronunciation: MEH-rin
Description: A Loyalist

Character: Molly
Pronunciation: MAW-lee
Description: Austell's cook at Totease

Character: Morai
Pronunciation: MOR-eye
Description: A Nothori warrior, leader of the Mossani Clan

Character: Morgan Angove
Pronunciation: MOR-gun AN-gove
Description: Emrys's friend and Cadoc's nephew

Character: Negan Aeland
Pronunciation: NEE-GAN AY-LAND
Description: A Gifted Valtanan woman, Efa's mentor

Character: Nev Bairstow
Pronunciation: NEV BEAR-stow
Description: Esari's Captain of the Guard

Character: Noa Rescorla / Aeden Ashae
Pronunciation: NO-uh ress-COR-la / AY-den a-SHAY
Description: A Nevedeno smuggler, Prince of Valtana, Aemylia and Novos's nephew

Character: Novos Penrose
Pronunciation: NOH-vos pen-ROSE
Description: Former King of Melrith, Aemylia's husband, deceased

Character: Owen
Pronunciation: OH-en
Description: A Nevedeno smuggler

Character: Peta
Pronunciation: PEE-tah
Description: An Esari solider

Character: *Raeth*
Pronunciation: RAYTH
Description: A death spirit residing in the Nijem Forest

Character: Roda
Pronunciation: ROH-da
Description: A Nevedeno spy

Character: Ross
Pronunciation: ROSS
Description: An Esari soldier

Character: Rumo
Pronunciation: ROO-moh
Description: A Loyalist

Character: Talan
Pronunciation: TAL-an
Description: Caja's brother, deceased

Character: Theo
Pronunciation: THEE-oh
Description: A Nevedeno smuggler, deceased

Character: Torr Voss
Pronunciation: TOR VOSS
Description: A successful merchant and sometimes smuggler

Character: Treave
Pronunciation: TREEV
Description: A Loyalist

ACKNOWLEDGEMENTS

As always, my deepest thanks go to my editor, Abby, for her continued guidance. Your insight and encouragement have helped this story truly take shape. Special thanks also to Peter and Caroline from Bespoke, whose incredible creativity and expertise have brought this book physically to life.

The Valtana Trilogy is a tale of love, loyalty, and sacrifice, but also a celebration of what it means to be a strong and powerful woman. I have said this before, but I owe so much to the women in my life who have shown me resilience, courage, and the power of standing tall no matter what life may bring. Their support and encouragement have carried me through this journey, and without them, these pages would never have been written.

And last, but never least, to my husband—you are my greatest inspiration and my heart's anchor. Thank you for your endless love, patience, and belief in me. This story is as much yours as it is mine.

Printed in Dunstable, United Kingdom

70601275R00228